Luke Smitherd is a former musi time writer. He has had various jobs over the years, including stints as a radio copywriter, an undercover singing waiter, a vacuum cleaner salesman (for four days, and never once took the vacuum cleaner out of the box) and one night as a podium dancer, during which he fell over and then smashed his legs into the podium railing trying to get up 'stylishly'. He is currently travelling all over the place while writing and can barely believe his luck.

Books By Luke Smitherd:

Full-Length Novels:
The Physics Of The Dead
The Stone Man
A Head Full Of Knives
In The Darkness, That's Where I'll Know You

Novellas:
The Man On Table Ten

Serial Novellas:
The Black Room, Part One: In The Black Room
The Black Room, Part Two: The Woman In The Night
The Black Room, Part Three: The Other Places
The Black Room, Part Four: The End

For an up-to-date list of Luke Smitherd's other books, his blog, YouTube clips and more—as well as to sign up for the Spam-Free Book Release Newsletter—visit
www.lukesmitherd.com

In The Darkness, That's Where I'll Know You
The Complete Black Room Story
By Luke Smitherd

Dedicated to anyone that ever referred to themselves as a Smithereen. Even if they were being ironic.

Acknowledgements

At the time of writing, the following people wrote a nice Amazon.com or co.uk review of my most recent novel *A Head Full Of Knives*, or sent a kind e-mail. It means an immense deal, not only practically—reviews mean people are far, FAR more likely to buy a book—but personally, as disappointments are abundant in the writing game, so any encouragement is amazing to receive, especially from strangers. I'm using here either the name you put in your Amazon review, or a shortened version if you sent me an e-mail. I don't want to ruin any witness protection programmes that might be in progress. And for those of you that have kept reviewing all along, I see your names when they keep coming up. You guys are saints in my book.

Thanks to:

Karenr, Buzzskin, Mark, Leo Hmailton, Mrs N.J Marshall, Heather Hindle, Mr S.D. MacMaster, C. Havard, Amazon Customer (so many of these, change your names so I can give you the recognition individually that you deserve!), MT, Angie H, Rhym O'Reison, Ventrisha "tvn", Samantha Dunbar, VAN, Esther4810, Clare Poppy Nobsack Gozdawa, Lockie "Lockie", Benjamin P Thurley, AngelaB, charlene hall, Mrs R K Lees, Sonya Moyes, T Selkirk, Glennccc, David A Willson, I. D. Ball "fastbutdim", R C Mansfield, Marmite, Girl on Fire "Spottsy22", jay8280, Hazel Clifton, Kai, scrooby1, MR W G HARPER, pandachris "pandachris", Simon Abrahall, Becca Ingham, saultrue, AllyBally, Canis Major, ChezisMe, Steve Gatehouse, Silversmith, simon211175, Gordon Draper, Johnathan H, The Fro, TerryHeth, Emma Hopewell, David Plank, MRS K DYE, Mrs Kindle, Katie, BigDog, fergus67, Bloomers, BoneyD, D. Maccauley "Don", Daisy, Joan Campbell, Chris Stothard, Mr. K. J. Dwyer, Shelly, Bruce White, Tina, ddaisey, Keith A. Stevens, Estefany Ortiz, Texasbelle "Texasbelle", Susan, pamela brooks, Mark (usa), Dannette Elaine Claderin "Write on, right now.", Faith S. Myer, SBKEsq, unclefester, Meg Julian, Harold Charlson, Laura Karoll, Siadina, Lisasun, Nancy Kephart, N. King "music princess", Bob Price, Paul A Ream Jr, Denise Davis, Peggy Brown, A. Lichtenstein, Holly T,

HB LEVESQUE, Denise Freeman, Cecilia "C.A.Rice", Maggie May "Maggie May", Russell, Judy Markham, Leslie Young "Fuzzette", SD, Kathleen Marion, P. Varady "izquierdo17", emily pittman, NitPicker "cclgoodstuff", Ann Keeran, nomare, Jay, T. Swift, Jody P, TClark, L.A. Otts, J.Ponce, deedee29, drac, Beatrice A. Walters "cat painter", Jason Nugent, Rick Novak Jr, Sharon F.Roy "Ditter S. Roy", Neil Novita, Chevy Rendell, amijames, SLB "Zoomama", Joanne G, Queen Tulip, Jennifer Chan, McG NY, mjoanne, Stephanie Wilkerson, C. Osborn "coffee nut", James Liston "Creating a better world, one review at a time", Fred K., Tammy S, Gaia, bluemoon1972, Melissa Quimby, Moises J Estrada, Jean M. Trickle, KatDaddy1414, sue, Double T, Gregor Notacow Mendel, Judie Lipsett Stanford, Melinda, janice m burgin, youknee, Propel Lover, Girl On Fire "Spottsy22", joanne bacon, Jo Cranford, Maz C, jay8280, Chi-Lover, SciFi Reader, Katrina, Nabbo, Barbara McShane, dogo, tracey dake, B. Shilling, Aaron Hubble, Kindle Customer, meredithbiblio, Caly, booknut, Lady R, Amazon Customer "Patty M", T, Kelli Tristan, Urbananchorite, KC "KC", Jacque Ledoux, Kelly Jobes, SciFIFan, swebby, Barbara "In Honor Of Books", James P. Morrison, R. Gaylor, Ryan, Amazon Customer "katecap", Jason Jones "tiredguy", Michelle Kennedy, Jean, wjmouse, and BSM.

Special mention to Barbra Smerz for editing my edits of Part Four out of nothing but the kindness of her own heart. That's some world class Smithereening right there.
Other proofreading by novelproofreading.com. Cover artwork by Mark Kelly.

PART ONE: IN THE BLACK ROOM

Chapter One: An Unexpected Point of View, Proof That You Can Never Go Home Again, and The Importance of the Work/Life Balance

***

Charlie opened his eyes and was immediately confused. A quick reassessment of the view, however, confirmed that he was right; he suddenly had breasts. Not very noticeable ones, perhaps, but when he'd spent over thirty years without them, even the appearance of a couple of A-cups was a real attention grabber. As he continued to look down, the very next thing to come to his attention was the material covering them; a purple, stretchy cotton fabric, something he had never worn, nor had he ever harboured any plans to do so. As he watched his hands adjust the top, he came to the most alarming realisation of all; those weren't his hands doing the adjusting.

The giveaway wasn't in the slenderness of the fingers, or the medium-length (if a little ragged) fingernails upon their tips, or even in the complete lack of any physical sensation as he watched the digits tug and pull the purple top into position. It was the fact that, while they were clearly stuck to the end of arms that were attached to his shoulders (or at least, the painfully skinny shoulders that he could see either side of his head's peripheral vision; his shoulders were bigger than that, surely?) they were moving entirely of their own accord.

1

He was so stunned that he almost felt calm. The bizarreness of the situation had already passed straight through *this is crazy* and out the other side into the utterly incomprehensible. Charlie stared dumbly for several seconds as his mind got caught in a feeble loop, trying and failing to get its bearings (*What ... sorry, what ... sorry, WHAT ...*) While, in that moment, he never really came any closer to coming to terms with the situation, his mind did at least manage to reach the next inevitable conclusion: this wasn't his body.

The loop got louder as these unthinkable, too-big-for-conscious-process thoughts instantly doubled in size, but got nowhere (*WHAT ... WHAT ... WHAT THE FUCK*). All Charlie was capable of doing was staring at the view in front of him as it moved from a downward angle, swinging upwards to reveal a door being opened onto a narrow hallway. A second doorway was then passed through, and now Charlie found himself in a bathroom. He wanted to look down again, to see the feet that were carrying him forward, to help understand that he wasn't doing the walking, to aid him in *any* kind of conscious comprehension of his situation ... but he quickly realised that he couldn't affect the line of sight in any way. The viewing angle was completely out of his control. Instinctively, he tried to commandeer the limbs that were attached to him, to move the arms like he would have done on any other minute of any other day since his birth, but there was no response. There was only the *illusion* of control; the moment when one of the hands reached for the door handle at the same time that he would have intended them to, as he reflexively thought of performing the motion simultaneously. What the fuck was going on? *What the fuck was going on?*

The crazy, unthinkable answer came again, despite his crashed mind, even in a moment of sheer madness—what other conclusion was there to reach?—as he saw the feminine hands reach for a toothbrush on the sink: he was in someone else's body—a woman's body—and he was not in control.

Incapable of speech, Charlie watched as the view swung up from the sink to look into the plastic-framed bathroom mirror, and while he began to notice the detail in his surroundings properly—tiny bathroom, cheap fittings, slightly grubby tiles, and candles, candles everywhere—the main focus of his concern was the face looking back at him.

The eyes he was looking through belonged to a woman of hard-to-place age; she looked to be in her mid- to late-twenties, but even to Charlie's goggling, shell-shocked point of view, there was clearly darkness both under and inside her green eyes (physically and metaphorically speaking) that made her look older. Her skin was pale, and the tight, bouncy, but frazzled curls of her shoulder-length black hair all added to the haunted manner that the woman possessed.

All of which Charlie didn't give a flying shit about, of course; thoughts were beginning to come together, and his mind was already rallying and coming back online. While Charlie would never describe himself as a practical man, having spent most of his life more concerned with where the next laugh was coming from rather than the next paycheque, he had always been resourceful, capable of taking an objective step backwards in a tight spot and saying *Okay, let's have a look at this.* While he was beyond that now—had he been in his own body, that body would have been hyperventilating—he was now aware enough to at least think more clearly. As the woman continued to brush her teeth, Charlie watched, and thought the one thing to himself that instantly made everything else easier:

This is probably a dream. This is fucking mental, so it's got to be a dream. So there's nothing to worry about, is there?

While he didn't fully believe that—the view was too real, the surroundings too complete and detailed, the grit and grime too fleshed out and realised—it enabled him to take the necessary mental step back, and put his foot on the brake of his runaway mind a little.

Okay. Think. Think. This can't actually be happening. It can't. It's a lucid dream, that's what it is. Calm down. Calm down. That means you can decide what happens, right? You're supposed to be able to control a lucid dream, aren't you? So let's make ... the wall turn purple. That'll do. Wall. Turn purple ... now.

The wall remained exactly the same, and the view shifted downward briefly to reveal an emerging spray of water and foaming toothpaste. The woman had just spat.

Right. Maybe it's not quite one of those dreams then, maybe it's just a very, very realistic one. Don't panic. You can prove this. Think back. Think back through your day, think what you'd been doing, and you'll remember going to bed. What were you last doing?

He'd met the boys, gone for a drink—excited about the prospect of one turning into many—the first night out for a little while. Clint's mate Jack had been over from London too, which was both a good excuse and good news for the quality of the night. They had ended up on a heavy pub crawl, and somebody had said something about going back to their place ... Neil. That guy Neil had said it. And they'd gone to Neil's, and then ...

Nothing. Nothing from there on in. And now he was here. As he felt hysteria start to rise, escalating from the panic that he already felt, Charlie frantically tried to put a lid on it before it got badly out of control.

You passed out. You had some more to drink and you passed out. That's why you can't remember what happened at Neil's, and this is the resultant booze-induced crazy dream. So wake up. Wake your ass up. Slap yourself in the face and wake the fuck up.

Charlie did so, his hand slamming into the side of his head with the force of fear behind it, and as the ringing sting rocked him, he became aware that he suddenly had a physical presence of his own. If he had a hand to swing and a head to hit, then he now had a body of his own. A body inside this woman's body? Where the hell had that come from?

There'd been nothing before, no response from anything when he'd tried to move the woman's arms earlier. He'd been a disembodied mind, a ghost inside this woman's head, but now when he looked down he saw his own torso, naked and standing in a space consisting of nothing but blackness. Looking around himself to confirm it, seeing the darkness stretching away around him in all directions and now having a body to respond to his emotion, Charlie collapsed onto an unseen floor and lay gasping and whooping in lungfuls of nonexistent air, his body trembling.

His wide, terrified eyes stared straight ahead, the view that had previously seemed to be his own vision now appearing suspended in the air, a vast image the size of a cinema screen with edges that faded away into the inky-black space around him. Its glow was ethereal, like nothing he'd ever seen before. How had he thought that had been his own-eye view? It had clearly been there all along, hanging there in the darkness. Had he just been standing too close? Had something changed? Either way, there was no mistake now; there was just him, the enormous screen showing the woman's point of view, and the black room in which he lay.

Charlie pulled his knees up into a ball and watched the screen as he lay there whimpering. That slap had hurt badly, and instead of waking him, it had added another frightening new dimension to the situation. He was terrified; he lay for a moment in mental and physical shock, and for now, at least, everything was beyond him. The words that he feebly tried to repeat to himself fell on deaf ears—*it's a dream it's a dream it's a dream*—and so he lay there for a while, doing nothing but watch and tremble as the woman made a sandwich, checked her e-mails on her phone, and moved to sit in front of her TV. She flicked through channels, thumbed through her Facebook feed. As this time passed—and Charlie still watched, incapable of anything else for the time being—he came back to himself a little more. He noticed that, while he was naked, he wasn't cold. He wasn't warm either, however; in fact, the concept of either sensation seemed hard to comprehend, like trying to understand what the colour red sounded like. Thoughts crept in again.

You can't actually be in her head. You can't actually be INSIDE her head. People don't have screens behind their eyes or huge holes where their brain should be. You know that. You haven't been shrunk and stuffed in here, as that's not possible. So this ... HAS ... to be a dream. Right? You have a voice, don't you? You can speak, can't you? Can you get your breath long enough to speak?

Charlie opened his mouth, and found that speech was almost outside of his capabilities. A strange, strangled squeak came out of his throat, barely audible, and he felt no breath come from his lungs. He tried several more times, shaping his mouth around the sound in an attempt to form words, but got nowhere.

Focus, you fucking arsehole. Focus.

Eventually, he managed to squeak out a word that sounded a bit like *hey* and, encouraged by that success, he tried to repeat it. He managed to say it again on the third try, then kept going, the word getting slightly louder each time until something gave way and the bass came into his voice.

"Hey ..."

With that, the ability to speak dropped into place, even if getting the hang of it again took a real physical effort. He at least knew *how* to do it now, his mind remembering the logistics of speech like a dancer going through a long-abandoned but previously well-rehearsed routine. He looked out through the screen with sudden purpose, determined to find out if she could hear him.

"Hey ... *hey* ..." he gasped, his lips feeling loose and clumsy, as if they were new to his face. Charlie sat up, hoping to get more volume behind it, more projection. He thought he had to at least be as loud as the TV for her to hear him, if she was capable of doing so at all.

"*HEY*," he managed, but there was no external response. Charlie's heart sank, and he almost abandoned the whole attempt. After all, it was easier and more reassuring to resign himself to the only real hope that he had; that this truly *was* a dream, and thus something he could hopefully wait out until his alarm clock broke the spell and returned him to blessed normality. Things might have turned out very differently if he had, but instead Charlie found the strength to kneel upright and produce something approaching a scream.

"*HEY!!*" he squawked, and fell back onto his behind, exhausted. Staring at the glowing screen before him, dejected, Charlie then saw a hand come up into view, holding the remote control. A finger hit the mute button.

Charlie froze.

The image on the screen swung upwards, showing the white ceiling with its faint yellowing patches marking it here and there, and hung in that direction for a second or two. It then travelled back to the TV screen, and as the hand holding the remote came up again, Charlie realised what was happening and felt a fresh jolt of panic. Without thinking, he blurted out a noise, desperately needing to cause any kind of sound in an attempt to be heard, like a fallen and undiscovered climber hearing the rescue party beginning to move on.

"*BAARGH! BA BA BAAA!*" Charlie screeched, falling forwards as he almost dove towards the screen in his clumsy response to the images upon it. The hand hesitated, and then the view was getting up and travelling across the living room and down the hallway. It looked like the woman was going to look through the spyhole in her front door, and as she did so, the fish-eye effect of the glass on the huge screen made Charlie's stomach lurch. He still saw the fairly dirty-looking stairwell outside, however, and realised that the woman was inside some sort of apartment block.

Charlie stared, trying desperately to pull himself together, and assessed the situation. She could hear him then; but she certainly didn't seem to be aware that he was there. So she could be as unwilling in all of this as he was?

It'sadreamitdoesn'tmatteranywayit'salladreamsowhocares—

He didn't believe that though. He just couldn't. There had to be some sort of explanation, and he couldn't be physically *in* her head, so this was ... an out of body experience? Some sort of psychic link?

Charlie surprised himself with his own thoughts. Where the hell had all of that come from, all of those sudden, rational thoughts? True, he'd been confronted with something so impossible that he didn't really have much choice but to look at the available options, but ... was he suddenly adjusting again? When this all started, he didn't even have a body, but one quickly appeared. Was his mind following suit? He was still trembling, his shoulders still rising and falling dramatically with each rapid, shallow in-breath of nothing, but his mind was at work now; the shock had seemingly been absorbed and moved past far more quickly than it should have been, he was sure. Would he be this rational already if he were in his own body? Whatever was going on, being here was ... different. He felt his mental equilibrium returning, his awareness and presence of mind growing. He was scared, and he was confused, but he was getting enough of a grip to at least function.

You have her attention. Don't lose it.

He opened his mouth again, got nowhere, reset himself, then tried again. "Lady?"

The view jerked round, then everything in sight became slightly farther away, very quickly; she'd spun around, and fallen backwards against the apartment's front door. The view then swung sharply left and right to either side of the hallway, looking to the bathroom doorway and then to the doorway of another, unspecified room. Charlie assumed it was a bedroom. He tried again.

"Can ... can you hear me?"

The view jerked violently. She'd clearly just jumped out of her skin, her fresh adrenaline putting all of her physical flight reflexes on full alert. It was a dumb question to ask—she obviously could—but even with his growing sense of control, Charlie's mind was still racing, his incredulity at the situation now combining with the excitement of finding that he could communicate with his unsuspecting host.

It was clear that she was terrified, and Charlie realised that he couldn't blame her. She was hearing a voice within the safety of her home when she'd thought that she was by herself, and Charlie could only guess what it sounded like to this woman. Did his voice sound as if he were right behind her, or was she hearing it actually coming from the inside of her head? Charlie couldn't decide which would be worse.

Get a grip, man. Of course she's going to shit herself when you start talking to her. Just ... try and think, okay? Think straight. You have to get out of this. You need her to talk to you; you need her if you're ever going to get this sorted out. Get a grip, get control, and think smart.

"Please, it's—" He didn't get any further as the jump came again, this time with a little scream; it was a brief squeal, clipped short as if she were trying to avoid drawing attention to herself. Charlie jumped with her this time, startled a little himself, but pressed on. "Please, *please* don't be scared. I'm shitting myself here too. Please. Please calm down—" The second half of this sentence was lost, however, disappearing under a fresh scream from the woman. This time it was a hysterical, lengthy one that travelled with her as she ran the length of the hallway into the living room, slamming the door behind her. Charlie heard her crying and panting, and watched her thin hands grab one end of the small sofa and begin to drag it in front of the door. The scream trailed off as she did so, and once the job was done, the view backed away from the door, bobbing slightly in time with the woman's whimpering tears and gasping breath.

Charlie was hesitant to speak again; he knew that he simply had to, but what could he actually say without sending her off into fresh hysterics? The answer was immediate; nothing. There was no way to do it easily. She would have to realise that she was *physically* alone at least—and safe with it—and the only way to help her do that was to keep talking until she accepted that there was no intruder in her home.

Not on the outside, anyway.

"I need your help," he tried, wincing as the view leapt almost a foot upwards and then spun on the spot, accompanied by fresh wails. "Please, lady, you're safe—" The cries increased in volume, to the point where he had to raise his voice to be heard. In doing so, Charlie realised that he now had his voice under complete control. And wasn't the blackness around him a fraction less dark now, too? "Look, just calm down, all right? If you just listen for two seconds, you'll find that—"

"*Fuck ooofffff!!*" she screamed, the volume of it at a deafening level from Charlie's perspective. He clapped his hands to the side of his head, wincing and crouching from the sheer force of it. It was like being in the centre of a sonic hurricane. "*Get out of my flat! Get out of my flaaaaaaat!!!*"

"Please!! Please don't do that!" Charlie shouted, trying to be heard over the woman's yelling. "Look, just shut up for a second, I don't *want* to be here, I just want to—"

"*Get out! Where are you? Get out!! Get oooouuuuuttt!!*" she yelled, ignoring him, and as the view dropped to the floor and shot backwards—the living room walls now framing either side of the screen—Charlie realised that she'd dropped onto her ass and scooted backwards into the corner, backing into the space where the sofa had previously been. Frustrated, terrified, in pain and pushed to his limit (it had been one hell of an intense five minutes, after all) Charlie let fly with a scream of his own, hands balled into fists over his throbbing ears.

"*JUST SHUT THE FUCK UP FOR A SECOND!!*" he screamed, and whether it was from using some volume of his own, or because her own screams were already about to descend into hysterical, terrified and silent tears, the only sound after Charlie's shout was that of the woman's whimpers. The view still darted around the room though, trying to find the source of the sound, a source well beyond her sight.

Charlie seized his moment. At the very least he could be heard, and *that* hopefully meant he could start talking her down. She was more terrified than him—of course she was, at least he'd had time to get used to the situation whereas she'd just discovered an apparently invisible intruder in her home—but he had to get through to her while she was at least quiet enough to hear him. Hysterical or not, she had ears, even if he appeared to be currently standing somewhere in between them.

"Look, I'm sorry for shouting like that, I just need you to listen for a second, okay? Just listen," Charlie said, as soothingly as his own panicking mind would allow. "I'm not going to hurt you, okay? Okay? It's fine, you're, uh … you're not in any danger, all right?"

"Where … where are you? *Where are you?*" the woman's voice sobbed breathlessly, small and scared. Her thinking was clear from the confusion in her voice; she was finally realising that she should be able to see the person talking to her, that there was nowhere in the room that they could be hiding. Charlie thought quickly, and decided that it was best to leave that one for a minute. He'd only just got her onside, and didn't want to push her over the edge.

"I'll tell you in a second. I'm, uh … I'm not actually in the room, you see. You're alone in the flat, and you're safe. You're fine. Okay?" She didn't reply at first. The sobs continued helplessly, but Charlie thought that they might have been slightly lessened, if only due to confusion.

"Wha … what?" she stammered, the view swinging wildly around the room now. "Your voice … what the fuck … *what the fuck is going onnnnnn ….*" And then she was off again, the hysterical screaming coming back at fever pitch. Charlie stood in front of the strange, glowing screen, his hands at his ears again while she bawled, blinking rapidly as his mind worked. After a moment or two, his shoulders slumped and he sat down. There was nothing he could do but wait, and let her adjust. His own breathing was beginning to slow further, and he was finding acceptance of his situation to still be an easier task than he thought; while it was no less mind boggling, his panic was dropping fast, and unusually so.

It's being in here that's doing it. It has to be.

Either way, he let her have a minute or two to calm down. Eventually, he stood and began to pace back and forth in the darkness—illuminated dimly by the unusual light of the screen—while he decided what to say next. His frantic mind kept trying to wander, to seize and wrestle all the aspects of the situation into submission, and failed every time.

You don't like the dark. You don't like the dark! Don't think about it, don't think about it … think about… wait … there's no breeze in here, no echo. It really is a room of sorts then, a space with walls on all sides?

He looked out into the darkness, looking for walls, and saw none; there was only seemingly endless blackness. Charlie thought it would be best not to go exploring *just* yet. Instead, he tried to control his breathing, and quickly ran through a mental list, double checking his actions and decisions of the previous few days before his night out:

Went to work. Did the late shift. Argued about sci-fi films with Clint. Helped Steve throw the drunk arsehole out that had started slapping his girlfriend. Went home, stayed up and watched a film because I had the Wednesday off. Met Chris in town—

And so it went on. By the time he'd finished a few minutes later—while he was no clearer about what had led him to be inside this woman's head—he told himself that he really *did* feel more capable of beginning to deal with things, and less frightened; in the absolute worst case, even though he didn't believe this to be the *actual* case, this situation was real, and had to be resolved. If he'd got in, then he could get out, and if this was the *best*—and more likely—scenario, where this was all just a dream, then he would wake up and all would be well.

Yeah. And if I had wheels, I'd be a wagon.

Charlie took a deep breath, and decided to speak again.

"Are you okay?" he said. The view jumped again, along with a fresh scream.

For fuck's sake.

"Look, we're not going to get anywhere if you keep doing that," Charlie said, not being able to keep the frustration out of his voice. "I'm sure you're a smart person really, so just knock the screaming and shit on the head and we can work together to sort this all out, right? For crying out loud, if I'm not *there,* I can't exactly do anything to you, can I? I know you're scared, and I know this must have been a hell of a shock, but I'm not exactly a million dollars myself right this minute. So, please … come on. Just … have a minute, sort yourself out, and then we'll … then we'll carry on," he finished, shrugging his shoulders in annoyed impotence. He knew that he was perhaps being a little harsh, but he couldn't help thinking that he had a bit of a flake on his hands here. Being scared was one thing, but a complete collapse like this was another.

Don't be a dick, Charlie, he reprimanded himself. *You don't know what she's been through before now. You might be squatting in her head, but you don't know anything about her.*

It was a fair point. She seemed to respond better to his last outburst though, and the sobbing was now drying up into skipping little breaths. She wasn't responding to his annoyance, Charlie thought, but it might have been the honest approach that got through. Sometimes people just appreciated it.

"Your voice …" she said, and her own was steadier, but uncertain. "Where—" She hesitated, seeming to try and find a different question to ask, something else to say that would stop her from repeating herself. She gave up. "Where are you? Where … where *are* you?"

She's not going to drop that one. Would you, in her shoes?

Again, a fair point, and Charlie decided that the honest approach had seemed to work before.

"Look … okay, I'll tell you," he said, trying to find words to describe the impossible, "and I don't understand it in the slightest myself, but it's … it's pretty heavy shit, okay? I mean, well, I don't mean heavy as in serious, as I've no idea what *it* really is, but I mean heavy as in … hard to get your head around. It's … *weird.* And we can't be having any of the freaking out stuff you were doing earlier, okay? I need you to work with me. Okay?"

Silence.

"Okay?"

Another pause, and then the view nodded quickly; a rapid, brief up and down motion that would have been barely noticeable to an outside observer, but seemed to Charlie as if her flat had been caught in an earthquake.

"Okay," she replied quietly, her voice breathy and small.

"Right …" said Charlie, speaking slowly and trying to prepare each word carefully. "I don't know how this has happened, or why, but the last thing I remember is being on a night out with my mates, we were out in ... wait ... hang on, where is this? Where do you live?"

"Huh?"

"Which city? Which city are you in right now?"

"Coventry."

"Jesus! That's where I live!"

"... okay."

In the brief pause that followed while she waited for him to continue, his mind grabbed the thought and filed it away for later. It might be relevant. Maybe they'd been somewhere in the city, been *through* something, something that caused a connection ...

It's a dream, remember? This is down to cheese and too many pints, or a bad kebab.

He dragged his wandering thoughts back on track, and continued.

"Anyway, *anyway*, we were out in Cov, and then we went back to someone's house, and then, I don't know, I must have fallen asleep or drank too much or whatever, but somehow ... *some*how ..."

He stumbled, tripping at the vital hurdle.

"What?" she asked, the view still scanning around the room, as if hoping to find the answers there.

"Ah ... ah *fuck* it, look, I, I, I woke up or whatever and here I am, in your fucking head. I don't know how I got here, and hell, I might be gone in the next five minutes for all I know, but I'm here, I'm in your head, here I am. That's it."

Silence again. Then:

"You're ... you're what?"

"I'm in your head. I'm standing here, in front of this, this ..." He waved his hands in front of the immense, ethereal screen before him, taking it in as yet another rapid flicker shivered across it. These had been happening constantly; later he would realise that this effect was due to her blinking. "This screen thing, okay, and everywhere else in here it's just black, and I'm stood here, completely ..." he trailed off, looking down at his genitals and deciding that it would probably be best not to mention the nakedness to a scared woman who is stuck in a flat on her own, "... completely without any idea as to what's going on."

Silence again. Then:

"A screen ... there's a screen in my head?" she asked. "What ... what screen, what the hell are you talking about?"

Charlie rubbed at his face, angry now, both with himself and her. Of course she didn't get it, it was un-gettable, but she wasn't even coming *close* to understanding and he was doing a lousy job of explaining it. He needed to get the important facts across if they were ever going to move on, and spare her the more intricate details. He needed a different approach.

"Look, don't worry about that, forget it, forget it. Listen. Right, okay, I'll start again. My name is Charlie. Charlie Wilkes. What's yours?"

There was a long, uncertain silence.

"Minnie," she replied, her voice shaking again. She was about to go any second, he could tell.

Talk her down.

"Are you scared to talk to me?" asked Charlie, as tenderly as he could manage. "You don't have to be. Talk to me. What's your surname? You might as well get used to talking to me, you know, as we need to talk to sort this all out, yeah? Come on. What's your surname?"

"I don't ... I don't like to ..." the tears were coming again, and Charlie knew he needed to stop this fast before she lost it.

"It's okay, have a second—" he began, but she cut him off, her voice rising.

"If I talk to you ... it'll get worse ... I think it's finally happening, I think it's finally happened and you're not real and I'm going cra-ha-ha-*haaaAAAAAAA—*" and then she was gone, wailing again ... but this time it was different. This time the screen went black and the sobs became muffled, turning into the low, mournful cries of someone who has given up. She'd dropped her head into her hands or onto her forearms, with her eyes squeezed shut as she cried, cutting off Charlie's view of the outside world. He realised in that moment why her earlier reaction had been so severe; this was someone not entirely comfortable in their own mind, someone already scared of finding voices in their head or visions of things that aren't there. He didn't have time to dwell on that, however, as he realised that Minnie's eyes being shut meant that he was now swallowed by total darkness. Terror came rushing in, threatening to take him and ruin the small amount of progress that he'd just made.

"Minnie, trust me, you're not going crazy," Charlie said, raising his voice almost to a shout to be heard over her noise. "I know it *sounds* crazy, this whole situation is crazy, but I promise you I'm the real deal! Okay? My name is Charlie Wilkes, I work in a pub—Barrington's, you know Barrington's?—I support the Sky Blues even though I never go to the Ricoh, I grew up in Oxford, I moved here, what, ten years ago? I like, ah, I like movies and books, uh, I like, I like music ... *shit,* who doesn't, okay, I like cheese, and I hate getting up early! The last film I saw was *The English Patient* on Blu-Ray, the, uh, the last thing I bought from the shop was a Pepperami and a can of Sprite! My favourite place to eat in Cov is the Ocean Restaurant, and I didn't vote last election day because I forgot to get to the polling station in time ... okay? Is any of this getting through to you?"

"*... you're not real ...*"

"I *am!* I promise I am! Look, if I wasn't real, right, and you were genuinely going crazy, don't the voices in crazy people's heads tell them to go and kill people, shit like that? Tell them that the government is run by lizards, and that they're Jesus come to, to, I dunno, stick forks in their asses? Well I'm not saying any of those things!"

Ease off, for God's sake. Don't start attacking her again.

"Look. All *I'm* asking you to do is listen to me. That's it. That's it. You know what, absolute worst case, you've gone nuts and you have a voice in your head. But it's not a nonstop voice, look, I can be quiet if you want, listen." Charlie stopped talking for a good thirty seconds before speaking again. "See? And I'm not nagging at you to do bad things. So it's not that *bad* of a bad thing, worst case. And best case ... I'm telling the truth, and you and I can figure this out together. Okay? So just, you know, chill out for a moment, take a nice deep breath, and let's talk."

He took a few deep breaths himself, trying to keep a grip—it was hard enough for him to keep it together, let alone having to try and do it for two people—and waited for her response. He closed his eyes, trying to pretend that the now-complete blackness that he saw all around him was of his own choosing, and that he could bring the light back any time he wanted. Her reply eventually came, so quiet that he could barely hear it even inside her head.

"Sorry?" he said, feeling suddenly hopeful. "What did you say? I didn't catch that sweetheart, I—" He jumped back as the screen blazed into life, her eyes opening as her head came up. He didn't have time to revel in the sudden return of the light, as her anger was already being directed at him.

"*Don't* fucking call me sweetheart," she snapped, her voice immediately strong. "I'm not your sweetheart, and I have a name. It's Minnie. I told you. Okay?"

Jesus, thought Charlie, kicking himself. He'd meant it as a term of endearment, trying to get her onside, and hadn't meant to patronise or insult. However, it seemed to have given her more of a kick up the arse than anything else he'd said so far, shunting her frightened mind back online.

"Okay, okay, fair point, I'm sorry," he said quickly, taking it back. "I just didn't catch what you said, that's all I meant." She hesitated to respond again, however, making a small noise in her throat that Charlie couldn't discern. Was she mollified by his apology or ... embarrassed by her aggression? Whatever it was, the sudden fire in her seemed to have died down as quickly as it arrived, as if she'd forgot, then remembered, the situation that she was in.

"I said my surname," she said quietly. She *was* embarrassed, Charlie could tell.

"Okay, sw—Minnie," Charlie said, correcting himself. "What is it?"

There was a heavy outlet of breath, and then something surprising; laughter, if a little snuffly in its execution. The light from the screen flashed off and on as she wiped her eyes.

"I don't like to tell people really, but I don't know why I'm embarrassed to tell you because obviously I've finally gone loony and you're not even real," Minnie said, laughing again and sniffing some more as she cleared the last of her tears. It was sad-sounding laughter, but there was also release in it, speaking to Charlie of an inner strength pushed beyond its emotional limits. There was another story here, Charlie knew, one that would have to wait. He decided that it was best to play along.

"That's right, you've gone crackers and I'm the result. Talk about adding insult to injury, eh?" he offered, smiling despite himself, and was rewarded with a small bark of continued laughter, sniffling and nervous, the view shaking back and forth as she shook her head resignedly.

"Yep, that's right ... Charlie, was it?" she said, looking up at the ceiling. "Sounds like a name I'd give to my lunacy-powered imaginary head-buddy. Jesus ..." She let out a sigh that ended in a final sniff. "Okay, *Charlie*, stand by to yuck your socks off like everyone else has my entire life, then ask the questions. Ready?"

Charlie wondered what the hell she was talking about, but didn't want to interrupt her flow.

"Yes. Ready."

"My full name ... is Minnie Cooper."

Charlie stared at the screen, suddenly lost for words. This had to be a dream, then.

"Are you ... are you ser—"

"*Yes*, I'm serious, my dad thought it would be funny, *yes*, my brother is really called Tommy, even though he insists on being called Tom, *no*, I don't like it, *no*, I won't change my name as it'd really upset my dad, *yes*, people find it funny, and *no*, I've never owned one. I think that's all of the usual questions. Got any others though?" she finished, sighing and chuckling in the quiet manner of someone who doesn't actually find anything in a sickening situation funny.

"No, I think that's all of them," Charlie said, sitting down and realising that they were finally having a conversation. "Well, I'd say it's a pleasure to meet you, but given the circumstances, I think that'd be a lie."

"Uh-huh," said Minnie with a sigh, the view leaning back and looking at the ceiling. "Keep talking, this really is something else. A real first, I have to say. Just ... great. Fucking *great*."

"It's for real, Minnie, I promise you. You have to take me seriously. Please."

"Don't worry, Chuck, I'm all ears. Go for your life."

Charlie winced.

"Do me a favour, will you?" he asked, scowling slightly.

"For you? Anything. Just name it."

Ignoring the sarcasm, Charlie responded.

"Don't call me that. It winds me up, and I'm stressed out enough as it is."

"*You're* stressed? Ah wait, of course you are. You're stuck in my head. You just don't know what to do with yourself, you little tumour you. I always thought that when my brain eventually went, it'd be a sudden haemorrhage, but I guess I'm going the slow way. Marvellous. Perfect way to leave a legacy, ending up wandering down the high street in my knickers, makeup smeared all over my face and babbling to invisible Chuck."

Ignoring the deliberate jibe, Charlie took in the room in front of him while he thought of his next move. It was as shabby as the bathroom, with a threadbare carpet and faded paint on the walls. A small table with two chairs stood in the opposite corner, and a bookcase—a full to capacity bookcase—was placed in front of the eastern wall. A fairly old TV had been placed in the corner to their left, with a knotted rug placed in front of it. She had done her best to make it homely, though; the candles were again in abundance, and there were many small picture frames all over the walls, each one with a candid photo of people she presumably knew. They were all quite faded, however, suggesting they hadn't been updated in some time.

Charlie realised that he was going to get nowhere unless he convinced her that he was for real, and so he turned his attention to finding a practical method for this. Almost immediately, he thought of one. He hesitated before asking the question, being forced to go somewhere he never really liked to. It had been a while ...

"Can you drive?" he said, trying to keep the tremor out of his voice and quietly hoping the answer would actually be no. She sniffed in response, and drew in a breath.

"I clearly shouldn't be allowed, but yes ..." she replied, her voice quiet and croaky like she was trying to hold back more tears. Charlie's heart sank a notch. *Dammit ...* he'd been hoping they'd have to take the bus. He *always* avoided being in cars.

"Where do you want to go?" Minnie continued. "I'm assuming this is the start of the bloody ... killing spree, right? Drive the fucking ... Fiesta through Tesco's shop window?" Her hand dragged across the bottom of the screen as she wiped her nose. Again, Charlie found himself wondering where he physically was; how could he be standing behind her eyes? He couldn't be. The screen would have to be, again, just a strange representation of them then?

First things first, Charlie. Plus, it's a dream, don't forget that, the voice in his head said ... but it sounded less confident than ever. Then Charlie realised that he was listening to a voice in his *own* head, and quickly pushed that thought away before his mind blew.

"My house. We'll go to my house," he said, firmly, pleased with his own idea and finding it infallible. "I'll tell you where the spare key is, and you can go in, hell, I'll tell you the password to my PC, you can go in there too ... all stuff that you couldn't possibly know. Right? And then you'll have to believe me. Okay? And then we can decide if this is, I dunno, a psychic link or an out of body experience or whatever, and then decide what we do about it. Tell me what's wrong with that, eh?"

Silence again, followed by another sigh and a headshake. Charlie was about to do some shouting of his own, when the view began to rise from the floor.

"Okay, whatever you say, Chuck, it's not like I had any other pla—sorry, Charlie, Charlie—let's go for a road trip. At least I'll have some company."

"You're up for that? That's great. Do you ... do you have a car of your own?"

"Only just, but yes. Hopefully it'll get us around Coventry and back."

Great. An old banger as well. This just gets better, thought Charlie, trying to smother his usual anxieties.

"Where the hell are we going, anyway?" Minnie asked.

"Radford," said Charlie, relieved at least that they were making progress and pushing thoughts of the dreaded passenger seat out of his head. A thought struck him. "Where are we at the moment, anyway?"

"Canley," she said, moving to pick up a black woollen coat from the living room table. "Costa Del Canley. Not too far ..." she caught herself, and gave a hollow laugh. "So it shouldn't inconvenience you too much." Then, quietly to herself: *"What the fuck are you doing, you crazy bitch ..."*

They moved into the hallway and the mirror came into Charlie's view, showing Minnie's face again. It was now red-eyed, with blotchy pink patches on her skin.

"Jesus, look at the state of me," she said, sarcastically, running her hands through her tight curls. "I'm in no state to be seen out and about with my very own man-in-the-head. Girl-about-town, man-in-the-head. Not every day I get to do this sort of thing, right?" Her face crumpled slightly for a second, about to go again, but she swallowed it back. She stared into the mirror for a moment, and as Charlie watched he was suddenly struck by an uncanny sensation.

It was only brief, but for a second Charlie had the utter conviction that he recognised her; that he knew her face like that of an old, long-forgotten friend, reduced to a hazy memory by a distance of years. Then just as quickly, the moment was gone, and Minnie was yet again just a stranger whose life he'd been thrown into.

"Charlie?" Minnie said, in a small, suddenly scared voice. *Or maybe not suddenly,* Charlie thought. He wondered if maybe the annoying sarcasm was her defence mechanism against the world, protecting the real Minnie when she felt as terrified as she did now.

"I'm here. I wish I wasn't—no offence—but I'm here."

"When we've been to your house ... if it's there or not ... will you leave me alone after that?" she asked. It was almost a plea. Charlie didn't know what to say.

"I'll try. I promise I'll try."

She carried on staring into the mirror, and then he heard her keys jangle in her hand. Minnie—and Charlie with her—was turning and walking out of the front door.

***

In all the years Charlie had lived in Coventry, he'd never quite got his head around knowing exactly where each area of the city ended and where the next began; knowing the quickest way between them was even more of a challenge. Riding inside Minnie's head—the pair of them inside her barely roadworthy Ford Fiesta—it became immediately clear that she didn't suffer from the same problem. He thought it best to be silent as they drove, even though he had questions; was she born here, what was her job, what the hell was her general problem anyway, other than having a strange man in her head (although he thought that if he did ask that, he'd phrase the question slightly more pleasantly). All of which he kept to himself, both out of politeness—Charlie was all too aware that he was effectively trespassing on her life—and the fact that if questions were asked about *his* life in Coventry, he'd never really be able to answer them all, as he knew that he couldn't really explain why he was still there.

He'd moved there for a girl, after all, and quickly realised that she wasn't The One (a lack of desire to do anything other than watch TV became rapidly apparent in their new domestic situation) and after moving out, he'd kept the same stop-gap bar job that he'd taken upon arrival in the city. He'd started off telling himself that he'd only work there while looking into doing something else—he had a degree in English, after all, and had thought about becoming a copywriter—but the same internal conversation had carried on for ten years, even when he was made manager of the venue.

These days, he didn't really even bother convincing himself that he intended to do anything else; life was good, the hours suited him, the work was mainly a sociable laugh, and he was lucky enough to have what he considered to be a good group of friends. If the city wasn't his first choice, and the pay wasn't spectacular, he supposed he didn't really class those issues as being enough reason to upset the status quo. Bottom line, he guessed that he spent a lot of time having fun, and that was what he loved best in life. Starting a family wasn't on his radar, held no appeal, but that wasn't because he was shallow; he just prized his freedom very highly.

And yet here he was, sitting trapped in a black room, with no knowledge of how he got there in the first place.

Even worse, he was trapped in a black room that was itself trapped inside a moving car, one of his least favourite places on earth to be. Visions of the past flashed before his eyes; the roll and flip of the light, the smack of weight on water ...

Charlie closed his eyes and breathed deeply, taking it away as best he could. Eventually, it was Minnie who broke the silence.

"You there, Charlie?" she asked, sounding businesslike. Minnie had seemed to relax once they were in the car; she had a job to do now, something to occupy her frightened mind.

"Yeah," he replied, sitting up and feeling keen to talk. As time had passed, he'd felt more and more guilty about his presence in her head, despite his previous annoyance at her hysterics. She'd been scared out of her wits, after all, and had done nothing, as far as he knew, to deserve any of this. Anything he could now do to be 'nice', he would do so, for her sake. "I'm here, just, you know, trying to respect your personal space. Well ... as far as possible, anyway." He chuckled slightly, trying to make a joke, but she didn't acknowledge it.

"Sat nav says we're nearly here," she said, referring to the phone software that was directing her. The modern hardware looked out of place where it was sitting, clipped in its plastic holder against the aging air vents of the decrepit vehicle. She hadn't recognised the name of the street when he'd said it, but Charlie hadn't even bothered to try and use it as proof of him being who he said he was. She'd only claim the same explanation that she'd used earlier, that of her own subconscious storage of something she'd heard, or seen once in passing, that was then forgotten by her conscious mind.

16

Charlie looked to the right of the view, clocking a shop he recognised as it went past.

"Yep, nearly here," he confirmed. He'd actually known that they'd been drawing near for the last few minutes, seeing the same old landmarks that he knew very well. *Thank God,* he thought. *Get out me out of this bloody thing.* He meant the car, and realised that he could have meant the black room as well. "Couple more streets down, on the left."

The day was bright, being morning and early autumn, and as Charlie dimly acknowledged this, a switch flicked in his head and a jarring thought occurred. *Was* it autumn? He'd just realised he had absolutely no idea what the date was, assuming all along that it was the next day after his night out, a Saturday, meaning today would be a Sunday. What if *wasn't* Sunday? Then what the fuck would he do?

He tried to steady his shaking hands in front of the screen's bright glow, and took a deep breath, wondering whether to ask Minnie.

One thing at a time. Last thing you need to do is give her another crazy concept to worry about. Let's do the bloody home visit first, confirm you're the real deal, then see what's up ... you get Sunday mornings off, at least. Good thing you're not supposed to be in work right now.

He opened his mouth to tell Minnie that it was the next turn, but the sat nav app got there first; she flicked the indicator without a word, and the Fiesta turned into Fynford Road. As Charlie laid eyes on his home street, he felt a sudden pang of longing; here was normality, here was his life, represented by the terraced street he called home. It wasn't the most glamorous street in the city by any stretch, but the rent was cheap, the building was sound, and he knew enough of his neighbours to say hello to that he felt there was a greater safety here. He wasn't friends with any of them, as such—they didn't make any more effort than a smile and a greeting, and neither did he—but they were acquaintances, good people as far as he knew.

Take a trip in their heads, buddy, double check. You don't bother asking permission, right?

Minnie pulled over in the first available space, and drew the keys out of the ignition. She sighed again, a heavy, resigned, I-can't-believe-I'm-doing this release, and the view swung up to the ceiling of the car. Charlie noticed that she seemed to have a habit of looking up when she spoke to him.

"Right. We're here. Which number am I looking for?"

"Seventeen. The one with the high hedge," Charlie said, as calmly as possible. He was excited now, the prospect of getting her fully onside filling him with anticipation. This would be the start of the process that got him the fuck out of there, and Charlie decided in that moment that if she helped him fix this, he'd give her some money towards a new car. Patronising again, perhaps, but he thought it was the least he could do.

"Of course it is. Doesn't hurt that it's also the one I've just parked near, right?"

She was persistent, he had to give her that.

"The hedge hides the door number from here. How could you know that one was number 17?"

She didn't reply, and simply unbuckled her seat belt.

"Let's just get this over with," she said, quietly, and opened the door. Charlie felt his shoulders drop, his back relaxing the instant she stepped out of the metal cage.

The view moved across the fairly empty street as she walked—at that time of day, as usual, most of the cars were gone—and approached the house, which was obscured, as Charlie had pointed out, by the high hedge sticking up over the small fence that ran around the edge of the miniscule, gravelled front garden. Her hand came into view, pushing open the low gate that was made from a different wood to the rest of the fence. Minnie's steps seemed to grow lighter once she was walking on the short, concrete path, as if she were worried about being caught trespassing. The scuffing sound of her trainers on the dull grey surface ceased, as she picked her feet up properly and put them down again with care.

"It's okay, no one's in," said Charlie, noticing the change and trying to reassure her. "Eric'll be out at work—sorry, Eric's my housemate—so there's no one to worry about." Minnie didn't respond to this, and instead the view began to cast about the front doorstep, looking for something.

"Where's this spare key hidden then?" she asked, her voice very low and discreet. "There's nowhere for it to be hidden under."

"You have to crouch down," said Charlie, whispering himself on reflex—not wanting the hiding place to be overheard—then realising that doing so was idiotic. He raised his voice again. "At the back of the step, on the right-hand side, the concrete's crumbled away slightly and left a gap. We stash it in there."

Without a word, the view lowered and then angled up, showing the upstairs windows as Minnie craned her head back, leaning in with her shoulder. A few seconds passed.

What ... did the curtain just move upstairs?

"There's nothing here," said Minnie, softly. "There's a gap, but no key."

"Of course there is," said Charlie, annoyed at what he took to be a half-assed effort on her part. "Check again."

"Charlie, I felt all round it. It's only a small gap, barely enough room for a key as it is, and there isn't one there. This is, as I suspected, bullshit." She didn't sound victorious, or even angry. She sounded scared, the word *bullshit* coming out almost as a squeak.

Eric. He's forgot to put the bloody key out.

"Eric's obviously forgotten to leave it out," Charlie said, frustrated now. This was typical; Eric, always so reliable, except on the one day that it was really required of him. "This means nothing. And hey, how would you have known the gap was even there in the first place?"

Minnie sighed, and the view moved to the floor in silence for a moment, showing one of her trainers pawing in aimless arcs on the path. Charlie's heart sank; despite the important point about the gap in the step actually being there, she didn't buy it, and was instead fearing the worst.

"Look, Minnie, I promise you—"

Both of them jumped as the front door opened. The view leaped a foot back from the step, and Charlie actually fell onto his backside in surprise. The floor in his darkened room was solid, and yet didn't hurt; it wasn't hard or soft, it was just something for him to stand on, it seemed. But there was no time to consider that.

The person responsible for the door opening was a short, elderly woman, looking like she was at least in her eighties. She was wearing a green jumper and jogging bottoms with an apron covering the whole ensemble, and her feet were covered with nothing but a pair of brown socks. Her white hair was scraped back into a high ponytail, though some of it had escaped in thin strands that stuck out in all directions. She wore glasses, and the expression on her aged face was a mix of confusion, suspicion and indignation.

"What are you doing?" she asked, looking Minnie up and down and putting a foot out of the door and onto the step, holding on to the doorframe with one hand. Minnie didn't answer, and the view continued to show the scene before her. Had he been of normal mind, Charlie would have realised that she was frozen, waiting for him to explain or give her a clue as to what to say; this wasn't the situation that she'd been told to expect, whether she believed him or not, and she couldn't exactly ask questions of her invisible companion to get the answers she needed without looking insane.

At that moment, however, Charlie simply wasn't capable of providing assistance. His blood had run cold upon seeing the old woman, and his world had been rocked even harder against its already battered and strained foundations.

He had never seen the old woman in his entire life.

His mind raced; Eric's mother?

No, you've seen pictures of his mother!

Had Mr Bansal, the landlord, hired her as a cleaner?

He's never done that in ten years, and he knows I'd hit the roof if he sent someone round without telling us first!

Had Eric invited her round?

What the hell for?

Everything drew a blank, while Charlie remained standing there gaping in shock. The mutual silence went on long enough to draw another enquiry from the old woman. Her free hand went up, palm out, and her head began to shake back and forth in slow defiance.

"I'm not interested, whatever it is. I don't want it. The sign says that we don't buy from salesmen, so we *don't* buy from salesmen. *Or saleswomen,*" she added, gesturing her hand up and down Minnie's frame. The view scanned around dumbly, as Minnie looked for the aforementioned sign. The old woman caught the look.

"*Here,*" she said, annoyed, and reached out and around the doorframe. She pointed to the front room window from the outside. "In the corner. You've seen it, I know you've seen it."

Minnie looked, as did Charlie, and his sense of shock dropped into straight-up terror. He felt like ice had just travelled around his entire body, and his mouth gaped at the sight before them. In the bottom left-hand corner of the window was a large, faded yellow sticker with black writing. It read:

NO DOORSTEP TRADERS, NO SURVEYS

The sticker had obviously been there for a very long time, peeling slightly at the edges, its surface bleaching after many years of catching the sun. Charlie didn't know how they'd missed it on the way in, due to its size, but it was clear as day to them now; to Charlie it was like a rubber stamp that declared his reality void. He'd lived in that house for ten years, looked out through that window every day.

There had never, ever been a sticker on the window.

As Charlie goggled uselessly, he heard Minnie's halting voice start up, coming to their rescue after realising she wasn't getting any help.

"Sorry ...madam ... but I'm ..."

"Pardon?" said the old woman, cutting Minnie off and speaking louder than she had before. She seemed to realise that Minnie was on the back foot, and looked like she felt she could take control of the conversation. "I can't hear you, I'm afraid, you have to speak loudly, speak up."

Charlie heard Minnie take a deep breath, and tried to come back to himself, to help, but got nowhere, seeing the gluey remnants of the sticker's previous, fully stuck edges, now left as ghosts of their former glory where the corners had peeled back.

Where the fuck did that sticker come from?? Who the fuck is this woman??

"*Sorry*, madam," he heard Minnie say, as if from far away. "I'm sorry to trouble you, but I'm not selling anything. I think I might have the wrong house, if I'm honest."

The old woman eyed her suspiciously, while her body seemed to relax slightly ... but not completely. Minnie's words—or the surprisingly confident tone she injected into her voice from nowhere—had had an effect.

"Wrong house ... who are you after then? What number are you after? This is seventeen," the old woman said, leaning out again and tapping the numbers stuck to the outside of the house. "*Seventeen,*" she repeated, as if Minnie hadn't heard

"Yes, this is the number I was given, but I might have been told wrong," said Minnie, sounding businesslike but not stern, not forceful. She was coming across like a softly spoken schoolteacher. The transformation was surprising and impressive. "I was looking for a Charlie Wilkes, is this his house? He might have lived here before, and moved?" The old woman scoffed in response.

"You've been told wrong, love, there's no Charlie Wilkes here," she said, almost looking satisfied by giving the negative news. "No one on this *street* even, and I know them all, apart from the Punjabi lot up the road," she added with a dismissive wave of her hand. "Who told you he lived here?"

"But he could have moved, maybe?" Minnie repeated, ignoring the question. "Did he live here before you?" Another scoffing noise came in response, the old woman leaning against the door frame and crossing her arms in front of her chest. She was no longer defensive or alert, but that didn't mean that her outward personality had softened in any noticeable way.

"Unless he lived here sixty years ago, but then I doubt he'd be anyone you'd know if he did," she said with an unpleasant chuckle. "My husband and I bought this house in 1954 and we've been here *ever since.*" She said this last part with great relish, enjoying her final pronouncement on Minnie's enquiry being incorrect.

Her words were a slap, and they catapulted Charlie into action.

"That's bullshit!" he yelled, thrusting an accusatory finger at the screen, veins standing out on his forehead. "That's fucking *bullshit,* she's lying! I've lived in this house for ten years, *ten years!* Tell her she's talking bullshit, Minnie, *I'm telling you, this is bullshit!*" His shouts grew into hysteria of his own, confusion fuelled by terror and a crazy, cold sensation all over his body. *They've done something to my house, someone's done something to my house and put me in here, this is bullshit!*

The only sound now was his heavy breathing, and the brief noise of a passing car on the road behind them. Charlie saw the old woman's face grow confused. He realised that Minnie hadn't responded to her—she'd been listening to Charlie's rant instead—and now the old woman was wondering what was going on again.

"So. Not here," the old woman added, waving a hand to emphasise Charlie's absence and waiting for a response from Minnie. Charlie looked past her into her kitchen—*his* kitchen—and saw souvenir magnets that he'd never owned pinning grandchildren's crayon drawings to a fridge he didn't recognise.

Wallpaper as faded and peeling as the sticker. Bran cereals on top of the cupboards, a half-eaten bowl of cat food.

This was real. This wasn't his house, and never had been.

"Minnie ... Minnie, I don't know what's—"

"I'm really sorry to have bothered you, madam," Minnie said, speaking suddenly and loudly, her desire to cut him off causing Charlie to panic and try and talk over her words.

"Minnie, listen—"

"I think somebody must have been—"

"Minnie, I'm *telling* you, listen to me—"

"—having a good laugh at my expense—"

"Please, Minnie!"

"—really sorry to have interrupted your day."

"Minnie, I'm here, I'm HERE!"

Minnie's last words to the old woman were choked back as her voice threatened to give way, and she turned before the confrontational hag could see her face collapse. The view hurried quickly back up the driveway, through the gate, and by the time Minnie had got halfway to the car her footsteps had quickened. They reached the Fiesta at a run. The door was flung open, and she dropped heavily into the driver's seat.

Charlie bit his own words back, not even noticing his surroundings this time, and let her get it all out. He was busy trying to control his breathing and get some perspective, to plan his next move. After a minute or two, he gave up. He didn't even know where to start. This was *insane*.

"I swear to God, Minnie, I have no idea what's going on," he said, clenching his fists and speaking with a trembling, low voice. "I know you're scared, but I'm, I'm, I'm ..." he trailed off. Minnie's hand struck the dashboard, hard.

"Dave, you *bastard*, you *bastard*, you *bastard*," she cried, her hand punctuating the word against the plastic surface. "All your fucking *fault,* you *bastard*, I *told* you—"

Dave? thought Charlie, his attention caught. *Who the hell is Dave, now?*

He decided to be quiet, and hoped that she would explain further by ranting to herself, but no further information was coming. A few minutes more passed, during which the occasional car drove by, and Charlie found himself wishing that she would look back at the house so he could check the upstairs curtains again, to see if the old woman was watching.

He was about to gently ask her the question when Minnie addressed him first.

"Charlie? *Charlie.*"

"I'm here, I'm here," he said eagerly, speaking as soothingly as he could manage.

"Just checking. Just checking I'm still *nuts,*" she said again with deep bitterness, slapping her hands together, hard. "Just checking I'm still a goddamn *statistic.*"

There was a pause, and Charlie took that as his cue.

"Who's Dave, Minnie?"

"*Dave,*" Minnie responded quickly, "is the reason I'm in this mess, that I'm sitting in a car talking to myself after dealing with some old bitch that I managed to wake up on a Sunday afternoon, after driving halfway across town because my crackers fucking junkie brain finally blew a fucking *gasket.* Turns out all those old government warning ads were *right.*" The view rocked sideways with this last word; she'd slapped herself hard across the head, and Charlie saw a few small droplets of saltwater fly away from her face.

Ah. There it is.

"Did Dave ... did Dave give you the ..."

"*No,* Dave didn't give me anything," snapped Minnie, sniffing. "Dave doesn't even use. Never has done. It was *Dave* that decided I needed persuading, dragging out of the flat for ... *socialising,* as he so charmingly put it. Thanks an effing bunch, mate," she spat, the view jerking backwards as she jammed her skull into the headrest of the seat. There was silence again, except for the sound of Minnie's heavy breathing. Charlie could see this was a very sore point indeed for Minnie, whatever had happened, and didn't want to upset her further despite his own panic. He was responsible for adding more weight onto already distressed shoulders, and he suddenly felt an impotent urge to hold her hand for a moment, to tell her it was okay to need help. He opened his mouth to do the same verbally, but the words didn't come, his brain too rattled and swirling to put instinct into conscious words.

"Let's just say," Minnie said finally, "that it … didn't go well. All right? And I don't think it's any coincidence that the next day, up pops a little voice in my head calling itself Charlie and asking me to go and visit old women, claiming they live in their houses." There was a pause, and the view swung back to the house; Charlie took his opportunity to look at the upstairs windows. The curtains were now still. "Bitch," muttered Minnie. "There was no need to be like that. I know I looked dodgy, but it was obvious I just had the wrong house. No need for that …"

"Minnie," said Charlie, taking her calmer demeanour as an opportunity to try again, desperation forcing him to push his luck. "Something's going on here. I don't know, maybe I'm just … remembering it wrong, maybe my memory's been screwed, I mean, to me, that's my home, and I know I work at …" An idea struck him.

We could check that right now, we wouldn't even need to go anywhere!

It was a thrilling thought, but terrifying at the same time.

What if the result is the same as this one …

"Minnie, grab your phone there for a sec? It's important. You're not crazy, and I think I can help prove it *right now*. Or at least, prove to me that *I'm* not crazy. I need you to do me a favour." She didn't respond, and continued to look out at the house. "Minnie? Can you hear me?" Charlie said.

"I can hear you, Charlie," she said quietly, the dry, protective sarcasm coming back into her voice but not quite making it. This time, it couldn't beat the fear. Her voice still had a crack in it. "Loud and clear."

"Facebook," Charlie said, excitedly. "Look me up on Facebook. I have an account, it'll say I live in Coventry, I'm all there. Easy." There was silence for a moment as she pondered this.

"Nope. Won't work, Chuck," she said, sighing and shaking her head as she deliberately used that name again. Charlie gritted his teeth and tried to keep a lid on his anger. "I could have seen your name on a mutual friend's profile, or even just seen your name in the paper, anything, and my subconscious has picked you at random and given you a little voice in my head. Seeing a name on a Facebook page, what would that prove?"

"I could … I could tell you what my last few status updates were about, and then you could check them and see if I was right. How would you know that?"

"Well, apart from the fact that I couldn't look at your statuses as we're not Facebook friends, Chuck. Unless your profile is Public?"

"I told you, stop calling me—"

"*Chuck! Chuckchuckchuuuuck!!*" Minnie suddenly screamed, and the jaded bravado dropped away completely as silent tears began. Charlie bit his lip, and waited a moment for the sobs to fade.

"Don't cry, come on. Listen, grab your phone and bring up Facebook a second. I know, I know, but just do it anyway. I'll tell you my password, you can log into my account, and I can tell you before you even see them what my last couple of status updates were." It was a great idea, one he was amazed he hadn't thought of before, but he was only getting silence again in return. It was maddening. However, without saying a word, she picked her phone up off the dashboard clip where she'd left it (*not the best idea round here*, Charlie thought) and held it in front of her.

"Yep, okay. Got it," she said. "Can you see that?" She paused for a second, thinking. "You can see what I see, right?"

"Yes," said Charlie enthusiastically. She wasn't totally sure, then, and that was good. "And I can see that just fine. Listen, go onto Facebook and log in as me. The e-mail address is cwilkes27@hotmail.com, and the password is Xanadu, that's Xanadu with an X."

He watched as she did so, his heart racing again like a small, buzzing engine. This would be proof. This would be *proof.*

It didn't work.

A familiar thumbnail image of his profile photo came up; a JPEG of the ELO spaceship. This image would have made Charlie almost weep with relief, as this was exactly as he'd always had it ... but sitting where it was, next to the reappeared e-mail and password entry screen accompanied with the words 'Incorrect Email/Password Combination' brought him no comfort at all. Quite the opposite, in fact.

"What a surprise," said Minnie, "no joy."

"You've done it wrong!" snapped Charlie, and immediately tried to rein himself in. His fear would make him lose control if he let it, and he *had* to keep her onside. All thoughts of concern for Minnie had temporarily disappeared. This was his *life.* He couldn't take another hit. This was something, *something* to grip onto with desperate hands, and he couldn't take this being proved false too.

She tried again without speaking. He watched the letters as she pressed them, watched them with laser intensity. She did it right. It still didn't work.

"Nope," she said. The practiced, cynical tone didn't hide her fear. Charlie rubbed at his face with trembling hands.

They've gotten to your account. Changed the details. If whoever has done this can put you in someone's head, they sure as shit can change your fucking Facebook password. Right?

Right. That *was* right. He tried to feel better, and he did, a bit ... but far from completely.

Does the account even exist?

"Can you search for my name?"

"What would be the point?"

Good question.

He wouldn't even be able to see himself, as she wasn't his Facebook Friend and had almost zero access to his profile; all she would be able to see was the ELO spaceship preview photo.

Some of your Facebook information will be visible though, won't it, even if she's not on your Friends list?

That was right.

"I'll tell you the point," he said quickly. "You won't be able to go through my profile, obviously, but the basic details will be visible."

"You think this address will be on here? It won't show the bloody house number anyway."

"No, no, that's not what I'm after. Can you just do it please?"

"Fine," she said, tapping at the screen. "Wilkes with a K-E-S, yeah?"

"That's the one." Minnie typed in *Charlie Wilkes, Coventry* into the search bar, and Charlie held his breath. The very first step was at least confirming that he was on there at all. His hands trembled, and he was unaware that his mouth was wide open.

The small ELO spaceship reappeared on the screen, then again as Minnie clicked on the preview and brought up the limited access version of his profile.

"I already said, Charlie, this doesn't really prove anything—" said Minnie, sadly, but Charlie interrupted her.

"No, no, I know, but look, look at the 'Works at' bit there," he said, a warm glow shooting through him as relief hit, blessed confirmation right there in undeniable black and blue on the screen:

Works At: Barrington's, Coventry

"See? That's where I said."

"When?"

"What? I told you earlier, I work at Barrington's." A pause.

"No, you didn't."

"I did! I bloody did!"

Another pause.

"Doesn't matter anyway," she said. "Same thing. Friend of a friend ... subconsciously tucked away. Whatever." The knuckles of her right hand came up to the bottom of the view, resting against her lip as her elbow was placed on the windowsill of the car door.

"Oh come on, remembering a name, but remembering where I work as well—"

"There are *autistic* people who can draw an entire city skyline from memory, and accurately too, because they can access parts of the brains that normal people can't," snapped Minnie, still looking at the house. "You've seen *Rain Man*, right? All the matches on the floor, counted straight away, the exact right number? The brain can do, and store, amazing things, if you can somehow access those talents. So don't tell me it's impossible. Why the hell am I even arguing with you, anyway? Just shut up and leave me alone. I need to think what the hell I'm going to do."

Charlie thought frantically, found something, snapped his fingers.

"It's Sunday today, right?"

"Yep."

That was important. He hadn't lost any time then, no period in between passing out and waking up here.

"Two p.m. My shift is supposed to start at two. And what time is it now, about eleven thirty? Okay. Go to Barrington's—"

"I don't ... I don't really go into pubs at the moment ..."

"Doesn't matter, just get a coffee or something, it'll just be families having a Sunday lunch right now anyway. Look, just do this for me and if it doesn't work then ... then ... well then I'm fucked because I won't have a clue what's going on. Just go there, have a coffee, and wait. Once it gets past 2:00 p.m., I should be there, and you can ask for me. They'll *tell* you I *should* be in, but I won't be, and they won't know why. See?"

"I don't get you."

"Think about it. You think you just happen to have somehow stored my name—and where I work—in your memory, and have gone nuts so you're dragging it out of your subconscious to create me, right?"

"Got it in one, Charlie."

Despite the sad, bitter tone in her voice, Charlie winced again. He didn't like *Charles* any more than *Chuck*. He let it go.

"Well, there is no fucking way that A: you know my shift pattern, and even if *somehow* you did, then B: you couldn't know that I wasn't coming today, right? Well, I'm telling you both of those things. So when it turns out that I *should* be in, just like I'm telling you, and I'm *not* in, you have to know that I'm real, right? The reason I'm not in work is because I'm in your head!" Charlie stopped talking, and held his breath. It had been an effort not to sound as desperate as he felt. Minnie's fingers drummed along the bottom of the screen, tapping across her mouth. The view then shook from left to right, accompanied by a resigned sigh.

"It's a good one, I have to admit, Charlie," she said, her keys coming up and slotting into the ignition. "And at the very least I won't feel like an idiot again, as you are at least *supposed* to be there." She sighed heavily, preparing for the short journey ahead, and turned the keys.

Charlie flinched as the engine rumbled into life; another car ride to get through first.

"Only problem is," Minnie continued, "what the hell are you going to say when we get there and it turns out you're *not* supposed to be in today? Or that you've phoned in sick? Or simply haven't updated your Facebook profile and you work somewhere else now? Hmm?"

Charlie didn't have an answer, couldn't begin to think of one.

"The house was wrong," Minnie added, with false, bitter breeziness. "Just because Facebook says Charlie Wilkes worked there at some point doesn't mean he still does, or that Charlie Wilkes's shift pattern matches what I've imagined it does. "

"Don't do that," snapped Charlie, his voice quiet but powerful now. "Don't say it like that. *I'm* Charlie Wilkes. I'm the guy."

Minnie drew in a breath to say something else, perhaps to carry on the argument, but then thought better of it. She flipped the indicator, and Charlie saw her hazel eyes as they looked into the mirror, catching her own reflection for a minute and looking at herself, looking through him.

"Okay, Charlie," she said, sadly. "Let's go to Barrington's." She turned the wheel, and the car pulled away from the kerb. This time, as they drove, Charlie didn't even feel the desire to talk, utterly lost in his own thoughts. He was more scared now than he'd been during all of this crazy morning, presented with the possibility—the unthinkable, impossible possibility—that Minnie might be right.

I'm Charlie Wilkes. I'm Charlie Wilkes. I'm Charlie Wilkes.

But he was also inside another person's head.

***

... the car flips, and he has time to hear her draw a sharp breath, realising that it's too late to stop it, handed over to fate and the twin forces of gravity and momentum ...

***

Charlie barely noticed the journey over to the city centre. Fear had turned to anger, and he began to think like a petulant child, thinking of ways to catch Minnie out, but they were all pointless, all able to be explained away with the same 'Subconscious Memory' excuse. He didn't think he could take hearing her say that again.

Somewhere inside, Charlie knew he was essentially being selfish, thoughtless, and tried to remind himself that he was the trespasser here. He was the one that had come to her, not the other way around. But like a cornered animal—and wasn't he exactly that, trapped and cornered?—his defences were up, instinct putting him into an aggressive stance. He tried to grasp his normal self, to find the man that would handle this situation best; friendly, helpful, the sort of person that would go out of his way to help a stranger if they needed it, ready with a smile and a kind word. But that man wasn't available just then. His every thought had turned towards proving he existed, and Minnie was not only the person who seemed determined to stop him, but the one who'd put the doubt into his head in the first place.

And so, once Minnie had parked the car near the cathedral, being lucky enough to grab one of the spaces on the small cobbled street nearby, he began to spit questions at her as she made the short walk along the street to Barrington's. They'd previously been sitting in silence all the way there, but free of the vehicle and drawing nearer to the pub, a growing sense of dread prompted Charlie to begin his interrogation.

"Where are *you* from, Minnie? What's *your* story?"

"What?"

"You have my situation, you've heard me tell you all about it. I know nothing about *you*. What did you do yesterday? Where did you go, for example? Do you even remember?"

The view stopped walking down the cobbled path, the Barrington's sign visible over the other side of the main road that crossed their path about a hundred feet away. A few people walked past the front of the pub, quietly going about their Sunday business. Charlie saw Minnie's hand come up holding her phone, moving to the left-hand side of her head.

"Listen to me, Charlie. This is really important."

Charlie realised what she was doing; using her phone to stop any onlookers thinking that she was having a conversation by herself.

"That isn't up for debate," she said, quietly and firmly, but with a slight tremor in her voice. "You aren't here to question me. You're in *my* head. Right? You're lucky I'm even bothering to come here, rather than being out getting myself sectioned. I will *not* have you doing that. It's the absolute last thing I need. Got it?"

Charlie bristled, not liking her tone; he liked being given no choice even less. The words *It's the last fucking thing I need being here in the first place too* came to his lips, but he bit them back. He knew could probably drive her legitimately crazy if he wanted to—stopping her sleeping, always talking, never giving her a moment's rest—and he knew that she didn't have the position of power here ... but hadn't he been thinking less than an hour ago that he didn't want to make it hard for her? And he did want to get inside Barrington's, after all. Arguing the point would only delay that, and there were other ways of checking who she was, subtler ways. It could wait.

"Right, got it," he said, but still saying it as if she were being unreasonable. It was petulant, but he felt like he had to salvage something from the exchange.

"Don't mess with my head, Charlie. I think it's already messed up enough as it is."

The phone went away, and the journey resumed again. Charlie strained to make out the interior of the pub from where they were, but as they drew closer, he thought he could see ... was it?

Yes! There's Claire, glass collecting!

A face he knew, someone he'd worked with for several years, and Charlie nearly wept with relief at the sight.

"Claire. That girl there. Her name is Claire, Claire Phelps, and you can ask her when you go in," he said, sharply. "Yeah, yeah, subconscious memory, fine, but the odds of doing it with *two* separate people, people who barely have any mutual friends outside of this pub? Bit of a stretch, don't you think?"

Minnie didn't answer; there was only the view, casting left and right in response. They'd reached the end of the cobbled path, and Minnie was standing on one side of the more modern main road now, watching for traffic. Being a Sunday, there was hardly any about, apart from a solitary bus coming from the right.

IN THE DARKNESS, THAT'S WHERE I'LL KNOW YOU

As Minnie waited for the bus to pass, Charlie looked through the pub window again, still just visible on the edge of the screen. What he saw there made his heart stop, made his lungs spasm and cause his body to instantly try and gasp for air like a cartoon character presented with a hot babe.

With awful timing, the bus slowly drew past, blocking his view for a few moments and giving him a tiny span of time to convince himself that he'd seen it wrong. He hadn't, of course, but it gave him enough brief, momentary hope that when the bus moved out of the way, and he saw through the pub window for a second time—the second sighting convincing him, and placing hope completely out of his reach—the impact was even worse.

A man had come up to Claire Phelps on her side of the glass, wearing the same matching uniform and saying something that made her turn and laugh, slapping his arm and nodding as she did so. Their relationship looked exactly as Charlie knew it to be; two colleagues that had worked with each other for years, as at ease in each other's company as two workmates can be.

The man on the other side of the glass was Charlie Wilkes.

***

Chapter Two: Minnie Leaves a Calling Card, If You Don't Want To Know the Result Look Away Now, and Charlie Sits Alone In the Black Room

***

Charlie's knees buckled, and he fell to the solid yet somehow impact-free floor again, one hand shooting out to break his fall without him consciously noticing. Minnie, unaware, was already beginning to cross the street, taking Charlie closer to the sight that had caused his world to be turned upside down for the second time inside two hours. All he could do was watch, a faint moaning sound coming from his mouth.

And that was what he did; watched as this other Charlie talked to Claire, wagging a finger at her as if scolding a child, watched as Claire slapped his finger away, sticking her chin out and extending the knuckles of a fist towards his face, shaking it at him. Watched as this other Charlie held his hands up in mock remorse, one of them holding a tea towel that was then suddenly thrown into Claire's face. Watched as this other Charlie sprinted out of view, laughing, as Claire snatched the towel away, also laughing, her face now red with embarrassment.

It was a typical incident between the two of them ... except it wasn't him. It was *another* him, one who looked and acted *exactly* the same as he did. One who was in his place of work—and several hours early at that, on a Sunday!—

31

and living his life. Charlie was dimly aware of an intense anger somewhere, boiling like hot mud deep inside him, but he was too shocked to experience it. He just continued to watch; Minnie's hand reached out and grasped the brass handle on the wooden door, pulling it open and entering Charlie's place of work.

Both Charlies' place of work.

The pub was the same as it had always been, a place that had never quite decided if it wanted to be a traditional boozer or a trendy city bar. As a result, it didn't really seem to cater to anybody's specific tastes, and became a place that people just ended up at somehow. Charlie had talked about changing the décor for years, but the owners never listened. It made money, and was the best performing of the five places they owned; by no means a runaway success, but never trouble, while the others seemed to haemorrhage money at an alarming rate. The owners had other concerns, therefore, and Barrington's was definitely subject to the 'if it ain't broke, don't fix it' rule.

So in both the main, large bar area—where Minnie was standing now— and the lounge room with its small wooden dance floor area, the oak effect wooden fixtures were still everywhere, from the tables to the chairs to the bar itself, jarring with the cream walls and modern downlighters attached to them. The music was trad jazz, massively at odds with the small number of families and people in groups of three or four eating Sunday lunches. The pictures on the walls were prints of famous works of art, creating a weird effect that just didn't seem to add up, along with large potted plants dotted here and there. The whole thing would have worked a bit better had they looked after it; as it was, signs of wear and tear were in abundance, from smudges and scratch marks on the previously polished metal of the light fittings, to cracks and gouges in the floor tiles. Nobody cared or even noticed at night—it was too busy and too dark—but in the brightness of the daytime, the place just looked shabby.

Charlie didn't see any of this though, nor did he wonder if Minnie had ever been in there before. He was already picking himself out near the far end of the bar—the man that Charlie had already decided he would refer to as Chuck, let *him* have that name—chatting and smiling with two seated couples as he cleared their plates. Despite himself, Charlie marvelled at the experience; he'd seen himself in a mirror countless times throughout his life, and also in camera footage that had been filmed while he was unaware of it at social occasions, so he knew how he looked from afar when moving and functioning. Seeing himself just a few feet away through the *screen*, however, was the most unusual thing Charlie had ever experienced (other than waking up inside a strange woman's head). The effect was the same as *being* there; the image quality was both unlike and superior to anything he'd ever seen on a man-made screen. Besides, wasn't he already seeing the screen as if it were his own eyes, already accustomed to looking through it ... and again, wasn't the blackness around not him not quite as dense as it seemed when he first arrived? Still unwelcoming and impenetrable, but ... less so? Things became familiar quickly in the black room, that was for sure.

32

Charlie watched mannerisms and expressions that were his own, and recognised them in a way that he would never have achieved when watching mere footage of himself in motion. Without a trace of vanity or arrogance, Charlie could have watched himself all day.

And there he was; taller than most at 6'2", but slim enough to take any sense of intimidation out of his height, reducing his visual impact. His smile was broad, as was his forehead, with slightly thinning blonde hair that still covered enough for him to get away with barely styling it, leaving it messy and free. In his white work shirt and black trousers, he managed the illusion of being smartly presented, even though outside of work he was never even close to it. Not that he didn't care about his appearance—far from it—but the look he preferred had always been one of carefree scruffiness. He felt it reflected his outlook on life; easy going, and looking for whatever experiences life threw at him.

When was the last time you actually had a real experience though, Charlie? Sure, you've got one right now, an absolute humdinger, but before this? What have you done? Look at your face. Look at that smile. Can't you see how false it is, now that you're seeing it from the outside?

Charlie snapped back to himself. Where the hell had those thoughts come from? It wasn't the time or the place; right here, right now, someone was living his fucking *life*, and here *he* was deciding that it was a good time for a bit of navel-gazing.

For some reason, Minnie was heading away from Chuck and approaching the opposite end of the bar. Confused, Charlie frantically tried to keep sight of his doppelganger, but soon he was off-screen as Minnie faced the mirror behind the optics full of cheap spirits.

"Go on then. Who's best to speak to here?" she muttered, the view dropping to look into the wood of the bar as she addressed him surreptitiously. Charlie goggled at the question; was she fucking nuts? Who was best to speak to?? How about the guy masquerading as him on the other side of the room, did she not think that might be a start?

Just as quickly, the realisation came; she had no idea what he looked like. She'd only seen his stupid ELO spaceship profile photo. Of course. She had no inkling that—in terms of convincing her that he was real—the absolute worst-case scenario had just happened. And compounding things further was the fact that he had no time to explain the situation either, as Chuck was now heading into view from the left-hand side of the screen. He'd obviously seen her waiting, and with his table-clearing task now complete, and no one currently behind the bar, he had gone back there to serve her.

Charlie's heart pounded with brutal force in his chest as he saw the other Charlie approach (*Chuck, he's Chuck, I'M CHARLIE*) leaving him unable to make a sound. He tried fruitlessly to warn Minnie, to tell her not to talk to this *fake* Charlie, this *Chuck*, but he couldn't. Upon seeing himself approaching, the sight had ceased to be fascinating. It was the most horrible thing he'd ever seen.

The smile was genuine this time though, he could tell, and that made it even worse. Chuck had seen that Minnie was alone, and he was clearly pleased and trying to turn on the charm. The thought made Charlie's head spin even more.

"Hi," said Minnie, as Chuck stopped directly in front of her sightline and framed himself in the middle of the view like some kind of awful, damning self-portrait. "Sorry to bother you, but I wonder if you can help me?" Her tone was confident, assured, and while Charlie knew that it was false, there was an unmistakable and genuine warmth underneath it, a tone he hadn't heard from her so far.

What the fuck is that?

When Chuck spoke in response, the words made Charlie rock slightly on his heels, as he already knew what they would be.

"Well, I'll certainly do my best to try, as long as you're not after money," Chuck grinned, raising his eyebrows as he made the little joke. It wasn't a chat up line, it wasn't even a stock line as such ... but it was not only the kind of the thing that Charlie knew *he* would say when something pleased him, but the *exact words* that had sprung into Charlie's head, unbidden, when he heard Minnie ask Chuck to help her. He felt so disorientated for a moment that he thought he was going to throw up, and wondered crazily if he could even do that when inside the black room.

You can't do that here, not in this place, this black room. That's what it is; the Black Room. This place is only for watching helplessly as your life disappears, while you lose yourself as others make jokes. This is where—

Charlie's spiralling consciousness jerked upright when he heard a new sound; Minnie laughing. It wasn't a big laugh—only a little chuckle—but she sounded as surprised as he was.

"No ... heh, no ... I just needed to ask you—"

Charlie suddenly heard another voice interrupt, a gasping, wheezing voice, and realised it was his own. Not Chuck's. His.

"That's me," Charlie gasped, straightening up off the floor and sitting up on his knees. "That guy. That's me. That's Charlie Wilkes."

Minnie's voice stopped dead, and Charlie saw mild confusion flash across Chuck's face.

"Ask me ...?" he smiled. Charlie knew that smile too, had felt it on his face before; it was his pleased, slightly smug smile, his smile that said *Hang on, is this girl interested?* It was a smile that said it was nice to know that someone might find him attractive, and he felt briefly embarrassed for Chuck, knowing the real reason for Minnie's stumbling hesitation. He wondered if Minnie had recognised the same thing. She still hadn't spoken, regardless. She was clearly frozen. Charlie froze too, trying and failing to think of a course of action.

"Are you ... is your name Charlie?" said Minnie, her voice almost a whisper, but Chuck didn't notice the tone, clearly delighted by the question. It looked like, as far as Chuck was concerned, she'd just confirmed what he'd clearly been hoping. Charlie supposed he couldn't blame himself (*Chuck, not me, I'M CHARLIE*) as he guessed Minnie was attractive, after all; he'd only seen her seemingly fresh out of bed, or red eyed, so he hadn't thought about it. To be fair, even if she'd been dressed and glammed up to the nines, he hadn't really been in a state of mind to be assessing the looks of the woman whose head he was stuck inside.

"Yes, yes I am!" said Chuck, a little too enthusiastically. Charlie winced internally, realising that not only would that have been *his* reaction, but seeing just how much of a goose he would have made himself out to be. "Sorry, have we met ...?" Again, Minnie froze in response, but only briefly; already she was fishing in her pocket for something, the phone then appearing in her hand.

"Sorry, I'm vibrating," she said, showing him the phone by way of explanation and then holding up one finger to Chuck as she turned away to take the 'call'. "Hello? Yes, this is her," she said, moving away from the bar. Charlie was impressed. She'd bailed, true, but she'd been put on the spot and had quickly remembered a good get-out when caught in the moment. Once she was out of earshot, she lowered her voice.

"What the fuck d'you mean?" she hissed. "I nearly just looked like a right idiot."

"I don't know!" Charlie hissed back, matching her secretive tone, then realising again that he didn't need to. "You'll have to excuse me, I've just found somebody else *living my fucking life!*"

"Well that was your last shot," said Minnie, through gritted teeth. "You're here, not in my head—and that's the big one—plus you don't live at that house, your shift time was wrong, all of it's *wrong*. You're not real, you're fake, and I'm ... I'm ..." she trailed off, breathing hard, and Charlie had a sudden idea.

"Ask him something," Charlie said. "Ask him something that there's no way you could possibly know."

"What the hell would that prove?" she asked, her hand covering the top part of the screen as she held it to her forehead. "Charlie Wilkes is there. There, behind the bar, not in my head."

"I don't know what it'd prove, but ..." said Charlie, searching to find what he was actually trying to get at, but realising he was onto something important, "... but it proves something, right? It proves that, at the very least, I'm real, surely? That something crazy is going on, but it's not you?"

Minnie hesitated for a long time. Then she said:

"Well ... what?"

"What?"

"What should I ask?"

"Okay ... uh ..." Charlie searched around, trying to think of something quickly, but Minnie helped him out.

"It's got to sound believable though. Like, why am I asking for him by name and then asking him some kind of personal question? He's just gonna freak out. Are you an expert in anything?" Charlie pondered this, and came to the conclusion that he wasn't.

"Uh ... no. I have an English degree?"

"That's not really gonna work. Wait, what about lost property?"

"I don't follow ..."

"Can I say I've been told you're the guy to speak to about lost property?"

"Yeah, I suppose, but how does that prove anything?"

"Well, when did you last work here?"

"Friday night."

"Do you remember anything being handed in?" Charlie saw where she was going with it. It wasn't exactly what he'd had in mind, but it was at least something Minnie couldn't know subconsciously. How could she know what had been handed in most recently? There was no way. If he could remember, and tell her, it would be undeniable proof of him being real.

He racked his brain trying to remember if anything had come in on Friday night ... there was something, wasn't there? A purse? A credit card? Wait ... a phone. A cracked Samsung. He remembered because he'd tried to check for an address book in it, so he could text someone who could then tell the owner where their phone was, but the battery had been dead. He hadn't even been working in the bar that night either; they'd come in here on their night out! He'd found it in the toilet on top of the cistern!

"Yeah. A phone, a Samsung. Big crack right down the middle of the screen. Ask if anyone handed in a phone *last* night."

"Why last night, if you weren't working?"

"I came in with some mates. Found it myself and handed it in."

"Right. That's what we'll go with. But this is the last one, Charlie. You have to shut up after this. All right? If this is more garbage ... you have to go away. Okay?"

Charlie said nothing. What could he say, even though he didn't have a choice about staying or leaving. The Black Room had him.

"Whatever you say."

Minnie put her phone away and turned back to the bar. Charlie immediately watched Chuck as Minnie approached, watched him pretending to be busy moving glasses around; exactly as Charlie had known he would be.

"Sorry, you were saying?" asked Chuck, apologising for no reason and using unnecessary politeness. It was something Charlie always did, and something he regularly told himself off for doing. He said sorry when people bumped into *him*; not because he was a coward, but out of a very English social reflex. Still, he saw it in himself and didn't like it.

Come on, Chuck. Show me something to like.

"Yeah," said Minnie brightly, turning on the false front, and Charlie noticed again how easily and convincingly she managed this. It would have been more impressive if it didn't speak of regular practice, of being something that she did on a regular basis to keep the world at bay. He wouldn't have even known this to be the case if he hadn't already seen her other side. "Apparently you're the guy to speak to about lost property stuff?"

Chuck looked slightly confused for a second, as Charlie had known he would; he wasn't the lost property guy—nobody was, specifically—but he quickly shrugged off the slightly unusual question and answered her.

"Well, I don't know why someone suggested me specifically, but I can certainly have a look for you. Missing something, are you?"

"Yes, my phone, it's a Samsung, black. Has it been handed in?"

"Hold on a sec," said Chuck, moving away to the other end of the bar and rooting around underneath. "I haven't seen one myself, but I'll have a double check for you."

Charlie froze. He hadn't found it. He was wrong about the phone as well. He was wrong about everyth—

"Oh, no, hold on, is this it?" Chuck said, straightening up and holding out a black Samsung phone with a badly cracked screen.

Charlie's heart leapt. It was the exact same phone! But Chuck hadn't seen it? Hadn't Chuck found it, the same way that Charlie had found it? It didn't make sense.

"Minnie, that's it, that's the one! That's the one I found! Ask if he found it."

"Oh great!" exclaimed Minnie, not missing a beat. She was doing well. "Was it you that found it?"

"No, no," said Chuck, bringing it over to her. "I don't know when this came in, to be honest, I wasn't working last night. Someone must have given it to another member of bar staff. Here you go," he said, holding it out with a smile. This one was definitely genuine, as Charlie knew. He was always losing things, so reuniting people with their missing items felt good. As he watched Minnie's hand go out to take it, he looked at the small black device with its unmistakably thick, single crack snaking its way across the phone's screen— beautiful, if aesthetically reduced proof of his existence—and he realised something.

"You've got to leave it though. Someone'll be looking for it."

He watched as Minnie's hand took the phone anyway, and felt a flash of anger; that was someone else's stuff!

"Minnie?" he said.

"Ah, no," said Minnie out loud, with a sigh, "This isn't mine. Mine's a Galaxy II, this is the older one." She sounded convincingly disappointed as she said it, handing the phone back to Chuck, who shrugged with an apologetic look on his face.

"Ah, sorry to hear it," he said, taking the phone but not moving away. "Never mind. Listen, do you want to leave your contact details in case it turns up?" Again, it was exactly what Charlie would have said, wanting to help return the right phone to this girl ... but Charlie thought Chuck sounded a bit too eager.

Am I ... am I trying to get her number?

"Oh, that'd be great," he heard Minnie saying, and saw her hand reaching into her bag for her purse. "I'll give you a card. I knew these'd come in handy for something one day." She pulled it out and handed it over quickly; too quickly for Charlie to read it. What the hell was she doing giving him a card? She didn't have a lost phone to be contacted over!

Chuck took the card and inspected it.

"Minnie Cooper?" he said, and Charlie saw him look up with a grin, one that almost immediately disappeared when he saw the expression that must have been written on Minnie's face. Charlie wasn't daft, and neither was Chuck, clearly; he knew when to abandon a line of approach with women when it wasn't going well. Despite himself, Charlie approved of Chuck's mental about-face. He watched Chuck glimpse at the card again. "Web design, eh? Tough work to make a living from, you must be good?"

Nice save.

"Apparently not," chuckled Minnie, and Charlie knew it was real, caught briefly by the question and somehow charmed slightly into giving a genuine response. "Gave it up a while back and started working on something else. Had the cards printed and just needed an excuse to use them up. But I still do it, if you know someone who needs any."

Chuck held up the card and flicked it.

"Not at the moment. But if I find anyone, I'll let you know quicker than greased-up lightning."

Charlie winced, hard, and saw that Chuck's smiled had faltered slightly too.

Quicker than greased up lightning? Oh, Christ.

That was one that Charlie hadn't known was coming, as Chuck was flustered and trying to be funny. But Chuck had failed, and he knew it.

"Uh ..." Chuck said, lost for a second. Minnie, to her credit, didn't let on. Or was her chuckling response real?

"That's one way of putting it," she said with a smile. "But listen, thanks anyway."

"No problem," said Charlie, holding up a hand as Minnie turned to leave. As Minnie walked towards the door, Charlie could have looked at the reflection of the bar in the glass, but he didn't. He couldn't bring himself to look at what he knew he would see; Chuck would be watching her go, smiling to himself and nodding, then looking at the card and grinning, delighted with the perk that just had been put slap bang into the middle of an ordinary day.

Lucky bastard.

***

"I wasn't going to take the fucking phone," snapped Minnie, as she walked back towards the car. "I had to at least hold it to have a proper look at it, make the whole act look real. What do you take me for?"

"Well I didn't know, did I?" Charlie snapped back, but he wasn't really paying attention; he was too busy trying to get a handle on what had just happened.

So there's another Charlie Wilkes ... or that's me, yet I'm here ... and he wasn't working last night either, just like me ... yet he's in this morning? So he's got a different shift pattern, or he's had to cover for someone? Either way, you've been replaced. Someone's gone to great lengths to get you out of the way, and erase the real you.

Charlie felt his chest tighten again, the panic dog scratching at the door.

No. Don't get frightened. Get angry, but don't get frightened. If someone put you here, then someone knows. Someone knows the answers, and that means you can find them and find out. You lose it in here, and you find nothing.

The thought was both sobering and strangely refreshing at the same time, probably because for once his self-nagging had actually had the desired effect. Personal pep-talks rarely had an effect on Charlie, so this was a strangely pleasant surprise. Whenever he tried to talk himself into a lifestyle change, he tended to end up falling back into old habits quite quickly, and being generally happy to do so. He was not a man who ventured far out of his comfort zone, and knew it. It was another thing that he didn't like about himself, yet was too comfortable to change it. Quite the vicious circle.

"Minnie," said Charlie, suddenly remembering his host, "look ... sorry. I didn't mean to kick off over the phone. You have to remember, you could be a kleptomaniac for all I know. But hey, that's got to make you feel better, right? You couldn't have known that the phone was there, so you know you're not going nuts, at least. So that's one problem taken care of."

There was no reply, and the view revealed nothing; the street still passed hurriedly by as Minnie continued to walk at a high pace back to the car.

"Minnie?"

"Just give me a minute, Charlie," Minnie muttered under her breath, clearly not wanting to look insane to anyone who might be watching. "I need ... look, I'm asking nicely here. Just ... don't say anything until I get back to the flat. All right? Can you do that?" She *had* said it nicely, too; her tone was soft, gentle, and calm in a way that he hadn't heard during any of this crazy, confusing day. She wasn't trying to manipulate. She was just asking him to let her think, and was trying to keep herself under control.

"Okay. Okay, no problem," said Charlie, in a quiet voice of his own. "Let me know when you want to talk. Just ... don't leave it too long though, yeah? I think I might go nuts myself if I had to keep quiet in here for hours."

"I won't," Minnie replied as she opened the car door and got in, sighing heavily as she settled into the seat, into her safe place. As the engine started, Charlie sat down on the floor, leaning back and propping himself up on his hands, giving a little sigh of his own.

You're real. You're real. Don't forget that. You've just proved it.

After a few minutes of the drive, and tired of chasing his own thoughts round and round, Charlie began to lean his head back on his shoulders, rolling it left and right (*not your real shoulders, of course, your body hasn't been shrunk and placed inside her brain. Brains don't have screens inside them, remember? This is your mind, it's your mind that's been moved, and your mind is remembering your body*) as a new idea occurred to him. Getting to his feet, he looked into the darkness again. When he'd first arrived, it was so thick and impenetrably dark that the idea of going farther into that space had been terrifying, and still was; he'd known, however, that if every other option was exhausted then he would have no choice but to plunge inside, looking for an exit or whatever might lie in the blackness, if there was anything at all. The thought had been smothered nonetheless, so terrifying and inconceivable that he couldn't even consider it unless he had no choice.

But he'd wondered earlier if it hadn't got a bit lighter, and when he looked now he was convinced that he'd been right. It *had* been lighter then, and possibly even more so now ... in fact, that wasn't the only thing that had progressed since he'd been here, was it? He'd gotten his head around the situation surprisingly quickly. And now that the room was lighter, and seemed to be more so than the last time he'd really regarded it, then that would seem to suggest that he was possibly becoming used to the lack of light in the situation visually too. Or the place itself was changing.

Can I affect it, then? Can I settle into the actual space more, as well?

With nothing else to do but be silent, Charlie decided it was worth a try. Turning his back fully on the screen—an unnerving task, being faced with nothing but that which seemed endless—Charlie peered into the darkness, surrounded by it while sitting naked, and listened to the sounds of the car as it drove along, his fear of the metal cage temporarily replaced by his curiosity towards the black one.

After a few minutes, Charlie had had enough, but with no other options, he forced himself to continue. Even when he heard the sound of speeding tyres on tarmac turn into the soft rolling of tyres pulling into a parking space, he kept his gaze on the blackness. He couldn't be sure—like the hands of a watch, any progress would be difficult to see happening, but unlike a watch there was nothing to gauge any potential difference by—and just when he began to wonder if it *was* in fact brighter now, Minnie's voice interrupted him.

"Charlie?"

And just before he turned back to the screen to respond, something caught Charlie's eye; the faintest detection of a shape in the darkness.

Something that *moved*.

Charlie leapt up, letting out a scream, and tripped over his own feet, tumbling backwards into the screen itself. Surrounded by an explosion of light for a millisecond, he had a moment to realise he'd fallen through it before landing painlessly on the floor on the other side. The image on the screen on this side was exactly the same, and so was the darkness that stretched away here; it would seem that the screen was the centre of this place. Jumping back up in terror, Charlie leapt through the screen once more and crouched impotently, trying to see while shield his naked body from whatever was shifting in the black space before him.

And it *was* shifting; now he'd seen it, the shape appearing as if it were a Magic Eye picture, it was almost impossible to un-see. There was faint movement in the darkness about fifteen feet away, and now he saw with dread that it wasn't just in the one spot either; it was here, and there, and then he knew that it was all around him. With a shriek, he jumped back through the screen to check the other side; yes, here too he was surrounded by a wall of barely visible and shifting *something* that had come for him out of the gloom. Charlie began to scream, his pressurised mind finally giving way and abandoning its tired attempts to stay calm during the most terrifying day of his life. He held his hands out in a pathetic effort to withstand whatever immensity had come for him.

"Charlie?! Charlie, what the fuck?!" Minnie was shouting, and Charlie's eyes darted to the screen, saw her hallway again, saw the keys go onto a small wooden hook on the faded wall. The normalcy of the sight was nightmarish, so close yet so far from the horror that Charlie was experiencing. He only just managed to find the clarity to speak, his mind blitzed by fear.

"There's something, there's something, something in, something IN HEEEERRRREE—" he gibbered, and Minnie's response was even more panicked, even more blurted.

"Wha, something, wha ... *Charlie*?!"

And as she spoke again, Charlie saw something that stopped his screams; partly out of confusion, but partly out of the realisation of possible salvation. With Minnie's voice—exactly in time with each syllable—the movement had increased over on the left-hand side. This movement, in the same moment, had also had the simultaneous effect of clarifying the positions of the barely visible shifting all around him; specifically, that while it was everywhere, it was only moving *on the spot.*

Nothing was coming for him, at least. All that had been revealed was something that had been there all along.

"Charlie!" Minnie shouted again, panic in her voice, and again, the movement quickened on the left, pulsed faster and kept in time with her speech. The shape of it all was still only barely visible in the darkness, but the *change itself* was clear.

"Hold on," squeaked Charlie, starting to breathe again, and sitting up slowly, feeling more than a bit foolish as he did so. He'd screamed, after all. As he'd continued to watch the moving darkness around him, as he saw where it turned and undulated on the spot, a theory had come to him. Was the moving thing not just ... a wall? Albeit a pulsing, twitching one?

"Charlie, what the hell are you playing at?" yelled Minnie, but it wasn't in anger; it was still fear, fear for him.

"I got ... I got a fright but ... I think it's okay. Give me a second, give me a second," he said, standing up and, after a moment's hesitation, taking a step away from the light of the screen, towards the black.

"Bloody hell," said Minnie, breathing out in relief, and *now* there was anger there ... and the simultaneous pulses with her voice in the dark were now in a different place too, moving more towards what Charlie saw as the centre. Emboldened, Charlie took another two steps closer.

About fifteen feet? Have the walls of the Black Room been this close all along, just hidden by the darkness? Did it just look *like this place went on forever?*

Two more steps, and now Charlie could make out the movement more clearly. It was as if the darkness was alive, churning slowly and gently ... but in slightly curved surfaces that went straight up; *walls* was as good a word for them as any, but it didn't seem to quite fit. It would do for now. As his gaze made its way up the wall, he realised that it seemed to arch right over and above his head, coming down on the opposite side.

"Are you seeing something? You've got to tell me what you're *doing* in there," asked Minnie, her voice a mix now of annoyance and concern. The darkness that was the wall pulsed directly ahead of him in perfect synchronicity with her voice.

"I think it's okay," Charlie said again, stepping closer still, inspecting it and not looking at the screen. "I can see better in here now. I'm just ... I'm seeing stuff. It's still really dark but ... I think I can see walls, but they're not like ... I don't know ..." It was hard to describe; a surface that seemed to be made of *nothing*, yet moved like it was alive.

"What's in there, anyway? You said something about a screen? What do you see?" Minnie asked. That was something, Charlie noted. She hadn't wanted to hear any of it before. Had she decided it was *all* real on the way over here? He seized the opportunity anyway, trying to explain it.

"It was all black before, but ... well, it still is ... but I can see better now. There's the big screen in the middle that shows me what you see, but the area around me seems ... smaller than I thought. It looked like it went on forever before. But the walls ... they're ...." he'd moved even closer now, only a few feet away, and he thought he could make out actual shapes. He struggled to find the words to explain what he was seeing.

When Charlie was a kid, he'd helped his dad wash the new family car one day in the summer. They'd been halfway through the first stage, which was soaping every surface on the vehicle up (the boring bit before the fun part, as far as young Charlie had been concerned: blasting the suds off with the trigger hose) when he'd moved onto the right-hand side of the car to do the driver's window, the side where the mid-afternoon sun was striking the hardest. He'd pulled his thick, water-heavy sponge out of the bucket and slopped a good load of foam onto the glass, then moved down to the rear passenger window, when a movement to his right idly caught his eye. Without really caring—he already knew what it was, the movement of the suds as they slid down the glass—he'd glanced over at the driver's window again, and was quietly entranced for a moment.

The bright sun had caught the oily texture in the cleaning fluid, lighting up its myriad colours as they danced and swirled upon the water that carried them. They looked incredible in that bright, hot sun, spreading over the glass and looking like a peacock's feather that had been turned into electrified liquid. It seemed alive, with a million different shapes and blobs pressing together, forming and turning, creating new shapes that were almost immediately lost inside the next batch as they appeared. It was beautiful. And then his dad had shot him with the ice-cold hose, having snuck up behind him, and claiming over Charlie's shocked squeals and outraged laughter that he'd been "*aiming for the window.*" Charlie had been very young. Of course, all that had been before—

Enough of that. Don't think about that.

This was almost the same visual effect, if only in terms of the movement; there were no colours here. As he moved within touching distance, Charlie could see the similar churn of shapes on the dark surface, liquid and solid at the same time, a dark oily thickness that rippled and rose, pulsed and ebbed. It was like watching tumbling muscle fibres that somehow moved so smoothly that they had the appearance of a fluid.

"The walls are what?" asked Minnie, and Charlie jumped back a foot in alarm as the surface in front of him came alive with each syllable.

"They move. They're black and they move," said Charlie quickly, as he tried to get his breath back. His words had failed to do the sight in front of him any justice whatsoever. "When you talk, parts of them move in time."

There was no immediate response. Then:

"Does the floor do it too?"

A good question. He'd been sitting on the floor, and hadn't felt any movement, nor had he noticed any. He looked down; the floor, while black, reflected the screen's light slightly. The walls were either too far away for it to reach, or they absorbed the light in a way that Charlie didn't understand; but over by the screen, now a good thirteen feet away, he could see that the floor area around it was smooth, and was indeed illuminated slightly by the light. The floor was made of something different, then.

He found himself looking at the screen, and realised that *screen* didn't do it justice either. The way it petered away to nothing at the edges, the way it was intangible—he'd fallen through it, after all—the way it hung in the air, the way the images on it reached his eyes in a way that he knew was more than just seeing them in front of himself. It felt, in fact, as if they were in *his* head, *his* mind, and yet somehow presented before him at the same time; after all, when he'd first arrived, there had been no screen and no room at all, had there? He'd been seeing Minnie's view as if it had been his own. Then something had changed. His view had changed, stepped back, and now there was the screen and the Black Room and his own naked body.

So what had changed? Something physical? Or just his perception of the situation?

"Charlie?"

"Sorry. No ... no, the floor doesn't move."

"Charlie, it's really weird when I ask you something and you don't reply. It's bad enough having someone in your head without having to keep thinking that they've disappeared."

Charlie rolled his eyes.

Ten minutes ago you wanted me to shut up completely. Make your mind up.

He checked himself, and mentally wound his neck in; he could see her point.

"Sorry, it's just really distracting in here. When you talk, the place ... it changes. It's disconcerting."

"I've been talking to you all day though. Why didn't you see it before?" She wasn't trying to catch him out. She was trying to work with him, to talk it through.

"It's changed in here, or I've gotten used to it … or a bit of both," said Charlie, watching the nearest part of the wall and waving a hand at it for no one's benefit. "I think it's been slowly changing since I got here, or maybe I have. I can see better, anyway."

Perception again …

He turned back to the screen again, and realised that he hadn't needed to squint either time that he'd looked from the black walls to the light screen in order to shield his eyes from the change from light to dark. Again, *screen* didn't do it justice. It was a *vision*, an *insight* … but those words weren't right either.

The view before him was that of Minnie's living room, from a low and crooked angle; she'd moved while he wasn't watching, and was now seated. Her head, Charlie could tell, was leaning to one side, perhaps resting on the arm of the sofa. Charlie walked back towards the image before him, running a hand through his hair as he wondered what his next move should be. A thought occurred to him.

"Are you okay?" he asked. It was genuine. He watched with slight amusement as Minnie sighed quietly, and then her hand and forearm came into view and up and over as she ran through her own hair, too.

"This is fucking nuts, Charlie. It's *nuts.*" The hand and arm fell back past the screen as they flopped downwards and into her lap. "But … you were right about the phone. Dead right. And no matter what I try to say to myself, there's no way around that one. Cracked, just in the way you said, and the exact same type of phone. And I can *hear* you, Charlie, and you sound perfectly normal to me, and you have the name of a real guy I've never met, at least not before today and not that I remember, at least … and there's all the talk of subconscious process bullshit that yes, *could* explain it away, but then you put it next to the phone thing and it *just doesn't have any weight anymore* … so it's all nuts." The view swung upwards again, the drab ceiling being displayed once more as her head rolled back on the sofa.

Charlie understood. What the hell would he think in the same situation? But most importantly—even if she hadn't specifically said as much—she sounded like she finally believed him. She'd just had physical proof, after all. He closed his eyes for a moment, and breathed deeply, not admitting to himself how close he'd come to disbelieving his own reality too.

Wouldn't a dream person think that they were real, too?

"Look, first things first," Minnie said, her head not moving, and Charlie noticed the wall pulsing on a fresh side now as she spoke. "You're standing in, in like a room, right? I mean, you are a body standing in a room, that's how you see yourself right now?"

Charlie briefly considered mentioning the lack-of-clothes thing again, and decided against it once more; doing so might well derail recent progress.

"Yep, that's right," he said, nodding to no one.

"So you can close your eyes, yeah? Put your hands over your ears?"

"Well, yeah, of course, but ..." replied Charlie, confused for a minute, then slowly began to get a dim realisation of what she was talking about, like seeing a bus in the distance but being unable to read its number. She didn't mean *that*, did she? But then, it had been a few hours ..."Oh. Do you, uh, do you need to ..."

"Yeah," she said, curtly. "Yeah, I do, I really do. Just don't look for a minute. Well, you won't see anything anyway, but oh *God*, that doesn't matter, I shouldn't have said that ... just ... listen, most importantly, put your fingers in your ears and hum or something. I'll shout you when I'm done. You'll be able to hear me?" As she spoke, the walls turned in many places, alive and feverish.

"Yes, yes, no problem," said Charlie hurriedly, almost as embarrassed as she was, closing his eyes as the view swung down from the ceiling and rose up. Minnie stood, and walked to the bathroom.

Charlie stuffed his fingers in his ears until it hurt and hummed like a lunatic for what seemed like an eternity, until he heard Minnie calling his name, just audible over his own noise.

"Done?" he asked, quietly. She didn't acknowledge the question, responding instead in a tone that was overly brisk and breezy.

"Does this help?" she asked, as the view crossed the living room and stopped in front of a mirror Charlie hadn't known was there. Her face was framed perfectly, more settled and awake now. She looked more alive, having had time to wake up, and her hair—while her curls would never be tamed—looked less like that of a lunatic. The dark rings were still under her eyes.

But those are actually some beautiful eyes.

For a moment, Charlie could see why Chuck had happily taken her card.

"I mean, seeing my face, does it help? I thought it might feel more like a normal conversation for you." Her eyes stared back into his, an air of nervousness about them, wondering if she'd done something stupid.

Charlie was taken aback; not only because here was more confirmation of her new belief, but because this was a step further. This was a gesture, a thoughtful, subtle, but unnecessary kindness. And, he realised, it was something he would have done in the same situation, wanting to put her more at ease.

"Yeah, that's much better actually. Good idea," he said, smiling. "So I guess this means that you're on board then? With me being ... you know, real?" He regretted the question as soon as it had left his mouth; it was too blatant, too blunt. But she didn't react badly. Instead, she merely looked away and shrugged slowly.

"Probably. I think so. The phone thing ... and sod it, you know, what else can I do? If you're real, the quickest way to fix this is to try and figure out what's going on. And if you're not ... well ... there's not a lot I can do about that, is there? Who knows, maybe working on it and trying to figure out what's going on is a good way of getting you out of my head, real or not."

It was good enough for Charlie.

"Okay. Well, good. That's good." He sat down on the floor, getting comfortable. How long had they both been awake, anyway? About two hours? Shouldn't he be hungry by now, or at least thirsty, or needing a piss himself?

Further proof that you don't have a true, physical form in here.

"So ... what now?" he asked, letting Minnie take the lead.

"Well ... I actually had an idea, on the way over here," said Minnie rubbing at the back of her neck gently, eyes moving away again, showing Charlie the floor. "It's pretty stupid sounding, but what the hell isn't going to in this situation?"

"No, no, please," said Charlie, intrigued.

"You know like ... *Back to the Future*?" she asked, eyes seeming to take great interest in her own skirting board.

"Of course," said Charlie. He was a child of the eighties, after all.

"You know in *Back to the Future II*?"

"Which bit?"

"When they go back to Hill Valley and it's all different. Where, you know. Where they changed stuff. Changed time."

Charlie understood where she was going. Marty and Doc's actions in the past created an alternate timeline in the future, where their town was changed beyond recognition. And here was Charlie's world, where he didn't live at that house anymore, and worked a different shift pattern. It was possibly the same thing, on a smaller scale. But it didn't fit; here he was, stuck in someone else's head. Where does that fit into time travel? And why would everything else be the same except him? And fucking *time travel*? Not only was that a step too far, but it was the same bloody time.

"I don't think time travel is a part of this, Minnie. Not wanting to be a dick, but I think even with all of this craziness, time travel is a bit much."

"No, I don't mean time travel," snapped Minnie, embarrassed further now that the idea she didn't even want to put forward was being called into question. "I just mean that there were two places in that film, weren't there? The Hill Valley they knew, and the Hill Valley they created when they changed the past."

"Okay, go on."

"Well ... what if this is just that? A different place?"

"But nobody's time travelled," said Charlie, confused. "No one's gone anywhere to change anyth—"

"*No*, forget about the bloody time travel," snapped Minnie, and Charlie could see her pale skin reddening, her embarrassment rising. "I just mean that this could be another place, somewhere that turned out differently to where you're from, that's all."

"But why would I remember my life? And more importantly, why is it only things about me that seem to have changed?" said Charlie, catching her drift and already beginning to poke it, to turn it in his head. He felt like she was onto something, and his questions weren't designed to find flaws, but to work at it, to work *with* her just as she was now trying to work with him.

"Where are you getting that idea from?"

"What idea?"

"That everything is the same apart from you? All you know is the date's the same and that you live somewhere else. You know nothing about what might or might not be different."

"Okay ... fair point," Charlie admitted. It was true, after all. He had no reason *not* to think he was the only thing that had changed, but he certainly hadn't explored any other possibilities. "Who's the president?"

"Obama."

"Prime Minister?"

"Cameron."

"9/11 happened?"

"Yep."

"Who won the league last season?"

"Manchester City, I think."

"Uh ... biggest film of last year?"

"*The Avengers*, probably. Or the new Batman one."

They both fell quiet, trying to think of new questions but also trying to avoid the obvious. Minnie said it first, eventually.

"It could be anything, couldn't it. We could go on all day and get nowhere."

"Unless we already *know* the only thing that's different," Charlie countered, shrugging to the darkness all around him.

"Maybe," Minnie replied, chewing her lip and thinking. Charlie turned back and watched the wall, finding the movement easier to make out; partly due to knowing what he was looking for now, and partly because, well ... wasn't it just easier to see now, full stop?

And were the walls churning faster?

"Minnie?" asked Charlie, not turning back to the screen as an idea occurred to him. "Do me a favour?"

"What's that?" asked Minnie, with a hint of suspicion in her voice.

"Can you remember ... Christmas. Christmases as a kid. Can you remember those?"

"Of course," she said, sounding confused. "I *loved* Christmas. Still do, I suppose, but it's not the same since we lost Mum. Dad just isn't as into the whole thing anymore, but I think he likes having me and my brother back. Why?"

Spurts of movement in different places, memories sparking in different spots.

"Can you remember the best Christmas? Was there a really happy one?" he asked, almost literally watching the cogs turn.

"Oh, yes ... but what's that got to—"

"I don't want to say just yet, it might spoil it. Just tell me about it?"

"Okay," she said, sounding unsure, but going with it, trusting him. "I got a Girl's World that year. You know them, the big heads with the hair that you can actually style? I wanted it *so* badly. Massively sexist and gender stereotyping and all that, totally, but I didn't give a shit about that back then. I just really wanted one. And Tommy got Megatron, and he was just going *nuts*, he was that happy—he hadn't expected it—and we just spent the afternoon playing with those while Mum and Dad joined in now and then. Dad even let me show him how to do plaits, and his were so lousy ... everyone was just laughing all day, and there wasn't even the traditional Christmas argument ... is that enough?"

Charlie didn't reply. He was too busy watching the explosion of thought all around him, the walls' pulses turning through fresh planes of movement in the dark. Strong memories, strong thought, new movements in other places. But the inside of a brain didn't look like this, didn't turn and pulse in this way, and besides, he couldn't be physically inside one and still be able to breathe. So what was this place?

If it wasn't physical—and it couldn't be—then it had to be mental, or simply his psychic energy or whatever placed inside hers ... but what about the room, and the screen? That was all very specific, very precise, too much to simply be some strange force of nature.

Unless ...

Charlie's own cogs turned, as he was dimly aware of Minnie asking for a response. A lifetime of comics and bad science-fiction TV was being referenced inside his head without him even being aware of it, dim thoughts making connections with long-forgotten memories that he didn't even know he had, questing for possible solutions. Had he been in a lighter place, he would have remembered his favourite line from Calvin and Hobbes: *I'm not dumb. I just have a command of thoroughly useless information.*

So this place could be ... a representation of her mind, then? Maybe it was simply how *his* mind made sense of the situation, how his own consciousness presented the meeting of their energies to him in a way that he could understand. It made sense to him; if he had to imagine being inside someone's head and seeing the world through their eyes, this would be the way that he pictured it looking.

Unless it's not actually in her head at all, Charlie. You have a body here. You can see it, you can feel it. It's right there, attached to your head. The Black Room could be—

"Charlie! For fuck's sake, *Charlie!*"

"Sorry, sorry, I was just—"

"I told you, don't *do* that! It's bad enough having a voice in your head without it suddenly going silent. Can you imagine what that's like?" She sounded really upset, and Charlie kicked himself. She'd only just started to believe he was real; his sudden silence would only tell her that he might somehow be a figment of her imagination after all.

"I'm sorry, Minnie, I just really had a whole roll of thoughts, I needed to finish them," said Charlie, turning back to the screen.

"Well you could have told me!"

"You're right, you're right. I just got an idea about this ... this room I'm in."

"Okay, tell me," she said, breathing out hard as she did so, calming down, embarrassed again. "Wait a second, I need to sit down. Do you mind?"

"No, no, please, sit. Take the weight off." As the view swung around and headed back to the sofa, Charlie regretted his last choice of words. Weight? She was painfully thin, after all. Weight could be an issue. Anorexia perhaps, or at the very least a lack of appetite that pointed to other things.

Or she could just be skinny.

The view dropped rapidly as Minnie slumped onto the sofa with a sigh.

"Okay, go for it," she said.

"Things happen in here, Minnie. In the walls. They change when you think, I mean when *you* think, or when you have an emotional response to something," said Charlie, sitting as well, cross-legged and naked in the dark. He was getting used to it, but still felt as strangely uncomfortable as he always had done when fully naked. Even here, in the Black Room, he felt like eyes were upon him. "I know I'm obviously in your head, but I think … I think what I see around me, the walls … I think it's a *representation* of your *mind*, Minnie. I think I can see your thoughts."

"That's pretty trippy," she replied, surprisingly calmly. "So … what do they do? They light up?"

"No, they just move, but in different ways and in different places. I couldn't really see them before, but I can now. I think I'm growing into this place, to be honest."

"Well don't get too bloody comfortable," said Minnie, a wry edge in her voice. "I'll be honest, I've had a bugger of a headache since you turned up."

"Must be my voice banging away in here all day. I'll try and talk a bit more quietly."

"Thanks," she said, sounding like she meant it. "It doesn't hurt more when you talk or anything though; I think my head, or my mind or whatever, just isn't used to having you in there. So when it all moves, doesn't it knock you about a bit? I mean, it must make it hard to stand up."

"No, it's not like that. The walls just kind of turn, and the floor …" he put out a hand and caressed the oddly smooth and unyielding, yet soft and comfortable floor beneath him. It was a complete contradiction, yet that was the only way he could describe it. He'd never felt anything like it. "The floor's different," he finished, not knowing how to say it. "It never moves. I don't know what the deal is with that."

"But of course, you realise that there's nothing like that actually inside my head," said Minnie, stating the somewhat obvious.

"I know, I know. Which leads me to one of two conclusions. They're both a bit Saturday matinee sci-fi sounding though, okay? So bear with me."

"Shoot."

"Right. One—and I think this is the more likely—my mind, for whatever reason, has been separated from my body and has been put inside yours by persons unknown. All of this, all of the stuff I'm seeing in here, is simply MY mind's way of processing the experience in a way I can understand."

"Well ... that does make the most sense in a loony situation, I guess," said Minnie, mulling it over.

"And the second one—which I think is more unlikely, but still one that we have to consider—is that the Black Room is man-made."

There was silence for a second.

"The what?" Minnie asked.

"Sorry, the room I'm in, I just think of it as the Black Room. Because—"

"—because it's black," Minnie finished, sounding like she was smiling. "Didn't really need that one explaining."

"No, I suppose not," said Charlie, smiling himself. For the first time on that crazy, frightening day, he felt like he was genuinely starting to relax a little. "But anyway, as I say ... could be man-made."

"You mean like ... some sort of ... projection room or something?" she asked. Charlie brightened. That was almost exactly what he'd meant.

"Yeah, pretty much. Like, I'm in here, and they're beaming me into you for whatever reason. This whole room could be one big organic machine, and this could all be some kind of test. It's loony as hell, and I have no idea how the hell they'd do it, but it's no loonier than what's been going on today."

"Mmm ..." murmured Minnie, thinking. Charlie heard fabric creak as she shifted on the sofa. "But what about the old woman, and your house, and, well ... you, at work?"

"Yeah, well ... I'd have to work on that one. But if they can do this, what else could they do?" Charlie offered. "Surely it's not outside of the realms of possibility to put an actress in my home, and remove my housemate? And if they can stick me in here, who's to say they can't stick someone else in my body's head, someone who can control it?"

"But your *body* would be in there with you. If you were in a man-made chamber thing," Minnie corrected, politely.

"Oh yeah. Got ahead of myself," Charlie muttered, shaking his head. "Well, like I say, I don't know about all that. But anyway, here's the thing; if they put me in here, there must be a door. Right?"

"I suppose so."

"So if it's okay with you, I want to poke at the walls a little bit. See if I can't find anything different, something that might suggest an entrance of some sort." Charlie gently bit his lip and waited for an answer, not knowing what to expect. If Minnie was someone who had reason to be concerned *before* all this about her state of mind, then he doubted very much that she'd be up for letting him prod her in the consciousness.

"Will you be careful?" she asked. She said it so gently that he was taken aback, feeling something soften inside of him. There was trust here already.

"Of course. I'll talk you through what I'm doing every step of the way, and if it sounds like I'm doing something that you don't like, just tell me and I'll stop instantly," said Charlie, genuinely wanting to reassure her; not just because he wanted her cooperation for the task ahead, but because he wanted to.

"All right then. Just go easy, okay?"

"I will. I'm heading over now," Charlie said, as he stood and made his way over to the nearest swirling wall. "Are you ready?" he called to the screen, once he was within touching distance of the wall.

"You don't have to raise your voice," Minnie said. "I can hear just fine." Charlie noted this; he'd had to raise his voice to be heard at all when he'd first arrived.

"All right," said Charlie, more quietly now, and cautiously beginning to raise his hand. "I'm going to touch it now." He was hesitant, and nervous. Up close, the black wall churned just like before, intimidating now with the speed at which it moved.

She's nervous too, then.

As Charlie watched the wall move, he was reminded of the image of cake mixture being whisked by a machine; folds and refolds and swirls, all turning on the spot. *So that's what it reminds me of,* he thought, *finally,* and with that he gently pressed his hand to the wall's tumbling surface.

To his surprise, he couldn't feel the folding texture he'd expected; his eyes said his hand should be bouncing around on the wall's shifting surface, but all he actually felt was a similar substance to the floor. Soft, yet unyielding ... but here, there was something extra, too. A vibrating sensation, thrumming away under his palm.

"Is that okay?" he asked Minnie.

"Are you touching it?" she said, sounding confused.

"Yeah," he said. "You don't feel anything?"

"Nothing at all," she said, sounding almost disappointed, "just this bloody headache, still."

"I'm going to push a little harder then, okay?" Charlie asked. After a brief pause, Minnie replied.

"Go for it," she said, sounding determined. As Charlie pushed, the vibrating sensation increased under his hand, almost like it was trying to push back.

"Still okay?" he asked.

"Uh huh," she said. He couldn't tell what she was thinking. *Ironic,* he thought. He pushed harder still. The vibration didn't increase further now, but it did seem to spread out across his hand, almost like it was *feeling* against his fingers, caressing their shape, tickling him almost. He realised that his heart was pounding against his chest.

"Still okay?" he asked again.

"Yes. I'm fine. Are you pushing harder?"

"Ah. Ah. Ah. *Ah.*"

"*Charlie?!*" shrieked Minnie, suddenly terrified at his gibberish response, but Charlie was, for the moment, incapable of clarifying the situation for her as the vibration had now shot up the length of his entire arm and slammed into his head, piercing his brain and bombarding his mind with images.

It wasn't painful; it was *stunning,* however, concussive with the force and strength of it all. The visuals were too fast to make any real sense of them—and on one level he could still see the churning wall and his hand

51

pressing against it—but he found himself recognising people and events that he knew he had never known.

Uncle Paul. Sam McGinty. Sarah Westmuller. Results day. Kevin's dog Misty, an ALSATIAN. The man with the cats in a box. Harry the manager. The boxing match at the social. Turning up to work with ladders in my tights—

He was right. This was her mind. He was seeing the layers of her mind.

—not being able to breathe and panicking, Jenny bringing me some Lemsip and grapes, Claire the Bitch's eighteenth, dancing in a nightclub while two years underage—

"Charlie, don't fucking do this—"

"I'm ... I'm ..." Charlie heard her, tried to find his voice, and nearly couldn't. "I'm okay ... I can see ... this is your mind, I'm seeing ... your *life* ..."

"On the screen, on the screen thing, you mean?" Minnie said, energised too now, speaking in almost a whisper.

"No, in my ... in my head ... I'm ... I'm going to push harder ... okay?" Charlie gasped.

"Does it hurt? Does it hurt you?"

"No, just ... intense ... *ah* ... but I'm okay ... ready?"

"Yes ... yes, all right," she said, breathing hard herself.

Charlie didn't respond, and instead pushed again, harder, the images still tumbling into and out of his head *(three hundred quid for fillings, left it too long, Euro 96 and being bored but watching anyway, James Pearson, my first pill in Ministry Of Sound)* but not changing in speed or pattern. He focused on the image before his eyes, not the ones in his head, and gritted his teeth as he got his body weight behind it.

Nothing changed. Then suddenly, the wall gave way beneath his hand.

Lots of things happened at once. The images stopped like someone had cut the ribbon of film in a projector, and Charlie found himself falling forward very fast, travelling with the force of his own pushing bodyweight. His arm disappeared into the wall up to the elbow, and his body fell against the surface surrounding the hole, his face and free hand slapping onto the wall. The images recommenced.

Charlie Brown Christmas special, Russ Abbott Christmas special, Who Wants To Be A Millionaire—

Charlie pulled his body and face back, and the images abruptly ceased again. He took a second to recover from his shock and get his bearings, and a second later he became aware of two things. One was that he *could* now feel the folds and turns of the wall, all around his forearm; they felt rough, like a dog's tongue, and warm, and exerted a tight pressure against him that made him feel, with fresh panic, that he might be stuck. The other thing was the fact that Minnie was screaming.

Charlie whipped around to face the screen and saw its light flickering on and off, as Minnie repeatedly screwed up and then opened her eyes, yelling. It was hysterical, agonised shrieking, and it was clear what the cause was. Turning back to the wall, Charlie pulled, and was horrified when his suspicions were confirmed; he *was* stuck. Frantically, he twisted and turned his arm, trying to get loose, but the tumbling folds of the wall seemed to almost have a vacuum effect, worse now that Minnie was in pain; they were moving at three times their previous speed. With desperation, Charlie got his feet up against the wall to push, then thought better of it; what if his feet went through as well? Straining, he planted his feet firmly on the floor instead and *leaned* away from the wall with all his might, blood thrumming in his temples as his shoulder felt like it was going to separate.

Minnie's screams hit a pitch that could shatter glass.

Something shifted in the right way inside the wall, and the vacuum popped. Charlie tumbled backward, his arm coming free, and as he dropped onto the floor with a heavy thud that yielded no pain, he was dimly aware that his arm was dry. He'd half-expected it to be wet.

Minnie's screams hit a crescendo and then turned into moans of relief and pain, the light in the Black Room dimming as her fingers covered her eyes. Charlie propped himself up on one elbow, quickly, and turned to the screen, feeling the awful quicksand-like pull of rapidly increasing guilt.

"Minnie, I'm sorry ... it just gave way—"

"What happened?" came the muffled reply, lost between her palms and her gentle, breathless sobs. "What did you do?"

"The wall, it just buckled under my hand," pleaded Charlie, turning back to the wall and being amazed to see a clearly darker spot where his arm had been. Already, however, it was closing. The wall healed before his eyes but with a shuddering, staggering action, as if it required a great deal of effort to do so. As he watched, the spot sealed over, and all that was left was the turning wall of Minnie's thoughts. "My arm got stuck inside ... I couldn't get it out," Charlie continued, turning back to the screen. "I saw things, Minnie—" He cut himself off, the intense guilt he now felt reminding him that the other parts could wait. "Are you all right? Did it hurt?"

The light from the screen suddenly tripled in brightness, her fingers coming away and revealing her living room ceiling once more. There was silence for a moment as she got her breathing under control.
"I'm okay," she said, bravely, sniffing. "But that ... bloody hell, Charlie. It was like you'd stuck a knife in my head. No, worse than that; like you'd twisted ... *me*. The whole world seemed to shift." Nothing but her breathing again. Then, incredibly, she added: "I'm sorry if I scared you. That just hurt so much."

Charlie gaped in the darkness. She was apologising to *him*?

"No ... look, I'm fine, I'm worried about *you*. Your vision's okay, no blurriness? No headaches?" he asked.

"Just the one I had before. I think I'm gonna need to stay lying down for a bit, though. I feel shaky."

"No problem. That's a good idea." He thought about telling her about the visions, her memories, but he decided better of it. He'd shaken her enough today, caused her enough anguish and upset, without telling her that he had access to her mental rolodex too.

"So ... no door, then?" she asked, breathing out as she settled. Her eyes narrowed; the screen dimmed.

53

"Not where I pushed, no. I know how much pressure I can put on it, at least."

"You can check again, you know. Other places. Just touch though. Don't push."

Charlie smiled, despite his breathless guilt. This girl was brave.

"Not today, I think. Not for a good few hours anyway."

"Okay. Christ, this headache ... you certainly didn't help."

"I'm *so* sorry—"

"It's all right. Really. You had to try, and I wasn't going to stop you. Look, I'm going to just put the TV on quietly for a bit. Do you mind?"

"No, not if it'll help you relax." Her hand swung past the screen, then travelled back the other way holding a remote. He heard the TV come on in the background, heard the volume dropping on it as she adjusted it to suit her aching head. A thought occurred to Charlie. "Minnie? Why did you give ... Chuck your card?"

There was just the sound of the TV for a moment.

"I don't know," she said eventually. "It just seemed to make it more believable, really. If I'd lost my phone, why wouldn't I?" She didn't sound right saying it—awkward, almost childlike—but then, Charlie had heard Minnie lie before, and it had been seamless. He had to assume she was telling the truth.

"Okay. I just wondered," he said, letting the matter drop. "I'll shut up for a bit."

"No," she said, sounding sleepy. "Talk to me. I don't like it when you go quiet. It's like you're lurking if you're there and not saying anything. Just talk quietly."

"No problem," said Charlie, smiling, finding himself feeling glad to have a break from the madness for a while. "What do you want me to talk about?"

"Tell me about your life," she said, sighing slightly as the screen turned to the left, facing the TV. "Talk about that. I want to know who my tenant is." Charlie wondered if she'd actually be paying attention if she was watching the TV at the same time, but he felt like he owed her; if that's what she wanted him to do to help, then that was what he would do.

"All right," said Charlie, rolling over onto his back and looking at the churning black ceiling. It turned above him like a boiling black sky. "Where should I start?"

"School ... what were you like at school?" Minnie said drowsily. She sounded like she was about to fall asleep, which wasn't something Charlie was looking forward to. Her eyes would close completely, and the Black Room would descend into total darkness. He didn't like the idea of that at all, but pushed the thought away. It had to happen eventually; he'd better just get on with things until that happened.

"Apart from being terrible at sports, a distraction in class, and obsessed with comics, I was a fairly average kid," Charlie began, putting his hands behind his head, resting them against that strange, smooth black floor. "By the way, you go next, you know. I like to know things too, especially when it comes to the women whose heads I'm stuck inside."

"Uh-huh, yes. Carry on," she muttered, and Charlie did.

As he talked, and time passed, the screen dimmed several times, and Charlie was certain she was about to pass out on him. His heart leapt nervously as he thought of being alone in the dark ... but every time it happened she would make a noise to indicate that she was still listening, or she would ask a question about what he'd just said, and he knew that she was still awake, just relaxed. Whenever he tried to bounce the conversation back onto her, however, she would brush him off, or say that it was still his turn. Charlie went with it. He was relaxing too; they needed a break, after all, on what was probably the most stressful day of both of their lives.

In a strange way, he felt that he liked Minnie, too; he'd already been impressed with both her bravery and her ability to bullshit on the spot. She'd been through the wringer—that much was clear already, both by her outburst in the car and her reluctance to come forth with details about her own life— but he felt like he would learn about her if he ended up being there long enough (*let's bloody hope not* his own voice said). Plus, it seemed like she already trusted him. There was a lot to be said for that, in Charlie's book. Trust was very big deal to him. And he found Minnie easy to talk to.

"... although I never really expected myself to still be in the bar trade by now," Charlie finished eventually, by now lying on his stomach. "I like it though, and the people I work with are a good laugh. You just think sometimes, though ... different paths you could have taken, and all that." He decided to give it another try. "So what did you end up doing?"

"Wugginonnatull," mumbled Minnie, and that's when Charlie realised that the screen was almost completely black and staying that way. The images on it were already squashed to a thin strip in the middle, blurred by her eyelashes, and this line of light was getting slowly smaller.

Charlie shot upright, opening his mouth to shout and wake her up, but something stopped him. It had to happen eventually, as he already knew—as he'd decided to accept—but it wasn't acceptance that prevented him from waking her up. It was that he *wanted* her to sleep, to have a rest from it despite his own terror of total darkness.

Madly, he found himself noticing the images on the TV screen in front of him, still just visible between Minnie's closing eyelids. The BBC were closing the news with a summary on the third round of the FA Cup so far, including the recent run of David vs Goliath upsets. Desperately yearning for the light from the TV—the *outside world's* light—Charlie even half-raised a hand towards the screen, reaching for it. Catching himself, knowing this line of thinking would help nothing, he closed his eyes as the Black Room grew darker and darker, forcing himself to breathe slowly and to at least have a chance of staying calm. He thought that if he *started* right, he had a better chance of not freaking out when the darkness smothered him completely. The sounds of the TV were still audible over Minnie's slow, deep breathing.

"*... and of course Coventry against Manchester United in a 3–1 upset at the Ricoh, after the controversial sending-off of Phil Jones just fifteen minutes into the match led to both a Clarke equaliser from the penalty spot and, seven* *minutes later, a screaming effort from Elliott that left David de Gea napping. United rallied magnificently, but Coventry were relentless, poaching a third before halftime, courtesy of—"*

Charlie's eyes flew open. He took a second while he frantically checked and double-checked it in his mind, the madness of the moment making him doubt his own memories, but he *knew* he was right.

He'd *been* at that game. FA Cup, third round, Coventry City Vs Man United. Clint's mate—he of the corporate connections—had a spare ticket going; Charlie hadn't believed his luck when he' been asked. Everyone in Coventry had wanted one.

But Jones had got a *yellow* card, not a red. He'd never been sent off. United had won 3–0.

Then Minnie's eyes closed, and the Black Room became a tomb.

Panic immediately closed a fist around Charlie's heart as he was plunged into a blackness of which he had never known the like. It was worse than he'd imagined, worse than he'd prepared for, and a weak cry escaped his lips before he could bite it back.

You can't wake her up. Calm down. Let her sleep. There's nothing in here but you. Breathe. Breathe.

Trembling, yet embarrassed at his own childlike panic, Charlie opened and clenched his hands repeatedly as he drew in air through his nose, tried to push fear out through his mouth. It almost began to work, but then the humming began, coming from all around him.

This time, Charlie didn't even try and stop the yell as fear slicked over his skin like a cold shower; he whirled around on the spot, crying out faintly. It wasn't a mechanical hum, nor a human-sounding one; to Charlie, the word that came to mind, the only image that he could think of, was *Monster*.

The sound was too low, too guttural to be made by any animal that he could think of. He listened more intensely, his head switching from side to side in the dark as he tried to catch any change in sound that might mean that the terrible source of the noise was advancing. Charlie slowly realised that it seemed to fade and increase, turn and waver ... it seemed to pulse.

Could it be ...

Taking a deep breath again—but holding it this time—Charlie put out a trembling hand and moved slowly forward, his fingers nervously splayed and twitching, as if the digits themselves were frightened of coming up against something in the dark. As he walked, the sound increased, dropped, raised behind him, coming alive in some places and dying in others.

You saw better in here after a while; all the time, you're getting better at being in the Black Room. You can see. You can see in the dark.

He opened his eyes, and the blackness was as impenetrable as ever.

Fuck.

One thing that was different, though, was the sound; even as it rose and fell, it got louder as he walked forward, as he approached the nearest wall. Charlie began to relax slightly. He thought he might be right.

When you touched the wall, he thought, *you saw things. You saw her memories. Her thoughts are in the walls ...*

As the humming reached its loudest volume yet, Charlie's fingers found the nearest wall in the dark, and the images came once more. This time, however, they weren't the tumbling kaleidoscope of clear pictures he'd gotten before, pictures arriving with the stated knowledge of what each one was; now it was purely a single moving image, with no other information than the visual before him.

Seen from Minnie's eye-view, Charlie saw people walking all around her, laughing, waving, talking, some arguing, some walking dogs, all of them under a cloudless blue sky. The horizon stretched along forever, and the sun shone warmly.

All of the people were walking upon the surface of the sea.

... and now the walls are showing you her dreams. That sound is Minnie's mind, dreaming.

Charlie began to laugh in the Black Room, relieved by the discovery and warmed in his mind as if the sun in Minnie's dream was shining upon him too. He watched as Minnie dove face first through the ocean's surface, seeing a town lying on the ocean floor, so far below that it gave him the impression that he was now flying. People were all around Minnie here, too, some swimming up from the citadel to the surface, others travelling inside clear, bubble-like capsules clearly designed to carry several lazier sea-people who didn't want to swim.

While the views and the adventure being presented to him were entertaining, there was no emotional connection this time either, in the way that there had been with the memories. This was more like watching a movie behind his eyes. Even so, it beat being stuck in the dark, and for the time being, lost in his relief, Charlie was content to watch Minnie's dreams. Eventually, the scene changed to a grocery shop, albeit one done up like a high-end boutique where the milk cartons replaced coats on coat hangers, where mannequins stood holding packets of sausages. After a while, Charlie decided to get comfortable, and sat himself on the floor, still making contact with the wall.

As many minutes passed—Minnie now having an argument with someone (who appeared to be an image of a real-life friend, perhaps) over who got to take the horse to school—Charlie began to wonder what had happened to the memories in the walls once the dreams began. Did they turn *into* the dreams? Or did the dreams just come to the fore as Minnie drifted deeper into sleep?

Hell, do you *get to sleep? Don't people go crazy if they never get to sleep?*

The dream-images themselves became more vivid, sharp, and colourful as more time passed, suggesting that Minnie was drifting into a different stage of sleep now, but the actual story being presented became more abstract. Things began to make less and less sense as time went on, and Charlie actually began to feel bored ... but not so much that he wanted to stop watching. Anything was better than only seeing the pitch blackness.

That was when he *felt* the wall move under his hand.

Charlie jerked his hand away, confused for a moment and convinced that he'd imagined it, but when the wall moved for a second time in the dark—moved forward so much that it already met his hand again without him even putting it back—Charlie knew that his first instinct had been right. The low humming sound all around him had grown louder, and the wall he'd been touching was now pushing against his body. It was actually moving him backwards, his feet finding no purchase on the smooth floor beneath him.

Oh no—

As the sound continued to grow in all directions, he realised that the walls were closing in on all sides.

Even in his terror, Charlie half-thought about the fragility of the wall, how he'd damaged it before and hurt Minnie, but it was different now, more solid; as if the surface of the wall had toughened as the weight of whatever lay beyond it pressed inwards.

There was no time to think, no time to plan. Terrified, Charlie pushed harder against the wall, trying to brace it, but he was still being pushed inexorably backwards. The humming grew and grew, sounding like a chorus of damnation, as the comprehension that he was about to be crushed to death exploded in Charlie's head. In a blind panic, he tried to punch through the wall again, hoping that the pain would wake Minnie and save his life, that she could stop this, but his fist bounced off harmlessly with no damage to the wall or his knuckles. It had clearly changed form now that it had begun this contracting process, had become solid and hardened enough to crush his bones to powder as her mind dropped into a deeper level of unconsciousness. The Black Room was being closed for the night. He could feel its density, and he felt frail and doomed against it.

"*Minnie! Minnie! MINNIIEEEEEEE!!*" Charlie screamed, not knowing what he expected her to do and not caring. It was the only thing he had, his only desperate option. There was no response from Minnie; she was too far under now to hear his voice, her mind removed and elsewhere. This was happening so suddenly, so quickly, that Charlie hadn't even realised that his mind wasn't receiving the images anymore. His feet scrabbled and slipped on the floor as he struggled against the wall, knowing the effort was pointless but having no other option but to respond with the helpless, desperate actions of a trapped animal. He couldn't see, he couldn't stop it, and there was nothing he could do. The humming became deafening in the darkness, devoid of any humanity or mercy, as it signalled the end of Charlie Wilkes's life.

***

PART TWO:
THE WOMAN IN
THE NIGHT

Three: There's No Place Like a Mutually Financially Agreeable Home, The Woman in the Night, Minnie Cooper: This Is Your Life, and Wikipedia Confirms Everything (As Usual)
***

—and now the car is upside down, giving him a more perverse view of the water; the sky that was previously above is now dropping away below him, visible through the windshield, and the river is rushing up to meet them, to claim them, and he feels something grasp his hand so hard it hurts.

"I love you," she says—

***

Charlie opened his eyes, gasping in a freakishly large gulp of air as he sat bolt upright, his hands trying to push against something that wasn't there and instead finding themselves tangled up in bedsheets. He saw the light, felt the linen, felt the bedding as it seemed to almost take on a life of its own, determined to ensnare his frantically struggling arms. His breath came in ragged gasps and moans as he looked around himself with wide eyes, taking in his unthinkable surroundings and failing to process them over and over again. As his eyes completed their twentieth sweep of the room, knowledge finally managed to penetrate his brain and the realisation connected; what he was seeing was real. He was not crushed, and was no longer trapped in the darkness. He was back. He was home.

The mess on his floor, his framed original movie posters, his large bookcase full of books that he never actually read more than once but couldn't bring himself to throw away; all was as normal. The room was as he'd seen it when he came home last n—wait, did he remember that? Where had he been again? On the town, with friends (*acquaintances*) ... but he didn't *remember* coming home.

Then the realisation that he was out, out, *out,* safe at home and *out* hit him, and his body turned into a wet rag. His strength disappeared and he could no longer sit upright. He fell back against the pillow with a cold sweat on his skin as relief turned into joy, and as the laughter began the joy gave way to a memory of terror. He'd begun to believe that he didn't even exist. The laughter turned into tears that went on for a long time, and Charlie's hands were clasped to his face all the while. He took them away and they flopped onto the bed, connected to limp and loose arms (*connected to your arms*) and lay there, shaking his head at the ceiling.

Christ ... that was a vivid dream. A vivid, horrendous *dream.*

Thank God it was over. That had just been awful, that feeling of total helplessness and loss. And that bit at the end, Jesus. He'd always been a little claustrophobic, but the walls closing in like that ... that was something else. And hadn't it all seemed to go on forever! Such a *long* dream! True, dreams often seemed that way, but wow ...

But ... was it all horrendous?

Still in his half-asleep haze, Charlie dimly remembered the girl. Yes ... the girl had been nice. Pretty, he thought, if a little troubled ... but she'd been smart. Even in his moment of intense relief and gratitude for his freedom, Charlie felt a slight, post-dream pang, feeling the kind of detached loss that comes after dreams in which a new friend is made.

But hadn't you seen her before, Charlie? Didn't you recognise her?

Charlie frowned. Where the hell had that come from? He'd never seen ... never seen ... her name escaped him now. He fumbled clumsily for it, felt for it, found it.

Minnie.

Yep, that was it. And yes, he'd never seen her before; the idea was stupid. Dream-haze stuff. He needed to wake up.

Throwing back the sheets, he leapt out of bed in a way that he hadn't since he was a kid, delighted to be facing the outside world.

The outside world!

He paused for a second, then held his hands up in front of his face and inspected them, turning his palms and fingers this way and that in front of the glowing lightbulb in the ceiling. He laughed, then kissed his own hands.

Fuck me, it's good to be back.

Stepping into his slippers and grabbing his dressing gown from its hook on the back of the bedroom door, Charlie bounded down the stairs into the living room. It was a mess, as usual; not the bombsite mess of the young student, however, but the mildly acceptable mess of the single bachelor. The living room was of a decent size, too, which minimised the impact of it all, and thanks to their landlord it was decorated nicely enough to look like a proper family home. Charlie would admit, when asked, that the majority of the mess was down to him and not his flatmate, Eric. Eric was quietly neat and respectful of Charlie's space, almost to a fault; Eric definitely wasn't the most forthcoming of guys, and Charlie certainly had no real complaints about him.

The man in question was sitting in front of him now, parked as always in the leather armchair nearest to the flat-screen TV. A freshly half-eaten bowl of cereal was left on the small side table next to him, forgotten while Eric immersed himself in whatever first-person shooter he was currently playing on the Xbox. Eric's presence seemed to cement Charlie's realisation of being home, and made his mood even better; oh yes, he was definitely out of The Black Room.

"Eric!" cried Charlie with a grin, spreading his arms wide as he stood by the door. This action made his dressing gown fall wide open, revealing his naked torso. Fortunately for Eric, Charlie wore boxers while he slept.

Eric looked up, slightly alarmed, with a look of confusion on his face. Eric was a few years younger than Charlie, but from his day-to-day demeanour you wouldn't know it. Just like the manner in which he kept his things, Eric was always neatly presented; his short-cropped black hair and perma-shaven face always made him look as if he was about to give a business presentation. All of which didn't mean that Eric was fussy; he wasn't. He just kept to himself and quietly got on with doing what he liked, which, a lot of the time, was playing on his Xbox. Charlie had never seen any of Eric's friends, although he knew that Eric had them. They would often call, and Eric would come back in after being gone for some time, with only the regular explanation of "been out with the chaps" offered up as a clue to what he'd been doing. Charlie had never been able to specifically pin down what Eric did for a living; all he ever got from Eric was "Finance" as an answer, and any further questions were met with diversionary tactics. Charlie had eventually stopped asking.

They weren't close, but Charlie did like Eric, and thought that the feeling was mutual. They'd talk briefly in the kitchen about anything interesting that had happened to them lately—usually Charlie talking more than Eric—and Charlie would ask for Eric's advice on things from time to time, usually receiving a sound explanation of what would turn out to be the wisest course of action for Charlie to take. They ate meals at roughly the same time together, sitting in silence in front of the TV until something came up on screen that

Charlie or Eric wanted to talk about. Overall, it was an arrangement that suited them both just fine; although, when Eric had first turned up, Charlie had been disappointed. He'd hoped Eric would be a new drinking buddy—or a new anything buddy—but it had quickly become clear that Eric had his own life, and politely liked to keep it separate. Charlie let him, respected his choices, and over time he saw why Eric had played it that way. They were just very different people, and it had been the right choice.

"Charlie," said Eric, nodding, his expression not changing. "Good night, was it?"

"I have absolutely no bloody idea!" cried Charlie, throwing his arms up. "But it's a glorious day outside, and I'm not at work until two, and intend to ... what time is it?"

Eric looked at his phone.

"Just gone ten."

"Then I intend to spend the next *four hours* outdoors until I have to go into work, and I think, actually, that I shall never spend any time indoors ever again!"

Eric eyed him suspiciously, then eventually seemed to decide that the matter didn't require further enquiry. He nodded, and then un-paused his game, turning back to the screen.

"Well, good for you. Glad you're in a good mood," he said, wincing slightly in annoyance as a death rattle from the TV indicated that he'd just bought the farm.

"Damn right I am," said Charlie, and then pointed at the half-empty cereal bowl. "What's that? Shreddies?"

"Raisin Wheats."

"Right. Any left? I think I'm out of cereal."

"Yes. Just don't go crazy with them."

"I won't, I won't."

Charlie turned and waltzed into the kitchen, revelling in the freedom of movement from room to room and glancing out of the window to take in the sunlight. Damn, he felt good. He had a day off tomorrow as well, a whole day to get out in this and ... Charlie paused in the middle of reaching for a bowl.

To do what? Go to the park and read? Go for a walk? Go to the gym? All three? He could, he had the free time, after all ... but no one else did. Anything he did, he'd end up doing on his own. But that was nothing new, nothing he hadn't experienced before; he did it all the time. He did plenty of social things to make up for it, though, things like ... he stood and thought, trying to remember the last time he'd done anything with real, close company. Even the previous night—or the beginning of it that he could remember—had been a rare Saturday night off, with a few work colleagues and their mates. Nice people, and a good laugh ... but that wasn't the same. It had been a good laugh, but ultimately, if they'd never seen him again they wouldn't be too bothered. That wasn't a judgement on them; it was just that they were acquaintances, not friends.

Charlie stood still in the kitchen, his arms limp by his sides and his good mood switched off like a lamp. Where the hell was all this coming from? What was the deal with all this damning self-reflection? Wasn't he thinking earlier, in the car with Minnie, about how he was lucky to have a good circle of friends? So these thoughts couldn't be true, could they?

Then answer the question. When was the last time you saw them?

He didn't know. But he wasn't that doing that badly, was he? He had real friends, like Chris and Terry. He didn't see them that often, true, but it didn't mean they weren't *there* for him. So why did he feel so lousy, and so ... lonely?

These aren't new feelings though, are they, Charlie? Maybe you feel them a lot more than you let yourself know. Any chance you got shaken up last night? Woken up a little?

Well, that was just—

"You need to text that lad, by the way," called Eric from the other room, interrupting Charlie's thoughts. "Neil, it might have been. He said to get you to text when you got up."

Neil? *Neil.* Clint's mate, Clint from work. He'd been out with the group last night ... but why would he want Charlie to text him? And furthermore, how would he have spoken to Eric? Charlie stuck his head around the living room doorway.

"When did he say this?"

"When he dropped you off last night."

"*Neil* dropped me off?"

"Yeah," said Eric, eyes intensely focused on the TV screen. "He came in the taxi with you. Said he wanted to make sure you got back okay, and that everyone else was too out of it to come with you."

Everyone else was too out of it? They hadn't been *that* bad, had they? But then, he didn't remember anything at all about the end of the night, so they probably had been. What the fuck had they done?

"I don't remember *any* of this, Eric," Charlie said, concern etched all over his face. "What was I like when I came home?"

Eric smiled, shaking his head as he went through his items onscreen, rearranging his death-dealing inventory.

"You were pretty out of it yourself, to be honest," Eric said. "It wasn't even that late, that's how I was still up. Must have been, what ... just after midnight? You just wandered in, mumbling to yourself, but you seemed to know what you were doing. You just toddled off to bed, and that Neil guy left his number for you. He seemed worried, but I think he was just being nervous. You seemed fine, just ready for bed."

Charlie looked on the coffee table in the middle of the room. The scrap of paper was still there, torn off the edge of what looked like a flyer, and covered in a fairly messy scrawl revealing Neil's number. Charlie walked over and picked it up.

"He couldn't have been that worried," Charlie said, examining the paper for no particular reason, "just letting me wander off to bed."

"Mm," agreed Eric, back into the onscreen action now. "Like I say, you looked fine to me. If you'd have looked bad I'd have kept an eye on you, but I put my head in about half an hour later and you were snoring. Hardly the actions of someone dangerously unconscious who's about to choke on their own vomit. You were quite happily asleep."

As he stared at the paper, Charlie wondered what Neil had actually been worried about if Eric's assessment of the situation was true. Had something happened earlier? Something bad that gave Neil so much cause for concern that he'd escorted Charlie all the way home?

There was only one way to find out.

***

"Hello?"

"Neil?"

"Yes?"

"It's Charlie."

"Fuck, Charlie! Shit, man ... man, that's a relief. How you feeling?"

"Absolutely fine. Thanks for taking me home."

"No worries, no worries ... I mean, I thought you were all right, but I wanted to be sure you got back. You were properly out of it before then, though."

Out of it? He hadn't even been that drunk ... had he?

"How much did I have to drink?"

"Drink? Uh ... man, I don't know. Six or seven pints? I don't think you were that drunk though. Pretty merry, like, but that's it?" There was confusion in Neil's voice; he didn't know why Charlie was talking about booze. A slow realisation began to dawn on Charlie, one that would also go some way to explaining his hyper-vivid dream.

"Neil ... what did we take?"

"Just a bit of ket," said Neil, as if he was explaining which brand of tea he had in the cupboard. "You were all for it, said you'd never tried it before."

Ket. Ketamine. A horse tranquilliser that had found its way into common use in clubbing circles ... or more importantly, club after-party circles. Neil was right; Charlie hadn't tried it before. He'd never been much of a drug user, but not out of any kind of piety; he simply couldn't afford to get into another expensive habit, and was always worried he'd become dependent on recreational drugs all too easily. However, he *also* lived by the mantra of trying anything once, and he knew that if somebody offered ketamine up, he wouldn't have said no.

"I don't remember that," Charlie said quietly, lost in thought. He'd heard the trips on ket were quite short though, only about fifteen or twenty minutes. But his time in The Black Room had gone on for *hours*, so it couldn't have been that. Unless it was some kind of aftereffect of the drug? Had the ket stirred something up in his head and triggered that crazy dream?

Did it also stir up some memories too?

What bloody memories?

"Really? That's strange," replied Neil, but too quietly. Charlie spotted the total change in Neil's tone immediately; intense relief had been replaced by caginess. It was obvious Neil had a reason to be so relieved previously, and now his sudden withdrawal meant that Charlie had brought something up that Neil was concerned about. He was clearly worried that Charlie didn't remember what had happened, worried that Charlie would *ask* what had happened.

"Did anything unusual happen, Neil? Did anything strange happen to me?" said Charlie, trying to sound casual but with every fibre in his body tingling. He wanted to scream *what the fuck did you do* down the phone, but managed to bite his tongue. Just.

"Nah, nah mate," said Neil, unconvincingly. "You just had a good ket trip, looked like you enjoyed it."

"Was Clint there?" asked Charlie, trying a different tack.

"Ye—" replied Neil, cutting himself off, realising his mistake. "I dunno, I think so," he continued, hurriedly, "I was pretty out of it myself, mate!" He finished the sentence with a forced, false laugh. Charlie let it hang in the air for a second before continuing.

"So if I asked Clint, he wouldn't say anything weird happened?" There was a pause on the other end of the phone before Neil came back on the line.

"I doubt he could tell you anything, man. He was fucked too." It sounded nervous, very quiet and sly. Charlie didn't really know Neil, and now he was starting to feel glad that he didn't; the man was starting to sound like a weasel.

"It was your ket, wasn't it?"

"Well, no, I mean, yeah, but everyone was asking about it, I didn't even suggest it. They all wanted to have some."

So that was it. Neil was covering his ass.

"Okay. Look, Neil, I'm pretty sure something happened last night, so just tell me. If I took it, it was my choice, and if everyone else is fine then I'm guessing there's nothing wrong with your stuff. But I need you to be straight with me."

There was a sniffing sound down the line, as Neil cleared his airways nervously, weighing it up.

"Well, look, I just didn't want to worry you man," Neil lied, picking his angle. "I mean, it's probably nothing anyway, we were all just pissing ourselves about it at the time, to be honest."

Because everything's funny on ketamine, idiot.

"You just seemed to go off on one for a bit, that was all," said Neil, trying to play down whatever had happened and sounding thoroughly unconvincing in the process. "I mean, y'know, normally people like, they just like, you know, chill out on ket. It's a thing, a bloody, ah, relaxant, right? It's a tranq. You're *supposed* to be super chilled, boom."

"Go on," said Charlie, leaning back against the wall as he listened.

"Aaaaah, well ... it's nothing, really. You started, like ... talking."

"About what?"

"Well, wait, not really *talking*," said Neil, and Charlie could picture him squirming on the spot. "You were like, kinda, shouting, sort of thing."

Shouting? On a tranquilliser?

"Shouting about what?" said Charlie, forcing a laugh, pretending he found the whole thing funny. He almost heard Neil relax slightly down the phone, imagined his shoulders unknotting while an amused, weasely smile spread across his face.

"Heh, well, just the usual shit, but, like ... louder. I mean, really shouting, man!"

"Ha ha! No way!" laughed Charlie's voice, while his face remained expressionless.

"Yeah, man!" laughed Neil, his voice at ease now, happy to offer more now that Charlie wasn't a threat. "We had to like, hold you down and shit! You started running about and shouting, when you were on the fucking *ket*!"

Sounds hilarious. Glad I amused you.

"Wow, man. So what was I saying?" Charlie didn't really know why he was pursuing the details; he had his answer, he knew what had happened to him, so why was he still so intrigued? It *had* been the weirdest, most vivid dream of his life though, and these thoughts about recognising the girl ... they did say that ket made people access memories vividly, that it opened up stores in the mind that you weren't even aware you had. Even so, he was asking the questions without really thinking.

"Oh, shit, what was it now ..." chuckled Neil, trying to remember the words. "It was so funny at the time, man, we were just off our faces and *pissing* ourselves at that shit ... uh ... something about a woman ..."

Charlie's blood turned to ice water, and he stood upright. Suddenly, he was very awake, everything in the room seeming to come into sharp, harsh focus.

"What about the woman?" he asked, speaking nearly in a whisper. Neil didn't notice.

"The woman, uh ... the woman ... shit ... ah, yeah! *The woman in the night, the woman in the night, the woman in the night*," laughed Neil, putting on a mock shouting-stoner voice to recount Charlie's rant of the night before. "Ha! We were all saying it man, and when Ben sat on you to get you to stay down and *you were still doing it*, man ... that shit was funny."

Charlie's legs started to feel weak. He let them bend, and he began to slide down the wall.

What are you even freaking out for now? It's obvious. You had a weird trip, and it carried over into your dreams. That's it. The answer is totally obvious. What the hell is wrong with you? It's completely self-explanatory!

That would have been fair enough ... if the phrase *the woman in the night* hadn't hit him like a sledgehammer, like a very important phrase that he'd known once before. Something very important that he'd forgotten somewhere ... he'd *known* that phrase before last night, hadn't he?

"Charlie? Charlie? You there?"

"How long ... how long did that go on for?"

"Well, that was the other thing, man. You must have been tripping for, like ... an hour and a half? Easy. Never seen that before. We were starting to get a little bit worried. Then you kinda came round, and were just really sleepy after that. You were barely awake, man, but you said you were thirsty, so we gave you some water and you just sat and drank it, just staring at the glass and shit. We kept asking if you were okay, and you just said you were fine ... but you just looked like you were fighting to stay fuckin' awake, and people said to put you in a cab. So I thought I'd better come too, just in case." This last part was said with a degree of smugness, as if Neil was waiting for praise for his selfless deed.

Selfless my ass, Neil. You just wanted to make sure I either didn't keel over after taking your shit, or wanted me off your property before I did. You fucking weasel.

"So who is she, man?" chuckled Neil.

"What?"

"The woman in the night, man! Ha ha, sounds like a bad porn film—"

He was cut off as Charlie hung up the phone and rubbed a hand over his face. He'd had enough of talking to Neil, but the idiot had just asked a very relevant question.

What does it matter who she was? It was a fucking dream!

Maybe so ... but there was some sort of a memory involved here. The way that phrase had lit up a part of his brain, a grubby, long-abandoned part that found itself suddenly bathed in the glare of floodlights, a part that said *YES, what took you so long?*

He felt drained, and then realised that his guts were making their presence felt. He needed to clear his head, needed a distraction for five minutes. Hadn't he spent all night having his melon severely twisted? He had to switch off. And he knew the combined solution that would do exactly that.

A comic, and a shit.

***

—and he squeezes back, desperate, even more scared now that he sees the terror in her, and begins to say I love you too *but the words are lost in the impact, the smack of metal on water—*

***

Twenty minutes later, Charlie emerged from the bathroom feeling refreshed and a great deal lighter, but still troubled. For a while, he'd almost forgotten all about the dream, the drugs and (*the woman in the night*) the telephone conversation he'd just had, but when he'd caught himself in the bathroom mirror on his way out, it all came slamming back; a jarring memory of seeing a shocking view in *another* bathroom mirror several hours earlier. A face that wasn't his, staring back at him.

It had been a nice face though, hadn't it?

On his way back up to his bedroom to think, he had to cross through the living room once more. He passed Eric again, who was still absorbed in his game. Without really knowing why he was asking, Charlie put a question to his housemate:

"D'you ever have really, really vivid dreams, Eric?" he said, looking at Eric's game and not at the man himself. "Like, where you have lengthy conversations with people, and everything makes perfect sense? I'm not talking dream-logic, I'm talking proper logic, even if the situation you're in is fucking nuts?"

"I don't really dream very often, I think," said Eric, still watching the screen. "Not since I was a kid."

Charlie thought about the amount of hours Eric spent in front of a screen, and was amazed. If Charlie watched even a bit of TV just before bed, he didn't go under quite as well and dreamed fitfully; he wondered how Eric hadn't sleepwalked into the path of a bus by now, or hadn't woken up naked in the butcher's.

"Never?"

"Not really," said Eric, shrugging. "Had a vivid one, have you?"

Charlie very nearly lied about it, but decided to be honest. What would be the point of lying? Plus, it was always a good thing to touch base with Eric, and this was something new. He didn't think Eric might rip him for it either, as would other people that he knew. In a way, it was the distance between himself and Eric that made it easier to be open.

"Yeah. Yeah, really vivid. It was fucking *nuts*. And there was this girl—"

"A-ha," said Eric, smirking slightly at the TV, "*that* kind of vivid dream. Well, spare me the details."

"No, no," said Charlie, smiling and running his hands through his hair nervously. He realised that he still hadn't dressed properly. "It wasn't that, but she was just real, man. It was like—"

"What was her name? She must have had a name," said Eric, raising his eyebrows as his character respawned onscreen for the umpteenth time. Again, Charlie nearly lied, and said that he didn't know, but he decided to tell the truth. It was a funny name, anyway.

"Ha, well, you'll like this one. 'Minnie Cooper.'"

This time, Eric's face lit up with surprised delight, turning in his seat now to look at Charlie directly.

"Ha! You're kidding! Did you know her as well, then?"

Charlie's skin nearly burst as the goose bumps hit, flashing all over his torso.

"*... what ...*" he said finally, his eyes looking like they would explode in his head.

"Minnie Cooper. Did you know her at school or something then? You don't forget a name like that, I suppose."

"Eric ... Eric, what the hell are you talking about?" said Charlie, squinting and rocking gently on his heels.

Eric looked confused, thinking that the conversational goalposts had been suddenly moved.

"Minnie Cooper," he said again, brow furrowing. "The girl you dreamed about. Did you go to—oh, wait, you didn't grow up here, did you, sorry. How do you know her then?"

Charlie tried to grasp at it, couldn't get it. Confusion reigned. Suddenly Eric was talking about a dream as if it were reality.

"I don't ... I didn't ... she's a dream. She was a dream. I dreamed about her," Charlie babbled, holding out a hand to Eric, showing him the lunacy of what he was saying. Eric just stared back, wondering if Charlie was somehow still high after all.

"Yes ... you dreamed about her. So where did you meet her in the first place?" Eric tried again, but with less conviction this time. He knew from experience that there was no point in trying to use logic with someone on drugs.

"I never have, Eric. I've never met her until she was in my dream," said Charlie, feeling idiotic and slightly light-headed.

Eric chuckled.

"Well, you must have done! Unless you know another Minnie Cooper, or your brain just happened to make up a girl with both an unusual name *and* the same name of a girl that I went to school with."

"You went to school with her? Did you know her?" asked Charlie, feeling a strange sense of urgency.

"Not really, it's just, you know, school. Everyone knows everyone's name. Skinny girl, big head of black hair—"

"Tight curls, like a poodle," interrupted Charlie, both wanting the answer to be yes and feeling terrified that it *would* be.

"Yeah, that's her," said Eric, sitting back in his chair and restarting the game, interest in the conversation lost. "Told you, you must know her from somewhere. Odd person to be dreaming about, but each to their own."

For a few moments, the only sound in the room was Eric's game playing, explosions and badly acted voice work filling the roaring silence in Charlie's head. The dream was intensely real again, a memory once easily dismissed now becoming like a fist.

He says he knows the girl you dreamed about. The girl you dreamed *about. Except he can't possibly know the same girl ... so then he just happens to know of another girl with the same crazy name, one who also happens to* look *the same as the one in your dream? Well, which sounds more believable; that such a coincidence could be true, or that you were really inside that girl's head, and that your entire world had changed around her? I know which one my money would be on.*

All of which might have convinced him, if not for his racing heart.

"Eric," said Charlie, needing to clear his throat to find his voice again, "let me just check I have this right. You went to school, in Coventry, with a girl called Minnie Cooper, who was skinny and had tight curly black hair. Am I right?"

Eric rolled his eyes, keeping them levelled at the TV.

"Jesus, yes. Look, my phone's on the table. Go on my Facebook, someone put an old school-year photo on there, have a look for yourself. She should be on there. Go into my photo albums, I think it's in 'Old Stuff.'"

Feeling like that moment was the real dream, wondering if perhaps he was still asleep, Charlie crossed to the living room table and gently picked up Eric's phone as if it were a grenade. His hand was shaking slightly. Moments later, Eric's Facebook profile was open in his hand, his photo albums folder opening up before Charlie's eyes.

Old Stuff.

The cover image for the folder was of an eighteen-year-old Eric giving the camera the finger; nothing yet.

You could leave this, right now. Walk away and forget it. This is a bad idea. I'm telling you, this is a bad idea. Once you open that up, if that photo's there, there's no going back. It was a dream. Write it off. Walk away. Walk away.

Why did his mind's instinct feel so scared? What did his subconscious know that he didn't? Charlie's thumb pushed the image onscreen anyway; what else could he possibly do?

The screen changed to the usual gallery of images, and Charlie spotted what he was looking for straight away; about four lines down, an unmistakable square full of pink and brown dots that was clearly a zoomed out image of several rows of teenaged faces.

This was pushed too.

Almost immediately, as the image appeared full screen, Charlie could pick out her hair; unmistakable in the row of blondes that she'd been placed in, as undeniable as a punch in the jaw. The face was at least fifteen years younger, the eyes far less haunted, even at a distance, but it was undeniably her. The girl he'd dreamed about, made undeniably real.

The woman in the night.

He thought he was going to be sick.

The Woman in the Night.

But he'd never seen her before last night, had never met her in his life, he *knew* this!

Are you sure?

Charlie's legs started to go for the second time that morning, and then something else started to go too. He barely made it to the upstairs bathroom in time before his guts came up through his mouth and into the toilet bowl, the stunned silence in his head now transformed into a screaming whirl of questions.

"You all right?" Eric's voice called from downstairs.

"*Uhhhh,*" Charlie moaned in response as he lay on the bathroom floor, confirming that he was indeed fine, even though he felt anything but.

But your house is here. Eric is here. Everything is the same as it should be, but in her head, your world—you—were replaced. Something else is happening. It was a dream, yes, but you must have met her, must have seen her. The same way she said she must have met you, remember?! You met her in passing somewhere; you were drunk perhaps, and dreamt her up out of your subconscious. Be honest, you liked the look of her, right? So why wouldn't *you bring her up in your dreams, why wouldn't your subconscious remember her face and her name?*

It all made sense, but it didn't work. Something about the realisation that Minnie Cooper was real had stuck in Charlie's mind like a shovel, had levered part of the surface of his mind up and revealed the edge of something that was possibly buried beneath … only it didn't just glint and catch the light, it buzzed like a bee, screeched at him to say *UNCOVER ME, I'M HERE, YOU'VE FORGOTTEN SOMETHING IMPORTANT.*

Then the shovel moved, soil shifted, something else came through. Her failed business.

She'd tried her hand at web design, right? You wouldn't remember that, surely. You can't even remember half the things your mates do for a living. You can Google her name and "web design," and if anything comes up you'll know something's going on. If it doesn't, then you can forget the whole damn thing.

It wasn't much, but it was something. Charlie staggered to his feet and went to his bedroom to fire up his PC.

Once it was ready (after much pacing back and forth while waiting, a time during which Charlie tried to think as little as possible), Charlie typed "Minnie Cooper Web Design" into Google, but hesitated before he hit the return key. He then realised that to weigh it up would mean to start thinking about the whole thing again, and instead just plunged his thumb down on the button.

Immediately, it came up.

Cooper Web Design, By Minnie.

"Coventry based web design offering … " Automatically clicking on the link, Charlie even recognised the colours and logo from Minnie's business card.

The woman in the night. The Woman in the Night.

It was too much. All too much. Charlie's arms slumped by his sides in the chair, jaw wide open and dropping his head down enough for his chin to rest on his chest. The slump was total. He tried to get at the problem, his mind only able to snatch segments of it once again.

Man-made. The Black Room could have been man-made, remember? That's what you said. Like a simulator. An experiment performed on people while they sleep. After all, you don't really know Neil, do you? How the hell would you know what he gave you? It could have been some sort of remote-connecting chemical, slipped into your bloodstream to receive outside signals to your brain, that they could then use to simulate ... an experience inside some random girl from Coventry?

It didn't sound likely. Not least because it begged the inevitable question of "Why the hell would they bother?" but also because it literally hadn't *felt* that way. The walls of The Black Room had been like liquid muscle fibre, tangible yet intangible, moist yet dry as a bone; he didn't think it was possible for them to exist physically and feel like that. And the way they'd changed, had pushed against him like rock ... and what the hell was all that about, anyway? He was about to be crushed to death, and then he'd just woken up? Or ... *or* ... had that actually been him being pushed out, being shoved out of The Black Room and sent home?

Are you nuts? Listen to yourself. IT WAS A DREAM. Don't you get it?

But it hadn't been. It simply hadn't been. Charlie knew it now, just as he knew the voice in his own head was now trying to lie to him, to protect him from having to deal with the madness right before his eyes. He'd known it the instant he'd heard Neil say the phrase *The woman in the night*, even if he'd not been immediately able to admit it to his weak, conscious mind.

Okay, yes. The Woman in the Night. Minnie. As insane as it sounds ... apparently you've somehow known them, or known of them, for a long, long time ... but in complete contradiction, you haven't *known them for many years. What the hell is that then? How does that work? Why The Woman in the Night, what does that mean to you? Where* were *you last night?*

Charlie put his hands to his face, and took a deep breath. He knew that he was only thinking about it in a practical way, scratching the surface of a ridiculous realisation that would blow his mind were he to fully comprehend it ... yet at the same time, the things that were coming up to his consciousness—dim and distant memories like dislodged and rising silt from the bottom of a lake, loosened into freedom by the ketamine—even though he didn't know what they were, they made it so much easier. This wasn't a *new* realisation. In some strange, unfathomable way, it was something he'd always known, something he was remembering again, and his mind, while still reeling, was also saying *oh yeah, I remember that ...*

So where were you last night? And why the hell is Minnie "The Woman in the Night"? Is it even Minnie that IS The Woman in the Night?

He didn't know. And his breathing was still rapid, his limbs still hollow and empty, his nerves still fried and wired, but he at least felt capable of functioning. He could plan, find out more. He would try not to think about it too much, to distance himself from it and make a plan. To be the practical, step-back-and-take-a-look guy that he prided himself on being able to turn into when the situation required it.

Okay. So what first?

Minnie. He had to find out more about Minnie. And Google was right there at his fingertips already.

Puffing out his cheeks, and trying not to think about what he was doing, Charlie typed "Minnie Cooper Coventry."

First at the top of the list of resultant links was the web design site again, but beneath that was the link for Minnie's Facebook page. The Facebook page might even have been there before, but Charlie had been so busy looking for the web design page, and so mentally screwed, that he hadn't noticed it. Either way, it seemed that there was only one Minnie Cooper in Coventry, at least. Charlie clicked on the link immediately.

The link was dead; Google's listing simply hadn't updated. In the top left corner was the Facebook logo, but with a message saying "This profile no longer exists."

She'd closed her Facebook profile then. Social media wasn't for everyone, that was for certain. He came back out of Facebook and looked at the next few links; other pages from her web design site, and then another Facebook link.

One titled "Minnie Cooper Tribute Page".

What ... the....

This was something else entirely. Charlie knew that there was only one reason why people set up Facebook tribute pages to non-famous people, and goose bumps broke out anew on his arms as he moved the cursor down to the link. He didn't want to click on it, and felt strangely scared to do so, but had no choice.

The page was public; he could read everything on it, and the description confirmed his worst fears.

Jesus ... Christ ...

There was what looked like a reasonably recent photo at the top of the page; Minnie smiling and holding a bottle of something. It was a genuine, full, happy smile, one that Charlie hadn't seen on her face while he'd been with her, and it showed him another side of her seemingly complex personality. The smile was transformative; she went from pretty to beautiful, a change lent even more impact when the accompanying header text cemented the fact that she would never smile again. The announcement was well meant, badly written, and full of typos (Charlie had never been pedantic enough to worry about typos; these people didn't have paid-for editors to work with, after all) but it certainly answered a lot of questions. As Charlie read it, his felt his stomach threaten to flip all over again. His hand went to his mouth without him realising.

"This page was set up for people to share there memmories of Minnie Cooper who was taken suddenly from us due to a brain hemmerage, she will be sadly missed. Please add your photos and pictures and stories of Minnie and please add a comment below her family would appreciate it NO HATERS THIS IS A PAGE FOR MINNIES FAMILY TO ENJOY, THEY ARE GOOD PEOPLE HOW WOOD YOU LIKE IT IF YOURE FAMILY MEMBERS DIED!! Be nice, have fun, peace, RIP Minnie.

UPDATE!!: The funeral is 3pm THIS SUNDAY at Canley Crematorium the family have asked that people that want to buy flowers instead donate to the Air Ambulance fund."

A brain haemorrhage?

She's dead? She's DEAD?

Stunned, Charlie scrolled down the page and read the comments, trying to get his head around the devastating opening paragraph but couldn't find any more information other than that which he could have expected; it was so sudden, she was such a nice girl, everyone liked her, etcetera etcetera. Charlie noticed that a large number of people seemed to be saying that they hadn't seen her for a while, though, and had wondered where she'd gone. There was also a handful of people that claimed to have spent time with her in Coventry near to the time of her death, people who'd said she'd seemed fine, physically at least.

But ... dead? I spoke to her this afternoon, she'd been fine! This can't be right, someone has it all wrong here!

But she hadn't been fine, when he thought about it. After all, hadn't he punched a hole in her mind?

The thought slammed into Charlie like an arctic wind, every inch of his skin turning icy cold with guilt and shock. He'd left her exhausted, asleep, an unsuspecting victim ... then he caught himself. There was no way all of this could have gone up so quickly, was there? Plus, when he'd left it had been midafternoon, and he'd woken up here this morning ... when had she died? In all of the shock and panic, Charlie realised he hadn't even looked at the dates of the comments. A quick glance at the most recent one told him that it had been posted a week ago; Minnie had been dead for at *least* that long then, and maybe a bit longer than that.

And it had been a Sunday, the same Sunday as today, had to be, because the phone had been handed in last night, *just like you found it last night. She was alive today ... so what the fuck is this?*

There were answers somewhere in all of this, Charlie knew, he just had to pick at it. At the same time, a strange leaden feeling had settled into his stomach, an almost physical weight that made him feel like he was unable to get up from the chair. He was, he realised, profoundly affected by the death of this stranger. He'd liked Minnie, he already knew that, but the realisation that she was gone highlighted the fact that he'd seen something in her that he could relate to; there had been something missing in her, he thought, and she knew it ... she was just trying to find out what it was, and how to get it back. As he sat in his swivel chair, thinking about Minnie, Charlie dimly became aware that he felt the same way about himself.

Plus, she was special. The Woman in the Night was special.

That was true, too, but he didn't know why. Yet.

Well ... when you think about it, "like" is a little loose, isn't it? "Intrigued by" is closer to the truth, right?

Charlie ignored the thought. A brain haemorrhage? That was just so goddamn unfair. She'd obviously stopped using the junk, and *this* was her reward when she was trying to sort herself out?

You don't know what's going on here. Maybe she knew too much.

The thought was an instantly sobering one. It didn't sound to Charlie like it would be out of the realms of possibility to give someone a brain haemorrhage if it kept something quiet—

Are you fucking stupid? SHE WAS ALIVE THIS MORNING, THIS AFTERNOON. Yet these comments go back over a week!

That was true. But if he'd really been inside Minnie Cooper's mind this morning—and Charlie believed that he had—then there was only one possibility left. The other Charlie, the other football result, the other shift pattern, another person living in his home that had lived there for decades … it all meant one thing.

The Minnie Cooper that died is a different Minnie Cooper. You weren't just in someone else's head; you were in another world.

There was no response, at first. Charlie simply sat with his hand on the mouse, staring at the monitor with his jaw set. If someone had looked at his face more closely, they would have seen it trembling slightly. This went on for several minutes as Charlie attempted to even *begin* to think about it. Nothing happened.

Eventually, the spell broke, and Charlie lurched out of his chair. This time, however, he didn't make it, and vomit that was mainly water splashed off the back of his bedroom door. It stank, and as he dragged himself up onto his knees, he realised that he would have to clean it up. In a way, he was grateful; he was glad of something normal to deal with, something relatively easy to fix.

Another world, another world, oh sweet jumping bollocks what the FUUUUUUU—

A few minutes later—delicious minutes of easy focus where Charlie gathered the various cleaning materials he would need from the kitchen—Charlie was working at the old carpet with a wet towel and beginning to peck again with his mind. In small bits, it was easier to deal with, and two things were already clear.

*Your Minnie might still be alive. (*Your *Minnie?)*

What you thought before—about the dead Minnie having been gotten to by somebody?—that could still be true.

The first thought gave Charlie a surprising amount of relief, while the second made him both intensely angry and scared. If that thought was true, then he'd potentially become part of something very big indeed, and involving ruthless people; but regardless, these were the people that would have killed this world's Minnie. If they had, Charlie silently swore that he would make sure they answered for that, if he was capable of doing anything about it. He decided not to think like that, though, for now at least. When he'd left, Minnie had been alive. This other Minnie had been dead for a week. If anything was going to happen to his Minnie, it hadn't happened yet; now he had a heads-up on the potential danger, he could see what he could do to stop it.

Okay, brilliantly heroic and all that, but what are you gonna do first, Johnny Big-Balls? Where the hell do you start?

Charlie stopped rubbing at the carpet—he'd done all he could with it anyway—and thought for a moment. It was a good question. All he had so far was the knowledge of what had happened to him last night, and that this world's Minnie was dead.

"This world's Minnie," man, this shit is CRAZY—

Charlie cut that thinking off as it would only slow him down, babbling in his ear like a backseat driver. He either accepted the situation and dealt with it, or he didn't; someone's life might be on the line. Even so, it was as intensely thrilling as it was worrying, for his Minnie's sake; he was potentially being called upon to save someone's life, something he had never been asked to do or had been able to do before. As severe a responsibility as it was, Charlie couldn't help but be excited.

So. A starting point. The funeral! It was today, at … where was it again? A quick scroll back up to the top of the Facebook page confirmed it was at Canley Crematorium. No one would notice another mourner turning up at the ceremony after all … but the question was, could he get away with being at the wake and asking a few questions? Charlie felt pretty sure that he would, but first he'd have to get the afternoon off.

Upon calling work, he'd felt a horrible anticipation that another Charlie would answer the phone; another Chuck, picking up the receiver and saying *I've taken your life again, Charlie, I'll always be here and I'll always fill your shoes*, but fear turned to relief as Clint answered on the other end. After answering a few laughing questions about how he was feeling after the night before, Clint confirmed that no, the upper management didn't know anyone had been out on the town Saturday night, and yes, he could cover for Charlie's hangover; they were quiet anyway. Charlie thanked Clint profusely—Clint was a good guy, and had always done well by Charlie—then he hung up and booked a cab for 2:30 p.m. Charlie didn't own a car, nor would he ever want one, and Canley was too far to travel by bike when he wasn't feeling one hundred percent. As much as he hated to get inside the dreaded metal cage again, it was a necessity; it just couldn't be avoided a lot of the time. Glad again for having a list of practical, easy-to-complete tasks to focus his mind on for the time being, Charlie started to run a bath and then got his black suit out of the cupboard, ready for lint rolling; he wondered where his black tie was. Everyone there was going to be saying good-bye to Minnie, and even if he technically wasn't, he had to look like them.

But that's the big question, isn't it, Charlie? Have you already said good-bye to Minnie, and you just don't know it yet? How do you know you'll ever see her again? And if you don't … what does that mean to you? You were so excited to be out, and so much has happened since, that you haven't really stopped to process that idea. What if you never see her again?

Charlie stood still for a moment. Eventually, he went back to his mental list: the bath, the suit, the tie. That was far easier.

***

It was a surreal feeling, seeing Minnie's coffin; having visual confirmation that Minnie was now trapped inside a box of her own. Charlie was sitting at the back of the small, ageing service room, which was still only two-thirds full despite its lack of size. It was populated by a crowd of about seventy, despite the hundreds of people on the Facebook tribute page all trying to outdo each other with their online displays of grief. Even though he was a short distance away, the coffin felt large to Charlie, and very imposing. He knew it wasn't really—Minnie couldn't have been more than five foot four—but it had a presence that Charlie was intensely aware of. Here, potentially, was *his* Minnie's future, and here he was without a clue as to what he was going to do about it.

Don't give yourself a hard time. That's what you're here to do, right? You're here to get a clue.

True, but it was the strangest sensation was being at the funeral of someone that, as far as Charlie knew, was alive in another world; or at least, another version of her was. He felt sadness and relief at the same time, and both of them tempered by fear of what might yet happen. Sitting there, he realised something; he desperately did not want his Minnie to die.

He thought he'd already identified Minnie's father, sitting at the front and sobbing hysterically; a big man both in height and breadth, still impressive despite his advanced years. His grey hair and beard were neat today, but Charlie thought that perhaps they hadn't been that way for the last week or so. A special effort had been made today for Minnie, for his lost daughter. The man was a wreck, his face continually going to his hands throughout the ceremony despite his bravest efforts to sit up and listen. It was painful to watch, and Charlie's heart went out to the man.

To the father's right, there was no female partner. Due to the fact that the far slimmer young man that was sitting with his arm around the father's shoulders was—even when the glimpses of his face from the back were only occasional—almost a male mirror image of Minnie, Charlie thought it was safe to assume that he was Minnie's brother. Charlie searched his memory for the name, found it; Tommy. Mum was either deceased then, or divorced and severely out of the loop as to what was happening to her children. The woman celebrant running the show was doing a good job, keeping her tone as sincere and un-robotic as possible, despite presumably having done several other funerals already that day. A tough gig, Charlie thought, and felt some respect towards her; this was a job that was more important than most to get right, and more difficult to do so.

As details on Minnie's life came out in the eulogy, Charlie leant forward to hear more clearly. Not just to try and glean some fresh information as to what might be going on, but because here were the facts that Minnie had done her absolute best to avoid talking about. She wouldn't like it, he knew, but he wouldn't tell her. And there was the question again, the one that had been rattling around in his head all day:

Are you ever going to see her again?

He didn't know, and with every mental repetition of the question he found himself becoming more and more nervous at the thought that he might not. For the umpteenth time, he told himself that he would find out that night; if, after the onset of sleep, he returned to The Black Room once more. That would be the only way to find out (apart from tapping up Neil for more ketamine, perhaps) and worrying about it wouldn't help. As ever, telling himself all this didn't help him relax even a little.

In the midst of all the details about Minnie's school life, and some funny stories, including one about trying to paint the dog black, a few items caught Charlie's ear in particular; Minnie had earned a degree in graphic design from the University of Bristol, and had spent a year working in a cafe in France without managing to learn more than a few sentences of French. There were glossed-over mentions of Minnie's *troubled times,* and her recent *getting her life back on track, going back into full-time employment in a supermarket.* Charlie supposed it wouldn't really do to specifically say "drug troubles" at a funeral, but working in a supermarket? Any job was better than being on government handouts—Charlie had no delusions of grandeur; he was aware that he worked "only" behind a bar and took pride in supporting himself, so he didn't have any snobbery towards Minnie's job—but Charlie somehow couldn't see Minnie being content doing that for the rest of her life.

Just before they were asked to stand, before the curtain came around the coffin and down on the final act of this world's Minnie's life, the celebrant explained that Minnie had always had a love of Whitney Houston's music (that was a surprise to Charlie) and that the song that was about to play was one of Minnie's favourites. Just before the closing lines of the ceremony were spoken, the celebrant reminded the assembled crowd that the wake would be held at the Bull's Head pPub. Charlie didn't know the venue, but Google or a cab driver would see to that. Some awful, generic Whitney number began to play (Charlie didn't recognise it) and the undertakers stepped forward to perform their bows of respect.

Minnie's father, nearly hysterical now and guided by the celebrant, walked out of a door in the front of the room that would take them into the garden of remembrance. The other mourners followed his considerable bulk; this part of the day was done. Charlie had to admit, it had been a good ceremony. The real mourners were here; Minnie would have been pleased. Let Facebook have the attention seekers.

Once Charlie arrived at the Bull's Head, he found it to be a nice, old school boozer, with a real fireplace in the bar. Here and there were original wooden beams and pieces of panelling so dark that they were almost black.

The wake itself was surprisingly chatty, with everyone but Minnie's dad talking to each other happily; while he was indeed talking to people, and receiving their well wishes and condolences with a sad smile, he wasn't giving much else out, and couldn't really be expected to be doing otherwise. It was clearly his brave face; his son was doing a better job of it. Charlie noticed that odd combination of emotions at work in the assembled crowd, the ones prevalent at most wakes; positivity (celebrating the deceased's life), happiness (reminded of their own mortality, people delight in conversation and drink), sympathy (for the deceased's family), reverence (for the deceased), and relief (they're not dead; it isn't their son, daughter, husband, wife).

Charlie waited until Minnie's dad was relatively alone, sitting only with his son at a small table in the corner. Getting to that point had taken a while. Charlie had wanted to ingratiate himself into some of the other mourners and ask questions, but they were all in tight little chatty groups, small pods of either families or friends, and all turning their backs on the other strangers to avoid small talk in such an important scenario. His only choice then was to simply wait until he could speak to the father and son on their own, the only people there with whom he would have a blatant excuse to walk up to and introduce himself.

Charlie had forced himself to only nurse the two pints of lager he'd gotten through while waiting. His nerves were so highly strung that the appeal of disappearing into the numbing arms of booze was all-too tempting, but he wouldn't allow it. He knew that he had to be totally on the ball, and ready to think on his feet should any difficult questions be asked. His paranoia was already through the roof, due to doing his best to look inconspicuous while standing alone at a wake. The fact that he was taller than most of the people there didn't help either.

Keep cool, Charlie, he thought, *no one's thinking anything about you. You could just be her milkman for all they know, or her next-door neighbour. There must be solo mourners at funerals all the time!*

He'd known that this thinking was right, but it still hadn't helped matters much. He'd felt too conspicuous, and after all, if his idea that Minnie had been gotten to was correct, who knew who could be watching? It was just as he'd decided that he was going to have to have a third Stella after all—or risk abandoning the task at hand altogether due to nerves—that his opportunity arose. Draining the last of his pint and dumping the glass on the bar, Charlie made his way over to their table.

As he approached, he could see that the father and the brother were now having a conversation, smiling gently. Charlie realised that he was about to interrupt what looked like the first moment all day that Minnie's dad had managed a happy memory without it wracking him with fresh grief. Charlie almost turned around, not wishing to spoil this important moment for the man, but then thought better of it; surely if the dad knew that there was a way that another Minnie might be saved, he would *want* the moment interrupted?

"Mr Cooper?" asked Charlie as he approached the table, hand outstretched. Both Coopers looked up at him. Of course. "Sorry, both of you, I mean. I just wanted to give my condolences. I knew Minnie only briefly, but we became very close friends." Relief salved its way through Charlie's body when both men smiled and nodded gently; they'd heard similar stories many times already today, and Charlie's well-wishes stood out no more than anyone else's. "This was just such shocking news," Charlie continued, "and I'm so sorry for your loss. I mean, it was just totally out of the blue. I only heard yesterday, and I just couldn't believe it."

"Yes, it was a massive shock to us all," said the brother, clearly wanting to do the heavy lifting for his tired and grieving father today. "How did you know Minnie?"

Charlie braced himself; he already had this prepared, having anticipated the question, but still had no idea if it might backfire badly or not. The only name he had that was related to Minnie's life could well be one that these two men didn't want to hear; Minnie had clearly known some dodgy characters.

"We were introduced by Dave," Charlie said, wincing internally and hoping that Dave, while he had been the guy that had encouraged Minnie to get out of the house, hadn't also been her drug dealer. "We kind of just became good friends after that." For the second time inside a minute, Charlie felt an almost crippling wave of relief as both men nodded again, smiling, and even exchanged an appreciative glance.

"A good guy, Dave," said Minnie's dad. He was wearing glasses now, having presumably taken them off during the funeral itself to cry. He looked good natured, round faced; his cheeks had the slight reddening of a social drinker. "He was a good influence on her, gave her a kick up the arse when she needed it."

"Yeah," said the brother, looking into his pint and nodding with a sad smile.

"Yeah, he is," said Charlie, frantically thinking about how he could start asking some questions. Was it normal at funerals to ask about the nature of the death? Surely not; it would be too painful, right? So how the hell was he going to get onto the subject? He realised that he needed to carry on talking, as it would be weird for him to just keep standing there silently. He opened his mouth to see what would come out. "It's just so unfair, after being helped so much by Dave, that this could then happen. Especially when she'd been doing so well." This last part was another gamble, but Charlie thought it a calculated one. From what he'd been able to gather both from the eulogy and Minnie's own hysterical rants when upset, she'd gotten herself clean and was working, although she'd recently had some kind of episode that she was worried about. Charlie doubted many people knew about that, if any, and even if they did, one episode didn't mean *everything* had gone wrong ... or rather, Charlie was gambling that it hadn't.

"She'd been doing great. Doing great," repeated the father, almost defiant in his statement. His eyes had come alive. "Sorted it all out, working again, got herself all fixed. It was too late anyway, the damage was done, but ... that's not the point ..." Alive eyes became wet, and looked away. The son touched his arm.

"You don't know that, Dad. You don't know that. They said it just happens sometimes, remember?"

His dad nodded silently, and put his hand over his mouth, his elbow resting on the table, looking away.

"I'm going to the bar, okay? Same again?" the son said, and the dad nodded, patting his son on the shoulder. The son turned to Charlie. "Would you like one, mate?" he said gently, offering that sad smile again.

"No, thanks," said Charlie, touched by the small kindness in this man's time of grief. He was about Charlie's age, with short, curly black poodle hair like Minnie's that was starting to go prematurely grey. "That's very good of you, man, but I'm driving, thanks." He regretted having to say no—he desperately wanted another—but this was too important to risk screwing up. Minnie's brother nodded and headed off to the bar, leaving Charlie with the dad, who was now wiping his eyes. Charlie felt suddenly very awkward. Minnie's dad saved him, however.

"Sorry, sorry, mate, silly old sod I am," sniffed Minnie's dad, looking up Charlie as he forced a smile and regained his composure. "Don't worry, everything's setting me off at the moment; everything's a reminder, you know? It's nothing you've said, don't worry." Charlie's heart melted. The guy was worrying about how *Charlie* felt?

"Hey, no, it's not, you know, it's, it's, uh, totally understandable," babbled Charlie, holding up his hands. "Jesus, I mean ..."

"How old are you, pal?" asked Minnie's dad, waving Charlie's words away and forcing another smile. "In your thirties, right?"

"Yes, that's right."

"You ever do drugs, if you don't mind me asking?" asked Minnie's dad. It wasn't an aggressive question—the man sounded friendly, and Charlie thought that the question was meant well—but there was major potential for upset here, and Charlie didn't know if the man had an agenda. Charlie looked at Minnie's dad's eyes; they were reddened slightly from a day of tears, but Charlie thought that was all there was to read in them.

"Yes, once or twice, if I'm being perfectly honest," Charlie answered, shrugging slightly. "I know that's obviously a sore issue, but you asked me an honest question, so there's an honest answer. I have." Minnie's dad nodded.

"Uh-huh. I didn't realise how many of your generation did. Just normal now, I guess. None of you seem to realise how it can get out of control." He shook his head, looking at the table.

"I think it's perhaps more that we don't consider how the outside world can turn *our* world upside down," said Charlie, "at the worst possible time, and how easy it then is to lean on bad habits for support. Even for smart people like Minnie." Minnie's dad considered this, then sighed and opened up his hands.

"You have to live your own lives, that's for certain," he said. "You do harm if you interfere, you do harm if you don't ... it's a bloody minefield. Sorry, I didn't get your name?"

"Charlie. Charlie Wilkes." As soon as the words were out of his mouth, he regretted it; he probably should have used a different name. He'd been caught off guard, relaxed in this man's presence. He held out his hand, and Minnie's dad took it.

"Don Cooper. Do you have kids?"

"No, sir," said Charlie. "Not even married."

"A wonderful thing, to have children," Minnie's dad said, wistfully. "But the *stress* ... Christ." He paused for a moment, lost in thought. Then he looked up, his eyes sad, the false front lowered. "Even so, this ..." He trailed off, waving his hand around him and gesturing at the assembled people. "It all just shows all the stress is pointless. Right? They're either gonna be okay, or they're not. Bugger all you can do about it. Not the drugs, and Tommy has hung his hat on that," he said, gesturing now in the direction that the son had taken, "and I have my doubts ... but they say this would have happened all the same? Just like that ..." he trailed off again, looking into his pint and radiating grief. Charlie stood there dumbly. This was painful to watch, and his heart was breaking for the man, but he had no words of comfort. Anything he thought of to say just sounded glib and pointless.

"Was it ... were there any warning signs at all?" Charlie heard himself saying quietly, the words seeming to come without conscious thought. It was what he wanted to know, but he couldn't believe that he was asking it. Fortunately, Minnie's dad didn't seem even slightly fazed by the question, answering almost as if he were on autopilot. And perhaps, by this point, he was.

"A little bit. She went a bit quiet for a while the week or so before she died. Distracted, really, not like her. Always so attentive normally. But you'd talk to her and you just knew she wasn't really listening, like her mind was elsewhere. And she always seemed to have a headache; I'd always have to have painkillers in for when she came round. That was a sign, obviously. She never used to get headaches."

Charlie's skin broke out in goose bumps again. He almost wanted to tell Minnie's dad to stop talking, to tell him that that was enough, thank you, he had to be going, and then he could turn around and leave. But he just remained standing there, helpless in the path of the speeding, runaway juggernaut of truth.

"And then she stopped coming round altogether. And that *was* funny, because Minnie always came round every other day. She was a daddy's girl anyway, you know, but after Sarah died, I think she worried about me a bit." His right hand when to his left, gently and absentmindedly caressing the wedding ring on his finger. Charlie didn't need to ask who Sarah was. Minnie's dad looked up at him, and now the tears were back.

"That was the worst part," he said, his voice cracking around words pulled like knives from his soul; they poured forth like a confession. "We didn't know exactly when she died, because she'd just stopped answering the phone. She was alone. And the last conversation we'd had ... it wasn't even a real conversation. It was like ... it was like she wasn't even listening to me at all, like she was just nodding in the right places. She'd just be holding her head, and you could see she was just trying to disguise the pain ... she was only there for me and Tom. You could sometimes even see her whispering to herself, trying to talk herself through it, and then you'd ask her what she'd said and she'd just brighten up, putting on this front ... she was always good at that. The headaches ... and then ... you could see she couldn't keep it up any more. She just said she had to leave, out of nowhere. And she gave me a hug, and for a second, she *was* there, I had her attention ..." The hand went back to his face, and his eyes and brow crumpled inwards. "She was in the toilet before she left. She thought we couldn't hear through the door. Talking to herself ... like ... someone else was there ..." These last parts were spoken into his hand, and Charlie knew that the man was done. Charlie couldn't hear any more anyway; he was struggling to take in the enormity of what he'd just learned, and he couldn't make this poor man recount any more agonising memories. Charlie suddenly felt like it was hard to take in air. He needed to get out of the crowded pub, needed to breathe.

"I'm sorry," Charlie almost whispered, and Minnie's dad held up a hand to tell him it was okay. Charlie hesitated, then put a hand out and rested it on the man's shoulder. Minnie's dad patted Charlie's arm, not looking at him, his sobs muffled by his other hand. As Charlie turned to walk away from the table, shuffling like a man in a dream, Tommy came the other way, holding a pint. His eyebrows went up as he saw Charlie; he had news to pass on.

"Hey, Dave's over there by the way, did you see him?"

FUCK!!

"Uh, no, I mean, yeah, I think so ..."

Tommy turned, looked over his shoulder, held up a hand.

"Dave!" he called. "Come here a sec."

FUCK!! FUCK!! FUCK!!

He turned back to Charlie, smiling pleasantly. Charlie returned the smile, but his was more like that of a grinning corpse. He was about to be utterly rumbled. His mind raced as Tommy talked.

"Listen, thanks for coming," Tommy was saying. "Don't worry if Dad got upset; anything's setting him off, it's hit him so hard. He'll really appreciate you coming over to pass on your respects. We're all a mess, to be honest ... he's just devastated more than most." He looked so sad saying it, that normally Charlie would have felt as moved by the son's words as the father's, but in that moment, as he saw the top of someone's head moving over through the crowd and knew that it was Dave, knew that in a second Dave would be in front of him and looking confused, all Charlie could think about Tommy was:

Nice going, asshole!! Shut the fuck up for a second so I can think of a way—heyyyy ...

85

Remembering Minnie's own trick, Charlie suddenly looked down at his pocket as if surprised, and then pulled out his phone. He looked at the screen, then sighed and looked at Tommy apologetically, mouthing the word *Work*; miraculously, Tommy smiled and held up a hand.

Charlie gave him a thumbs-up, then turned away and began speaking to his imaginary caller.

"Hi? John, is it important? Okay, explain what's happened ..." Charlie began to walk, very quickly, and kept up the conversation until he was outside the pub. Even then, he kept the phone to his ear, and didn't turn back to face the building either, until he'd flagged down a cab and was on his way back to Radford.

Even though he was stuck inside a car, Charlie breathed a sigh of temporary relief and guilt. That had been far too bloody close; plus, he'd just walked out on a man who was opening up to him, a stranger. He told himself it had been for the best, that he didn't want to cause an awkward scene on a difficult day for a grieving family, but it didn't help any more than telling himself that he'd been there for Minnie, to save the other *her*. As the buildings sped by, and his heartbeat began to slow down again, Charlie turned his mind back to what he'd learned, and the dark feeling sank back into him. A cold sweat broke out on his skin, and he tried to think of ways around it, but there were none. It wasn't definite, by any stretch, but the coincidences were too great to dismiss; all the similarities were there. One thing he was certain of now; no one had deliberately silenced Minnie. This was something else.

This Minnie had gotten headaches, progressively worse ones. She'd seemed distracted, and Charlie didn't think it was just because of the pain; nor did he think Minnie whispering to herself had been her trying to "talk herself through it." And then she'd had a brain haemorrhage and died.

His Minnie had gotten constant headaches while he was inside her head. And to anyone else watching, it would look like she was talking to herself too. He didn't want to admit it—couldn't even begin to believe it—but he had to accept that the following was true: this world's Minnie had also had a Charlie in her head. Another Charlie, just like him, and it sounded like he ended up being in there for some time. Eventually, her brain couldn't take it anymore.

Charlie was betting that, just like him, that other Charlie hadn't even meant to turn up in this Minnie's head either. And if the pattern stayed the same, that meant that Charlie was going to keep ending up inside *his* Minnie's head too.

So if he couldn't figure out how to stop himself from ending up inside Minnie's head, then eventually ... he was going to kill her.

***

Eric was out when Charlie got home; that was fine. He had too much on his mind as it was, without stopping for small talk with his flatmate ... and then felt bad as soon as he had that thought. Eric was all right. "Small talk" was too dismissive a term for their conversations, and did them both a disservice. But how did you ever become close to someone if things never progressed *beyond* small talk? Especially when one of you was so cagey. Still, it was a friendship, of sorts.

Throwing his jacket onto the bed and undoing his tie, Charlie signed into his PC and immediately brought up Google. He typed a sentence into the browser—

Out of body experiences

—and hit enter. Straightaway, as usual, Wikipedia came to the rescue, and immediately his eye was caught by a link in the summary box:

Chemical Induction

Well, well, well.

Clicking upon the link, the page immediately leapt to the relevant paragraph; Charlie couldn't believe what he read. But not because it was contradictory, but because it seemed to confirm everything so perfectly:

"OBEs induced with drugs are sometimes considered to be hallucinations (i.e., purely subjective), even by those who believe the phenomenon to be objective in general. There are several types of drugs that can initiate an OBE, primarily the dissociative hallucinogens such as ketamine, dextromethorphan (DM or DXM), and phencyclidine (PCP)."

Except his experience *hadn't* been a hallucination; there was no doubting that now. And what were the odds of ketamine being on that list? Okay, sure, it was a hallucinogen, so therefore you could have guessed that it might be there, but Charlie hadn't known that ketamine was classed as such; he'd only known that it was a drug. For a moment, a feeling of stupidity passed over him. He didn't even know what kind of drug it was, and yet he'd put it into his body based on the drunken words of a stranger. He was too old to be doing shit like that. Either way, here was ketamine on a list of out of body experience-inducing drugs, and here *he* was having taken some and consequently experiencing time out of his body ... and inside someone else's. Wikipedia didn't have anything to say about *that*, but it didn't matter. The cause was there; he just had to figure out how to stop the effect, if the post-ketamine change in his mind turned out to be permanent. Indeed, there was no guarantee that last night hadn't just been a one-off, but somehow, his experience had been more than imaginary, and if he was the same as whichever Charlie had ended up in the dead Minnie's brain, then he was going to keep having them.

And what about the Charlie that was in her brain when she died? What do you think happened to him?

Charlie sat bolt upright in his seat. That was something that he hadn't considered. Minnie going to sleep seemed to have pushed him back to his own world, but he'd been sitting in there for quite a long time—a good hour or two—before the walls had started to contract. So if death was even vaguely quick, he'd still be in there when it finally happened. Even if it wasn't, and Minnie dipped into sleep before death, again, he'd still be in there, as the walls wouldn't have had time to contract, or before whichever late-stage process of unconsciousness that had actually pushed him out had begun.

Don't panic. You know what caused it now for certain, and you also know the end result, which might well have been more than the other Charlie and Minnie knew. Plus, you might not even end up back there unless you take the drugs. Hell, the other Charlie might have been taking them constantly to get back there just out of curiosity, neither of them knowing what the end result was going to be. Right? Plus, if you didn't know what damage you might be doing, wouldn't you do that? Wouldn't you take the drugs again to try and go back? You want to see her again, don't you?

Yes. Charlie did.

The realisation felt like it should have been shocking, but it wasn't. He *did* want to see her again, and as soon as he acknowledged it consciously, it just felt right. He wanted to see Minnie Cooper again, and more importantly, he wanted to see her alive. There was a connection there, that was all he could say, and it felt like something old and important. But he wouldn't make it happen, wouldn't risk her life; he would never touch any drugs again, if doing so meant that she would be safe. And just as he thought of that concept—he would never see Minnie Cooper again—he felt a dull wrench in the back of his stomach.

Hey, don't forget, you could well end up killing yourself as well, asshole. Just a minor detail that you might want to consider.

True. Plus, panicking and worrying weren't going to help anything. This was research time, time to see what he could find out that might help the situation in case he *did* end up there again without the drugs. He took a deep breath, slapped his cheeks gently and went back to the Wikipedia page.

Some time later, after trying and failing to find any information about out of body experiences that wasn't already covered by Wikipedia, Charlie turned away from the PC and rubbed his face with his hands. It was all getting too much again; too many things kept coming up from the depths of his mind, more detritus from the depths of his subconscious, and his confusion, frustration and growing desperation were building. As if summoned by his own need for distraction, the phone rang.

It was Mr Bansal, the landlord. Normally, Charlie tended to let calls from Bansal ring out—he always left a message, and it was usually just to let Charlie know that he was going out of town, and that Charlie was to pay the rent to Bansal's brother if Charlie wanted a receipt—but today, he answered. The call was welcome.

"Charles?" asked Mr Bansal down the phone. Charlie winced. His landlord never called him Charlie.

"That's me," answered Charlie, still rubbing his eyes. "What's up?"

"Sorry to call you on a Sunday, Charles, is this a bad time?"

"No, no, it's fine, it's fine."

"Okay. Just to tell you that I have to book a man to come round before Wednesday to check the boiler, is that okay? When is good for you?" *Wednesday* and *When* were pronounced *Vednesday* and *Vhen*, Bansal being born and raised in Mumbai. His English, however, was excellent, and the only remaining trace of his accent was in his mispronunciation of Ws into Vs. Charlie often wondered if it was actually a deliberate affectation.

"Tuesday, do it Tuesday then. Tuesday afternoon, late as possible," Charlie said, thinking around his shifts.

"Okay, thank you, I'll let them know. Everything else okay?" This question was always asked, regardless of the nature of the call. It was both a responsible question as a landlord, and a reminder to Charlie to look after the place. Charlie already had his usual answer ready, when something occurred to him.

"Yeah, everyth ... actually, Mr Bansal, there was something. This might sound like an odd question, but, who owned this house before you? Have you had it a long time?"

"Yes, very long. Why?" *Vhy?* There was a slight note of confused suspicion in his voice, and Charlie supposed it was a weird question that any landlord would be suspicious of. He thought fast.

"We just keep getting these letters, that's all. I wondered if they might be addressed to the previous owners?" Charlie winced. That was dumb thinking. No one in a rented property got letters through that weren't addressed to them and thought they might belong to the previous owners; they would assume a previous *tenant*. Fortunately, Bansal didn't seem to notice at first.

"Who to?"

"The Johnsons," Charlie lied, hoping that the previous owners hadn't been, by coincidence, called Johnson.

"No, no, not that I know of. Tenants before you, uh, were Carter, Wiltshire, and ... ahh ... Gardener. I've owned that house, oh, twenty years at least, you two are the only other ones living there in this time. No Johnsons. And the owners were the Whitlocks." *Vhitlocks.*

"Oh, right. Never mind, then. Twenty years, eh?"

"Yes, yes. First one that I ever bought, actually," said Bansal, sounding as if he was smiling, enjoying the memory.

"I think I might have known them, the Whitlocks," lied Charlie, having not grown up in Coventry, but Bansal wouldn't know that. "When I was a kid. We had a Mrs Whitlock help out at the school."

"Oh yes?" asked Bansal, sounding like he was asking out of politeness rather than interest. "Small world, yes?"

"Yeah, I never knew why she left the school. Isn't that a funny coincidence though, eh? How come she sold, in the end? Did something happen to her then?"

"Hmm, I think ..." said Bansal, trailing off as he tried to remember, "... yes, I think her husband went to jail, actually? I think it was jail. Then divorce, and she sold the house. Something like that."

"Well, well. Guess you never know what the future holds, eh?" said Charlie, his voice flat, lost in thought.

So that's why. The old bitch's husband got busted, and she sold the house ... yet over in Minnie's world, he's as free as a bird. So Coventry's Miss Charisma is still living there, and old Chuck is obviously shacked up somewhere else.

The possibilities were suddenly endless, and Charlie felt light-headed all over again.

"Very true, very true," said Bansal, clearly wanting to wrap things up. "Okay, Charles, I'll send you a text once I know what time, okay?"

"No problem," muttered Charlie, and Bansal said good-bye and hung up. Charlie flung the phone onto the bed, and after a moment's hesitation, dived after it, burying his head under his pillow and moaning. He wanted to shut out the world and its myriad new layers, perspectives, realities, as well as his own memories; they threatened to resurface, freed from their carefully forged shackles. He lay there a while, breathing steadily, feeling very tired and letting his body relax.

You can't lie here. You might go to sleep. You're not ready. You haven't learned anything!

But what else could he do? There was no guarantee that sleeping would take him back to Minnie's world without ketamine anyway, and he obviously couldn't stay awake indefinitely (he'd learned that lesson in the eighties after watching *A Nightmare on Elm Street* at far too young an age, managing only forty-eight personally enforced hours awake before falling asleep on the back of the bus during a school trip). He'd read the bloody Wikipedia page and there was nothing to help, and what could he find anyway? "How to stop having out of body experiences"? Who the hell ever needed to know that?

Might as well have a look. You never know.

Reluctantly, Charlie admitted that that was true. Sighing, he got up off the bed and went back to Google. It was nearly six in the evening.

***

Chapter Four: The Loneliness of the Long-Distance Cyclist, This Cubicle Is Occupied, Charlie Looks At the Last Ten Percent, and A Ceramic Mug Leads To a Surprising Discovery
***

The many hours after that were not pleasant for Charlie Wilkes. Fruitlessly searching Google, he got nowhere; he found various techniques covering everything from presleep relaxation, to a change of diet before bed. Amazingly, it seemed that quite a few people wanted to *stop* having out of body experiences. He hadn't known that it was a regular enough thing for anyone that they'd *need* them to stop. Of course, the religious elements were there, saying that OBEs were due to influences on both sides of the fence; some were saying that it was God's will, others were saying that it was the work of malevolent demons and that the best cure was to see a priest. Other, more realistic interpretations were along the lines of the Wikipedia entry; the whole thing was a hallucination, and those afflicted would be best to see their doctor. Charlie thought the latter would certainly be worth a try, and made a mental note to book himself an appointment in the morning. He suspected that it probably wouldn't help in any way, but he did entertain the slim possibility that sedatives *might* help; sending him into a deeper level of unconsciousness might affect the way his mind travelled (*is that even the right word?*) at night.

In any instance, Charlie thought that what was happening to him was far more severe than any of the instances listed online, and therefore highly doubted that any of the doctor-free remedies that he'd read, like a self-massage before bed (in both senses of the phrase) or even an actual massage would make much difference to his situation. He decided, however, that if he found himself in The Black Room once more, he would try anything, would even risk being carted off to the nuthouse on his doctor's advice. Eventually, by around 8:00 p.m., he gave up, and tried to shut it all away, tried to put it out of his mind for the time being.

What's the point in worrying about it if you don't even know that you'll go back without the ketamine? This could all just be a waste of time, and let's face it, you're not getting anywhere with Google. You've made a real effort; you've done your best. Just try and relax. Your head's taken a major kicking of its own in the last thirty-six hours, and you need some downtime. Hell, even sleep now if you can, or put a film on.

The sleep window, however, had passed. After all the searching and stressing and staring at a computer screen, he was absolutely wired, his mind having changed from exhausted confusion to a crackling whirlwind of pressing questions and frightening ideas.

So he went for the film option, popping a Blu-Ray into his bedroom player, but he couldn't settle; deciding that the TV in the living room was much bigger than the one in his room anyway, Charlie opted to watch the film downstairs, especially as Eric was out on another one of his mysterious social occasions. He actually wished that his housemate was in, thinking that a conversation about anything might help take his mind off his concerns. After a while, he shifted back upstairs to watch the rest of the movie, thinking that lying on the bed might help him relax a bit more. By the time the film ended, he was more wound up than he'd been in the first place, frustrated by his own inability to focus and—although he wouldn't admit it—his inability to prevent his mind wandering back to the most pressing concern; that all he had between the likely death of Minnie, and the possible death of himself, was a hope that he didn't end up back in The Black Room at all. True, it was a big loophole; why would he go back without the ketamine, after all? As he'd already considered, there was a possibility that maybe the dead Minnie's Charlie had *kept* taking it, not knowing the harm that he was doing, but just the fact that there was a *possibility* that he could go back weighed very heavily on his already rattled mind.

By now, it was around 10:00 p.m., and Charlie was nearly climbing the walls. In a sudden burst of action, he leapt out of bed, grabbed his coat, and headed downstairs, fetching his bike from the hallway. He was still in his white shirt and trousers from the funeral, but he didn't care. Once outside, he swung his leg over the bike's seat and began to pedal, the wind feeling refreshing against his face and the growing sense of speed emptying his mind, his legs pumping in the cool night air. All the buildings around him were dark—the city shut down as usual on a quiet Sunday night—and the streetlamps lit his path as he pedalled through the streets without a destination in mind. Charlie wished he'd done this hours ago, with a whole evening ahead of him just to pedal and keep going. The world was his oyster, freedom was just the push of a pedal away, and he feared that soon he would be confined once more; confined in a space that might mean his own death, and the almost certain death of the girl he couldn't get out of his head.

The problem is more that you *can't get out of* her *head, Charlie.*

However, after an hour, Charlie realised that he didn't cycle anywhere near as much as he thought he did, or at least not for any great length of time; freedom had infinite appeal, but his body's own limits soon meant that rest had infinite appeal *plus one.* He was approaching a pub, and it seemed like a good place to stop and let his legs begin to feel like they belonged to him again. It was nearly 11:00 p.m.; maybe still in time for Sunday last orders, hopefully?

It was, somehow. Charlie sat in a corner with his pint of lager, and found himself hesitant to drink it. Would even booze have the same effect on his sleeping consciousness now, the ketamine having dislodged something in his mind? Many times he put the glass to his lips, and yet never took a swig. The risk was too much, and he could have kicked himself for being so stupid as to buy a pint in the first place. At the same time, he was so frustrated that he could have kicked anyone. Couldn't he even have a goddamn pint now? He was sick of the headfuckery of it all already. He was sick of feeling frightened, and found himself fervently wishing not to go back to The Black Room, for both of their sakes.

And there it was again; that simultaneous sting that came with the thought of never going back, however scared he was. He would never see her again, and it was more than simple interest that made the thought so untenable. There was something *big* there, something that he'd just glimpsed an edge of, like a child seeing the foot of an elephant and being dimly aware that there was much, much more to the thing than that. Resisting the temptation to throw his pint at the wall, Charlie got up to leave, telling the elderly men at the table to his right that he had to go and that the pint was perfectly untouched if they wanted it. He pedalled off into the night, and once he found himself on a relatively deserted street, he let out a frustrated scream into the night air.

It was gone midnight by the time he returned home. It looked like Eric had come back, as his coat was hanging in the hallway and his keys were sitting on the living room table. Charlie's legs were now like lead, and his face and ears were ice cold from their second bicycle journey of the evening. He hoped he would sleep now, that the physical exertion of all the pedalling would have tired him out enough to do so. He just wanted it *done* now, wanted to know, wanted to find out if The Black Room was inevitable or not. He wanted to call someone. Someone from his own family, maybe? They hadn't spoken in a long, long time, and even when he was in contact, even when he'd still lived at home, they hadn't really had a proper conversation since ...

Stop.

All right.

He headed upstairs and paused outside Eric's door, trying to see if the light was on in there; the glow underneath the door was dim, suggesting that it was only lamp light. Eric was probably asleep, and Charlie didn't want to inflict this horrible restlessness on anyone else. He went to his own room, took off his clothes, and lay down on top of the bed with the lights off and the curtains open. He always shut them under normal circumstances; tonight, he wanted to see the stars.

Charlie began to wait.

After several maddening hours, during which he was convinced that he might finally be dropping off, only for his mind to latch onto another facet of the situation and carry him rudely back to the land of consciousness, Charlie fell asleep.

***

His eyes opened. In front of him was a pair of knees, pale and almost bony, upon which a mobile phone was resting, held between a pair of slender-fingered hands. Underneath that was a pair of ladies' underwear, wrapped around said knees and seemingly tying them together. The phone's screen showed a list of emails; the user was checking through them. In front and to either side of the knees was a set of sheer beige walls; *no*, the front wall wasn't a wall at all. It was a door. This was a toilet cubicle.

As his confusion cleared, Charlie realised four things almost simultaneously: the first, as he looked farther to his left and right and saw the imagery end, saw the edges of the glowing screen that displayed them and saw the darkness beyond where the walls turned and undulated in the gloom, was that he was back in The Black Room. The second realisation, coming as it did with an almost shocking moment of delight, was that he would be able to talk to her again, that he could see Minnie again, that he could be with her and feel the connection that he hadn't noticed until it was gone. The third followed instantly on the heels of the second, slugging him in his guts and ensnaring him in a grip of despair that doused his high spirits like a rancid, ice-cold shower, his misery worsened by the depth of the fall from his previous high; it was the remembrance of what being in The Black Room again meant for Minnie. He was dimly aware of what it might mean for himself, also, but in that moment his concern was only for her. Regardless, he had to speak to her, to let her know that he'd arrived, and as he opened his mouth to speak, the image on the screen finally hit home, finally made sense, and the fourth realisation landed with a confused bang. His shocked words spilled out of his mouth halfway through his opening sentence, interrupting himself before he realised what he was saying.

"Minnie! Can you hear me, I'm ba-*OH JESUS, YOU'RE HAVING A SHIT!!*"

The second part of Charlie's outcry was lost in Minnie's own squeal of startled terror, as the phone flew out of her hands and the view shot upwards. The knees pistoned out of sight as she leapt off the toilet, and her saw her hands fly past the screen as she clapped them to her mouth, screaming in panic. Charlie tried to rally, immediately realising what he'd done.

"Oh, oh wait, sorry, sorry, I just, I just, ah, I got a shock, everything happened at once, I only just saw I was here and then, then, I saw that you were—"

"*Charlie!*" gasped Minnie, her breaths coming in rapid, sharp inward squeaks as she found herself in a whirlwind of realisations of her own; Charlie was back, he was back in her head, it was nothing to be scared of, what the hell did he have to shout like that for. "*Oh Jesus, Charlie!* You just, oh Christ, oh Jesus, you just, you just, oh God—" he'd seen her ON THE TOILET— "Fucking *hell*, Charlie! Close your eyes, cover your fucking ears, I'm in the bloody loo! Now, close them *now!*"

The view swung downward as her hands began to reach for her underwear, and then realised what he might be seeing. The view swung sharply back up. The room then was immediately plunged into total darkness as Minnie screwed her eyes shut. In his panic, Charlie didn't even care. Minnie was still screaming over his frantic placatory noises. It was getting to be a familiar sound.

"Jesus, Charlie, just close your eyes, *close your fucking eyes*—"

"Yes, yes, right, sorry, I'm doing it now, okay, you're good, clean up, no, sorry, I mean—"

"*Charlie!*"

"Right, right ..."

To Charlie, all was quiet in The Black Room, his senses plugged tight as Minnie went through practices that Charlie—even as a more enlightened man than most—could not begin to conceive of occurring, much less want to imagine. To do so would be like trying to imagine the Easter Bunny getting fisted in front of Charlie's mother. After a while, Charlie thought he might have heard Minnie say something like *I'm finished*, but he thought he'd wait another minute or so just to be on the extra-safe side. Once he was certain that the muffled sound he was hearing was Minnie repeating his name with greater and greater urgency, Charlie uncovered his ears and opened his eyes. Upon doing so, not only did he immediately see that was it certainly okay to look now, but the sight before him had a double impact—another multi-part shock within the space of a few minutes—the two halves of it coming together and creating a force greater than the sum of their parts; it took Charlie's breath away.

Minnie had moved to stand before the mirror outside of the cubicle, so that he could see her; reflected in it, he could see that they were inside some kind of public restroom. That was of no consequence for the moment, however. Framed before him was Minnie, but a different Minnie than before; this was a Minnie that had prepared to face the outside world, giving him a glimpse of the Minnie she could be when at her best, and not the scared, nervous, fragile girl that he'd met the day before. It wasn't in the makeup, or the prepped and tamed hair (although, Charlie would later realise, they couldn't be ignored; the difference was notable) but was instead found in the fact that this was a Minnie who'd had time to steel herself, who'd had time to bring her inner strength forward to face the outside world. It wasn't one of her fronts, either; she'd set herself into a different mode. True, her eyes (brought out even more by the eye shadow and liner, the darkness around them highlighting the fascinating colour within) were currently looking both startled and furious, and the hair, while pulled back, seemed like it had recently been disturbed in its moorings (Charlie felt his caught-out schoolboy self step forward from his memories, head bowed) but the physical package and sense of character was quietly overwhelming in its impact. That was the *first* impact; it was certainly a day of mental hits that came in groups.

The second was something that he'd already realised upon arrival, now coming again with not only a deeper impact, but without any of the negativity at its heels. There was none of the gloom, for how could there be any now that he fully appreciated his previous thought? Now that he realised its enormity, and the surprising amount happiness that came with it, the glow that filled his body with warmth? For the moment, consequences be damned. He felt unbeatable, like he was more than up to the task of stopping anything that might threaten either of the two of them. The strength of it was so shocking, so unexpected.

You've seen her again. Here she is. Here she is.

And of course, now he'd been back to his reality, and had been reminded of the long-buried name from his past, it seemed ludicrous that he didn't recognise her the first time; how could he have forgotten? He might not know how, or when, or for how long, but he had always known her face, hadn't he? How hadn't he recognised it? And here she was.

The Woman in the Night.

"*CHARLIE.* Unplug your bloody ears, will you?" Her breath was still coming in heavy pulls, but it was slower now, her jaw set and her composure returned; returned enough to look angry, at least. And, Charlie wondered, perhaps a little relieved too? She seemed to have gotten herself together awfully quickly, after all.

"I'm here, I'm here," Charlie said, stepping back from the screen. He hadn't realised how close he'd moved to it. "Um ... sorry about that. I literally just turned up—"

"That's nice, Charlie, glad to hear it," she said quickly, holding up a hand and closing her eyes, raising her chin and shoulders in defence against the very recent and painful memory. The screen went out again as she did so. "And obviously this little incident never happened, and shall never be spoken of again, under pain of death or torture, end of subject, yes?"

"Fine," said Charlie, unable to resist smiling in the blackness. "Sorry if I scared you, though."

"Yes, great, that's the end of it, no apology necessary, thank you very much," snapped Minnie, and then opened her eyes to reveal herself again, eyebrows raised. She was back in control once more, competent again; the Minnie that had time to prepare for the world was a Minnie less easily shaken than the one he'd met yesterday, a more capable Minnie. Charlie liked this side of her. Minnie raised both of her hands now, and spoke. "Now, enough of all that, tell me, *where the hell have you been?*"

"Minnie, I was back! I was back in my body!" Charlie cried, eager to bring her up to speed. The thought of telling her the bad news flashed through his mind and was immediately sent to the back; that could wait. Plus, weren't they going to fix it all anyway? Of course they were. He wouldn't let her down. How could he have worried? And anyway, Minnie would want answers immediately, would be desperate to find out whether their theorising had been anywhere near to the truth or not.

"What?"

"You went to sleep, right? When I was last here, you went to sleep in front of the ... hold on, what day is it?"

"Monday, but anyway, sod that, tell me what *happened—*"

"Sorry, sorry. When you passed out, the fucking walls in here started to push inwards, like a trash compactor or something. I thought I was going to be crushed to death!"

"*No ...*" gasped Minnie, leaned forward over the sink and holding herself up on her arms. She was rapt, fascinated, her jaw wide open. But, Charlie noticed, the edges of her lips were turned up slightly in a smile; she wasn't just excited to hear the info. She was pleased to hear it from *him*. Charlie couldn't believe it (wouldn't she have been pleased when she woke up and found out that he was gone? Or would it have made her doubt his reality all over again?) but then he realised that it must mean she knew it too; there *was* some kind of connection at work here.

"Yes!" cried Charlie, almost laughing now, delighted to be sharing the story, delighted at her total focus on what he had to say. "I was absolutely crapping my pants! And I was like, *Minnie! Minnie!* And you couldn't hear me, you were too far gone, and—oh, Minnie, *I could see your dreams!*"

"What?!" Now it was Minnie's turn to laugh-shout, delighting in their coming together, revelling in the torrent of vital and exciting information. "No *way!*"

Of course she is. She's been wandering around since you left unable to share any of this with anyone. And now you're back, and you can both spill your guts to your hearts' content. You're the only two people in the world that are a part of this, the only ones who understand.

"I can prove it! You had one about people walking on the sea, and they lived in a city—"

"—under the water! Oh my *God!!*" This last part was a shout, her hands flying to a face that was lit up with amazement. "That's unbelievable! That's—

wait, what happened with the walls? They, they started to come together? What happened to you?" Her expression changed so fast that it was almost comical, the worry lines appearing in her forehead, her hands coming forward, imploring.

"I don't know, I just woke up back at home, and it was Sunday morning. I think … I think that as you dropped even further under, whatever happened to your mind as a result meant that I couldn't be in there anymore. It pushed me out! And when I got home, I was back in my house and everything. Minnie, you were right—well, kind of—about the different place idea! It's, it's, it's like the same world as here, but there's just a few differences, like the same football matches happening but having different results, different people living in different houses because their lives went a slightly different way, I mean, it's … Minnie, it's another world. We live in different versions of the same world! Can you believe it? That's why there's another me here in *this* world, and on a different shift pattern at work at that!"

Minnie's face remained the same; Charlie knew she was just trying to process it all. Even when she'd already thought of the same idea, it was another thing entirely to find out that your crazy science fiction theory was true.

"Oh my God …" she whispered, her head shaking silently as she stared at the mirror. "When I woke up on the settee, it was dark outside, and … you were gone …" She looked stunned now, even paler than usual. Charlie worried that her legs might give way. Her eyebrows crinkled upwards on the inner edges, sadness creeping into her expression, worry. "I panicked. I thought I might have done something to you by falling asleep, at first. I was like a crazy woman. I just kept saying your name for about an hour, kept going back to the mirror and repeating it, hoping you'd reply."

Hoping?

"And then I got to thinking that maybe something like what you actually just said had happened, that you'd gotten home somehow, and that seemed to make more sense; I was pleased after that, but I just found myself thinking that I'd never know … and that it might eventually drive me crazy." Her face was totally blank now, and the view of the mirror had dropped slightly. Her previous joy seemed to have been sucked right out of her, remembering her doubt and fear, remembering a time when, once again, she'd become her own prison, her own system of torment. "And then, after a bit longer … well, I suppose … it's understandable … I started to think that maybe I'd imagined the whole thing. I mean *everything*, not just you. Even the headache that I'd had all day. I thought that might be either psychosomatic, or the sign of a tumour or something, one that fucked my brain and made me hear voices. All of it seemed false, the old woman at the house, even the proof with the phone when we went to Barrington's, and I started to believe that maybe I hadn't even been there …" Her mouth straightened for a moment, like she'd remembered something. Charlie's face had also fallen, both at her account and at the sound of the word "headache." The on-screen view straightened up slightly, back to its previous position.

98

"It wasn't nice, Charlie," said Minnie. "It put me in a bad place again. Christ ... I have to say ... I'm really glad to hear your voice."

Something shifted inside him.

"And I'm really glad to see you, Minnie, really glad. It's—"

"Hang on, how did you get back here? What happened?"

She'd cut him off, and he understood why, but he still felt a sting.

"Right, okay, well when I woke up—"

There was a slight bang off to the left and the view swung in that direction, revealing a short woman in her forties who was wearing a work tunic and a name badge that Charlie couldn't make out. The bang that Charlie had just heard was her opening the door to the ladies' room.

"Minnie, Sarah needs to go, her taxi's here, come on! She's right on my case, and Phil will be down in a second, you don't want another bollocking."

"Sorry, Linda," said Minnie, her usually impressive acting abilities failing to produce natural-sounding speech. "I'm coming now, I'll be there in two seconds." The woman at the door rolled her eyes in a good-natured way, and turned to leave, closing the door behind her. As the view swung back to the mirror, Charlie suddenly realised something that he'd previously missed, something that his eyes had taken in but his brain hadn't registered in all of the excitement; Minnie was wearing the same tunic and name badge as her colleague. Minnie was at work.

The checkout job. That's a supermarket tunic. So she has the same job in this world.

"*Shit!*" Minnie snapped in a stage whisper, slapping the sink in frustration. She looked up. "Look, I've got to get started, as I'm already on my last warning," she said, leaning earnestly towards the mirror and talking in a low, intense voice, the words coming out in quick staccato. "But I want you to keep talking. I want you to explain everything you know, everything you found out, *everything*, okay? I won't be able to reply most of the time, but there might be times when I can, all right? Can you notice if I nod in there?"

"Uh, yeah," replied Charlie, many questions of his own upon the tip of his tongue but knowing that Minnie was having to rush.

"Then I can do one nod for yes, two nods for no, okay? I'm really sorry Charlie, I can't tell you how much I want to talk to you about all this, but I was lucky to even get this job; if I lose it then I'm screwed, and the boss hates me already. Jesus, and this headache ... I can tell you're back. I've been fine since I woke up, and as soon as you're here it's pounding away already."

"It's okay, it's okay, go, go. I can talk, and you can tell me all your stuff later," said Charlie, heart sinking at this news even while he savoured the words *I can't tell you how much I want to talk to you* and selectively missed off *about all this*. The view swung towards the door once more, and as she walked, Charlie began to sift through all the information he had to pass on, wondering where to start and how to bring up the extremely difficult parts of it.

"Go on then, talk," said Minnie, sounding exasperated and full of disbelief that Charlie wasn't already falling over himself like before. Her hand came up into sight, grasping the door handle, and then stopped. She hesitated, then spoke.

"Charlie, this is going to sound stupid asking *this* out of everything, but ... when you watched my dreams. Did that happen on its own? Or did you have to do something?"

"I did something. I touched the wall," said Charlie, confused. There was a pause, her hand remaining on the door.

"Okay. Look ... I really ... could you not do that, this time?" she said, quietly. "That ... it just freaks me out. I don't know what it was like in there for you when I'm asleep—well, pretty dark I assume—but ... that's a big deal. I'm not ready for that."

She was asking, not demanding.

"Okay. Okay, Minnie."

"Thank you. I hope you understand."

She opened the door that led into a short white hallway, then went through another door at the other end. The view now revealed an expansive, clean-looking supermarket, the strip lights bright overhead in the high ceiling, with a surprising amount of people in the building for a Monday ... daytime? Charlie realised that he didn't even know what time it was. Minnie was muttering something under her breath, but even from Charlie's close-as-possible proximity, he couldn't make it out.

"What?" he asked, turning his head fruitlessly; the sound, though barely audible, was still all around him, but he couldn't make out the words.

"I said, *can you hear this*," said Minnie, slightly louder, but still muttering while trying not to move her lips, her voice sounding like that of a bad ventriloquist. "But I guess not. I can't talk this loudly on the checkout, though, not most of the time anyway." She made her way through the shoppers, towards a till where a stressed-looking woman was making *come on* gestures and tapping her watch. "Okay, anyway, get started. It was worth a try. I know you'll have questions too, and I'm so sorry I can't help properly now."

"Don't be stupid, it's not your fault," said Charlie, appreciating her concern. "Look, you settle in, I'm just trying to figure out where to begin." Minnie had reached her checkout now, and the woman—Sarah, presumably— was standing up and shaking her head, grabbing her handbag from the floor of her booth. Minnie couldn't reply to Charlie at this range, not with Sarah so close and a small queue of three shoppers waiting.

"Sorry, Sarah, get out of here. Thanks so much for holding on," Minnie was saying, as Sarah stepped out of the booth and Minnie took her place. "I owe you for this." Sarah didn't reply, but instead nodded stoically and patted Minnie on the shoulder as she left. It wasn't forgiveness, but there wasn't a grudge being held either; Charlie had a feeling that Sarah had been guilty of the same crime before, and she wasn't going to hold it against Minnie even if she didn't like having it done to herself. Minnie took Sarah's place at the till.

"Hi," she said to the elderly lady at the front of the line, who smiled and returned the greeting as Minnie took the first item of shopping and ran its barcode over the reader. Charlie watched as she went through the rest of the old woman's shopping and took in his situation, trying in this moment of calm to settle his mind into the fact of his return. Only when Minnie cleared her throat for the second time did Charlie get the hint.

"Shit, sorry, I was just settling in after all the panic. Okay, okay. Uh ... right."

The ketamine.

"Okay. Look, reading between the lines, it sounds like you've had bad run-in with drugs in the past, and I'm not someone who takes drugs as a rule, so don't worry about that, *but ...*"

Charlie sat down as he began to talk, making himself comfortable while wondering how the hell he should approach the tricky subject of her counterpart's death, or if he should bring it up at all. He went through the story of the day he'd just had, starting with the ketamine discovery. He then realised that he was getting ahead of himself, and went back to waking up in his bed in the house that he was *supposed* to be living in, and trying to find out via his landlord who the old woman might have been. Throughout all of this, he kept stopping, thinking Minnie was talking to him, but realising each time that she was only addressing the customers, asking them the same checkout questions about help with bagging and store cards. Charlie then moved on to his downstairs conversation with Eric, during which he realised that Minnie was real and that they did, in fact, exist in some kind of separate parallel universes.

"You were along the right lines with the whole *Back to the Future* thing, I think," said Charlie, now propping himself up on one elbow and lying on the floor of The Black Room. He was positioned near the far wall, directly opposite the screen. He made sure he wasn't touching it—he didn't want extra complications just then—but he found that with a greater distance between himself and the screen came a greater sense of space, making The Black Room less claustrophobic. He wasn't at all surprised to see that the room was lighter again still, the churning walls now clearly visible in the darkness from any range (although "light" was not a word that could really be associated with The Black Room. Even the ethereal glow of the screen only stretched so far in that space). Whatever kind of connection there was between them, it was increasing.

Despite Charlie's relaxed position, the eagerness with which he was talking was anything but. So keen was he to tell her everything, that he had to keep restraining himself in order to keep his account coherent; the downside to it all was that she couldn't respond or share her thoughts on the matter. He knew that she was as electrified to hear it all as he would have been, though; the rapid tumbling of the walls was testament to that.

"So I Googled you," said Charlie, his mind now made up about what he was going to tell her. He'd decided shortly after he'd started talking, as soon as the silence on the other end began; he couldn't tell her now, couldn't give her such frightening, devastating news when she was at work and couldn't even respond without sounding like a lunatic. The solution was simple; gloss over it for now (she couldn't question him about any bad attempts to talk around it anyway) and tell her the truth later, when they could actually talk about it. "And you were on Facebook, just like I was when you looked for me. I didn't see you in person or anything, but the pictures on there were definitely you." All of which was, of course, technically true. As he watched the screen, and saw a girl in her early twenties handing Minnie her credit card, he realised that he'd pretty much brought her up to speed … apart from one other important detail, and it wasn't the news of her other self's death either.

"And … well, that's about everything. I wondered if I'd even come back, to be honest, and it took me forever to get to sleep, but … here I am. It looks like sleeping brings me here, but *you* sleeping sends me back. There was something else, though, man … I wish you could talk back, I'm desperate to hear what you have to say about all this."

The next customer on-screen was passing their items along, but Charlie heard a dim, muffled noise that sounded like it might have been Minnie trying to talk under her breath. Charlie smiled and sighed at the same time.

"If that was you, Minnie, I can't hear that either," he said, frustrated but touched at the effort. "I appreciate you trying though. The yes and no thing would be useful if I had questions that could be answered that way, but I'm really the one with all of the new info here. Anyway, look, there was something else that Neil, the ketamine guy said, and it really triggered some kind of memory or something. Well, I don't think I can call it a memory because I don't really remember anything, but it certainly had an effect. Apparently, when I was under the influence, I really freaked out. I kept ranting about 'The Woman in the Night.' Does that mean anything to you? Because it certainly does to me, even though I don't know what that meaning actually *is* … but it was like a lightbulb coming on when I heard it. Ring any bells?"

The screen moved up and down once, twice. A no.

"That's disappointing. Shit …"

He looked around himself, trying to think what to say next.

"So … that's everything, I think. On the major plus side, we know I exist, we know you exist, and neither of us is going crazy."

Just leaves the small matter of her eventually having a brain haemorrhage, thanks to you gate crashing her brain.

Charlie sighed again, then sat up and ran his hand through his hair distractedly.

"*Aaaaah,* I just wish I could talk to you about this! What time do you finish here?"

The view moved downwards and to the right for a moment, to the keypad of Minnie's till. Charlie saw two of her fingers rest deliberately on the edge of it, side by side. *Two o'clock.*

"Right. Early shift, eh? Uh … what time is it now?"

The view swung up to the till display; the tiny LED readout there showed it to be just before one.

"Not too bad, then. I just have to kill an hour."

He looked through the screen, at the next customer who was already advancing. It was a man in his thirties, covered in what was clearly fake tan applied in such a ludicrous amount that he resembled an orange mannequin.

"Bloody hell," said Charlie. "What's he trying to do, blend in at a varnish factory? He looks like Julio Iglesias ate a streetlight."

There was a muffled barking sound, and the view jerked. The man turned in mild surprise, and for a brief moment Charlie had the sensation that Mr Fake Tan was looking directly at him, that he had heard the remark. Then it made sense; Minnie had laughed, bitten down on it, and the man had turned to look at her due to the sound.

"Sorry, I sneezed," said Minnie, her voice dripping with embarrassment. Charlie grinned in the darkness, pleased, and feeling mischievous. The man, meanwhile, didn't look convinced, and went back to placing his items onto the till. The next one along was a bottle of hair removal cream, of all things. It was like God was *giving* Charlie the go-ahead.

"Ah, of course," said Charlie. "One must always prepare the canvas before applying paint."

The screen began to shake up and down, very gently. The man didn't notice, engaged in passing along a packet of butter. Charlie couldn't think of anything for that, so instead just said:

"Ask him if he wears ladies underwear."

It was stupid, it was puerile, it wasn't even funny, but the screen went on shaking all the same, the walls of The Black Room turning in a different pattern altogether now, more angular and spiked in their movements. Next came a packet of apples, which was also no good, but then manna from heaven; a nine-pack of toilet roll.

"Nine-pack. Obviously gets through a lot. Likes his dinners. Point at the toilet roll and ask if he likes his dinners." Charlie was giggling himself now, knowing that what he was saying would only amuse a three-year-old, but helpless nevertheless. It was a rush, being normal like this in the craziest situation possible, making Minnie laugh at stupid jokes in a secret, shared moment. The screen was shaking harder than ever, and the strain in Minnie's voice was evident when she spoke.

"D'you … ahem … ah … do you have a points card?"

The man shook his head without saying a word, lips tightly pursed as he punched his number into the chip and pin machine. Charlie felt a bit guilty—the poor sod hadn't done anything, after all—but he couldn't shake the giggles now, as the woman coming up next in the queue was putting down a packet of haemorrhoid cream. In ordinary circumstances, it wouldn't have been funny in the slightest, but in that moment, the sight of that innocuous packet sent Charlie into hysterics, and forced Minnie to pretend to be having a coughing fit. Eventually Charlie got himself under control, and by the time he'd finished, he saw that the screen was shaking less too, and was now only lurching occasionally as the last of the giggles subsided.

"Sorry, sorry," he said, holding up a placatory but unseen hand. "I'll stop, I'll stop." There was brief gap in the queue at that point, as the elderly man in a beige coat standing at the end of the till was only just beginning to empty his trolley. Minnie seized her moment—finally, there was enough of a gap in the human traffic for her to talk—and hissed in a voice that was barely audible to Charlie, but low enough for the old man not to hear at such a distance.

"You're gonna get me in trouble!" she scolded through gritted teeth; but Charlie could hear the last echoes of laughter rippling in her voice, the smile in the sound. *"Listen, I've only got a bit longer to go, keep quiet until two and then I'm all yours. I'm already on my last warning! Unless you have any more news?"*

"That's about everything, I think."

Oh, apart from the bit you're really, really gonna hate ...

"Okay. Sorry, Charlie ..." The old man was advancing from the other end of the till towards her, smiling, as his now-unloaded shopping began to travel along the conveyor belt.

"Look, don't be silly, you've got to keep your nose clean, after all."

The screen made a brief nodding motion, once, indicating her agreement, and so Charlie lay back on the floor and put his hands behind his head. He had time to think, at least, to get his thoughts and ideas about the situation whittled down in his mind, to get a coherent set of theories together. He didn't think the Room was man-made anymore, at least. Not unless this had all been going on for an extremely long time, as his gut told him that his connection to The Woman in the Night had been.

It's definitely her, isn't it? The Woman in the Night is Minnie.

Well of course it was ... and that didn't help things one bit.

Okay ... well, what else do we know?

Charlie pondered the question. There were differences between the worlds, subtle ones, but differences nonetheless. Minnie was dead in his world, alive in this one, and he'd never moved into his house in Radford in Minnie's world because there had been someone else living there for decades ...

But when you were last here, it was Sunday, wasn't it? And when you woke up back in your world, it was Sunday again.

This was true ... Charlie settled back to think about it. It must have been around six p.m. on Sunday in Minnie's world when he'd left before, and he'd woken up around ten in *his* world on the same Sunday morning ... so that meant his world was around eight hours behind? He double-checked it; it was at least four in the morning by the time he'd passed out Sunday night, and in this world it was nearly one in the afternoon now. He must have been here for about an hour, so he'd gotten here around 12:00 p.m. ... that confirmed it. There was about an eight-hour time difference between the worlds. Did *that* mean anything?

No.

Hmm.

Charlie stared at the ceiling for a few minutes, watching it as it turned. His mind drifted vaguely and aimlessly through different possibilities, different ideas, but he soon realised that he was getting nowhere; plus, it seemed that even in the middle of the impossible, humans were still capable of boredom.

At least you've got light this time. Not like before, when she went to sleep. That was worse.

But then he'd been able to watch her dreams ... and with that, a thought struck him.

Is it as simple as a mere privacy issue? Don't you think that was a little suspiciou—

Charlie cut that thought off in its tracks. His mind was wildly speculating again, considering all the possibilities, and he didn't think for one second that Minnie was anything but on the level. He *knew* she was. The Woman in the Night was on his side. He knew that at the very core of his being, even if he didn't know how.

Okay, okay. But what if there's something that she doesn't even know *she knows? You didn't know about the ketamine; you'd forgotten. She used to do drugs, too. There could be something in that.*

It was a good point ...

Not forgetting that you don't remember where the hell The Woman in the Night comes from anyway, or what that name means to you. And if the Woman is Minnie, how *is it Minnie? There might be something in her head that you can access, something that she can't or won't.*

It was hard to argue against the logic, Charlie had to admit, but she *had* asked him to stay out of her dreams. True, she wasn't dreaming, but if he could access her thoughts and memories (as he had before, when he had her permission the last time he was there), that was still pretty much the same thing, and almost definitely worse; bad enough that he was in her head without asking, but to take away the last veil of privacy would be a trespass too far.

Well, hold on; you don't even know if you can *do it. Sure, you found out the last time you were here that you could* see *her thoughts, but not that you could sift through them, or if you could choose to search for, say, prior memories of you? Why not just try? If it turns out that you can, then you stop without really looking at anything, and can have the conversation about permission later and see if she lets you have a real search.* Then *you can argue it out with her. Hell, even if she says no, would you leave it at that? You're trying to save her life! To save both of your lives, potentially! This is bigger than privacy! She can have all the privacy she likes when she's buried six feet und—*

Okay, that was enough. The point was made. Charlie sat up and looked at the right-hand wall, scratching his chin as he did so. A test made sense, at least. He wouldn't be really looking at anything, and it would mean that he knew if he could actually do it *before* having what would no doubt be a difficult conversation with Minnie, one that could be avoided entirely if it turned out that targeted mind-reading/memory sifting wasn't even an option. So technically, there wasn't really any harm in an experiment, and crucially, it'd give him something to *do*. He didn't like to be secretive about it, not with Minnie, but if he said anything about it now she couldn't say anything back anyway, and it might stress her out. Best just to run a little test and then know what the options were.

You're trying to save her life. You don't know how long she has, because even in your world it sounded like the headaches were coming for a little while before she died. It might be different here. There isn't time to waste.

Convinced, Charlie stood and made his way over to the right-hand wall. The extra light, or *perceived* extra light, threw the swirling, turning surface of The Black Room's walls into greater relief. Was there a texture to them too, a slight grain? With their unending movement, Charlie couldn't be sure. He glanced over his left shoulder to the screen, seeing another shopper waiting patiently as their items went through the till, a line two or three people long standing behind them.

It's just a test. You're not really looking, not being nosy. It's all right.

Charlie turned back to the wall and raised his right hand. Slowly, he moved it forward until it was pressing against the smooth, odd-feeling surface, again amazed by the visual and sensory contradiction of moving wall and stationary surface. As he pushed more firmly, just like he had in the daytime the last time he was here—

With Minnie's permission—

—being careful to not go too far and smash through like before, he waited to see if anything happened. This time it did, with shocking force, and although he tried to aim it—tried to carry out the experiment properly and see if he could somehow search for a specific subject—thought was impossible in that initial moment.

Later, he would think:

When she was asleep, her brain was in the right alpha-wave state or whatever to "broadcast" her dreams to you more gently ... oh, or maybe it was just an extension of the whole room-getting-lighter thing? Or maybe dreams create a more passive feed? The connection has obviously been growing the whole time, and maybe it was just a case of you not being in The Black Room long enough the first time you touched the wall, that's why it wasn't such a sheer, unrestrained force?

Charlie's entire body tensed up as if electrocuted, and his own thoughts were drowned out in the roar of Minnie's mind. It was a psychological hammer blow, *no*, it was like standing in the path of a riot hose of consciousness. The feelings ripped through him, the images lost this time with the sheer speed at which they tore through his mind, anxiety, paranoia, warmth, warmth directed at someone, new, fresh, hopeful, then back to something else now, panic,

(*whatsthepanicwheredoesthatcomefrom*)

sadness, loss, determination, panic again,

(*THEREgrabitTHEREyouhavetodirectit*)

and thought returned to Charlie just for a moment, enough for him to choose a passing emotion, snatching it out of the mental stream like a bear grabbing at a salmon, picking *Panic*, and now she is in a bar, and it isn't the sort of place that she used to go, but she'd gone there on Dave's advice because Dave was right, none of the other crowd would be there, none of the people that would bring back any bad memories or who would make an already difficult situation even more difficult. Small steps, that's what Dave had said, even though he doesn't have any idea of how big this first one is for her, being out again, being *clean* and being out again, how long's it been, a year? Year and a half? And this place is *busy,* too busy if anything, and already her heart rate is picking up and she's starting to sweat, worrying now that the perspiration will make her top stick to her and show her ribs, the ones that are still on painful and accusatory display even though she's been back on solids for a while and has actually put on weight, has put on weight and *still* she looks emaciated, to her eyes at least, but then when had she ever approved of what she saw in the mirror in the last five years? And Dave is holding her hand and leading her through the crowd

(*Barrington'sthey'reinBarrington's*)

and constantly turning his head back to smile at her in a way that he thinks is reassuring but it's not because she can see the worry in his eyes. This has taken weeks, weeks to get her out of the house after months of rehab and cold turkey and vomit and cold sweats and night terrors and bones that feel like broken glass under her skin. *Just an hour,* he'd said. An *hour amongst people and an orange juice each and then home.* And she'd said yes, fully believing that it would be okay, that she was ready, but she hadn't expected this *many* people, this throbbing mass of pressing and breathing humanity, a queue at the bar four people deep. She'd forgotten about this, forgotten what it could be like, had expected a quiet bar with plenty of space and this is just too much. What had Dave been thinking? This place was a really, really bad choice. Her heart has turned into a jackboot against her chest, and the sweat is now flowing freely down her back even though it's not even hot in there, reminding her of the withdrawals, the endless hours of nausea and despair, that place she never wanted to be in ever again, and her skin suddenly begins to prickle like a million stabbing needles. Needles, goddamn needles again.

(*waitthat'senoughyouknowyoucandirectitnowyouhavetostop*)

Her wide eyes swing back and forth, taking in the venue as she frantically looks for a safe haven or bolt hole, and doesn't see one, in her panic she can't even see the exit, and the tightness in her lolloping stomach becomes a slashing blade. Then Dave turns to her and asks the worst question he could possibly ask at that moment:

"What do you want?" he says, gesturing towards the bar and the crushing, nauseating bundle of people before it.

And she knows. She suddenly knows, and it's a thought she hasn't had so badly, a *need* she hasn't felt this badly in months, something she'd left behind ages ago, and it is terrifying.

What she really wants—what she really *needs*—is to shoot up. Then everything will be okay.

And Minnie pulls her hand out of Dave's, taking in his shocked face for a second, hears him start to say her name but she is already turning and bolting for the door, blindly pushing her way through people and sobbing, nearly falling as she does so.

(thatsenoughyouhavetostopNOW)

Charlie cried out as he broke the connection. He saw a sharp movement out of the corner of his eye and turned quickly to his left, facing the screen; Minnie had jumped at the sound, the latest shopper at the till also looking startled due to Minnie's sudden jump.

"Uh, sorry," Minnie was saying, fumbling for an excuse and rallying magnificently as usual. "I just got a static shock from this chair, always happens!" The shopper smiled and nodded, happy to accept the excuse because, of course, they didn't really care any further than an explanation.

"Sorry," Charlie said, once Minnie had commenced running the items through once more, "I just tripped over my own feet mucking about in here, clumsy idiot," he lied, feeling a cold sensation on the back of his neck. He'd made it even worse by lying, and had already gone too far before that. That wasn't just a test. That had turned into prying. Had it all been his fault, though? The rush had been so powerful, the hit of the memory so intense, that it had been, ironically, like a drug in itself ... but that wasn't an excuse. He could have stopped at any time.

Isn't that what all the addicts say?

Maybe, but that was a lame attempt at a justification, if ever there was one. He'd gone too far. Charlie sat cross-legged on the floor and closed his eyes, setting his jaw and gritting his teeth in annoyance with himself. The fact that he'd been successful was cold comfort. It was good to know that he could at least pick up on certain things in her thought stream, or emotion stream, or whatever it was, and therefore could possibly investigate her consciousness further with Minnie's help—

—and PERMISSION—

—but he would still take it back if he could. He'd made a mistake. He wouldn't mention it to Minnie, and would simply ask, as planned, to look through her subconscious later.

And feel like an asshole for the rest of the time.

He sighed heavily, darkly, the good feelings absent, replaced by guilt. Trying to think more practically, he considered how much stronger the hit of Minnie's thoughts had been this time, how much more intense it was. There was no doubt about it; his "physical" connection to The Black Room, to Minnie, was growing. However, he'd just majorly tarnished the emotional one, on his side at least.

Look at the positives. That "test" of yours might turn out to be a big help towards saving her life. Yeah, you could have waited until later, but when a life is in the balance, it's all about the end result, right?

It didn't make him feel better. That was a very personal and dark memory he'd just seen. It was clearly a memory of the experience she'd mentioned in the car outside his/the old woman's house, and it had not been his to take without permission.

Maybe, okay, but it's done now, and you've added a practical tool to your arsenal. Remember that.

He decided to try and do that, as it was too late to do anything else. He realised that he'd been tracing circles on the strange, black floor with his fingers, and drew his hand back, deciding to think practically. What would he ask her to do then, or for her permission to do, to help use this new discovery to their advantage? He began to make a list in his mind, to prepare to use the rest of that day's time as efficiently as possible. He would make it right.

By the time Minnie had finished her shift, however, Charlie was no further forward. He couldn't really seem to get his thoughts straight without having somebody else with whom to talk things through. He wondered if it was because he hadn't actually been unconscious at any point for the last two days. Sure, his *body* had slept, but his mind had spent the night awake in *another* body; how did that fit in with getting essential, rest-giving REM sleep? He didn't feel physically tired now, and hadn't really felt that way when he was back in his own body either, but was it affecting his ability to think straight?

The view stood up, as Minnie's replacement appeared for the handover; a girl several years younger than Minnie, with cropped hair. She looked absolutely crestfallen to be starting her shift, but gave Minnie a tired smile as the two of them exchanged pleasantries. After Minnie's hand was seen touching the girl's shoulder in solidarity, the view swung away as Minnie began to walk along the backs of the row of tills, towards the door marked "Staff Only." Immediately, she spoke to Charlie.

"Charlie?" she said, quietly, but loud enough for Charlie to hear now that she wasn't being observed by waiting shoppers.

"Here," said Charlie, the dark feeling in his chest lightening now that he was engaging in conversation again, and getting to talk to the one person that he most wanted to.

"Sorry about that," said Minnie earnestly, sounding slightly breathless as well. Was she excited to talk to him, too? "That shift seemed to go on for*ever*. Typical that it was one of the busiest Mondays I've ever had. Hang on, can you hear me okay?"

"Clear as a bell," said Charlie, a smile spreading across his face seemingly of its own accord.

"Great. Look, I'll be out of here in five minutes, I just have to get my bag. You must have been bored out of your mind, I'm so sorry. I just really had to be on the ball today, I've had a few … issues lately. Well …" The view panned left and right quickly, and then looked down, showing her feet as she walked. "A few freak outs, if I'm honest," she said, talking into her chest. "I've had a couple of emotional days. It's not been easy adjusting. Very embarrassing, and I'm not proud of it, but … there it is." The view swung right, and Minnie's hand was seen pushing open a door that opened to reveal a small beige room with a block of lockers on the left and a tiny kitchen on the right. A low table, covered by magazines and surrounded by foam-padded chairs, sitting in the middle of the floor. Mercifully, there was no one else in there. Automatically,

Minnie moved over to the small, simple mirror mounted on the wall. Her face came into view, smiling.

"You know what's weird?'" she said, her breathing now slightly fast. "I wouldn't have said what I just said to anyone other than Dave or my family. I mean, I couldn't. Why the hell can I say it to you? Maybe I couldn't, face to face."

Charlie beamed, nodding. He knew exactly what she meant. Minnie now chuckled slightly, and shook her head, the view dropping to the floor again.

"And that too," she said, head still shaking. "What I just said, just *then*. I can't believe I just said *that*. Sorry. Maybe that's just really weird."

"No," said Charlie, a little too quickly, "It's not. Not at all. There's something going on here. And I think ... I think The Woman in the Night is you."

The view popped back up to the mirror, showing Minnie's surprised face. Charlie immediately regretted spitting it out like that—he'd just gotten excited—and nervously wondered how she would take it, what she would read into it.

Why are you worried, anyway? You're in her head, Charlie. It can never be anything more than that.

What was that supposed to mean?

"What do you mean?" she asked in a small voice, biting her lip slightly. Her eyes searched their reflection in the mirror as if they were his, looking within him. Then she caught herself, shook her head, and held up a finger. "Bag," she said, firmly, letting out a sharp breath. "Then we can get the hell out of here and talk properly."

"Okay. Good idea," said Charlie, relieved, while Minnie opened the combination padlock on her locker and took out her bag. The view then turned and headed towards the exit, and open conversation.

***

"Right. Okay," said Minnie, now that Charlie had finished going through everything for a second time at Minnie's request. They were back inside Minnie's car—much to Charlie's displeasure—and pulling onto her estate. "So if this whole Woman in the Night thing was triggered by the ketamine ... and it's something that you think you remember ... then you think the ketamine had some sort of deep recall effect?"

"Nicely put," said Charlie, nodding, still sitting on the floor of The Black Room. "And yes. On some level, I recognise you, Minnie. You're a memory, and I don't know how that's possible. You're a memory that feels like it's from a long time ago, and that can't be right as I remember you as an adult. If it's from as far back as I think, and I'm talking about *years* ago, like when I was a child, then the memory of you should be one of you as a child as well."

"So what the hell does that mean?" said Minnie, pulling the car over and killing the engine. She absentmindedly checked herself in the rearview mirror before unlocking the driver's door and getting out.

"I've no idea. Plus, there's something else; it's gotten a lot lighter in here."

"Really?"

"Yeah. Whatever's going on, I think it's getting stronger. Or our minds are merging more, or something. I don't know, but I can certainly see more in here." He didn't mention his other reason for thinking so—the fact of his trespass—and again felt the stab of the unshared secret. It was a blockade between him and Minnie.

"Wow ..." Minnie said, mulling Charlie's words over as her keys went into the lock of her front door. "I'm just trying to think if I have anything like that myself. If I remember *you* in any way, you know?"

The twist of guilt in Charlie's stomach was an almost physical pain, his prior actions brought forth again and souring his happiness of sharing and talking with Minnie.

"Do you need to eat?" Charlie asked, suddenly keen for brief change of subject. He'd just been given the perfect cue to bring up the matter of going through her memories, and now it was here, he found himself lost for words. He'd just needed a moment to get the question straight, had been caught flat-footed. There it was again, his brain being somehow slow on the uptake, easily knocked off-balance and confused. Now she'd said it once though, he told himself, he could always bring it up again.

"Hmm, I do actually. Do you ... do you not get hungry in there?" she asked, the screen showing her bag flying onto the settee.

"Apparently not," said Charlie, shrugging. "Not tired or cold either, by the looks of things."

"Why would you be cold?"

"Uh ..."

Well, she was honest with you. You can at least be honest about this.

"I don't actually have any clothes on in here," he said, wincing as he said it. "Not by choice," he added, hurriedly. "It's just the way I turned up. Au natural, as it were."

Minnie considered this.

"Typical," she said, finally, opening the door to the kitchen. "First naked man in my flat for a long time, and he's inside my head. Just don't get any man-sweat on my consciousness though, okay?"

"I'll do my best," said Charlie, smiling. "Do you need five minutes to chill out, or whatever? Just to feel like yourself after work, before we start getting our heads in a mess trying to figure this out?" It seemed like a stupid question, but he did want her to be as comfortable as she could be. Who knew, maybe being as relaxed as possible, as often as possible, might delay the inevitable. Plus, a more relaxed Minnie would surely be someone with whom it would be easier to put his head together, so to speak. He could certainly do with the thinking help, that was for certain. There was an unusually long pause; so much so that Charlie felt compelled to say her name again.

"Minnie?"

"Sorry, yeah, I was just thinking about time, that was all," she said, sounding uncertain. Charlie looked around him; the walls were turning in yet another new manner. "I, uh … I have a thing tonight, I've not really had a chance to mention it to you. I can cancel, in fact, I probably should, well, maybe I shouldn't, but I think it might be important …"

"Well, not necessarily," said Charlie, not forgetting about the urgency of the situation but wanting to be helpful, not wishing to disrupt her life unless it was necessary. "I mean, we might not get anywhere, and then you'd only be sitting here effectively on your own for no reason. Let's just see how we do, eh? And then, if it leads nowhere, you might as well go and do your thing."

"Yes, but it's not really that simple …"

She suddenly sounded genuinely concerned, speaking with the kind of worried sigh reserved for people who have gotten themselves into a real mess. Charlie didn't miss the tone.

"Minnie, what's going on?"

There was another lengthy pause.

"Look, you're right. I need five minutes," she said, quietly. "Let me make a cup of tea and just get my head together. It's going to sound weird, but I need to think about the best way to explain it. I was so excited that you were back that I just wanted to hear everything you'd found out, then I remembered and I couldn't tell you about it while I was on the till, and then I needed to get everything straight again on the way home so I was properly up to speed. Plus, if I was honest, I was putting off telling you … ah Jesus …"

"Eh? Minnie, what's happened?"

"Nothing, I just … give me five minutes? Please?"

What could he say? Was he to refuse her five minutes, when he was trespassing inside her head, unbidden? He had to respect her wishes, especially after his previous actions, even if he had to suppress a sudden desire to grab her and shake her and make her tell him what the hell was going on. His knuckles whitened.

You've got to play it cool, Charlie. You're on her turf in the worst way. Plus, it's never going to be an option for you to grab her in any way, regardless. Never hold her.

The thought had an instantly calming effect. Charlie let out a sigh of his own, one of resolved defeat.

"Okay. Okay. But you're being really mysterious, Minnie, and there's enough mystery here as it is."

"I know, it's just … it's a tough one, that's all. It's best if I get my thoughts together first. I need to relax or I'll just make a mess of explaining it."

"Yeah, fine. Best get on with it then, I guess. Whack some Whitney Houston on and drink your tea." The last part was meant to be a mild rib, intended to lighten the mood, but the view suddenly became very still and the walls around him seemed to almost change direction; Charlie realised that the lighter blackness of his surroundings enabled him to see changes in her mental state reflected more clearly in the walls.

He'd said something wrong. What had he said?

"You okay?" he asked.

"Why did you say that about Whitney Houston?"

Oh, shit. The funeral. You only know about that because you went to the funeral.

Panic set in, Charlie's mind's sluggish state affecting his usually quick bullshitting muscles.

"Well, anything. Music. Put some music on—" Charlie began, talking without thinking and trying clumsily to brush the question off.

"Yeah, but you didn't say just 'music.' You specifically said Whitney Houston … and you meant it as a joke," said Minnie, her voice quiet. Charlie couldn't read it. "You meant it as a joke taking the piss out of me. I could hear it. I never told you I was a fan, and I don't have any CDs on display. Why would you specifically say her?"

Guilt and mental fatigue worsened Charlie's on-the-spot panic to a point that he hadn't felt since he was caught stealing chocolate from the corner shop when he was nine years old. He knew the assumption that she was leaping to, and it was wrong, but the principle was still the same; he *had* looked at her mind, even if it wasn't where he'd gotten his knowledge of her musical tastes from.

"I just meant, like, music, and, she … she's a …"

"You did something in there, didn't you?" The view faced the countertop, showing her hand gripping the mug she'd gotten out to pour her tea into. Her voice was low, firm, all of her prior confusion and concern now gone.

"I didn't pry, no, if that's what you're saying," Charlie said, hearing the pleading tone in his voice and hating it, knowing how bad it sounded. He *had* done wrong, but not in the way she thought; he hadn't been cunning, hadn't sifted and sorted and indulged curiosity after curiosity. He'd experimented, and he'd let it get out of hand, and he *was* wrong for that, but not as wrong as she was thinking. "I just wanted to see if I could guide the visions that I got, if I could search for specific things, and if I could then I was going to—"

"Specifics? I *specifically* asked you not to look at things in there, Charlie," said Minnie, cutting him off with a calm tone that made Charlie even more nervous. "I took you at your word. I trusted you." There was an edge in her calmness, a dangerous one, and the view was as steady as a surgeon's knife.

"And I didn't go against that, Minnie, I would never do that," said Charlie quickly, holding his hands up to the screen. "You know I wouldn't, not on purpose, you know you can trust me more than anyone. I don't know how you know that, and I don't know *how* I know you know that, but it's true. Right?"

"Boundaries are important, Charlie. They're very important to me," said Minnie, her breathing becoming heavier. "I was laid bare in rehab, humiliated by myself beforehand, and forced to confront and reveal everything about me. It was worth it, but it was fucking hard. I only just got my pride back. And I asked you. I *asked* you."

"Minnie, please listen—"

"That last ten percent! That's mine! That's the very last bit that everyone gets to keep!"

Charlie stopped, confused. What was she talking about?

"The guy in the corner shop or whatever, then work colleagues, then acquaintances, then friends, then true friends, then lovers. That's the fucking order. I thought about this a *lot* in rehab." The mug banged down on the countertop to emphasise the word, injecting further bitterness into the sentence. "And even the lovers, they don't get that ten percent. They never get your *very* private thoughts, the little dark ones that you think and aren't even sure that you mean. The ones that the privacy of your mind *frees* you to think and dismiss without fear or judgement. No one ever gets them. That's the way it needs to be, or we'd all just spend all day long disgusting each other or giving the very last of ourselves away."

Charlie just stared at the screen, stunned.

"It's the last part of ourselves, Charlie. That's all we can claim if everything else goes. And you just decided to help yourself." She sounded so disappointed; that was the very worst part, Charlie realised, and the thought helped him to find his voice. He couldn't let that be.

"Minnie, I promise you. I made a mistake, I held the connection too long and I saw some stuff. I never intended to pry. I'm so sorry, I've been feeling terrible about it ever since, but I swear to you that I would never intentionally betray you. Hell, if nothing else, we absolutely have to be able to trust each other in this—"

"Yes! We do!" interrupted Minnie, barking angrily, a sad and bitter break in her voice, and she banged the mug again on the counter. It shattered, leaving her holding the handle.

"Fuck!" snapped Minnie, the view leaning down as she flung open a lower cupboard with force. Her hands took out a dustpan and brush, and then she began to silently sweep up the fragments of ceramic mug. This went on for a few moments, an oppressive silence filling both The Black Room and Minnie's kitchen.

"Minnie, I meant what I said," Charlie muttered eventually, needing to break the moment, to fill the silence. "I would have never even tried the experiment if I realised that it would bother you so much." There was no reply, her hands still busying themselves with the cleanup operation. Charlie, now standing dumbly in front of the screen, found himself considering what she'd said. Was that true? Ten percent?

His thoughts were broken by, again, a small number of things suddenly happening at once: a sudden, stabbing pain in the lower part of the index finger on his right hand, and Minnie letting out short yelp.

"Son of a bitch," she said, sounding like she was feeling sorry for herself now, and Charlie watched with growing horror as her right hand came towards her face. He already knew what the problem would be, as he brought his own hand into view in front of his eyes.

Onscreen, sticking out of the lower part of Minnie's right index finger, was a small fragment of ceramic mug, embedded when she'd had enough of just using the brush and had decided to grab for a few pieces. It was about a half inch long. Minnie grunted in both pain and annoyance as she pulled it out of her finger and flicked it away. Charlie's finger hung in the air in front of his eyes, confirming what he already suspected and filling him with a newfound sense of dread. There, with the blood beading gently in a line half an inch long, was a corresponding cut on his own finger.

The connection was indeed stronger. Lethally so. The day before, when he'd punched a hole in The Black Room wall, it had caused Minnie great pain, but had resulted in nothing for Charlie. Now, however, it seemed that an injury to Minnie led to a corresponding injury to Charlie; and when Minnie's brain eventually haemorrhaged, Charlie's would as well. If he didn't find a way to leave Minnie behind forever, they were both definitely going to die.

Charlie felt the strength go from his limbs, and sat down before he fell down. The cut didn't hurt as much as he thought it should have, the pain perhaps slightly dulled in The Black Room, but he could feel it enough for it to be like a nasty beacon of unpleasant truth embedded in his hand. Charlie hung his head quietly, while Minnie scraped the broken, damning fragments of mug into the bin.

**

She went into the living room without a word, and sat on the sofa. Charlie didn't know what to say. Was she still angry? Embarrassed? One thing was absolutely, categorically certain now; no matter how he or she felt, there was no time to fuck around anymore. The mug sealed it once and for all. They had to get this show on the road. If she wasn't going to be forthcoming, he had to put his foot down, like it or not. He began to try and find the right words for the businesslike approach, but Minnie got there first.

"I believe you," she said quietly, but her voice was different now. Softer.

Eh?

"Sorry?"

"I believe that you weren't trying to pry. I believe you when you say that it just went a bit too far."

"Uh ... okay?" Charlie couldn't believe the change, but he wasn't going to question it. He let her speak. Minnie sighed first, however, heavily and thoughtfully, and the view swung up to the ceiling, flashing Charlie's mind back to the previous day when Minnie was cowering on the floor in hysterics. That seemed like the behaviour of a different person now.

"I believe you because I think ... ahh, because I think that if I was in your shoes I probably would have done the same thing, and it would have gone the same fucking way, okay?" It was a confession, and a hard one, but she'd said it. "It doesn't mean I like it, but I'd be a hypocrite if I said I couldn't see how it could happen. And ... you're right. I know you wouldn't ... you know. Pry. And no, I don't know how *I* know either." Charlie's breath caught.

It's true for her as well. It's true for her as well.

"And now ... NOW I've gone and spilled my fucking guts again, and said all that stuff, and I've embarrassed myself again and laid myself bare and *shit* ..." She slapped the sofa gently in frustration. "What a dick."

Silence.

"You didn't," said Charlie, gently. He was stunned by her honesty. "You were just angry, and rightly so."

"I meant all that though, Charlie. Everything I said. Even with you."

She stiffened slightly, as soon as the words were out. *Even with you.* Her realisation was clear, written in the way that the screen froze and the cogs in the walls of her mind jarred slightly.

"Uh ... I don't know ..." she said, lost for words, sounding confused and embarrassed, as if the previous sentence had come unbidden to her lips. She sounded surprised.

"Look ... I get it," said Charlie, both elated and crushed. His own words hung shakily upon his lips. What could they do? What could they ever do together? But still ... *still* ... to hear her say it, even if she didn't seem to really know what she'd just said ...

Weren't you the one just deciding that there was no time to fuck about?

Right. Fucking *hell* ... but that was right.

"Okay, I understand. And with regards to what you said in the kitchen, I'm not sure I agree with that way of looking at things, but I understand. And with the dreams and all that, you know that I won't look at anything without your permission. Right?"

The screen nodded.

"Okay." She sounded like she was smiling.

"Right. Right. You still need five minutes?"

"Oh ... Jesus ... I forgot about all that ..." said Minnie, the view becoming slightly covered as her right hand went to her forehead.

"Minnie, just tell me. Come on. You know I'll understand."

"Yes, I know, but this is—" she was interrupted by the muffled sound of her phone ringing inside her bag, which was still lying where she'd flung it onto the sofa. "Hold on, I'll just get rid of this." The hand moved away from her face and out of shot, followed by the sound of rummaging while feminine accoutrements clattered off one another. It came back, holding her phone and revealing the name onscreen as she looked at it:

OTHER

"Oh ... Christ," she said, snatching it quickly below eye level. "Talk about fucking lousy timing."

"It's okay," said Charlie, meaning that she could take the call but feeling confused at the same time; she obviously didn't just mean that the call was interrupting the conversation.

"No, I mean ... well, listen ..." She hesitated as the phone continued to ring insistently, demanding to be dealt with like a squalling child. "Shit ... shit ... sod it, this is as good a way to start the explanation as any, I guess. But just ... don't jump to any conclusions until you've heard me out, okay?" She waited for a response as the phone continued to blare. For the second time in five minutes, the sense of dread returned as Charlie began to have a suspicion about what Minnie had done.

No. She couldn't have.

"Minnie ... did you ..."

"You'll see, I'll explain everything, but just—look, I've got to take this."

She pressed ANSWER and the phone disappeared off the right-hand side of the view on its way to her ear. Charlie jumped to his feet.

"Minnie—"

His fears were then terribly confirmed, suspicion, confusion, anger and jealousy all jostling and yelling inside his head in their attempts to take the number one spot as he heard his own voice respond to Minnie's phone greeting, heard it through Minnie's ears the same way he'd heard it coming from behind the bar at Barrington's.

"Hi, Minnie, just wondered if you wanted me to swing by in a cab to get you, or if you were going to make your own way there?" said Chuck's voice, full of the phone levity that Charlie knew so well from his own conversations.

"Hi, Charlie, no, it's okay, I've got an early start so I'm gonna drive, but I really appreciate the offer. See you at seven," said Minnie. Again, she sounded like she was smiling.

***

PART THREE:
THE OTHER PLACES

Chapter Five: "It's Not You and the Other You, It's Me," A Date With Destiny, Shared Memories, and A Major Revelation at the End
***

Minnie hung up the phone and sighed, preparing herself for the confrontation that was about to happen, while Charlie's mouth worked uselessly. Shock had taken his words. There was silence for a second, the air heavy with apprehensive tension from Minnie's side, and confused anger on Charlie's. It was he who broke the moment, and then the air was filled with chaos instead.

"*Chuck*? Are you fucking *kidding* me?"

"Wait, Charlie," said Minnie, sounding quiet and calm, "you don't understand, I said I'd explain—"

"What's the deal here?! What the fuck is going on?"

"Charlie, listen. *Listen*—"

"Bollocks! Jesus Christ, you lecture me about trust and then you're out batting for the other team? When did this happen then? Did you go back to Barrington's?"

"No, I've not been back since we—"

"Then how the hell did you set up this little *rendezvous*? And why didn't you tell me?!"

"Hey, now that's not fair, I haven't had a chance, and I was bloody well going to—"

"Were you? *Were* you?"

Charlie felt sick, like he'd been winded by a heavy blow to the stomach. Half of it was the betrayal, and the other half—more than half, if he was honest—was violent, impotent jealousy. It was bad enough to hear Minnie simpering like that down the phone, to hear the sudden and complete removal of her attention from the Room at the sound of Chuck's voice, but it was all infinitely and uniquely worse; the other guy in this situation was *him*, so why wasn't it *actually* him? He could obviously do the job just as well, and had every right to be the one to do so. But it wouldn't be him. It wouldn't be him. It would be Chuck.

*Chuck. Mother*fucker.

"Look ... I'm not going to answer anything if you're not going to listen," said Minnie, trying to sound firm but not succeeding; there was a tremble in her voice. "Do us both a favour and let me speak, and you might even feel better afterwards. Okay?"

Charlie scowled in the darkness, clenching his fists.

"Yeah, right," he said, scoffing like a child. "I'm sure I'm gonna love every second of this. How could you do it?" He realised it was a stupid question ... but at the same time, it wasn't. She knew it, too. It wasn't a betrayal because there had been no agreement, and there was no way of there ever truly being one because he was stuck inside her head, but all the same ... she knew what he meant. Didn't she? She'd said so. *Even with you.* That had said it all.

"I'm perfectly within my rights to do whatever I want," she said, the tremor in—and the volume of—her voice beginning to rise. The words had cut Charlie like a blade, even if she didn't really mean it the way she'd made it sound; it was just bravado. "But just shut the fuck up and you might even get your ego massaged a little, *okay?*"

The last part was so intriguing and so clearly a reluctant confession, given up only as a necessity, that Charlie did actually dial things back.

"*Fine*," he said, but the venom was mostly for Minnie's benefit. Even so, he sounded like a sulking teenager. "I can't wait to hear it."

Minnie didn't reply, but the view travelled the short distance across the living room to the sofa, and dropped sharply downwards as Minnie let her weight fall onto the cushions. She sighed again, and the view panned down to her hands, where her fingers began to play with her nails. She paused before speaking, trying to reset.

"I will say, it's a bit fucking rich you getting on your high horse with me after doing *exactly* what I asked you not to do," she said, breathing slowly as she spoke, trying to stay calm. Charlie went to speak, but bit his lip. She had a point. "But I can understand how you feel about this, and I accepted your apology so I shouldn't bring up what *you* did and then go on about it ... but it still needed to be mentioned. Anyway ... look, do you remember when we were about to leave Barrington's? And I gave Char—Chuck my old business card?"

Another crushing fist of nausea punched Charlie square in the guts, but he said nothing. He remembered the moment she was talking about too, and he remembered thinking that it was an unusual thing to do—leaving contact details regarding a missing item that would never turn up—because the phone had already been found.

"Well ... this might sound stupid," said Minnie, "but ... I think you'll understand. I think you'll know the kind of thing I'm talking about. Anyway ... I felt *compelled* to give him my card. It felt like it would be a mistake to walk out of there and not leave some sort of contact. I know that almost doesn't make any sense, because, well, he's you, and you were literally with me at all times, but ... to see him ... hell, to see *you*, in the flesh ... it felt like *we* were meeting for the first time. It felt like that was the way it *should* have been; in a bar, on the street, introduced by a friend ... and it just, well ... it felt like the most natural thing in the world. And then I went outside, and I felt guilty almost straight away, and that's fucking idiotic because I'd only just come to terms with you being in my head, let alone feeling any kind of loyalty. That's why I said I needed to think, and then by the time we'd gotten home I'd started to deal with the more immediate issue of having a man in my head that I now believed was real."

The fingers stopped wrapping around each other, one hand pushing the other away in nervous frustration.

"And then all the other stuff happened, and then I went to sleep and you were gone ... and that was so tough and weird when I woke up, and I *missed* you, Charlie, I really missed you after one day, can you believe that?" Charlie could, and did, and his heart leapt a little in a sick, confused and hopeful bounce, knowing the final result of all this but still somehow hoping that it would be different in the end. "And I nearly rang him so many times, wanting to hear your voice ... but I didn't, because I thought it wouldn't be *you*. He wouldn't know the things you know, even if he was the same person; he wouldn't have shared the day that we'd had. Just that little difference would have been enough to mean he wasn't the same. That ten percent, that last ten percent." The leap was higher this time, Charlie thanking God for that ten percent, and for The Black Room that housed it.

"But then ... he rang me," said Minnie, and the softness that came into her voice—barely audible, but there nonetheless—was like an ice cold blanket on Charlie's growing excitement. His face fell, the hidden nature of his physical form allowing for total openness of expression. "And he said—"

Charlie already knew what he said; in a flash, in the split-second moment that he considered what he would say in Chuck's shoes, he knew. He could have spoken along with Minnie word for word, were she not giving her generalised version of Chuck's sentences. But he knew the *exact* details of it: *Hi. This may be a little forward, because I know you left your card just to get your phone back, but ... well, I couldn't help wondering if you wanted to go for dinner tonight. At the very least, it's a free meal, even if the company is the stalker barman from your night out ... plus, I know this great Italian place over in—*

"—Italian restaurant in town. And I just said yes without thinking, because Charlie, *it was just like talking to you.* We just got chatting, about salad and vegetables that we like and don't like, of all things, and it was just so easy, you were saying about how you like—"

Charlie didn't want to hear it, didn't want to be party to their early-stages conversation, but he knew the answers, of course; he liked peas, because they always seemed like a more friendly vegetable, but lettuce tastes of soil.

"And then ... oh, oh God Charlie, I don't want to say it ... after that, it was like ... like we had our *own* ten percent, a conversation that you weren't part of. There's *our* ten percent, and then there's mine and his too, but both of them are *you.* And on the phone there was a connection, a total connection, but it wasn't you at the same time, and ..." She sighed, slapping her thighs gently with her hands. "Plus, I thought there might be another reason to go too, a chance to maybe talk to you, I mean to *him*, shit, and who knows what might come up that might help us figure out what's going on? If nothing else, that's a reason to go, right?"

Charlie didn't reply. He thought he was going to throw up, and that set him off wondering wildly if he even could *be* sick in The Black Room; if his body wasn't really here, what food could he throw up? What food had his current form actually consumed? Wasn't he just a visualisation of his own consciousness or something, The Black Room itself just a visualisation that he could understand? So he couldn't have a belly full of food ...

"Charlie ..."

You knew you could never hold her anyway. You knew it. What were you expecting? How can you say you love her if you would have her be alone, just because she can't be with you?

His brow furrowed at the thought, in self-pity and surprise. It was the first time he'd thought the word, the first time he'd admitted it to himself; the drama of the moment had brought forth the truth, and the accompanying full realisation of the impossible gulf between them settled into him like a physical weight. He could never have her. He could *never* have her.

Why are you feeling so strong, so quickly? What's the goddamn link between you two?

"Charlie?"

His mouth moved again, trying to respond and let her at least know that he was still there, but his lip began to quiver and his nose twitched and he didn't trust himself to be able to complete the sentence. The weight was sorrow, and it was getting heavier.

"Charlie, are you there?"

"Uh," Charlie managed, and he began to blink furiously, to cut this growing indulgence off as quickly as he could. He tried to give himself a reevaluation of the facts; he was here to save Minnie. That was the point. This was *Chuck's* world, not his, and *he* was the intruder here; whatever the connection was between himself and Minnie, the correct connection should be Chuck's, not his. It needed to happen, he needed to let it happen, and also, she was right; there could be a lot to learn from Chuck, he could be another piece of the puzzle. If he was falling in love with her—if he wanted the best for her—he had to let her pursue the natural order. He had to help her observe, to find the information that would help save her life. And wasn't Chuck the same as him, after all? He could envy Chuck's opportunity, for certain, but envy the man, envy Chuck's qualities? They were exactly the same as his own! Everything that drew Minnie to Chuck drew her to him as well. Shouldn't he be proud?

So Chuck gets his Minnie and mine's dead? That's fair?

He was aware that he should feel guilty for thinking such things—he was not the wounded party in his world, the dead Minnie and her family clearly were—but in that moment, all Charlie felt was a tightness in his chest and a dying sensation in his heart. He'd known he was drawn to her, but a vague awareness of true desire is quickly and fully realised when the possibility for obtaining that desire is taken away.

"Please listen, Charlie," Minnie was saying, sounding like she was pleading, *willing* him to understand, but Charlie was sitting on the floor now, his eyes closed in a pained expression as he tried to pull himself together, to at least smother it all down until he could function and get the job done. He had to. "Even what I just said, that isn't explaining it right. This ... it's both of you, do you understand? It's not him over you, it's *you*, just ... like, in two different forms. Like there's you on a Wednesday, and you on a Thursday, and they both are the same person. *Aaaah*, no, I mean ... it's *all you*, Charlie. Talking to you in my head, and talking to you on the phone, and later there'll be talking to you in person ... and it's all the same person, and there's something going on with them that feels ... like home. And isn't it the same for you and Chuck? You know the me that knows about you, he'll only know the me that doesn't, the one I show him ... but they're both the same person. I ... I can't explain it better than that."

Charlie opened his eyes slightly, feeling like he was beginning to grasp her point, but not thinking that it made any difference. Maybe she was right, but that didn't mean he ... it didn't mean Chuck ... wait, it was all him? The whole point was him?

Bollocks, are you *physically taking her out to dinner tonight? Are* you *the one sharing a bottle of wine with her?*

These were angry, pained thoughts, and as such were like warm water on Charlie's cold psyche; he began to turn towards them, but the other part of his mind that was saying *but she'll be with you, she'll be with you and enjoying your inner thoughts, your mind, told by your lips, like watching yourself talk in the mirror.* It was a colossal headfuck, his rampant emotions battering his ability to rationalise, and behind it all was the knowledge of the task he had to perform. With a superhuman effort—he loved her, after all—he was able to stamp it all down, to give her a response, to *focus*. For her sake.

"I ... I understand, Min," he said, hearing himself abbreviate her name on instinct, using such familiarity, and his face crumbled as he realised that that would be how a married couple would talk; a level of quiet, mutual ownership. He screwed up his eyes and bit his finger, hard, the pain getting him back on track. "Look ..."

"No, you don't, I can tell, listen, it's *you*, Charlie, he's *you*—"

"Minnie," interrupted Charlie, the steadiness in his voice surprising him. It was a performance worthy of Minnie. "I get it, I just ... I need a bit, okay? You had a bit of time to get your head around stuff last time, and this is ... it's a lot to understand."

It's more than that, man. It's a lot more, and a lot worse.

"Just sort yourself out, uh, make some food or whatever, get yourself ready, and uh, let me just ... you know. Think." He kept his voice steady, and perhaps, he thought, that was due to there being some truth in what he was saying. There *was* more to think about here ... and maybe he could even come to terms with it enough to be able to get on with things, as unlikely as it seemed. No matter what, he *had* to suck it up.

"Okay," said Minnie, sounding unsure. "I know, it's almost impossible to get. Look ... would you like me to try and sleep? I feel like, as weird as it sounds, like I *want* you to come with me, because I think you'll understand what I mean ... not that wanting you here sounds weird, because well ... I do ... but I think *you* don't want to be here now, and I really think you should be because you'll see what I mean—"

"No, no," said Charlie, trying to figure out what the hell she was blathering on about. He didn't understand it, but if he'd had insights about this whole situation that had turned out to be right, couldn't Minnie have had them too? However much it might twist in his gut, he thought that it might be best to trust her judgement; that didn't mean, however, that the anticipation would be any easier. "Just ... sort yourself out, as I say. I'm not gonna pretend that this is easy, but ... okay."

"You'll see, Charlie," said Minnie, a gentle certainty in her voice. "You'll see what I mean. I'm gonna eat first, then start to get ready."

"Okay. I'm ... I'm probably not going to talk much, all right? I feel ... I feel a bit sick."

There was a brief silence, Minnie not knowing what to say to this.

"That's fine," she said eventually. "I understand. I'll probably just check you're still there from time to time though, okay?"

"Okay."

"Look ... this is the last thing I'll say about it, all right? I know I'm repeating myself, but ... it's *you*. Tonight, Charlie, I'm meeting *you*. No one else. That's the best way I can put it."

Charlie thought he might have caught a sense of it, a dim understanding that might have made everything all right, but it was a slippery, fleeting thing, glimpsed for a moment and then gone.

"Okay. Sort your food out."

IN THE DARKNESS, THAT'S WHERE I'LL KNOW YOU

Minnie hesitated, as if she was about to try and explain further, but then the view simply moved up and down in a nod before travelling upward again as Minnie stood and made her way into the kitchen.

The next few hours crawled by for Charlie; he saw Minnie choosing a light microwave meal even though the start of the date was still several hours away, and her evening meal therefore even further than that; a daytime soap was watched as she ate her chilli chicken and noodles, the only talk between them being when Minnie occasionally checked to see if Charlie was still there. His confirmation was brief, and invited no further discussion. He wasn't sulking, he was just locking himself down, riding out the time by trying to lose himself in the show, and did the same later with the music that she listened to as she prepared herself.

It was an unusual feeling to say the least, watching someone make themselves look their best before they went on a first date with him, while knowing that it wouldn't *be* him; he witnessed the normally hidden anticipation, observed the meticulous creation of what would be passed off as an effortless process. Before she got in the shower, she sheepishly asked if Charlie would turn his back on the screen. He obliged, and told her so.

Thoughts would try and creep in:

She would keep this whole part secret from me if it were our *first date. I can see all this because I don't matter. It's* not *me. It's* him.

Won't she hate it, knowing that I'm watching her in first-date mode, seeing her putting on her first-date front? Unless she's different with him, unless he's let inside that last thirty, twenty percent? Does he get to be inside that last ten after all, while I'm inside her fucking head *and I still don't even get let inside that?*

What if she brings him home? Do they fuck while I'm still here? Would she do that?

This last one stuck harder than the others, and he wanted to ask, but knew that to do so would be crude and inflammatory. With that thought, his heart sank. He knew that—until tonight was over at least—a wedge was now between them, even if he seemed to be the only one that was holding it there. Minnie seemed certain that tonight he would see her point, that it would all be okay, and Charlie tried to cling to that mental lifeline as a way of smothering the sick feeling in his stomach.

Other times he tried to flat-out ignore the head-twisting thoughts, tried to move away from them and focus instead on a sound, or a visual point on the bedroom wall reflected in Minnie's dressing table mirror, reminding himself to keep it together and to be on the ball tonight for anything that might help solve the riddle of The Black Room ... and then he would again see her retouching her makeup, and it would be like a kick to his heart.

Grow up. You've got a job to do.

But it wasn't that easy.

After several hours that felt a lot longer than they actually were, the view was finally moving along the corridor that ran through the centre of Minnie's small flat, and stopped in front of the door. There was the sound of jangling keys as they were picked up, and then silence as Minnie paused. Ordinarily, Charlie knew, she would have moved to the mirror to talk to him. Now, her reasons for not doing so were painfully obvious; she was fully, socially made-up for the first time since Charlie had arrived. He'd seen her getting ready, of course, but to engage him in conversation while in that state would be to rub the date in his face. However she might think the evening would resolve Charlie's concerns, she was trying to protect him for now, and Charlie hated her for it, hated himself for his own vulnerability. He couldn't help it.

"Charlie?"

"Yep."

"Just checking. Last chance for me to cancel this. You know what I think, but you're the one that has to come along in the end. I think it would be a big mistake to call it off—for your part as well as mine—but I won't make you do something that you don't want to."

His anger lessened, but the sick feeling grew.

"It's okay," he muttered. "Let's just get it done."

"All right," she said quietly, and those were the last words spoken between them until the car journey was over and they'd arrived at the restaurant.

The sight of the entrance was usually one that filled Charlie with a small sense of warmth; he loved the place, its food and its décor both being exactly to his taste, and being back there normally made him relax instantly. But tonight, the sight of its dark window frames and contrasting, light-coloured venetian blinds made his tension grow even greater, made his shoulders knot up like cordwood. As Minnie made her way to the door, the warm light from within spilling through the glass and out onto the street, Charlie could see The Black Room's walls tumbling in new, energised ways. Minnie was excited.

A short, pretty woman in her twenties greeted Minnie at the door, carrying a clipboard.

"Hello there, are you meeting someone?"

"Yes," Charlie heard Minnie reply. "Table is booked under the name of Wilkes, I think?"

My name. My name.

The woman glanced at the clipboard.

"Ah yes, if you'd like to follow me?"

She led Minnie towards the back of the restaurant and around a corner, the venue seeming larger on the inside than it appeared from the street as it extended inwards. The walls were painted a warm yellow, with dark wood panelling on them that reached to waist height. Scattered everywhere were random paintings from mismatching periods that somehow worked together with the ornate, almost gothic light fittings to create a charming, bohemian effect. Like Barrington's (but in greater, almost ridiculous numbers), there were large potted plants everywhere, in this case ferns.

Don't let him show up. Don't let him be here.

But he was; as they rounded the corner, Charlie saw his own face light up, saw himself raise a hand and stand to greet Minnie, saw the obvious delight in his own eyes, and his heart sank. Chuck was wearing exactly what Charlie would have worn, of course; the fitted black shirt he'd bought in London (the one with the sharp collar) and his favourite grey slim-fitted jeans. On his wrist he even wore his good, "special occasion" watch.

"Hey," said Chuck, grinning. "You made it."

I knew you'd say that, asshole.

"Certainly did," said Minnie quietly, slightly shy now but stepping closer to him. They shared an awkward moment, and Charlie knew what Chuck was thinking; does he go for a kiss on the cheek here, or ... what? As he could see by the movement onscreen, Minnie was similarly unsure, but then they both chuckled slightly and went for the kiss option. The awkwardness was broken, and the moment had served to put them both at ease; what might have been a bad start had ended up being the best one possible.

Charlie watched all this and again had that flash, that brief glimpse of understanding, and again it wasn't enough. He'd had it the second Chuck had hesitated in going in for the kiss, and in the nanosecond before the comprehension left he'd felt the darkness inside him lift. Charlie sat up slightly in The Black Room and thought, watching as Chuck sat down and the view similarly lowered to a seated level, showing Chuck in annoyingly complimentary candlelight. That had been twice that he'd seen the edge of something, twice that he'd nearly grasped what Minnie had been talking about ... and twice was enough to give the amount of credibility to her suggestion that everything would be okay, enough at least to calm his mind slightly and leave him able to watch without going mad.

Okay ... this isn't a good situation, not by a long stretch ... but there's something going on here. She might be right. Just watch. Just watch, and try to relax.

"Did you find the place okay?" said Chuck, picking up and opening the menu but not looking at it. "You're certainly nicely on time ... but not fashionably late. I'm disappointed. You should have kept me waiting at least twenty minutes." Charlie heard Minnie chuckle, and noticed the nerves in her voice—she was still too aware that Charlie was there—but he was only dimly aware of registering all of this. It was Chuck's words that he was fascinated by, had become electrified by.

Although Charlie had had a previous moment in Chuck's presence when he'd known what the man was going to say next—to a point where he could have almost lip synced it with him—this was different. That had been a casual conversation, but this was Chuck on a date. This is what he would have said if he were in Chuck's shoes with a girl he wanted to impress, a girl he wanted to like him, and Chuck's words suddenly brought out an empathy in Charlie that was like a magnet, drawing him towards his other self. It was *incredible*.

Chuck's cheeseball date-banter was something Charlie hadn't expected, even though he should have. He'd come into the evening feeling at his most adversarial, his most jealous, and had seen Chuck as a hated rival, ridiculously. And it *was* ridiculous, he now saw; how could he be jealous of himself? As soon as Chuck had sat down and spoken—he'd gotten it briefly with Chuck's opening line, but it had taken another sentence to bring it all home—he'd heard it in his voice, heard himself in the other man's shoes, and realised that they were completely *his*. And it was already growing, as part of his mind heard Minnie's teasing riposte (*It's only because I wasn't bothered if I impressed you or not, I'm only late for the important ones*) and was already responding to it, mentally holding up his hands and saying:

"Ouch, good comeback. Okay, okay, you win. But the *important* thing is ... do you like Italian food? As I've eaten here an embarrassing number of times, so if you're not much of an Italian eater, I can tell you what to go for on here and—"

—what to avoid like the plague ... and here's where I actually find out you're a big Italian food expert whose—

"—grandmother I'm trying to teach to suck eggs," finished Chuck, cocking his head with a self-effacing sigh and looking down at his menu. Minnie laughed, her eyes still on Chuck, the view framing him perfectly.

"Keep digging," she said, but that nervous edge was still in her voice; she wasn't herself, not yet, but Charlie already knew that she would be, that he, that *they*, would put her at her ease, that even Chuck would notice it and that the perfect solution would be a little bit of—

"Okay, well, at the very least we should get some wine—"

Ah shit, she drove—

"Wait, you came in the car, didn't you. Okayyyy, well they do some great soft drink cocktails here."

"Ah, I can always leave it. I have a later start tomorrow than I thought, so I can always pick it up in the morning if I need to," said Minnie with a shrug. Chuck grinned, pleased, a happy smile that ten minutes ago would have made Charlie want to kill him, but now he felt it too; he knew what Chuck was feeling, just as he felt the words come to the back of his own brain and mouthed them along with Chuck's voice, feeling an empathy that was beyond explanation:

"Well, okay, the night is young after all, and we'll see how we feel, right?"

Charlie felt so good that he didn't even notice his heart hammering in his chest or his blood pumping harder through his veins, his delight at the situation matched only by the sudden and dramatic turn in his mood. How could he have got it so wrong? The sensation was so intense, so *instant*, that it could almost be mistaken for a psychic bond, but it wasn't that at all. It was different, but just as strong; he was *there*, after all, sitting down for a romantic meal with the girl that he knew he should be with. Chuck's words were his words, his responses were Charlie's responses, and Charlie knew exactly how Chuck felt in such an uncanny, emphatic way that he shared in the feelings himself. It was bizarre, but wonderful, and hearing his response come from Chuck's lips was exactly the same as if he were the one saying it, as if he were the one on the opposite side of the table.

Right then, as he heard Minnie say *Okay* with a smile in her voice, and saw the slight furrow in Chuck's brow that he knew came from noticing of Minnie's air of discomfort, Charlie knew that this would be the most magical night of his life; he just had to remove that discomfort, a job that would be extremely easy.

"Minnie," said Charlie, and saw the view jerk ever so slightly in response. He wasn't listening to Chuck—to *himself*—as he already knew that he was saying *Everything okay? You seem a bit ... uncomfortable? Is this place all right for you?* "It's okay. It's totally okay! I get it. I wish I'd listened to you, I just didn't understand. But you were right, you were completely right. You understood it before I did. So please, relax. Let's just ..." He hesitated, both in trying to find the right words and then, when they came, feeling a sting from knowing again that no matter what, his actual arms would never get to hold her. But in that moment, it didn't matter, the sting could come later; tonight, he had a date with her, with The Woman in the Night. With Minnie. "Let's just have a good night," he finished.

As he watched the screen, he saw her expression change through the relaxation of Chuck's; the brow unknotted and he smiled, a pleased smile that Charlie had never really seen before because it only came when he didn't think about being watched. It only came when he was lost in the moment.

"Everything's fine," said Minnie, and in her voice was a warmth that confirmed why Chuck looked so pleased. The nerves were gone, and only delight remained. "I just suddenly thought that I might have left the door off the latch, but I just realised I can text my neighbour to get her to check, so no problem; and you know what, sod it, I *will* leave the car. Let's order some wine."

Charlie watched as her hands fished her phone out of her bag, his mouth miming along with Chuck's—and his—response of *Okay, let's see what we're gonna have and we'll get something to match, even though I haven't got a goddamn clue about the wine menu.* The view remained on the screen as Minnie typed, letting Charlie read what Minnie wanted him to see:

OH GOD, I'M SO GLAD. I KNEW IT. YOU UNDERSTAND NOW, DON'T YOU? THIS ISN'T ABOUT HIM, YOU, AND ME. IT'S ABOUT YOU AND ME, JUST IN A DIFFERENT WAY. THIS WAY, WE GET TO DO IT HOW IT *SHOULD* HAVE BEEN. I KNEW IT, I DON'T KNOW HOW BUT I DID. AND I HAVE TO SAY ... YOU SCRUB UP WELL.

Charlie grinned. This was all so insane, but so wonderful, to be on *both sides of a date* with someone so special, and better still, to know that she felt the same. The familiarity mixed with the excitement of *un*familiarity ... it was unique. It was magical.

"Tell me that," said Charlie, "I love compliments. I'll give you one right back, and I'll mean it." Minnie's hands worked, and the text on the screen expanded.

HA!!! THIS IS SO FUCKING WEIRD!! AND YOU'D LOVE THAT I BET, WOULDN'T YOU, HAVING YOUR EGO STROKED? WELL, I SHOULDN'T, AFTER YOU BEING A SULKY, AGGRESSIVE LITTLE SHIT EARLIER, BUT I GUESS YOU DIDN'T UNDERSTAND :-S OKAY, I'LL SAY IT, BUT NO MORE OF THIS 'COS WE HAVE TO DO THE NIGHT PROPERLY. PLUS I DON'T WANT YOU THINKING I'M A DICK FOR BEING ON MY PHONE ALL NIGHT.

Charlie chuckled, but his face was red from Minnie's pointing out of the way he'd acted. She understood why he had though, and he wasn't surprised by that fact. It was Minnie, after all, and wasn't that surely why he'd come to her in the first place? It couldn't be coincidence. He'd come to The Black Room for a reason, come to The Woman in the Night, and the reason was surely connected to the fact that they were meant to be together. Charlie had never believed in fate, but Minnie had made a believer out of him.

"Okay, you'd better put it away and make with the nice-nice, but just remember to play hard to get. I'll see right through it, of course, but I'll appreciate that you tried." He felt warm all over, giddy.

HMM, WELL YOU DO DESERVE IT, I SUPPOSE … I DO LIKE THAT SHIRT.

There was a pause, and then her fingers moved again:

THANK YOU, CHARLIE. I KNEW YOU'D GET IT. I KNEW YOU'D BE HAPPY. I WOULDN'T HAVE SAID YES OTHERWISE, BUT I KNEW I COULDN'T EXPLAIN IT UNTIL I GOT YOU HERE. I JUST WANTED A NIGHT WITH YOU SO MUCH.

Charlie suddenly found it hard to breathe, but found his voice nonetheless.

"Me too. And thank *you*. Okay … let's go."

The phone screen was locked, and it disappeared back into the mysterious depths of Minnie's bag.

"Sorted," she said, and Chuck smiled back at her, that delighted grin brightening his face again, one that only got bigger when Minnie added, "I have to say, you look great tonight. Much better than you did in your work threads."

"Thank you very much," said Chuck, as Charlie mouthed it with him, "you're not looking too bad yourself either; *great* about sums you up too. I *think* we can just about be seen with each other, don't you?"

"Oh, you don't need to worry, I don't know anyone in here, I think," chuckled Minnie, and the waiter arrived to ask what they'd like to drink. As Charlie settled onto the floor of The Black Room with a smile on his face, his only regret in that moment was that he wouldn't be able to taste the wine. Other than that, for one evening, everything was all right; everything else could wait.

IN THE DARKNESS, THAT'S WHERE I'LL KNOW YOU

***

It *was* magic. As time passed, they learned about each other's lives, their families—Charlie (*Chuck*) was a little evasive on that one, as he always was, but that was only inside his twenty percent, and could come later—their hopes and aspirations, yet feeling like they'd known each other since the day they were born. Finding mutual ground, deeply held and shared beliefs and convictions, and an instant rapport; a deep comfort from the presence of the other, a feeling of *I can do no wrong here, I am accepted totally* despite the excitement of the new.

There were juxtaposed differences too, of course; Minnie liked to run. Charlie found it boring and inexplicable. Charlie liked comics. Minnie found the idea laughable. These almost insulting differences of opinion bore no ill will, and instead made them both smile and highlighted the parts that they had so profoundly in common.

By the time they reached dessert, the hours having flown by, Charlie (*Chuck*) found himself spilling his guts about things that he didn't even know that he'd felt. The truth about his life, how he *was* unfulfilled, and how he wasn't quite sure how he was going to fix it, how he hadn't really admitted to himself that he had been coasting because it was easier than facing up to the truth. It was madness, the sort of thing people never confessed to on a first date because they wanted to paint themselves in their very best light, and keep their failings to themselves. But here, it was all right, because he knew that it would only bring them closer together. He was proven to be correct; Minnie in turn told him about her "screwed up" past, and how she'd only just gotten herself back on her feet. As she did so, Charlie reached out his hand in the dim light of The Black Room. Chuck did the same in the warm light of the restaurant and took Minnie's hand across the table; neither Minnie nor Chuck nor Charlie seemed to notice that they'd done it, the movement as natural as breathing. He almost wished that he could see her face, but really, he didn't need to. He could see exactly how it looked by the way that Chuck's eyes were holding Minnie's, that she was returning the intense stare and the smile with equal delight. After all, hadn't he seen her face before a great many times? The face of The Woman in the Night? He just didn't know *how*, but it didn't matter, not tonight.

She confessed about her early experiments with drugs after her mother died (Charlie came out of the moment for a second at that point, reminded of how he already knew about her mother being gone ... but the thought passed just as quickly as it came) and how it had gotten out of control. Again, this was *madness* for a first date but acceptable here, no, more than acceptable, *desired*. How she'd started to get clean, ran her own very small business for a while, then losing it when she'd begun to struggle with the workload, and watching it all fall to pieces around her once she got back on the needle. Charlie felt bad, and he (*Chuck*) asked if she was okay on the wine, like he'd talked her into it;

normally such a question would have felt like he was insulting his dinner companion, but he knew with Minnie it would be okay. It was. She smiled, raised her glass in front of the view, and said wine was different. Charlie returned the gesture with an empty hand, not noticing that he was doing it as he watched Chuck carry out the motion simultaneously. Charlie saw the glass as being in his own hand. They toasted.

"Someone's still being a bit cagey though," said Minnie, as the wine glass came away from the bottom of the screen. "I've seen your 'lack of ambition' and raised it, upping the ante with 'Minnie Cooper: My Drugs Hell.' But don't think I didn't notice how you skipped over the bit about your family, there. Come on. This has been a very on-the-couch date so far, so don't hold back on your half of it."

Charlie's, Chuck's, *their* smiles faltered, and their heads lowered slightly, their mouths now held in a stiff, pretend smile that was utterly alien to the sincerity that had been there before. Charlie looked up through his eyebrows to see Minnie's other hand cross the table, this time being the one to make the gesture as she gently took hold of Charlie's fingers.

"Hey," she said softly, with an empathy that was as clear as rain, "it's all right if you don't want to tell me. I'm sorry, I was only teasing. If it's hard to say, you don't have to. It's only early days anyway—" She stopped suddenly, her arms stiffening as she realised what she'd said. Even though they both felt it, even though they both knew what was going on, she'd put it on the table with her words. Even though they both knew, deep inside, that it was okay to say so, it was still a big confession, and as such carried with it a vulnerability. Chuck looked up at her again, breathing in deeply as Charlie did so, and withdrew the hand that he'd taken hers with earlier. He moved it across the table to take her fresh hand where it sat on top of his left, sandwiching hers between both of his. He and Charlie smiled; of course it was okay to tell her, just as her confession to him had been. They knew.

"Sorry," Charlie (*Chuck*) said. "Reflex action. It's not something I talk about normally. I haven't talked about it for years. It's kind of ... well, it's hard to think about, and I don't wanna end up acting weird tonight as a result." He smiled and looked at the back of her hand as he gently stroked it. They were so close already, he knew, in such a frighteningly short space of time. He looked up at her, and smiled again sadly. "I just don't want to blow it, being perfectly frank."

"You can't," said Minnie, and the soft warmth in her voice made Charlie's shoulders melt, the fear and tension that had appeared with the introduction of the subject now melting away. Of course he could tell her. He *needed* to tell her.

"Well ... you asked for it," Charlie and Chuck said with a sad chuckle. They looked down at her hand once more and began to speak, transporting them back to a past that they seldom returned to but whose grip they had never escaped.

IN THE DARKNESS, THAT'S WHERE I'LL KNOW YOU

***

It's match day, and they're late. Normally, Dad would be driving, dropping Charlie off on the way to work, but after four shouts of "Hurry up" followed shortly after by an ultimatum, followed by a countdown, Dad had yelled his disappointment and had gone to the plant. It's only half Charlie's fault; he hadn't been able to find his football boots, but if he'd gotten up on the first of three visits by his mum, he'd have found them in time. Charlie is ten years old.

Mum is driving him now, of course, and she's deeply unhappy about it, her incorrectly guilty conscience having got the better of her after seeing Charlie's miserable face at the breakfast table. She's regretting it now as she drives, her occasional sighs and tuts developing into quiet admonishments and then loud ones. She hasn't got time for this, after all, with the rest of the holiday packing and the house-tidying to do before they fly off to Majorca in the morning, and the more she thinks about it, the angrier she's getting. How could Charlie be so selfish? It's not as if she and Mark don't have enough to do as it is, and Charlie's been so sullen lately—as well as getting bad reports at school—doesn't he care that they're working their backsides off to make sure he's fed and looked after?

By this time they're out of the village, heading across the bridge that will take them over the wide river and on towards their destination. And Charlie is sitting in the passenger seat, of course, scowling and staring out of the window with his arms folded. He isn't responding to a word she says, and it's making her even worse. He didn't say thank you after she'd told him to get ready quickly, get ready and she'd take him. He didn't say a word, and has had that annoying pout on his face ever since his dad had stormed off to work. Doesn't he realise that he's the one who's in the wrong?

Charlie doesn't. In fact, Charlie is furiously ruminating over how unfairly he is treated by his parents. Always believing his teachers over him, always telling him off, always telling him to be quiet. It's not fair. And now he's going to be late and miss the warm-up, so he'll have to be a sub for the match. It's not fair. It's not fair.

"Are you even listening to me?" she says, exasperated by his silence, and Charlie knows why she's getting angry and continues to glare out of the window, saying nothing in order to get back at her some more. "Charlie!" she snaps, immediately furious due to his deliberate impertinence. Charlie still doesn't answer, knowing that his silence is working but also getting angrier with her; she's always shouting, why can't she just give him a break for once? He decides he's not going to say anything at all, no matter what she does, even if it means that he doesn't get to play. He's temporarily taken by that childish madness that a lot of us never lose, that destructive instinct that is both a rush and a sense of failing. In that moment he wants to show her, to get back at her for all the perceived wrongs she's done him.

"Right!" she snaps, and he knew that it was coming. She pulls over, and turns the car around, heading back the way they came along the country lane. Her jaw is set in grim determination, both in righteous anger and deep upset;

135

she didn't want him to miss the game, that was the whole point, but while it breaks her heart, the little shit can't get away with this. Expecting a yell of complaint from Charlie, her frustration and anger only increases when he simply continues to stare out of the window. "I hope you're happy," she says, her face reddening. "You've annoyed your dad, you've infuriated me, and now you don't get to play football. No one wins, thanks to you being so selfish and ungrateful. I don't know what's gotten into you lately, Charlie, but this attitude of yours has got to stop!" Still the silence in return, and Charlie is getting angrier too. All she ever does is shout, all Dad *ever does is shout, all his teachers ever do is tell him off ... why doesn't everybody just leave him alone?*

"Look at me when I'm talking to you!" shouts Mum, and it is *a shout as she reaches boiling point, and when all she still sees is the back of his head in response, she takes one hand off the steering wheel and slaps Charlie's leg, hard, the bare skin on display where it sticks out of his football shorts. Charlie jumps in his seat, pain and surprise and anger shooting through him and out along the length of his arm as it uncoils reflexively and slaps his mother back, striking her on* her *leg with equal force.*

Almost immediately, he realises his mistake, righteous anger turning into vapour as his mother stares at him, her mouth forming a perfect O in her shock. Not just a mistake; a big *mistake, the biggest. The O disappears as her lips begin to curl back into a furious snarl, and Charlie cringes away in his seat as the words* I'm sorry I'm sorry I'm sorry *start to reach his mouth, knowing that they will be drowned out anyway by the screaming that is about to thunder out of his mother's throat. Neither of these vocalisations get to happen, however, as this brief period of shock and anger has been enough to distract his mother from the road, from their return journey towards the bridge, from the fact that the car has drifted enough to be about to hit the edge of the old stone bridge's left wall dead-on. His mother sees it nearly in time; a brief glance away from her son to check that all is still well on the road turns into a wide-eyed, bleached-skin stare as she lunges for the wheel and wrenches the car away from the looming bridge-edge, but in her panic she sends the vehicle the wrong way, the desire to simply be* away *from the impact being bigger than any logical thought. Charlie screams as the car begins to skid down the embankment, but even then the change of direction hasn't been enough to avoid the wall's end-edge completely; the far right-hand side of the bumper clips the stone at full speed and crumples, as does the wheel-arch and the tyre, the impact combining with the sudden drop of the bank and the car's momentum to spin the entire vehicle into the air. Charlie sees the water before it seems to turn, and then everything—everything—goes into a very strange slow motion. Later, he will remember it this way, remember his mother's next words even though she couldn't possibly have had time to say them, but he will always be certain that she did.*

The car flips, and he has time to hear her draw a sharp breath, realising that it's too late to stop it, handed over to fate and the twin forces of gravity and momentum, and now the car is upside-down, giving him a more perverse view of the water; the sky that was previously above is now dropping away below him, visible through the windshield, and the river is rushing up to meet them, to claim them, and he feels something grasp his hand so hard it hurts.

"I love you," she says, and he squeezes back, desperate, even more scared now that he sees the terror in her, and begins to say I love you too *but the words are lost in the impact, the smack of metal on water, and then his head hits something very hard and everything goes black.*

Some time afterwards—he doesn't know how much, but will later think that it couldn't have been long—he is revived by an intense, freezing cold feeling on the top of his head, along with a dull pain. It takes a moment to figure out where he is, the inverted nature of his surroundings making him confused, but then he gets it; he is in the car, upside down, held in his seat by his seatbelt. Water is running in around the edges of the door, and quickly. He looks dazedly through the window to his left; all he can see is silt-filled water, lit from above by the midday sun. He is submerged, then, at least to the point where his body is underwater inside the car. He remembers the pain again, still not fully conscious, and looks down, or rather up from his perspective; the cold feeling on the top of his head turns out to be from the rising water that has been rapidly pooling in the roof of the vehicle, filled enough now to be touching even the top of Charlie's short stature, having risen well past the top of the passenger window. This realisation snaps him into full consciousness, causing the pain in his head to double, as it penetrates that if the water is touching the top of his *head, then his mother, much taller than he, must be—*

He can't see her face. From the shoulders up, she is covered by the murky water, black inside the car where the light doesn't penetrate as much. She is very still.

Charlie screams, then screams louder as the pain increases with his cries, and he frantically struggles for the seatbelt clasp. He finds the button and the clasp lets go, and Charlie's screams are muffled with a splash as he falls the very short distance upwards, out of his seat and into the pool of water in the roof of the car. The water isn't deep enough to cushion his fall; for the second time, he hits his head, and is knocked unconscious underwater.

The next thing he knows, he is in the ambulance gasping for air, and his chest is hurting very badly. There are people around him shouting excitedly. After that, it's only remembered in flashes. Waking up to find his dad crying by his bedside in the hospital; waking up to find a nurse changing his drip, and her saying soothing words that he can't remember later; the journey home, his dad silent, his dad staying *pretty much silent for all of that first week and all of the second, right up until the funeral; of being in the toilet cubicle at the wake, and overhearing the conversation between his drunk uncle Shaun and some other guy, of hearing the words* Dead when he was pulled out of the water, *and being confused, surely they mean when* she *was pulled out of the water, but that brings the horrible, awful, unbearable pain and guilt again and he starts to cry into the sleeve of his child's suit.*

Weeks pass. Dad barely speaks to him anymore, and Charlie is sad all of the time. He's sent to a psychologist, of course, and Charlie likes him, but the psychologist doesn't help much, and doesn't remove the lead weight inside

Charlie's heart. He gets headaches a lot too, but doesn't say anything to Dad about them. Dad doesn't really seem to want to talk to him, and so Charlie keeps the headaches to himself. They don't eat together; Charlie's meals are left on the table. At night, he hears Dad crying. Charlie doesn't sleep much.

But when he does, the funny dreams come.

It's always different; sometimes she's young, only a few years older than Charlie. Sometimes she's on old lady, as old as Grandma was before she died. Sometimes she's about Mum's age, and those aren't so nice, but most of the time it's bliss; it's the only time that he feels normal again, feels happy, and Charlie begins to look forward to the night times as the best part of his life.

He can never talk to her, though, and that's the bad part, but he gets to see her, gets to watch her life like it's a film, and later, he can move around in it like a ghost. It's never very clear though, and the sound is far away, with words difficult to make out, but she's there, she's always clear, and she's close and it's wonderful. If she's out with friends, he gets to go along, gets to float around the table; he can't move too far away from her, but that's okay, because he doesn't want to anyway. When she's older, she's always married, and always to a man that looks very familiar to Charlie, and he wishes the visions were clearer so that he could make the man's face out; but sometimes, they're both even older and have kids, yet other times they're the same age and don't. Sometimes she works in a supermarket, other times she works with computers that Charlie doesn't recognise, speaking into a little black block that she holds in her hand like a telephone, but it can't be a telephone because telephones don't look like that. But there's always the blurred man too in these later-day ones, while the Woman is always as clear as a bell.

He feels like she's the most important thing in his life, this woman, and his times in the night with her are the things that young Charlie looks forward to more than anything else, the times with this woman in the night. It's his secret though. He doesn't want to tell anyone, doesn't think they'll understand.

One day, at a family gathering, a christening, about a year after the accident, Charlie's Aunt Sarah comes to see him, a kind but concerned smile on her face. His dad is off somewhere, having left Charlie to his own business, and by now that's okay. Nowadays, time in the same room as his dad just makes Charlie feel uncomfortable. Aunt Sarah sits next to him in the corner of the pub, and strokes the back of his head. Aunt Sarah is nice; she comes around to visit sometimes, and looks after Charlie when his dad has to go away. His dad goes away a lot, and the expression that's on her face right now is one that Charlie sees whenever she looks at him.

She asks how he is, and how he's doing. It's what she always says, and Charlie gives the same answer: okay. She asks about his friends, and school, and if he hangs around with people his own age much; Charlie thinks about it, and says not really these days. It's something he hadn't really thought about before, but now that it's brought up, he supposes that he spends a lot of time on his own now, reading. Escaping. He doesn't say that to Aunt Sarah, though.

She says that it's important to get out of the house, to do things, to see people, and Charlie just nods, but then she repeats it, stroking the back of his head again and looking so worried that Charlie decided to confess that he does have a friend. Aunt Sarah's face lights up, and she asks who. Cautiously, Charlie tells her everything, and watches her face go from smiling, to amused, to confused, to concerned again. When he's finished, the look on Aunt Sarah's face is worse than when she came over in the first place. The smile is still there, but now it looks totally false. Charlie can see this, even as the eleven-year-old that he now is.

When they get home, Charlie's dad calls him into the living room. He makes Charlie sit in the armchair opposite him, not on the settee next to him like he would have done in the past when he wanted to talk. He asks Charlie to tell him what he told Aunt Sarah, and Charlie is angry because he told Aunt Sarah that it was a secret. He says he doesn't want to say, and Charlie's dad rubs his own face and quietly repeats that he wants Charlie to tell him. Charlie says it's a secret and then his dad goes crazy, screaming at him and telling him how he still hasn't learned, he still hasn't learned anything and then he starts slapping Charlie about the head and telling him to do as he's told, do as he's told, do as he's fucking told for once in his fucking life and then drags Charlie upstairs, throwing him into his bedroom and saying that he's going to fucking well sort him out. Charlie doesn't answer back as his dad leaves and the door slams, but he does cry to himself, and even seeing The Woman in the Night later doesn't make it okay, seeing her on that occasion as a sixteen-year-old graduating from high school.

The visits to the psychologist stop after that, and Charlie instead starts seeing a different doctor, one that asks him different kinds of questions and then Charlie is given some tablets to take. They make him feel funny before bed, and he sweats a lot more than he used to, but he doesn't complain to his dad. They don't talk at all anymore, but worse than that, even The Woman in the Night is harder to see now. It used to be like he was inside *the blurred rooms and environments with her, floating around; now it feels like a dream. Soon after that, it's like he can't see her at all, the visions turning into a mess of even murkier colours and sounds, and then he stops seeing her altogether. It's devastating; his only happiness, his only retreat taken away forever, but he thinks that at the very least his dad might be happy now, perhaps even happy enough to let him stop taking the tablets. He tells his dad that he doesn't see The Woman in the Night anymore, tells his dad quietly after entering the living room and seeing his father sitting in the armchair looking at the wall with the TV off. His dad looks at him like he doesn't remember who Charlie is for a moment, then says quietly:*

"It never happened, Charlie. Remember? It never happened. You imagined it." His words are slightly slurred, and Charlie wonders how long his dad has been drinking like this, broken by his wife's death and unable to deal with the madness of the son he now despises for something as simple as lying in bed too long on a Saturday morning. Charlie doesn't know what to say, and so he agrees.

"It never happened."

There's a moment, and for a second Charlie thinks that they might hug and go back to the way they were before. His dad appears to be considering it, but then he goes back to staring at the blank spot on the wall, and it's as if Charlie wasn't even in the room.

Eventually, Charlie comes off the tablets, although not for some time. He waits, as the weeks pass, for the effects to wear off and to see The Woman in the Night again, but she never comes back. And after a while, it seems so distant and impossible that Charlie begins to think that maybe his dad was right after all; maybe he did just imagine it. And maybe it's for the best, he tells himself. Maybe it's better that way, better that his dad doesn't have another burden to deal with, and so Charlie decides that there was *no Woman in the Night. It was just a crazy time, the aftereffect of a tragedy. And so Charlie begins to forget, begins to make himself forget everything from the crash onwards (he'll never forget that of course, never let himself be relieved of the guilt of what he did) and everything to do with the weird stuff after his mum's death; that means the conversation with Aunt Sarah too, the strange overheard conversation in the toilet, his dad saying* It never happened; *all of it was imaginary too. All he will remember is that his dad was never the same after his mother died, and that all of it is his fault.*

***

Chapter Six: I Am the Resurrection, Whispering (Bitter) Sweet Nothings, An Unexpected Message, and An Even More Unexpected Visit
***

Chuck finished his story. In fact, he'd finished it some time ago, and was listening to Minnie's heartfelt sympathies with a grateful, embarrassed and sad smile on his face, but Charlie wasn't listening to Minnie's words. His heart was pounding and he was almost crying; he and Chuck had stopped being *they* the minute that Chuck had reached the end of his tale, as Chuck's story had ended way before Charlie's did. Charlie couldn't blame him; he'd long forgotten the rest of the story himself, about the visions and the pills and The Woman in the Night. He'd forgotten it *all*.

But he remembered now, and the truth was like a tidal wave.

By relaying the story along with Chuck, and experiencing the uncanny feeling of an actual shared dual memory, he'd remembered his past in a vivid way that he never had before ... and it had all come flooding back. Chuck's story had concluded with the car ending up in the water and saying how his mum had drowned but *he made it out*; Charlie now knew the rest, even if Chuck didn't remember, or if he wasn't prepared to say it.

But now it seemed almost ridiculous, not remembering those nights; of *course* he recognised Minnie; hadn't he seen her enough times? It was his dad's fucking fault, the man who had first become a stranger, and then no more than an echo of Charlie's past once he was old enough to leave home. That had been just fine with Charlie by then. It was *that* bastard that had made him forget, and it was just another reason to hate his dad more than he already did. He'd long given up on trying to understand his dad's reasoning, trying to fathom how a grown man could blame a child for a simple mistake, and found it a lot easier to hate him instead; even the hate had been forgotten in recent years, the man becoming no more than a dim, seldom-recalled memory, but right now the anger burned inside Charlie. Not that there was much room; the sense of wonder and confusion that filled Charlie was even stronger still.

You've known of her almost all of your life. No wonder the connection is the way that it is, that sense of instant, easy rapport!

How did you forget this?! They made *you forget. It was weird, and they smothered it.*

You were dead. You drowned, you died, they resuscitated you, and they never told you. They never told you!

Did it affect your brain, then? Some kind of minor brain damage that changed your perception?

The Wikipedia page! One of the out-of-body experience causes was drowning! But you didn't remember drowning, so you didn't realise ...

Charlie watched Minnie stroking Chuck's hand, not knowing that the connection was, temporarily at least, broken. He heard the sincere sympathy in her voice, saw the mix of embarrassment, relief and gratitude in Chuck's face and realised something else.

He doesn't know. Chuck doesn't remember either. He's not experiencing this like you are, isn't experiencing every memory more strongly than he ever has before because he isn't aware of simultaneously sharing his thoughts with someone else. *You have to trigger it. You have to make him realise what he's forgotten ... the answer could be in there somewhere, Charlie!*

"Minnie," said Charlie, but it came out as barely more than a whisper, Charlie's throat having dried up as he'd lost himself in his own revelations. He still couldn't believe it; he now knew how he'd begun on the road to The Black Room. He'd seen other worlds as a kid, *wait*, that was right, worlds *plural*, different Minnies and different lives in different points in time with ...

Wait ... there was always a guy with her too, wasn't there? When she was older? There was always *a guy with her, and although you couldn't see him properly he always looked ... familiar ...*

Charlie's whole face went slack.

It was you. Wherever there was a Minnie, there was always another you. In any universe ... you're always supposed to be together.

Charlie sat down before he fell down.

But your Minnie died. And this Minnie is Chuck's. You shouldn't be here.

That was the truth, and it was unavoidable. The thought was full, solid, and heavy with a factual weight that pushed everything else out of the way. The force of it was blunt, and there was no despair, no jealousy this time; it left Charlie utterly numb instead. He saw them together, saw their hands across the table, and although he had first seen Chuck as a rival, and then as an extension of himself, now he also saw completion, and a sad, distant satisfaction. He had to preserve this at all costs. He had to save Minnie's life and allow his other self, the other part of him, to live the life that they were owed. He saw all of this, and felt it click into place. He loved her, and if he couldn't have her, then not only should she be happy, but he wanted her to be with *another* him. Charlie knew that he had a job to do.

"Minnie," Charlie said again, this time with a firmer, more assured voice, his breathing steady. The view jerked just a fraction; he'd surprised her, thinking that Chuck would still be speaking for both of them. "Sorry, I didn't mean to startle you." Charlie was surprised at the clarity of his speech, at the quiet resolve there. "I need you to ask Chuck something for me; I think it might be important." The view bobbed up and down slightly, but Charlie couldn't tell if it was from Minnie telling him to go on or if she was nodding at what Chuck was saying, talking as he was about how he'd ended up in Coventry. "I need you to ask him about *after* the car crash. I know that's gonna feel a bit awkward, but trust me, he won't mind. Ask him if there was any trauma or anything. Trust me on this." He knew she would; she trusted him completely, as he did her. When Chuck had reached the point where he was talking about starting at Barrington's, and paused as if he was thinking what else there was to tell, Minnie did as Charlie had asked.

"Can I ask you something?" she said. "If it's too painful to discuss, you don't have to say, but it's something that worries me a little bit about your story. For you, I mean ... I just picture you as this little kid having to deal with something so big." Chuck smiled a little bit, and shrugged.

"Go for it," he said. "It's okay. You won't upset me. I feel like ..." He trailed off and looked at his wine glass, smiling and toying with it like he'd caught himself saying something embarrassing.

"Like what?"

"Probably shouldn't say it, but then this is easily the most dirty-laundry-airing first date that I've ever been on, so I think I'm not changing the tone at least ... but, well, I feel like I've known you for ages. I feel like you can ask me anything." He smiled, but with a faint trace of worry around his eyes; Charlie then saw it disappear, and knew that Minnie had smiled back.

"Okay," she said quietly, and with great affection. Charlie knew that was for him as well, and it warmed him, made him feel proud ... but not like before. That feeling was already distant, like a memory. It was affection for everything that he was, and that couldn't mean more to him than it did ... but again, he knew that he shouldn't be there. "After the accident. With your mum. Did you ... you must have had some major emotional trauma after that. I just wanted to know how you handled that, what they did to help you." It sounded natural, but then in this instance it probably was; it was perhaps a normal thing to want to know after a story like that. Chuck nodded without a word, and again shrugged, raising his eyebrows in an *ah well* kind of fashion, but the sadness was back in his eyes.

"I think ..." he began, and then paused, staring into the distance, lost in thought. "It would have been worse if I'd *really* seen anything. You know? I mean ... yeah. It was pretty horrendous as it was." He fell silent again, his fingers finding the stem of his wine glass again. Charlie watched, rapt. "If you mean trauma from my mum dying, then yes, of course. It was devastating ... who gets over that, you know? I never did. If you mean the actual crash itself, then I think I was at least lucky in that respect. I remember the car hitting the water ... and I just was going for my seat belt clip straight away, on autopilot almost, just moving without thinking. I thought my mum would be doing the same thing. If I'd known she wasn't ..." He trailed off yet again, and Charlie saw Minnie's hand find his again, almost pulling it off the stem of the wine glass. Chuck smiled sadly, but it didn't reach his eyes, and he didn't look at her. He was back in the river.

"I would have gotten to hers first. I would have made sure of it. I tried to get my door open but it wouldn't go, and then I thought about winding the window down, even when I was panicking. I said Mum, go out the window, and just ... I just assumed that she was doing it! Self-preserving little fuck ..." Chuck smiled bitterly, but his eyes were wet. "I got out, but the car was already pretty much under. I'd made it worse, you see ... I'd let the water in when I opened the window. If I'd stayed in the car and waited for help, it might have been okay. The water might have taken longer to come in. All you could see by the time I made it out to the surface were the tyres, sticking up like a dead animal on its back. I waited for my mum to appear, and she didn't ..."

"It's all right, I didn't mean to get back into the accident, I didn't want to upset you," blurted Minnie, her hand gripping his so hard that her knuckles were white, but Chuck held up his free palm; he was going to continue. Charlie was desperately glad. This was electrifying news.

He got out of the car? He wasn't knocked out when it hit the water? He never drowned?

"No, no, it's probably good for me," said Chuck, sniffing slightly and grinning, his old self returning for a moment. "Although probably not the slickest behaviour on a first date."

"Don't be ridiculous," said Minnie, sincerely. "I asked. But if you don't want to tell, don't. I'm all ears if you do." Charlie nodded, and carried on.

"I swam round the other side of the car, and tried to open her door," he said, eyes drifting away once more. "It wouldn't budge. I thought it was just the water holding it shut, and nearly ruptured every damn muscle in my body trying to get it open. It never occurred to me that it would be locked. I should have gone round to the other side, gone back in through the window, undone her belt, dragged her out ..."

"You were ten," said Minnie, firmly. "There's no way in hell that you can be blamed for not knowing what to do. Do you really think you could have done all that underwater, let alone have the strength—at ten years old—to drag a grown, unconscious woman out through a car window?"

"Even so. I climbed out in a panic and scrambled up the bank, looking for help. I flagged down a passing car—I don't know if they would have seen us otherwise—and two guys came back with me. They looked terrified for me; I can still see their faces."

Charlie leapt to his feet, a fresh memory hitting home. Chuck's assumption was wrong. They *would* have seen Chuck, and Charlie knew that because they saw him in *his* world! He remembered them, they came to the funeral! Jesus, he could even remember their names, couldn't he? A Steve … and John! Steve and John, they were students or something, weren't they? They were the ones that had pulled him out of the car! His dad had introduced them and told Charlie to say thank you, and they'd looked a bit uncomfortable … they'd *known*. They'd known what had happened to him, down there in the water, maybe they were even the ones that had brought him back. But not Chuck … he'd gotten out. Like the football score and the old woman in the house, here was another difference between their worlds, and Chuck knew nothing about The Woman in the Night. But Charlie did.

"They tried to get her out. Eventually, one of them went in through the passenger window. I remember him coming out, having run out of air, and told the other one to take me up to the top of the bank, and to try and find a phone. He muttered something else, I couldn't hear it. Me and the other guy … what was his bloody name … John, I think. I only saw him again at the funeral. We got in his car and drove to the next village and got to a phone. Steve, the other one, he did get her out in the end. I found out later, but … y'know … so I never really saw anything, as I say. I didn't even see her body at the funeral. I blamed myself for everything, and still do in many ways, but the psychologist helped a lot. I saw him for about a year, but it was necessary, I think, even if he was just pretty much repeating himself. It was good to hear. My dad didn't help in the fucking slightest, but that's another story."

Chuck sighed heavily, and looked back up at Minnie, trying to keep his jaw steady. She took both of his hands, and the pair of them said nothing. Charlie thought that she might have been waiting for a further instruction from him, as well as wanting to comfort Chuck. It was strange; here was Chuck, talking about the death of the same woman that Charlie had known, but it didn't have the same effect on Charlie at all; the story was too different to the version he'd experienced. It was almost the complete reverse of the uncanny connection that he and Chuck had shared earlier, this part of Chuck's life so alien to the memory that Charlie had now uncovered. It was just like hearing someone else's sad life story. Charlie marvelled at this; he would have expected it to still be too close to home for him. It was interesting to know, however, that his dad obviously didn't end up any less distant, even without Charlie giving him the extra burden of his son's nighttime weirdness.

"It's okay," Charlie said to Minnie, "I've got what I need. You don't need to quiz the poor bastard any further."

"I shouldn't have asked," said Minnie, and Charlie felt, for the first time that night, that she was talking just to Chuck. It stung a little. "I just worried that you didn't get any help at all. It's so sad."

"A toast," said Chuck, freeing one hand and picking up his wine glass with a smile that looked less forced this time. "To childhood misery."

"Indeed," said Minnie, toasting him, and while Charlie kept an element of restraint, he couldn't help but feel the connection to Chuck drop back into place as he realised exactly what he was going to say next.

"Now, to answer your next question," said Chuck, gently wiping his eyes after sipping from his glass, "eight inches, if I'm really in the mood."

Charlie smiled, despite himself, and Minnie burst out laughing. It was a joyous sound.

***

Soon after, it was time to leave; the restaurant was closing. Charlie had settled back into his previous position on the floor, but it had become more difficult; before, he had allowed himself to be a part of it, doing exactly as Minnie had intended. Now, he had to keep reminding himself to step back, step back, but it had been almost impossible, drawn in by every one of Minnie's responses and feeling Chuck's answers before he even said them. It was an indescribable wrench to tell himself over and over that he wasn't a part of this, however right it felt, and that he was there to save *their* future together, not his. The best way of doing it was to remind himself, again, that he would also save his own skin at the same time, but that didn't seem to matter all that much. He loved her.

Waiting outside in the cold, Minnie had taken Chuck's arm without a word, and they'd huddled together. They'd stayed that way, silent and content, all the way back home in the shared taxi. As it pulled up outside Minnie's block, there was the first truly uncertain moment of the night as Minnie went to get out of the cab; she went to give him a kiss good night, but hesitated. Chuck didn't say a word, and stared back at her. If he had been watching any other man in this situation, Charlie would have felt deeply uncomfortable. As the man in question was Chuck, another version of himself, Charlie was simply as fascinated to see what came next as Chuck was.

"I really, really want to see you again," Minnie said, quietly.

"I want to see you too," replied Chuck. There was a moment of silence except for the metallic thrum of the taxi's engine.

"I'd invite you up, but … it's not that I don't trust you. I just want this to be …" She couldn't find the words, but Charlie nodded, his face serious.

"I know. It's okay."

Minnie leaned forward and kissed him, deeply, and her hands found the back of his head, were in his hair. Charlie couldn't see—Minnie had closed her eyes—but he knew that Chuck would be holding her too. If he was honest, he knew that Chuck would be restraining himself from letting his hands wander further, but he also knew that Chuck *did* understand. Charlie did, after all.

Eventually, she broke the kiss, and Charlie saw Chuck smiling as the view pulled backwards.

"I'll wait until you're inside," he said, and they kissed again, briefly. Their hands stayed entwined until they were at arms' length, Minnie disembarking from the cab, and then she let go as she stepped back and closed the door. All the way to the building, the view panned back and forth from the front door to Chuck's smiling face, seen through the back window of the taxi. Once she'd opened it, she turned and gave Chuck a final wave, and then stepped through the doorway, closing the door behind her with a sigh. She stood in the darkened hallway for a moment, swaying ever so slightly. She wasn't drunk, exactly, but she'd had enough wine for an outsider to notice.

"Charlie?" she said, quietly.

"I'm here," he said, not knowing what to think.

"It's the strangest thing," she said, letting out another sigh and sounding like she was smiling with it. "I've had this ... amazing evening with you, and you've left, but ... you're still here."

Charlie smiled, sadly.

"Yep," he said. "He meant it, you know. He did understand."

"No, *you* meant it," she said, leaning on the wall, the view swinging down to her feet as she pulled off her heels. Charlie didn't have the energy to go into it all, and she *was* mainly correct, after all. "Besides, even after all that ... Jesus, I can't explain it. It's just so fucking *weird!* You're the same, the pair of you, and yet ... well, you're even closer, Charlie. You know everything he does, and he *is* you, and yet we've been through more together ..." She fell silent again for a second. Charlie didn't say a word.

"Charlie," she said. "Where does this leave us? All three of us? I didn't think any further than tonight. It was wonderful, I know that. What's happening?"

Charlie, of course, didn't have an answer.

"Charlie?"

"Yeah. I'm here. I ... well, look. Here's what's going to happen now. You're going to go upstairs, and get into bed, and you're going to go to sleep. And I'm going to be sent home when you do. And the next time I come back, we're going to try and figure this out some more. I learned a little bit about the differences between me and Chuck tonight, but now isn't the time to go into it; you're tired, several sheets to the wind, and this can wait until tomorrow. Okay?" He sounded more assured than he felt; he thought that maybe he'd picked up a few things from Minnie in the pretending stakes. It occurred dimly to Charlie that this was now *his* last ten percent.

"Charlie?"

"Yep."

"You feel it too, don't you? It's impossible, and it's weird, but ... right? You do?"

His head felt light, his limbs airy and weightless.

"Of course I do. Completely."

He meant it.

"I think I love you, Charlie."

But she isn't yours. She isn't for you.

"I love you too, Minnie."

You can't say that.

But he had.

"Okay," said Minnie, almost in a whisper, and neither of them said another word before Minnie got into bed and fell asleep. This time, when her eyes closed, the darkness was light enough to see the walls of The Black Room turn, and as requested, Charlie did not watch her dreams. He sat and thought deep, dark thoughts, and waited for the walls to come together and send him home.

***

Charlie woke up, dazed and bleary eyed. There was no surprise this time, but there *was* relief; he'd known what was supposed to happen when the walls came together, after all, and it had all been a hell of a lot less frightening when he could actually see what was going on ... but even so, feeling the rock-solid surface of the wall behind him and seeing another one getting slowly closer had been unnerving. Feeling the softness of his mattress and duvet against his body was a delight. Waking from being in The Black Room may have only felt like waking from a dream, and it meant leaving Minnie behind for a while, but it was still extremely good to see the reliable and wonderfully normal four walls of his bedroom.

He looked at his alarm clock; it was gone four in the afternoon. That made sense; Minnie got home around midnight, and he'd already worked it out that his world was eight hours behind hers. It was a good job, then, that he was working six in the evening until closing time that day, otherwise he'd have been in some serious shit ... but even then, Charlie found himself thinking that he didn't care even if it *did* come to that. He looked towards the curtain, watched the greyish light that was leaking in through the window.

The two of you were supposed to meet. You would have met in this world at some point, your *Minnie and you. You could have had what you'd seen in your dreams.*

Christ, it was almost unbearably unfair. She'd died because somewhere, out in all the worlds that he'd seen as a child, was another Charlie who'd had the exact same bang on the head, the exact same drowning, had taken the exact same drugs twenty years later that Charlie had. It sounded impossible, but if the worlds were infinite—and with all the possible, microscopic variations that could occur between them all, why should he believe they would be anything *but* infinite—then it was absolutely likely to have happened. Hell, there could be a Charlie out there with the exact same life as

148

his in every way, except that one day one of them had toast for breakfast and the other one had cereal. And that other Charlie, the one in the exact same accident, had travelled between the worlds in the same way that he had, and having that Charlie in his world's Minnie's mind, his *intended* Minnie's mind, had killed them both.

And Chuck had gotten out of the car immediately. He hadn't developed the same abilities, so he was oblivious to all of this, but the poor bastard was going to lose *his* Minnie too if Charlie didn't find a way out of this. Charlie had at least accepted Chuck's role in all of this, and didn't want to see that happen to him. Charlie didn't want it to happen for all the obvious reasons, but now realised that he wanted a happy ending for Chuck's sake as well. He liked the guy—how could he not? Chuck was almost exactly the same person as himself—and the idea of another him being cheated out of a chance with his Minnie was too much for Charlie to think about. His newfound empathy with Chuck was too strong.

He sat up in bed, trying to shake both the cobwebs in his awareness and the self-pity in his heart. Neither of those would do anybody any good, and he couldn't afford to be complacent. As he looked around for his jeans, he tried to get this moving.

Okay, what have we learned? Well, there's—

His train of thought cut off as he caught sight of his phone's screen. There were two alerts on there; one that said *Missed Call* and a message from voice mail saying that he had *1 New Message*. The missed call was interesting; he hadn't put his phone on airplane mode before bed, and it was still set to normal mode. The phone would have rang and vibrated then, and that always normally woke him up. When he was inside The Black Room, then, could he not be brought back to consciousness until Minnie went to sleep? That *was* an interesting possibility ... could that be useful?

He picked up the phone as he mulled the idea over, and called his voice mail, assuming it to be work checking that he was still coming in; he'd called in sick the day before, after all.

It wasn't work. He recognised the voice, but couldn't place it immediately. Once the caller identified himself, his skin broke out in goose bumps and his mind began to race.

"Charlie ... we need to talk. This is Tommy ... listen. I know that you didn't know my sister, I know that you don't know Dave, and I know that you were lying to my face at her funeral."

Tommy.

Christ.

Tommy sounded so flat and direct that it was frightening in itself, even without the things he was saying. Charlie was utterly busted, and he already realised that Tommy would have had to have gone to some trouble to track down his number; this meant he really, *really* wanted to talk to Charlie ... and this was a man whose sister had very recently died. What the fuck had happened then? What the hell did he want?

Fuck ... fucking hell ...

The message continued:

"I've also found out some other things from my dad as well, things that make me extremely keen to talk to you. I haven't called the police yet, because I haven't made up my mind what I think about it all. I'll be honest with you, if it turns out that things have gone one of the ways I think they might have done ... well, I won't be bothering with the police, Charlie, if you get my meaning. And I know people too ... I'm sure you understand."

Tommy sounded capable of murder, his voice so dead and yet ready to snap that Charlie couldn't picture the words coming out of the same man he'd spoken to at the wake, that sad but friendly guy who'd appreciated Charlie coming to the funeral. Charlie found himself wishing desperately that he'd given a fake name. Why the fucking hell hadn't he given a fake name?

"So you want to make it your number one priority to come and talk to me and give me your side of the story. I promise that, when you come and meet me—tonight, six o'clock, at the Burnt Post—nothing will happen. I want to hear you out. I might be wrong, and you might have a proper explanation for all of this, and I might even end up buying you a beer and saying sorry."

There was a pause, and then a snort that was either a chuckle or someone choking back emotion.

"Just be there, Charlie. This might all be completely wrong, but I've stopped giving a fuck about that. Just fucking be there or I'll come and get you, and I won't be alone."

There was the sound of movement, and then the computer voice came back on:

"To repeat this message, press—"

Charlie cut off the voice mail call, dropped his phone on the floor, and ran his hands through his hair. While he didn't know how Tommy had gotten his number, it was obvious how he'd been rumbled; after Charlie had bailed from the wake because Tommy had called Dave over, Tommy would have explained to Dave that Charlie was outside on the phone. *Charlie who?* Dave would have said, and not only that, Charlie hadn't come back again either. But that still didn't explain Tommy's animosity towards him. Yes, it was bit odd that someone would have come to a funeral and lied about their reasons for being there, and then suddenly disappeared as well, but it wasn't like Minnie's death was suspicious or had any foul play involved; Minnie died from a brain haemorrhage, after all, and had been showing signs of severe mental deterioration before that. So what the hell had Tommy's dad said to him to piss Tommy off so much?

Either way, he didn't have much choice other than to go and meet Tommy; not just because the man was threatening him—and Tommy could be bluffing about that, of course—but because there might be some answers there, and Charlie didn't really seem to be getting anywhere with regards to actually *stopping* himself going to The Black Room. One thing was for certain, at least; when he got to the pub, he'd better have a decent explanation for being at Minnie's funeral.

IN THE DARKNESS, THAT'S WHERE I'LL KNOW YOU

***

Minnie's intercom buzzer went off; in a brief moment of confusion, she thought it was her alarm clock.

"Charlie?" she said, without thinking. She'd passed out with him there, after such a wonderful night ... the memory came back, and its warmth replaced the empty feeling that she had upon realising that he was gone. With a smile on her face, the buzzer already forgotten as she started to drift away again, Minnie closed her eyes and rolled over.

Bzzzzzzzzt.

Her eyes jerked open again, this time coming back to full consciousness. That wasn't her alarm; that was someone pressing the call button to her flat. She then registered the lack of light in the room; looking at her clock, she saw the time: *2:13 a.m.* It was after two in the morning? Who the hell was calling now? The area wasn't the nicest, sure, but she immediately began to worry about any smackheads that might be wandering around. She'd never *seen* one, of course, but in the dark, all alone, her mind easily played tricks.

Don't be an idiot. It's not a smackhead, and even if it was there's two sets of doors between outside and up here. It might even be—

She sat up, excited. Might it be Char—Chuck? As she corrected herself, she realised how she'd not used his name at all over dinner, not able to call him Chuck to his face, but not feeling it appropriate to call him Charlie, even though he *was* Charlie ... either way, she threw on her dressing gown and made her way to the intercom by the front door. Had he forgotten something? If it had been anyone else, the thought of someone coming to her flat in the middle of the night two hours after the date had ended would have seemed weird in the extreme, but with Charlie? No chance. She picked up the intercom's handset.

"Hello?" she said, her mouth close to the receiver. She found herself hoping that it *would* be Chuck. Even though she didn't want to rush anything—it would be so easy—she still wanted to hear his voice, to have him near.

"*Minnie?*" said the voice on the other end. It was Chuck; a little jolt ran through Minnie's body. He sound sheepish, embarrassed. "*Look, I'm so, so fucking sorry to be calling on you in the middle of the night like this. I tried your phone, but it was turned off.*"

"It's okay, it's okay ... what's happened?" He sounded so worried that she could almost picture him hopping from foot to foot. Her excitement was replaced by concern.

"*I ... shit ... look, I need to tell you something. It's gonna sound like the weirdest fucking thing in the world, and I'll understand if you never wanna see me again afterwards, but I think it could be really, really important. I wouldn't even tell you any of this, if I didn't think ...*"

151

Minnie froze, and waited for him to finish. She suddenly knew what he was going to say next, even though it couldn't be true.

No WAY ...

Chuck sighed, sounding exasperated with himself, and highly stressed.

"... if I didn't think you'd been having some very weird stuff happening to you, too."

NO FUCKING WAY ...

"Minnie ... fuck it, I'll just say it. Do you have ... have you been having voices in your head? Maybe even one that ... Christ ..."

NO! FUCKING! WAY!!!

"... maybe even one that sounds like me?"

Minnie dropped the receiver, where it bounced off the skirting board with a clatter and hung loosely at the end of the cable. As she stood in her hallway, head pounding and mouth gaping as she stared at the phone in shock, she could hear Chuck's tinny-sounding voice coming through the receiver's speaker.

"Minnie? Are you there? Ah ... fuck, listen, please don't freak out ..."

She grabbed the receiver back up in a flash, and found her voice.

"You ... you'd better come up."

***

Chuck sat on Minnie's sofa, his head in his hands, as Minnie brought him through a mug of tea. He looked up as she came in, and took the mug from her with a sad but grateful smile.

"Thanks," he said, and she smiled in return, sitting next to him and holding her cup with both hands. They were silent for a while, neither of them knowing where to begin; Minnie also had to deal with the unusual feeling of having a man in her home again. She felt like she should be nervous, but with Chuck it was different. Yes, a male presence was strange, but at the same time ... Chuck looked like he belonged there. And she couldn't help but thrill at the feeling of having him close again.

"So ... firstly," Chuck said eventually, looking down at his mug, "I guess this is the most important thing by a long way; *do* you know what I'm talking about?" He looked up when she didn't answer immediately, and the fear in his eyes was almost painful. He *needed* her to understand. Minnie nodded, the movement barely noticeable. She was scared too, this unusual and unknown world—a world that she'd entered only two days ago—now seeming to open up into a vast gulf beneath her feet, one that could swallow her whole and change everything forever. Chuck let out a breath that seemed to take the weight of the world with it, but he didn't *look* relieved; he could see Minnie's fear, clearly, and felt the same himself. He reached out and took one of her hands, and she grasped his back gratefully.

152

"Okay," he said. "Okay. Well … that's a hell of a start." He smiled slightly at her, but the worry was still in his eyes. "Should I … look, why don't I go first, because … well, I think I know a lot of your story, and I'll get to *how* I know that in a second." He looked concerned again, perhaps worrying that Minnie would think he'd been snooping on her somehow, but Minnie didn't think that was true. She'd let him tell her, and then draw her own conclusions. She trusted him completely.

"Okay. You start," said Minnie, and forced a smile for Chuck's benefit. He nodded, and looked back down at his cup.

"It, uh … it started yesterday," he said, his voice faltering, clearly more scared than he'd been letting on.

Yesterday … so maybe after me and Charlie came into Barrington's? Interesting …

"I was on a break at work and was checking my emails on my phone out the back. You'd, uh … you'd come in earlier, and asked about the phone …" He shrugged slightly, squirming on the settee. His embarrassment was clearly at maximum, knowing how much he sounded like a stalker. "I heard Jerry shout something from the kitchen—Jerry's the chef—so I went back inside and asked him what was up … he looked at me like he didn't have a clue what I was talking about. I said that he'd called me, and he said that he hadn't, and I just thought it was some kind of bullshit wind-up, you know? Staff get bored on a slow day, and really have nothing better to do … and I was about to go back outside again when I heard it again, but properly this time."

Minnie wanted to blurt out *heard what* … but she thought she already knew. She gripped Chuck's hand more tightly.

"It wasn't Jerry at all. It was this voice, inside my head, saying *Can you hear me, Can you hear me* …" He looked up at her for a second, and saw her wide, unblinking eyes, checking her reaction. Minnie couldn't do anything but nod, but it was enough to tell him to go on. "I jumped out of my fucking skin," he said. "I asked Jerry how the hell he was doing that, and he just looked pissed off. *Fuck's up whitchoo,* he says. Then I hear it again, and the room just starts spinning as I freak the fuck out. I feel like I can't breathe, and I'm just panicking, and Jerry's looking at me like I'm a nutcase. So I run out of the kitchen and into the disabled toilet, as I feel like I just need to be shut away somewhere safe. I'm not thinking straight, you know? And this voice is still going all the while, and it's freaking out now, shouting *You can hear me! You can hear me!* And I'm shouting at it to shut up, shut up, and eventually it does, just for a bit. I think it was giving me time to calm down. It worked too, I suppose; just when I get my breathing under control and am starting to think that maybe I'd just had some kind of hallucination, it goes, very calmly: *You're not imagining this. Please help me. I'm really scared.* And all of a sudden it's all just *so* crazy that I just give up and say what do you want? And when it replies, it just sounds so goddamn terrified—and *I've* calmed down just enough to actually take in what it's saying—that I find myself listening to it … and we start to talk."

He looked at Minnie again, as if he wanted her to say something.

"Go on," she said, squeezing his hand.

"The voice said that it didn't *want* anything," Chuck said, looking at Minnie. "It said that it had just gone to bed and woken up inside my head, but not *in* my head really, it said that it was in, like a, uh, like a room, hexagon shaped, one with blue walls with these two kind of big windows in one end that were oval shaped, like eyes."

"*Blue* walls?" asked Minnie, interrupting.

"Yeah," said Chuck, looking confused. "Why d'you ask?" Minnie waved her hand, annoyed with herself.

"Doesn't matter, I'll explain when it's my turn. Carry on."

"Okay, okay. Well, she said that—"

"Wait, wait," said Minnie, interrupting this time but not taking it back. "She?"

"Uh … yeah," sighed Chuck, nodding slowly and looking away. "That's, uh … that's the other kinda … dodgy part."

Minnie waited for him to say what she knew was coming next. She couldn't believe it, but she knew it anyway.

"The voice was a woman's," said Chuck, slowly, not wanting to say it but needing to. "The same woman that had come in earlier that day to ask if someone had handed in a phone. The same woman that I took out to dinner tonight … the same woman that's sitting next to me right now." Minnie wanted to put her hand to her mouth, but that would have meant letting go of his. "She said that her name was Minnie," Chuck said, "and that she was scared and wanted to go home."

***

Charlie pedalled harder, his tired legs carrying him and his bike towards the Burnt Post. It was a farther distance than he would normally cycle, and his legs were still aching from the previous day's exertions, but he thought it necessary in case Tommy's promises of an amnesty for their meeting proved to be false; if he needed to get away quickly for whatever reason, he wanted an escape method that was quicker than running and didn't rely on there being a taxi present.

It was only around five o'clock, but he wanted to get to the pub before Tommy. He wanted to make sure that he had a seat near an exit, and with a good view of the front door so he could gauge any possible accomplices that Tommy might send first. He'd thought about bringing some backup of his own, but then thought against it; he didn't want anyone hearing what Tommy might be accusing him of, plus none of his friends were tough guys or, sadly, close enough to be called on for a fight on a random Monday evening. He also—perhaps foolishly—thought that Tommy had been telling the truth about nothing happening that evening. He'd seemed like an upright guy at the funeral, and while he was clearly very upset about *something*, Charlie thought

154

that if Tommy said that this would be a safe meeting, then it would be. After all, if Tommy had managed to get hold of Charlie's number, he probably knew where Charlie lived as well; it didn't hurt to be careful though, and Charlie planned to be *very* careful.

He had his story ready, too; in fact, all he'd done for the last hour was pace the floor of his bedroom, going over and over it in his head, ironing out all of the kinks until he'd got his simple excuse as ready as he thought it could possibly be. It all just depended upon what Tommy had to say, which hopefully wouldn't completely disprove Charlie's story before he even had a chance to say it.

Charlie was glad they were meeting in a pub, at least. He really felt like he needed a fucking drink. Charlie pedalled on, as the grey sky above seemed to grow darker.

***

"Me? You think I've been in your head?" said Minnie, even though she knew that wasn't what he meant. She just wanted him to confirm the unthinkable.

"What? No, no, not at all," said Chuck, putting his cup on the floor and taking both of her hands in his. "Not you, it was … well, I think you know what it was. It was … another you. From somewhere else." His eyes bored into hers, pleading with her to stay with him on this. A thought occurred to Minnie.

"Is she there now?" she whispered, not knowing what she wanted the answer to be.

"No," said Chuck quietly, shaking his head. "We think she comes here when she goes to sleep, but leaves when her body wakes up back … you know. Home. She just suddenly disappeared about an hour ago. That's what happened last time she was here, too."

So his Minnie travels to the Black—no, the Blue *Room when her body sleeps, and not when her host does …*

"Was … was she there tonight?"

Chuck looked away and nodded solemnly, expecting a rebuke from her. She immediately lifted his chin back up to face her directly.

"It's okay … I understand," she said. "You're right. I …" Now it was her turn to feel embarrassed. Even with Chuck, she felt ridiculous saying it out loud, but she still had to say it. "I have another you that comes to me, and talks to me in my head. He was there tonight, with me. He didn't even want to come, at first, because … well, because he was jealous." Chuck's eyes were wide now and there was almost a relieved smile on his face.

"I would have been," he said, nodding, and then they caught a moment together as it lit up between them, and were kissing the next; not a passionate, frenzied kiss, but the tender, mutual reassurance of two frightened lovers comforting one another. When they broke apart, Chuck breathed out through his nose, heavily. "How was he tonight in the end?" Chuck said. Minnie smiled.

"Exactly how I thought he would be," she said. "I couldn't explain it to him at first. I couldn't make him understand that talking to *you* was exactly the same as talking to *him*, and that there was nothing to be jealous of. He totally got it though, once we all got together tonight." She smiled at the thought, but again, another thought struck her. "You? I mean ... well, me, I guess?" Chuck nodded, gently raising his eyebrows and pursing his lips.

"Much the same, I think. She didn't get mad, or openly at least ... she just went very quiet. I knew what was going on, but I also knew she'd understand once I saw you. And yeah ... she got it." Chuck smiled properly now, his hand finding Minnie's once more. "Hell, it was only when she told me her name yesterday, and I remembered your business card, that I recognised the voice! It nearly blew my fucking *mind* ... and when I told her that I'd met you already that day, she went bananas. She wouldn't have it, said that the last time she'd been in Barrington's she'd caused a right scene and had gone running out of the place!"

"Christ ..." said Minnie, gasping slightly.

"What?"

"That's true. I *did!!* And that *would* have been the last time too, if I hadn't been in yesterday, which I wouldn't have been if not for Char—the other Charlie. *Jesus ...*"

So this is what it's like. Knowing that there's someone else living the same life as you ... how the hell did you get your head around this, Charlie?

"I thought I was just going crazy at first," said Chuck, almost chuckling at the memory, more relaxed now that Minnie had confirmed that she understood, that she was a part of it. "I mean, you'd come in earlier, and I thought that you were pretty, and ... well, I'd be lying if I said I wasn't glad that you left your card. I mean ... I took that—rather hopefully—as maybe a little bit of a come-on, if I'm honest. Was I right?" he added with a slight, cheeky grin, shades of the normal Chuck coming through. Minnie raised an eyebrow and smiled, despite the madness of the situation.

"On with the story, please," she said, smirking.

"Okay ... well, I tried to make her prove it; I got her to tell me some stuff I couldn't possibly know, about her family member names, that kind of thing? A quick search on my phone confirmed that it was all true, and that *really* got my attention. I mean, I'd never seen these faces or names in my life, so this *had* to be for real. It didn't make it any easier to properly accept, mind, but at least it was proof. After that ... just talking to her, well, *you* ... once you start, it's amazing what you can quickly get used to. You start off just thinking well, I might as well go with this, and if I'm crazy then I'm crazy. You just accept it, right?"

Minnie grinned, nodding her head.

"I know," she said. "And as for your 'proof' techniques ... I'm not surprised that you did that stuff. You did the exact same thing in my head to try to get me to believe *you.*"

"Fucking hell," said Chuck, shaking his head in amazement. "Great minds ... well, identical great minds, so I suppose that really shouldn't be a surprise ..."

Minnie realised that Chuck had accepted the online proof as all the proof he needed, unlike her, but it made sense. Not only was it Chuck's idea, and one that Charlie had also considered to be enough, but he didn't have all the drug-related-mental-breakdown paranoia that she'd had.

"After that," Chuck said, "I claimed I was sick and went home. I'd certainly put on enough of a display in the kitchen for them to think that there was something wrong. We—me and the other you, I mean—went back and forth for a few hours, theorising like a pair of idiot scientists ... we came up with a few things, and I kept suggesting that we should go and see you, to see if you knew all of this. I mean, *you* of all people turn up—and asking for a type of phone that Mi ... that the other Minnie said she didn't even have—and then later that day I get a Minnie in my head? Too much of a coincidence, right? But she didn't want to yet, she said being around you would freak her out too much. She wanted to go over everything else first, to see if we could figure something out before we went down that route. Plus, she said that the address on the business card you gave me was wrong too, said she still lived at home, and she found that suspicious; she thought you might be trying to lure me somewhere that I shouldn't go."

"Sounds like my thinking," said Minnie. She sighed, feeling a stab from the barbed blade of her old depression even as she noted that the other Minnie lived at a different address to her, just like Charlie and Chuck.

Yep. Loony fucking Minnie, the emotional wreck, terrified by the craziest situation imaginable, and unable to face anything that might tip her even further. I wonder how the hell she managed to not just break down into a big sobbing ball inside his head.

"Christ ... I wonder what the hell she's still doing living at home though?" said Minnie, and for the third time that night, a big thought struck her, and this one was the biggest yet. "Oh my God ... maybe the Minnie in your head is the one from the Charlie in *my* head's world ... we've got to find out if that's true, to get them together, that could be the answer to all of this ..."

Yes, but is that a sting of jealousy you're feeling about that idea? He's sitting right here, *you crazy cow. They're the same person.*

Chuck nodded calmly.

"I did think that this might be the case. That your Charlie and ... wait, I'm getting ahead of myself. I have to tell you how I know about you having ... you know." He pointed at the side of her head, and raised his eyebrows.

"Oh right, yeah, go on. Sorry, I'm getting you off-course, this is all just so much to try and take in."

"I know, it's fine. I'm going off-track myself, to be honest. Well, after a few hours, she just ... left. Vanished. Obviously, I found out the next day that she'd woken up at home, but at the time it was fucking awful. I started to feel like I'd imagined the whole thing, and even worse, if it was true then I'd never know what had happened ... man ... it was just horrendous. I freaked out. Again."

"Me too. I know," said Minnie, smiling at him, letting him know all was well.

"Thanks. I mean ... anyway. I don't have to tell you, you get it. But I had your card; I would have rang that night, but it would have been a stalker-y enough phone call to make at the best of times—I was only supposed to call you if I'd found your phone, remember—but it was late by then and I didn't want to make it seem even worse. So I waited until the next day. She'd said not to call, but as far as I knew she was gone and not coming back, and I needed ... I needed to know, you know? I had to see if there were answers out there. Can you imagine living the rest of your life with an unresolved mystery like that? So I called you the next morning."

Minnie nodded. She knew about that.

"And then, at around the same time as the first time, she came back. I don't know how it is with your guy, but the times for this place and her place are totally different. She'd been here for about four hours, having arrived in the late afternoon, but she'd slept for about nine in her world. That's just fucking crazy."

What did Charlie say the difference was? About eight hours difference between them? So the passing *of time between Charlie's world and here is the same, even if the hours don't sync up ... so maybe it's not a Minnie from Charlie's world? Fuck, how many worlds* are *there?*

"She was pleased, I think. I know I was ... but then I told her what I'd arranged, and she freaked out. I mean, full blown hysterics. Not jealousy, if it sounds that way to you, but scared. She was really scared of seeing another her, saying it would send her crazy. She begged me not to go, but I insisted ... and then she told me about still doing the drugs." He held up a hand. "It's okay, Minnie. We can talk about that another time. I'm not judging you at all."

Minnie was confused for a second; then she got it.

"Wait ... is she still using?" she said. It was Chuck's turn to look confused now.

"You ... you're not?" he said, sounding timid, realising what an incorrect assumption he'd made, and how big.

"No! I've been clean for ages! It was the hardest thing I ever did in my life! I told you at dinner that I was!" It was hard to keep the anger out of her voice, and Chuck kept his hand up.

"Okay, I'm sorry! I just wondered if maybe you were just *mainly* clean and still did recreational stuff or something!" he said, quickly. "You have to remember, I've got a Minnie in my head who thinks she only got there because she tried ketamine for the first time, and most of the time she seems fine, and she's just like you! I thought that maybe you'd glossed over the truth a little at dinner, and I would understand if you had because it's so personal! Be fair, eh?" He shrugged slightly, keep his hands high as if to say *you see my point?* She did.

"Okay. Carry on," she said, holding up her hands too and sighing. She didn't apologise back, though.

"Eventually, she conceded," said Chuck, moving rapidly on, glad to leave the subject behind. "She had to. She'd done the whole Facebook thing on her end, and said that there was another me in her world, but that she'd messaged him and not had a response. She'd been too scared to go into where Facebook said he worked. The only lead we had left was, well … meeting up with you. Which I'd already arranged."

"Was that the only reason you arranged it? To get answers?"

Charlie looked at her and frowned, but his mouth kept smiling. She knew what that meant.

"*Anyway*," he continued, "at dinner, as it turned out, everything was fine, as I've already said. We met up, and … well. you know. But, right at the end … just after we kissed …" He hesitated, trying to find the right words. Minnie sat forward. "She was confused at first … she couldn't figure it out. And I was halfway home in the taxi by the time she realised what had happened. She just seemed to have this eureka moment, like it all suddenly clicked into place." He shrugged again, pointed at Minnie's forehead once more. "She realised that she'd sensed the other guy," he said. "The other me."

Minnie blew the air out of her cheeks.

"Woah …"

"Yeah. I couldn't really freak out back, as the cab driver would have thought I was crazy, but as soon as we were home we started going on about what the hell it all meant. We agreed that I had to tell you, but I didn't want to scare you off in case I was wrong. And then, with perfect fucking timing, she vanished again. I wasn't scared that time. I was just pissed off at the inconvenience of it."

They both chuckled, hands intertwining again.

"And I think I must have spent the last two hours wearing a hole in my carpet, plucking up the courage to come over here and risk ruining the best night of my life by making myself look insane … but how could I not, after the other Minnie had said that? Not only was it an excuse to come straight back, but it would help both you *and* me, we'd both be able to relate to the other about something urgent and crazy. So … here I am." Minnie put her hand to his face, and he trembled slightly, closing his eyes.

"You don't look insane," she said.

"Mm," he mumbled, enjoying her touch, and then opened his eyes. After a second, he spoke. "Do you love him?"

She hesitated. Then:

"Yes. Do … do you love her?"

"Yes. I don't know how it's possible, how any of this is possible, but … yes. It's so right it's indescribable."

"So that means …"

He smiled, breathed heavily, slowly.

"Yes."

His hand caressed her face in return now, the pair of them staring into each other's eyes. Something passed between them, and it was a moment that was nearly seized again, but Chuck stopped it.

"Wait ... wait. There's other stuff to talk about. Coffee. We need coffee, we need clear heads. Right?" He looked at her with a pained expression, as if he wanted her to disagree and say *fuck the fucking coffee, come here*, because he wasn't the sensible one, the practical one; he never was, he was just *trying* to be that way for once because this was all so important. Minnie knew that he was right; they needed to stay focused.

"Right. Coffee. Yes. Go, go. Jar's in the cupboard." She grinned, and gestured away to the kitchen. He nodded, and grimaced slightly, jokingly expressing his disappointment, and left the room.

By the time he came back, Minnie was glad of his idea; her head was spinning so much from all of the evening's revelations that she felt like she *would* sleep if she didn't have some. Would he want to stay? Would she let him if he asked?

Chuck handed her a steaming mug, sitting down and shaking his head. He put his coffee on the floor, and rubbed at his face.

"Well. Well, well, well. This is a fine old load of bullshit, eh?" he said. She chuckled and sat back against the arm of the sofa, sipping at her coffee. It was a moment to relax, a brief respite from the maelstrom of craziness, and the coffee tasted good, if a little more bitter than she liked. Chuck clearly preferred his coffee strong.

"Do you mind if I just have minute to process all this?" she asked, enjoying the moment but meaning what she said. "It's a lot to take in, and I think I need a decent caffeine hit before we continue." Chuck held up his hands again, agreeing utterly.

"I think that's an excellent idea. I know caffeine is supposed to make you more stressed, but I feel like I need it to help get my brain back in order." He picked up his mug in his right hand and rested it on the sofa's arm, and awkwardly gestured to her with his left. "Would you, uh ... do you wanna lean on me?" She smiled and nodded, and moved over to sit up against him, leaning her back against his chest as he draped his left arm over her stomach. Neither of them said another word, and Minnie sighed; she hadn't felt this comfortable in a long, long time.

After a while, Minnie thought that the coffee should have been working; instead, she felt more and more relaxed, and drowsy. She felt that she could quite happily leave everything until morning, and sleep on the sofa wrapped in Chuck's arms. She went to suggest that maybe they should do just that, but all that came out was a murmur. Chuck seemed to notice this, but miss the point; he gently moved her sideways, so that she was propped sitting up against the opposite sofa arm, and then Minnie felt him move away. She opened her eyes. Chuck was now positioned almost identically to her, seated opposite, but with his arms draped along the top of the sofa; one running along the back, the other running along the sofa arm, his fingers gently drumming. He noticed her looking at him, then smiled and rubbed at his top lip.

"Yeah ..." he said thoughtfully, as if he were assessing her. "I think you're about ready. So tell me; how long has that cunt *really* been squatting in your head?"

Minnie tried to register the question, but found she couldn't; her thoughts were sluggish, but even through the fog in her brain she vaguely thought that she should be pretty shocked by what Chuck had just said. She felt nothing, however, and now she found that her arms wouldn't respond properly. She found herself dimly aware of a memory, one of an abnormally bitter coffee, and struggled to sit up, but found that she couldn't; all she managed was a slight wriggle. Chuck saw her body begin to shift, and his smile became a scowl as he quickly sat up; his shoulder shot forward, and his heavy fist slammed into her jaw in an explosion of pain.

***

Charlie chained his bike up outside the Burnt Post, and thought of Minnie; he pictured her fast asleep, alone but happy. In that moment, he envied her. He sighed and walked up the short steps to the door, preparing to wait for Tommy and whatever madness was no doubt coming to him next.

PART FOUR: THE END

"He was tired of the routine. And there was a point where he just kind of gave up. He couldn't face being 40. And he resorted to stimulants. There's a dark side there, a really dark side."
-Priscilla Presley

"From the very fountain of enchantment there arises a taste of bitterness to spread anguish amongst the flowers."
-Lucretius

"There is always inequality in life. Some men are killed in a war and some men are wounded and some men never leave the country. Life is unfair."
-John F. Kennedy

"The closing years of life are like the end of a masquerade party, when the masks are dropped."
-Cesare Pavese

Storm clouds are raging all around my door
I think to myself I might not take it anymore
Take a woman like your kind
To find the man in me.
-Bob Dylan

Chapter Seven: The Other Black Room/Chuck's Story – Part One, A Quiet Un-Relaxing Pint, The Knot Grows, and An Accidental Tip-Off
***

Minnie woke up and didn't know where she was. Almost immediately, the pain in her mouth flared up; what the hell was that from? She tried to put her hands to her face, and discovered that it wasn't possible because they were tied to the back support struts of the chair upon which she found herself sitting. This realisation reminded her of everything that had just happened; confused and horrified, memory struck like a jolt of poisoned caffeine. She let out a gasp of intense fear that was muffled by the ball gag in her mouth.

A ball gag? Chuck, oh Jesus, Chuck, *he did this, he hurt me, how could he do this, what the fuck is going on—*

She realised that she was still dressed, to an extent; she was wearing the vest and shorts that she'd been sleeping in. Even as fear stampeded through her like a pack of rabid, yelping dogs, this thought brought some relief. He hadn't assaulted her sexually, then. The ache in her jaw was doubly intense, due both to the residual pain of Chuck's punch and from keeping her mouth wedged around the ball gag. Her limbs were responding now, twitching away—*drugs, fucking drugs again, he drugged me, what the hell did he put in my drink*—but she couldn't move her arms or legs fully, bound as she was to the chair with something hard and thin. She felt the seat beneath her bare legs, and realised two things at once; one, that she didn't own the solid wooden chair that she was tied to, and two, that she was no longer in her own home. The second of those revelations ramped up her terror even more. As she looked around herself, trying to assess the room she was in, she probed around her lips and jaw with her tongue and almost immediately felt a lance of fresh, stabbing pain as it found an unexpected hole. Chuck had knocked out one of her lower teeth. Her lip was split as well, and the coppery taste of blood was all around her mouth.

Her breathing was rapid as she continued to look around frantically; even in the dark, with the curtains drawn, she could see that this was probably a room in an older building, the low ceiling making her think of a cottage. The sky outside, spotted through the very thin gap at the top of the curtains, was a dark, navy blue as opposed to black. Dawn was only just beginning to think about breaking—it would not be fully light outside for a good hour or two—so the gloom inside was almost total. It looked like there were beams above her, perhaps? It was hard to tell without more light. She thought that she could feel loose old floorboards with her toes, their shape coming through the threadbare carpet—

Is he still here?

Panicked anew, she peered as hard as she could into the dark, subconsciously noting the shadowy clutter around her that was a clue to the life lived in this home. She listened intently for any sounds coming from the rest of the building; she heard nothing.

He could be hiding.

That was true; even if he was gone, she had to get herself under control, had to calm down and think because if she couldn't, she was fucked. Between the pain and the terror and the confusion and the fucking awful, unthinkable betrayal of it all—how could he do this, *why*, how had he been so sincere and, and, and *perfect*—

Please, you've got to get it together. You can't think about that. It can come later. Whatever and whoever Chuck really is, you have to think of a way out of this. Look at what he's done. He's fucking dangerous. He might want to kill you, and at the very least it looks like he wants to hurt you very badly. You're alone, you don't know where you are, and you're tied to a chair.

Did she dare scream? Would there be any point with this gag in her mouth? Plus, she'd noticed a few more things in the dark; a fireplace, a grandfather clock, individual armchairs as opposed to a sofa. The walls weren't flat, and seemed to bulge inwards slightly. It all pointed towards her first guess being correct, that this was an older building, and if that was the case, it meant that the walls were thick and sturdy. Even worse, it was probably at the very least detached. If she was right about this being a cottage or farmhouse, she could be right out in the middle of nowhere. Plus, a scream might bring Chuck running, if indeed he was currently in the building.

Oh Christ, oh Jesus, oh please God help me. I'm so fucking scared. How could he do this, how could he do this, how could he fucking do this—

STOP IT!

She began to cry, despite her own wishes, and her tears were red hot on her cheeks. She realised that she was desperately thirsty, and that realisation made her desire for water, an immediate close second to her desire to be out of the chair. She tested her bonds behind her; what the hell had he used to tie her up? That thin and hard material was digging into her wrists and ankles. She then got it; a plastic restraint handcuff, the thin plastic tie that a lot of US police used on TV. It hurt, and she thought that soon her circulation would be cut off to her hands. She had to think of something before her hands didn't work properly.

What the fuck can I do? What the fuck can I do? Where is he, he's in here somewhere—

With each hand strapped to either side of the back of the wooden chair, a few tests of its sturdiness suggested that it was too solidly built for her to snap or bend out of place. A few more minutes of terrified struggling— flinching at every creak made by the floorboards upon which the chair rested—confirmed this.

Oh Jesus, Charlie, where are you? I need you, where are you—

Wait; was Charlie crazy too? The thought was unthinkable, but then, she'd felt the exact same way about Chuck before ... this. Could Charlie be the same? Could he be the same, and not even know it? He and Chuck were duplicates of each other, weren't they ... she felt sick, and very nearly threw up as she moaned and and lolled around in the chair. The room spun, and it wasn't a residual effect from whatever Chuck had doped her with. It was despair, fear, and almost worse than everything else, it was the devastating betrayal she felt. How? *How?*

"You can't get free, Minnie. Sit still. Sit still and listen, or you'll regret it. You'll regret it. You'll regret it."

Minnie froze, her heart seeming to leap into her throat. Every nerve in her body, every neuron in her brain, was firing at full capacity. The voice she'd heard acted upon her body like an electric shock.

The door to the living room wasn't clicked shut, she now noticed, and instead had merely been pulled against the frame. It was now opening, to display the speaker's outline in the dark. She could now see that there was a distant light switched on somewhere in the depths of the building, revealed now behind the speaker as the door opened, and it cast them in faint silhouette. He'd obviously been standing behind the door all along. Hiding? Listening? Of course he had been. He'd been waiting. Teasing her.

Chuck was standing in the doorway now, framed by it. It was still too dark to see his expression, any effort to do so made harder by the dim light behind that covered him in shadow. She could only see the slow, heavy rise and fall of his chest and shoulders as he breathed deeply in and out. His head hung forward, indicating that he was looking up at her through his eyebrows. She could hear that he was breathing through his mouth.

The crease-free outline of his body told her that he had removed all of his clothes, and Minnie saw—realising that she really *could* reach an even higher level of terror—that in one hand he carried a small paring knife. He slowly raised the arm that held it, cocking his head to one side as he looked her up and down and pointed the tip of the blade at her face from the other side of the room.

"I have some questions," he said, low and deeply intense. There was a tremor in his voice.

***

Charlie looked at his watch. Ten past. Was this all some kind of fucked-up wind-up then? He'd polished off one pint almost immediately to calm his nerves, but had been sitting and nursing a second one ever since, with his eyes on the front door. He'd perched himself at a table that was nicely within a skip and a jump of the fire escape, with his bike initially parked just outside it. He'd then realised the stupidity of chaining his bike up, given the possibility of the need for a speedy getaway, and had subsequently unchained it and placed it outside the nearest window to his seat, where he could keep an eye on it.

He reminded himself yet again that the *real* likelihood of needing to actually 'escape' was quite slim; Tommy would hardly try anything in a public place. Although he'd threatened Charlie quite ominously, there would then be witnesses to connect the two of them if he brought the boys in to give Charlie a beating in a crowded boozer. If Tommy thought that Charlie had really done something to his sister, he certainly would want to handle the business end of things away from watchful eyes, and not in a crowded pub. And it *was* crowded, surprisingly so for a Monday night. An explanation was given when Charlie noticed small posters dotted here and there for a quiz night. Part of his brain made a mental note, despite his nerves. He liked a quiz, and in a desperate yearning for normalcy he decided that if all of the weirdness ever blew over, he'd come and have a go. The thought of all this being 'over'—and everything that might mean—made his stomach turn, so he went back to watching the door.

Earlier, a pair of suspiciously large looking men had entered and made their way to the bar, where they'd been standing ever since. At least twice, Charlie had caught one of them looking at him, upon which the big guy had looked away immediately. Potentially not good. Maybe Tommy really did mean public business ... or maybe their eyes were just wandering about the pub.

The door opened, and this time, unlike the other thirty or so other times it had been some other person or a chatting couple, it *was* Tommy. While the Minnie-like wiry hair was of course the same as the first time Charlie had seen him, his eyes were different. Before, even at the funeral, there had been a

170

brightness, a liveliness about them. Now—just like the hair—Tommy's eyes matched Minnie's, the way that hers had looked when Charlie had first seen them; haunted. They scanned the room, and picked Charlie out almost immediately. Tommy didn't react in any way, and simply began to make his way over, winding through the tables full of quiz teams. His head was slightly down now, making the dark circles under his eyes appear even darker. He clearly didn't want to be seen, didn't want to be connected to Charlie if things ended up … going further. Charlie swallowed, and sat up straight.

He looked Tommy over as the man approached. He hadn't really sized Tommy up before, and noticed now that the genetics shared between Minnie and her brother went beyond the hair. He was skinny, and pale, and a good deal shorter than Charlie's tall frame. Charlie still felt wary; Tommy now looked like the crazy kid at school, the one smaller than everybody else that was still too twitchy to mess with. You knew that kid would go further than you were prepared to, and without a second thought.

Tommy passed the two guys at the bar, and Charlie watched for even a hidden acknowledgment between them; there wasn't one. Tommy reached Charlie's table and locked eyes with him, drawing out a chair without looking at it and sitting down. He was wearing an old donkey jacket, grey t-shirt and blue jeans—a far cry from his funeral suit—and Charlie realised that he had no idea how old Tommy was. Looking at Tommy now, Charlie would have put Tommy at around the same age as himself, perhaps a bit older.

They stared at each other for a moment, Tommy not saying a word, Charlie listening to the blood pulsing in his ears. Every now and then, Tommy would look away, or up in the air, his lips set so hard that they were almost white. It was as if he were either trying to contain his anger, or stop himself from crying. After this went on for an interminable length of time, Charlie decided to break the silence.

"Do you want me to go first?" he asked, trying to sound assured, confident, and succeeding at doing so for the most part. If he was going to try and bullshit his way out of this, he thought that he needed to sound like he knew what he was talking about. Tommy glared at him for a moment, and then theatrically opened his hand and leant forward in his seat, giving Charlie the floor. A scowl briefly flashed across his face; Tommy was furious, but clearly not a man used to being in a confrontation. He didn't know where to begin, which Charlie took as a good sign. If Tommy *really* suspected Charlie of some kind of foul play, or had made his mind up completely that Charlie had done something, he wouldn't be hesitating like this. Maybe the talk on the phone had been some Cooper-brand posturing. Having seen Minnie in action, Charlie could believe it.

"I haven't got a fucking clue what all this is about," said Charlie, as calmly as he could, "or why you're leaving threatening messages on my phone. But you're right about me not knowing Dave, and you're right about me lying about being at the funeral. I can see why—if something bad has turned up—you're going to think I'm involved. But I'm going to tell you the truth, and I can't say any more than that." He took a deep breath before continuing; Tommy's eyes looked red around the edges, like he'd been crying, and they bored into Charlie's. "No, I don't know Dave, that's true, I only know the name. That's why I bailed from the funeral, because I knew he wouldn't know me ... but I also worried that he might know *my* name, thanks to Minnie." Charlie hoped he was pulling a believable face, and maintaining eye contact with Tommy was difficult.

"Dave, he's ... I've been through a lot of changes lately," said Charlie, putting on a good show of squirming in his seat, "and back when I used to hang around with Minnie, she used to talk about him a bit. I thought he sounded like a goody two-shoes, to be honest. She said he was worried about her using, and that I should meet him. I didn't want to, but I kept saying to Minnie that I'd think about it ... I had no intention of doing that, obviously." Charlie picked at the arm of his chair, hesitating before he went into the next part, the part that was most likely to piss Tommy off. It was a fairly audacious lie, but so far he was impressing himself; he didn't know that he could lie this well. But first, he had to go through the build-up.

"Minnie and I were introduced by a ... mutual friend?" said Charlie, acting like he hoped Tommy would take the hint. When Tommy shook his head, annoyed, Charlie deliberately looked embarrassed and said the next part quietly. "Our dealer?" he said, turning his hand.

"What was his name?" said Tommy, quietly. The only part of him that moved was his mouth.

"Everybody called him Sparky," lied Charlie, having thought the name up on the way over. He thought Tommy might want to know more about this fictional dealer, and had already prepared a way out. "I didn't know his real name. I heard he fell out with some bad people a while back and got a major kicking. He moved away after that, and around then Minnie decided to kick the habit, so ... well, I didn't see her very much after that, and I found a new guy to sort me out with whatever I needed." Charlie's heart was thudding so loudly in his chest that he was sure Tommy would hear it, but the man's face was inscrutable. Charlie *thought* that Tommy believed him so far, but the question was whether or not he would want to take things further when Charlie was finished.

"So what was *your* relationship to my sister?" said Tommy, taking a deep breath in through his nose and letting it out, the word *your* dripping with thinly-disguised contempt. Whether he believed Charlie or not, it was clear that Tommy seriously didn't like him. Charlie wondered, yet again, what the hell Tommy had heard from his dad.

"Well, it's kind of awkward to say, you being her brother and all," said Charlie, squirming in his seat again, and for real this time, wary of what he was about to say. The build-up was over; here was the big lie. "After we met one night, we went back to hers, and ... you know." Charlie stared at Tommy, whose hairline moved as he bristled in his seat. Charlie nervously continued. "And after that, we'd either meet up at hers, or mine, and we'd use together, and ... well. We were single, we both wanted to do it ... it was convenient, and we both liked each other, and it was nothing more than that, okay? It was just

172

that, mutually convenient. And then, when Sparky left, and Minnie quit after Dave finally beat her down on it, we kind of stopped seeing each other after that. I mean ... I only heard about the funeral the day before, and ... I had to go." Charlie let out a breath of his own, and nodded as if to say *I'm being honest, like it or not, that's what it is I'm afraid.* Tommy continued to stare at him, his elbow on the arm of his chair, one finger against his mouth. He didn't respond.

"What did you expect me to say to her dad and her brother on the day of her funeral?" said Charlie, pushing it now but feeling the need to seize the moment. *"Hi, your sister and I were friends with benefits and we used to do drugs together, so here I am as a reminder of the darkest side of her life?* I panicked. When you guys asked me how I knew her, I wasn't prepared, I only came over to pay my respects ... I didn't want to be the junkie guy, and I wasn't even sure you knew Dave, so I said I was a friend of his. It was stupid, but I didn't think it really mattered. I certainly didn't expect *this."*

Charlie actually felt a great deal more confident now. He certainly couldn't have performed it any better, and to his ears at least, the explanation sounded completely plausible, even likely. It was all down to what Tommy had to say.

Tommy took his finger away from his lips, and pointed it at Charlie, where it bobbed slightly. He stared at Charlie in silence.

"Let me tell you something then," he said after a moment, neither confirming or denying that he believed Charlie's story. He leaned forward, resting his elbows on the table, his face totally expressionless. "Let me tell you what my dad said to me."

***

Chuck slowly walked over to Minnie's right, never taking his eyes off her. She watched as he moved past her, walking over to a small dining table behind her that she hadn't noticed. He picked up another chair. There were only three still around the table, and Minnie realised where her own chair had come from. Her breath came in rapid, hyperventilating gasps around the edges of the ball gag. Where the fuck was this? Chuck carried the chair across the room, and placed it about five feet away from where Minnie was sitting. He moved slowly and steadily, as if he was stalking her even though she was completely at his mercy. His breathing was steady but heavy, inhaling and exhaling through his nose. He sat down slowly in the chair, regarding her for a second, and then he raised the knife again. Though he was well out of striking range, Minnie flinched. Chuck wagged the blade, then turned it back and forth in the air.

"Is he back in there yet?" Chuck said, quietly. Minnie knew who he meant. She shook her head rapidly, her eyes pleading. The rubber straps of the ball gag, pulled tight across her cheeks, were already slick with her tears.

Chuck leaned forward, resting his forearms on his knees, but keeping the knife pointed at Minnie. It had a relatively short blade, and looked nasty and vicious to Minnie's terrified eyes. It was perfect for jabbing and gouging, its short blade and handle allowing for fast action and plenty of torque. Minnie didn't own a knife like that. "You mustn't lie," he said, nodding slightly, his expression hard to see in the dark. "I'll know if you lie. I can find out." He raised the paring knife and tapped the flat of the blade against the side of his head. "Charlie knows things," he said, his voice flat and lifeless.

You're not Charlie. You're not fucking Charlie!

Or is this Charlie? Is this what Charlie really is, too?

He leant back again, watching her, and scratched at his upper thigh with his fingers.

"I'm going to take the gag off," he said. "I'm going to take the gag off, and you have to stay quiet. If you *don't* stay quiet, I'm going to take this," he held up the knife, "and I'm going to stab you in your eyes, then I'm going to bury it in your throat. Do you believe me?"

She nodded, rapidly. He returned the action, slowly, and then got up and made his way round to her chair, undoing the gag at what felt like arms length. He slipped it off over her head, and while the relief in her aching jaw diminished, the movement set off the nerve in her punched-out tooth and she bit back on a scream. Chuck moved around to the front of the chair once more, keeping the tip of the knife pointed in front of her face, standing again at arm's length.

He suddenly jabbed it towards her. The point came frighteningly close to her eyes, and Minnie let out a gasp of terror ... but it wasn't a scream, and the blade didn't connect. She'd passed the test. Chuck wagged the tip of the blade at her, and sat down once more, again not taking his eyes off Minnie's face for a second.

"Questions," he said, laying the paring knife across one of his thighs. "Remember; honest, now. I really, really need to know a few things, as there's a lot here that's new to me, and I don't understand it. I need to know what's going on with this guy ... he worries me a lot. I can check, you know. I can check if you're lying."

Charlie? He means Charlie?

"Charlie?" she whispered, frightened to speak but needing to know. Her voice was barely audible, so terrified was she of reaching a noise level that Chuck would deem too loud.

"Yes?" replied Chuck, darkly.

"No ... I mean ... are you talking about Charlie ... in my head?" Her voice shook, and Minnie hated the weakness in her voice. She was a victim again, it seemed, and worse than she'd ever imagined possible.

Think, girl. Come on. Please.

But she was scared out of her wits.

Chuck raised a finger, slowly, and pointed it towards his chest. The gesture was deliberate and threatening, and Minnie knew that she'd said something wrong. She nearly wet herself.

"*I'm* Charlie," he said, and his voice was low and threatening. "Not him. He's a fake. He's a fraud. He's nothing. He's a trespasser."

"Yes, yes," babbled Minnie. "You're Charlie, you're the only Charlie. He's … fake, yes, he's fake, I'm sorry, I'm sorry." Fresh tears spilled out onto her soaking face, and she tried to keep the sob out of her voice, but she couldn't help it as she verbally betrayed the man she loved. She wanted Charlie, *her* Charlie.

He's not here! You have to rely on yourself, so get it together! You have to!!

Chuck pointed at her again, with just his finger this time.

"Don't do that again … " he said, the end of the sentence rising slightly. Minnie understood exactly what would happen if she did.

"I won't, I won't, it was a mistake, I'm sorry." She was sounding like a madwoman, rattling her words out so fast that they almost slurred together, spittle and tears and blood mixing on her lips. "Where … where is this?" Chuck nodded.

"Doesn't matter. And that's correct, it was a mistake, " he said, and cocked his head, as if he was trying to look inside hers. "He isn't in there … is he? You're telling the truth … I *think* you are. Can you ever tell the truth? Are you even capable? Either way it's hard to tell from here. Maybe I should go in there. What do you think?

A thought occurred to Minnie, and it was so startling that she started to ask it … but she stopped herself. Not before she'd drawn in a giveaway breath, however; Chuck saw it, and picked the knife up, wagging it.

"Go on," he said, his head jerking back the other way. His head movements were birdlike now, sudden and twitchy in comparison to those of his body. Minnie swallowed. She couldn't say *it's nothing,* as he wouldn't buy it—and if what he was saying was true, lying was pointless—but on second thought, what she had to say was a safe question anyway. Wasn't it?

"Is she … is *she* in there now?" she asked, her voice shaking terribly. She had to know. The thought that there could be another her trapped inside him, or even worse, one that was like *him*, was extremely difficult to think about. But she had to know. Chuck seemed to be taken aback by the question, sitting slightly more upright in the chair as if he were confused. The moment then passed.

"*Ohhh* …" he gasped, finally getting it, and then burst into uproarious laughter, actually slapping his naked thigh with his empty hand as he did so. Minnie shuddered in her chair. "Oh, *Christ* no," he said, gasping out the words as he cackled gleefully, his head thrown back. "No, no, no. That's just … no. Sorry, I forgot about all that. Oh, that's funny. That's … oh, that's classic." His laughter subsided, and then he fell very quiet as he began to slide the edge of the knife's blade along his other thigh in a shaving motion. This went on for some time, Chuck seeming to be entranced by the movement, or the feeling of it. Minnie didn't dare disturb him. When he finally did speak again, he didn't look up, and his voice was airy, almost as if he were half asleep.

"*That,*" he said, cocking his head again and watching the metal glide up his leg, "was all a load of bullshit, I'm afraid. No Minnie. Not in here. I suppose

I'd better explain, really. I'm in no rush. I want to take my time, anyway. I've decided that I'm going to let fate decide my course of action. The problem *is*, you see, that I just can't make up my fucking *mind* about the best way to go about this ... and I have two options. Neither of which, it has to be *said*," he shrugged as he said it, "goes very well for you, but then, that's the whole point. It's just a case of which is the best for dealing with ... *him*. And, you know, I just *don't* fucking know. This is all totally unprecedented, and if I knew all of the rules then it'd be fine, but only have a thin idea at best. Typical of you, Minnie. Typical of you, fucking everything up. Fucking bitch. Fucking *bitch*. Why can't you just tell the truth? The Queen Of The Liars. The Queen Of The Liars." He spat at her then, and Minnie flinched, biting down on a scream in such a way that it made her sound like a startled dog. Chuck laughed, and leapt out of his seat to stand upright, cackling and hunching over like an excited crowd member at a fight. He drew his hand back to strike her, and Minnie flinched, but then he stayed there, hand held in the air, trembling slightly. Minnie re-opened one eye, and saw him frozen like that, breathing heavily, as if undecided, and then he sat back down with a gasp. Minnie remained where she was, pressed as far back into the chair as she could be without knocking it over.

"You'll keep. You'll keep," said Chuck, nodding and breathing heavily through his nose, moving his head up with each breath.

What ... what the fuck was that?

A part of Minnie's subconscious put a few things together, and let her know.

Look at where he's sitting. How far away he is. He didn't touch you then, and when he took the gag off you it felt like he was standing at arm's length ... is there a reason? He's not certain about something, is he?

Minnie was still beyond terrified ... but a part of her was watching, assessing. If he wanted to take his time, that was good, because it gave *her* time. And that meant she still had a chance ... but Chuck was clearly massively unhinged, and she had to be *extremely* careful. If he was wary of something, that was good, but it didn't mean he wasn't crazy enough to bypass his own boundaries.

Try and stay calm. Try and stay calm. Keep it together.

But then she looked at the knife, and thought of her situation and what he had threatened to do, and knew that keeping calm was easier said than done. Chuck leaned back on the chair, his eyes still on Minnie, and blindly felt around behind him. He eventually came across that which he clearly knew was there: a lamp. He turned it on, and the gentle-glow bulb provided enough light to see by, but it only barely illuminated the room.

It lit the left-hand side of Chuck's face though, and to see it almost made Minnie start crying again. There was no trace of the man she'd eaten dinner with there, no pity or remorse. His face hung slack except for his top lip, which was curled into a slight sneer, making him look like a dull preacher of hate. His eyes were dead and unfocused as they regarded her, but she knew he was watching intently, and that she shouldn't take his dazed-looking expression as a sign of witlessness. It was more like there was so much hate and anger behind those eyes that his face had given up on trying to express it.

"No, there's only one Minnie here. Only one Minnie I'm concerned with," he said, and pointed a finger at her, cocking his thumb like a pistol's hammer. He dropped the thumb onto his hand, and recoiled the finger like he'd fired it. "*You,*" he said. "You, the bitch, the fuck-innnng bitch, the Queen." Only his mouth moved when he talked, as if it were disconnected from the rest of his face. He continued to lean back on the chair, rocking it slightly, staring at her. "So yeah. I like this story. I'd like to properly spill my guts. Then I'd like to properly spill *your* guts, a-ha. Always a good one." He let the chair drop forward, and as it landed he fell forward with it, hunching right over in his seat, his chest touching his thighs. He looked up at her and grinned grotesquely. Again, the movement of his mouth didn't reach his eyes, while they showed that he was completely insane. "*Hnnnnnnnnnn,*" he said, and it was deliberate. It was for her benefit, goosing her. It worked; Minnie flinched like she'd been poked in the ribs. Chuck giggled, and sat up.

"All bullshit," he said, folding his arms and sitting back. "All bullshit. No other Minnie, all the other stuff, all bullshit, bullshit. I think you were foo-ooled, Minnie. I think so. I'll never know for certain, of course. You're the expert. But imagine that, if I did? The Queen Of The Liars, beaten at her own game."

What other stuff? And I'm The Queen Of The Liars? What the fuck?
Let him talk. Stay calm.

"I'll start at the beginning, shall I?" he said, looking away to the clock on the wall. "Plenty of time, I think. It should have worn off by now, but maybe there's some kind of residual effect? Who knows? But plenty of time, I'm sure. Doesn't matter if it turns out otherwise."

The drug? What did he drug me with? A residual effect on me? I don't feel drugged any more. Just scared out of my goddamn mind.

"Either way, it works out okay. Not for you, though."

Minnie said nothing, sitting trembling in her chair.

"I didn't get out of my mother's car, of course," said Chuck, sighing slightly. "I died in there. Did the *faker* tell you that, too? Even if he didn't, the same thing must have happened to him. It *must* have done. He's here, after all. How else could he be here? Maybe he doesn't even know it. But he died too. He must have died. And like me, he must have been brought back by a helpful hero or heroine or trained doctor. And like *me,* he must have been dead long enough to come back ... *different.*"

***

Generally, the human brain will not reach full recovery if resuscitated after more than three minutes of clinical death. It can happen, but it is uncommon. After pulling the boy from the car, Steve tries fruitlessly to resuscitate him while John goes for an ambulance. No-one knows it—as no-one could know how long the boy had been unconscious underwater—but by the time the ambulance arrives, Charlie has been clinically dead for four minutes.

Meanwhile, the other *Charlie, in* his *world—Chuck—due to Steve spilling the tea from his thermos in his lap while driving, and having to pull over to sort himself out, making them reach the bridge and the overturned car in the water later than they otherwise would have—has been clinically dead for six.*

No-one knows, therefore, of the minor medical miracle of Chuck's almost instantaneous recovery, least of all him. He gets headaches, and a lot *of them, almost every hour, and some so blinding that they make him want to curl up into a ball and cry, but he keeps them to himself. His dad is* not *to be bothered, he knows.*

He overhears the conversation in the toilet at the wake, and for Chuck, something clicks; he knows that they're talking about him. *He thinks about this, and wishes that he* was *really dead. Then he would be with Mum, and he wouldn't feel so sad all of the time. A little part of him dies inside.*

Then he starts to see The Woman In The Night, and during those times, all is well. At first, he simply finds himself in the same room as her, and each time she's different, but then things move past *that. Things get so much bigger than that, and quickly, and at first it's a huge amount for his young brain to understand.*

One night, he sees two of her. Two moving images of her floating before him, like TV screens made of clouds. To either side, and above and below those ethereal images, he can feel that there is something else too ... he just can't see *those, try as he might. The images he* can *see are blurry, and the features of the people in it are hard to make out (as always) but one of them shows the Woman with a child. The Woman is dressing her daughter for school. The other is The Woman at school age herself, at Chuck's age. While seeing a vision of The Woman In The Night is normal for him now (it happens every night after all) seeing* two *of her like this, seeing these two undulating shapes—like dreams compressed into selectable boxes—is wonderful. Laughing, he reaches out to the younger Woman, more drawn to her due to her similar age, and finds himself disappearing into her image, pulled through the screen and into her world; now he finds himself seeing her the way he normally does, with Chuck circling the room like a ghost, experiencing the Woman's life, filled with its warmth. He always struggles to hear anything properly; on many nights, he barely even catches a single word.*

Chuck wakes the next morning, breathless and excited. The next night it is the same again; two cloudy images to choose from, a sense of something else around them, and before him is a teenaged Woman arguing with her dad (Chuck will take her side. He always does, even if he can't hear the argument) and a slightly older, university-aged Woman, becoming stressed over her revision. Chuck makes his choice, and again disappears into one of the Woman's worlds for a night of escape.

At the christening, Aunt Sarah comes to him, asks how he's doing. Chuck nearly tells her the truth, but thinks better of it; this new development in the night-times, this new way of entering the Woman's world, speaks of a growth. He is changing, he thinks, as he grows older, and there is more development to be had. Whereas before, it was his lovely little night-time escape, one that he had grown to see as normal in his own, child's way. Now he thinks otherwise. There is more to come, something big, *he thinks.*

"I'm fine, thanks," he says, and gives her a hug. He means it. He loves Aunt Sarah.

Time passes, and Chuck's night-time world grows. Soon, two images become three, becomes four. By the time Chuck is thirteen years old, he can see up to twenty-six different images—twenty-six different worlds, he now knows— before him, and knows that there are still more to be found. He can feel the rest of them, as always, above and next to the others, just out of sight. He wonders how many there may be in total, or even if they have an end at all; the thought both thrills and terrifies him. They are slightly clearer now too, the world around the Woman coming more into focus, even if it will never be quite *right. It's always hard to see, all of it blurry ... except her. One night, the one word he hears is her name: Minnie. It is a revelation. He will not hear it again for many years.*

His night-time adventures have, in many ways, enabled him to cope with the daytime world, providing a comfort that his father does not or cannot. That's fine by Chuck, although sometimes he does become sad when he remembers the way that things used to be. Those days feel like they happened to someone else, but Chuck just gets on with things. His dad buys the food, pays the bills, and drives him where he needs to go; he fulfils his practical responsibilities, and Chuck takes his comfort from his friends as much as he can. When Chuck develops into puberty, another element enters the worlds of The Woman In The Night: desire. Whereas before, The Woman was a form of comfort and warmth—her presence soothing to Chuck—now the teenager-to-twenty something versions of her have an effect on Chuck that he at first finds confusing, then pleasing, then frustrating. In the worlds where she is near or past his mother's age, however, Chuck is still young enough to see her in that role. There is, as there has always has been, a familiar, hard-to-see man in all of the older Minnies' worlds, and he makes Chuck feel guilty for some reason. If only he could see him more clearly, learn his name, because an idea has started to form in Chuck's mind, a suspicion, and he knows that it is dangerous. It is a very, very dangerous thought that he can't allow himself to think about. The night worlds are separate. They've always been *separate. That knowledge is all that allows him to view his waking life as separate from his sleeping one. The idea of allowing the two to cross over, to even consider it ... it makes him shake, even the very concept of it. He is even sick once. It's too thrilling, too mind-blowing. He pushes the thought away, smothers it.*

It can't be true. It can't be true.

The presence of the young adult Minnie becomes a frustration that is almost too much to bear. In his night-time state, he doesn't have a body, just an awareness, yet despite the absence of hormones and male anatomy, his mind still knows how to be aroused, still remembers. It's a torment, but he has become an addict. Afterwards, when he awakes, he masturbates furiously, a strange sense of shame following immediately after doing so. He begins actively avoiding the worlds where she is older, nearer to his mother's age, feeling awkward at the idea of them, but that is becoming easier and easier; by the age fifteen, he has a nightly choice of over fifty worlds. They are all different, every night, and Chuck begins to think that it's not the world, but his perspective upon them that is changing, as he seems to see them from a different point each time he sleeps.

His school grades aren't as good as they were, Chuck being more interested in girls and having a laugh with his few friends than his education. They find him a little strange, he knows, but he is at least accepted as part of the group. The Woman In The Night is a separate part of his life, and now as normal and expected to him as waking up each morning; he isn't interested in actual relationships with the girls around him—after all, how could they compete—but like every young man, he is more and more interested in sex. When he loses his virginity at sixteen, he enjoys it, but he can't help picturing the young woman versions of Minnie as she does so. He feels guilty about it afterwards, feels that he has been unfair to the girl he's slept with. She's one of his few female friends, after all, and it was only a combination of mutual physical desire and experimentation, but she deserves better than that. He lies with her afterwards, strokes her, talks to her, wants to let her know that she has his respect. She finds his words odd. He can't help imagining how it would have actually been if it had been The Woman In The Night. Chuck's confusion grows, and a little knot inside of him tightens up and threatens to grow as well.

When he realises how he has to improve his schoolwork if he wants to go on to do his A levels and then university, Chuck knuckles down. He's not too sure what he wants to study, but he is sure that he wants to live the university life. There will be girls there, and he wants to meet more, as he has begun to have a sneaking suspicion, that old, dangerous idea that is so glorious and bright and tempting but terrifying and all-encompassing that he becomes light headed and dizzy that if he should even consider it ... but it won't go away. He knows that if he lets it take hold, then it could be the end for him, and so tries again to tuck it away in a little corner. But now it is getting harder and harder to forget that it's there; the Woman's world is easier to see than ever, and the suspicion is starting to become a solid knowledge that he must deny for the sake of his own sanity. Just as Minnie's world is clearer than ever now, the man in it is often even more so. It has to be true. If only the sounds were better, if only he could hear the man's name just once ... he continues to smother it, but it is growing, as is the knot inside him.

At night, there are over seventy worlds now, and Chuck is beginning to be interested only in the Minnies in their twenties, the teens having less appeal. He sees himself as a man, after all, and less of a boy. The mother/lover confusion has all but left him. For the first time in a while, as he enters one of the older Minnies' worlds, he sees her shower. It's not the first time he's seen her naked, of course, but this really is a woman, after all, not a girl. Part of him feels like this is spying, an intrusion, but the majority of him feels that this is nothing of the *sort. He knows her intimately now, her most shared secrets, or at least those that she says out loud. He didn't ask for this, he reminds himself; he sees her when he sleeps, and has no choice about it. He has seen her future husband and lover (and there is that suspicion again, more than a suspicion,* IT'S OBVIOUS, ACCEPT IT, *but he pushes it away as he knows that to do otherwise would be to risk everything) but doesn't see him as a rival, somehow. He knows that he is an interloper (*NO YOU DON'T, YOU KNOW THE TRUTH, ADMIT IT*) and tries to tell himself that he is lucky to be here at all. He watches that Minnie shower, and the frustration becomes unbearable. He wants to wake up so that he can fix it, but he can't. As ever, he has to watch, and wait. The knot grows.*

He passes his GCSEs, begins preparations for his A-levels. Then one night he watches Minnie and her husband in their bedroom.

He has seen Minnies with other men a handful of times over the years, but this is the first time in a while. He is past the point of worrying about the decency of seeing any Minnie naked now. He is glad to watch, but frightened of what the experience would do to him, whether he could handle it, especially with this *man. This is not just some university lay, some drunken, excited teenage fumble, an ill-advised screw in an alleyway outside a nightclub. This is this Minnie's lover, her future husband, and the meeting of the bodies in front of him is not occurring only in lust, but in love.*

It's too much, but he's made his choice now, picked this world, and he can't take his eyes away until his physical body awakes. He hears her moans of pleasure, watches her small, bare breasts as she arches her back, and if he had a mouth he would let out a moan himself, one of pain. Minnie is clear to his eyes; she's always clear, the one thing that's always clear in these worlds. He hears the man gasp, her husband, her partner for life, the one that is always there in all of the worlds, and watches his blurred hands roam over her body, clutching at her hips and pulling her onto him, pulling himself into her. Rage, frustration, lust, jealousy, all boil within the spectral essence that is Chuck in that room, and at the worst possible time he hears Minnie speak with clarity, catches the one word that he thought *might have been said so many times but he never dared to believe, confirming and freeing the devastating truth that he has been denying for too long:*

"Charlie, oh Charlie..."

It is like a bomb has gone off inside Chuck's head. It is devastating, and it tips him over an edge that he has been walking precariously along for years. Here is truth, undeniable, suspected and desired and yearned for and terrifying in its implications in so many worlds now (the worlds at night are now well over a hundred) and knows that he cannot tell himself otherwise anymore, it's undeniable, they even have the same fucking name *so why does he even pretend to not know it.*

The mouthless presence that is Chuck manages to scream to himself THAT'S ME, THAT'S FUCKING ME *and he knows that he is in big, big trouble. The now paper-thin wall between his day and night existences has been torn apart, and he is left with the knowledge that in every world Minnie finds him, or he finds her, and yet in* his *she has not yet appeared. He has to live with the knowledge that because he* should *meet her, he somehow has to function normally and still make sure that it happens naturally, organically ... it seems almost impossible, and worse, it's the thing that he wants with every fibre of his being, a lifetime of unattainable obsession now revealed as, in theory, attainable.*

All of these other Charlies he has seen with her, none of them seem to have lived the night-time life that he has; they don't worship her, don't fall down dead at the mere fact of her being able to touch them, have never spoken of their past adventures in the night. Chuck has to confront the terrible reality that, in all of the worlds, he is unique. He is the only one that has spent half of his life worshipping at the altar of The Woman In The Night, and he has already become a very, very different person to them as a result. Different to the men that the Minnies love.

He has to live with the knowledge that, had his nights have been normal, he would *have eventually met The Woman In The Night, married her, spent a lifetime with her, an existence almost unimaginably blessed to Chuck's mind. He has spent years telling himself that it's alright, that he is only seeing a life that he cannot have, that he is lucky to be even seeing her; now he knows that it is a possibility that it could be his after all, and it is a terrible burden. It is the burden of knowing the path that he needs to walk, knowing the risk of the ultimate loss should he fail, and worst of all, knowing that he is* not the man he is supposed to be ...

The terror of failure is too much for Chuck. This is the ultimate performance anxiety, the ultimate choke. Another man might sit back and think amazing, I can have her after all, and let it happen, *but Chuck knows that he is different. And even in all of his nights of observation, he cannot piece together how it* should *happen yet. He can't follow a script that he doesn't fully know, and in the process of trying to do so he might ruin it entirely. It's not even just a question of finding her—that could be easy—but of finding her in the* right *way, and at the* right *time of her life.*

He knows that he is not the Charlie Wilkes that he should be. *He has indulged too much, observed too much, obsessed too much, allowed himself to be cocooned in it. He should have told Aunt Sarah, should have even told his father. They could have helped him stop it.*

And worst of all, Chuck must live with the knowledge that he will be obsessed with finding her and meeting her, correctly, at the right time, with the possibility *of having her or losing her, for every conscious and unconscious minute of his adult life.*

He drops out of school, quits his A-levels. What would be the point of staying? It would only be a distraction. He knows he doesn't meet her at university anyway; he's seen a lot of university times with her and hasn't seen himself during any of them. He knows they don't even meet immediately after *university either, for the same reasons; in all of the worlds, Minnie is never with him until what looks like at least her late twenties. He's caught their age difference twice, on times when it's her birthday and they tease one another— they do this relentlessly, playfully—that she is four years younger than him.*

Charlie decides confidently that any time from his current age of nigh-on eighteen until at least the age of twenty-four is safe; he doesn't need to worry about missing their meeting until after then. She will be twenty then, and he has definitely seen her as being older than that, in countless worlds, and single. But the wait, the unbearable wait...

He will throw himself into his work. Into planning.

The first thing he does is buy a notebook. He spends three days noting every relevant fact that he can think of, the things he already knows to be universally true about her. Despite nearly eight years of observing various periods of her life, there is less concrete information available to him than he'd like. The night-times' complete lack of clarity make it difficult to take everything in, but there are things he notices, single words that come through, and in such a way there are many things that could be put together. However, even those details tend to be lost the next day, like a dream that had vivid parts at the time but remembered only in glimpses later. He wishes fervently that he'd always taken notes upon waking...

The facts that he is fairly sure of are the ones that he has seen or heard the most repeated examples of, the ones that seem to occur in most, if not all of the worlds. He begins to write them in his notebook, the notebook that will become so utterly precious to him over the years. One fact is the most important of all:

Minnie lives in Coventry. Eventually, he must move to Coventry, once it nears the time that he and she should meet.

He gets a day job in a plastic manufacturing plant. He took the first thing he could get. As long as it pays the bills and lets him keep his head down in the day, he's happy. He gives his dad some rent out of his first pay packet, and his dad takes it without a word. Again, it's all fine with Chuck. As long as he can stay focused, quiet, and above all, calm, *he's okay. If he can keep a lid on it, he's okay.*

The nights come, and they are his real *life. Everything else is just maintenance. He finishes work, and the time before sleep is either spent trying to disconnect as much as possible, distracting himself with pornography or video games, or in planning, tweaking and refining his notes, honing either that which he already has or trying to figure out where the new bits fit in, deciding whether or not they're something he hasn't seen before.*

After all, he enters her worlds every night; though the audio has slowly gone from being almost non-existent to extremely patchy in the past, nowadays it has become clearer than it has ever been, the breakthrough of hearing his name seeming to open a floodgate, a new connection to the worlds forming. That, in addition to his increasing age—he's always gotten steadily better at seeing and hearing the worlds as he ages—means that by the age of nineteen, he can overhear fifty percent of what's being said, and his confidence in his sacred notebook grows. How many countless occasions would he have the opportunity to hear a deeply loving couple discuss their history, even if it is in broken sound? He knows it's all there for him to piece together; he just has to write as many notes as he can, no matter how minor they might be. Every time he hears something new, he will remember it, note it down upon waking. He has years to work it all out, to make sure it happens, to make sure that his awareness of what should *happen won't ruin its chances of it* actually *happening.*

By the age of twenty, inside two years of starting the notebook, he has it; they always meet in a bar in Coventry, at place that he apparently works. He doesn't have its name...

But what, *his brain asks him, worrying and panicking as usual,* if your world doesn't quite follow that rule? You've had it confirmed several times, after listening to their stories and hearing their loving reminiscing ... but what if it doesn't happen that way for *you?*

He can't think about that. He has to get his head down, to press on, and the knot inside him continues to grow. It can never be undone, now.

Just before his twenty-first birthday, he confirms—after hearing it for a sixth time, as this is too big to be sure of from just one hearing—that they meet in 2014. Later than he thought. An extra two or three torturous years of waiting on top of what he already feared enduring? He grits his teeth, and reassesses. He still intends to be there long before 2014, to be safe ... but not too long. He can't meet her too early. She might be there already. She has to be the person she is at that age that they should meet, the person that will love him.

But you're not the person *you* need to be. You never will be. You've seen what none of the others have.

The other thought comes:

You might as well go now. You could find her, even if she isn't in Coventry yet. You could hire a detective, *they* could find her, even if you can't. Why waste all those years that you could be together?

And he wants to, so badly ... but he can't risk it. She might not be ready. He weeps at night, before sleep, with the frustration of it all, claws at himself and leaves long welts in his skin. He's found that he's started humming without realising it. He notices people staring at him on his way into work. He doesn't care ... but then realises that it might draw unwanted attention to himself, and so he tries to stop it.

By the age of twenty-two, he has managed to satisfactorily confirm the name of the bar where they will meet: Barrington's. He looks it up. It doesn't exist. Yet, he reminds himself. Bars open and close all the time. He'll keep checking. There's years yet.

It occurs to Chuck, during one of his more lucid daytimes, that the worlds can't be infinite. He sees over three hundred of them now, at his last count, but there's too many similarities for there to be an endless number; if they were infinite in their amount, one world would be infinitely different from the next, the odds of finding two close enough to be recognisable verging on the impossible. The main threads in terms of his and Minnie's lives are always roughly the same, and the worlds must only be mere ripples apart from one another, some worlds only being as different as the fact that people blinked a few more times that day. What was that idea? Chaos theory? Load of bullshit. Even so, he still feels that there are more of them out there, just out of reach, so there must be a few extra at least; with this, he concludes the thought, before moving onto another aspect of the Minnie situation as he works at his station.

184

Such analyses, of course, are all he thinks about these days, and now the knot almost fills him entirely.

How wonderful, he thinks, that he can see so many worlds laid out before him, but in all of them he always sees her.

Years pass, the notebook grows. He joins a gym, tries to make up for his shortcomings—he's chubby these days—but knows he can't go too far, as he has to be just right. He can't get muscular. The others aren't muscular, but look like they take care of themselves more than he currently does. He hopes that he can wear the veil of the Charlie Wilkes that he needs to be, and hopes that it is enough to make her believe.

Even on his low wage, living at home has meant that he has saved up a considerable amount of money. This is good; this will help him when the time comes to move, should he be out of work for a while.

During his twenty-third year, at an age where he can hear almost all of the sound perfectly, where the vision of the worlds is at ninety percent, he sees a night-time Minnie in a bar that he has never seen before. He is beside himself. Is this it? Is this their meeting? But no ... he can tell it isn't right. Even if it wasn't for the fact that he can't see himself working there, at least on that evening, she doesn't look right. Too young, but only just. She is with a large group of people, and she doesn't really seem to know where she is. She's swaying, her eyes wide and her pupils dilated. None of them are drinking much; it's one of her junkie times again. Chuck has seen a few of these over the years, and they're always difficult to watch, but fascinating like a burning car by the roadside. As he follows the group out of the bar and into the night, his heart sinks as he knows that, yet again, he still hasn't seen that vital meeting.

During his twenty-fourth year, however, he finally witnesses it. It's an almost religious experience.

She enters the bar with a male friend. The place is busy; a Friday, a Saturday, or perhaps an England game. But then he sees no shirts, his mind assessing and taking notes after years of practice. She looks nervous; she's even sweating slightly. The friend pushes through the crowd, leading her by the hand, but she hangs back. She's terrified (this must be, Chuck thinks, during her post-rehab days. He has copious notes) and her friend can't see it. She's about to bolt, but then he sees himself appear wearing street clothes (he's not even actually working there that night, Chuck realises, he can't believe it) and touch her nervously on her shoulder, a confused smile on his face, and then Chuck KNOWS, SWEET JESUS THIS IS IT, THIS IS FINALLY IT, HE'S SEEING IT.

He sees her turn as if she's been stung, sees her friend turn his head sharply as he feels the movement travel down his arm, sees himself hold an apologetic hand up. Her face is already changing, relaxing, a slight look of confusion on her face too.

"Listen, this is going to sound like the world's worst come on," he hears himself say, a cheeky but embarrassed grin on his face, "but I swear to God I know you from somewhere. You're not from Oxford, are you?"

Minnie's friend doesn't say anything, watching the interaction. He's concerned for her, knowing her fragile state. Minnie stares in silence for a second, her confused eyes searching this Charlie's face. *It's already happening. It looks to Chuck like a sunrise as the expression on her face breaks into a smile, as he sees her remembering a piece of her old self and delighting in it, delighting in how such a bullshit question has brought some part of herself back in a moment when she was preparing to flee.*

"You're right," she says, chuckling, and trying to hide the relieved tears that are springing to her eyes. "That is a terrible come on." *Chuck sees himself laugh, and shrug.*

"I mean it!" he says with a grin. "Seriously. If I was going to go for a really terrible come on, I was going to ask if this phone was yours. Found it in the toilet," he says, holding up a Samsung phone with a cracked screen. "I figured at the very least you'd have to be nice to me in order to get a free phone out of it. You can't really tell me to bugger off and then still get this. The screen's cracked, but it's kind of nice ..." *Minnie laughs again, a curious look on her face that seems as if she's trying to understand why this man's terrible patter is soothing her tension. The leaden scales that have been sitting on her mind are sloughing off as he speaks, delight and comfort replacing them.*

"You should hand it in," she says, mock-shaking her head, grinning at the returning confidence in her own voice, coming back to her like an old friend she had thought long dead. "Prove you're a nice guy."

"Hmm, then you'll just bugger off if I go and—oh, sorry mate," he says, spying Dave holding her hand behind her. "I didn't mean to—" *Dave can't excuse himself quick enough, holding his own hands up now, smiling. He's just seen a Minnie that he hasn't seen for a long time.*

"No, no," he says, "She's just a friend of mine. Actually, Minnie, I've just seen someone over there. I'll be in the corner if you need me." *She turns to Dave, who takes her hand in his briefly and raises his eyebrows. She pauses for a second, worried, and then that smile breaks through again like light from behind a cloud. She nods, biting her smiling lip, trying not to let Charlie see. Dave returns it with an equal grin, and grips her hand tighter for a second, then moves away.*

"Tell you what then," she says, turning back to Charlie. "I'll come with you. You hand that in, you——————-drink" *Chuck doesn't get the whole sentence, but he thinks her lips said* you buy me a drink *during the lost audio,* "and then I'll decide if you're a nice guy or not."

Chuck can see it, can see her almost glowing at the realisation that she can somehow be her true self for now, after less than a minute of talking to this man. It's crazy, but what else could he expect? Their bond travelled across countless worlds, after all. He watches the night, watches their amazement at each other. If he had a body here, Chuck would be weeping uncontrollably all the way through. He feels like a pilgrim witnessing a miracle. For the first time, he worries briefly about his state of mind, but lets it go.

When he wakes up, he calls in sick and spends the next few days making and clarifying frantic notes. In the nights to come, he pays even more attention to his doubles' movements and mannerisms, the meeting that he has witnessed putting even more nerves and tension under his skin, behind his eyes.

IN THE DARKNESS, THAT'S WHERE I'LL KNOW YOU

By the time he is twenty-six, he has seen it again. It's in a different world (Minnie's hair is a lot shorter) but the conversation is roughly the same. He has re-read the meeting section of his notes so many times that he notices any minor differences, and adds to the notebook when he wakes. Something vital is picked up; the menu on the wall. 'Winter menu.' They meet in winter, then.

By the time he is twenty-eight, he thinks he knows a lot of the major differences later in their lives; in some worlds, Minnie has been in a car accident herself and they can't have kids. In all the others, they have a boy and a girl. Chuck doesn't know how he feels about that. He doesn't want to share her. The accident means she spends a lot of time at home, and ends up successfully developing her web design business. In the other worlds, she works her way up the supermarket ranks and becomes a manager, or leaves altogether and becomes a stay-at-home mum. His notes are now vast; he knows so many of her likes and dislikes, he knows her like she is already his wife.

At thirty, he finally moves to Coventry. He knows that they meet in 2014 at some point, and that is three years away. He thinks that this gives him more than enough time to get a job at Barrington's (it now exists, he knows, having checked Coventry business listings an endless number of times every week) but minimises the amount of time he would live in the city and thus the risk of possibly bumping into her too early. When he moves out, he doesn't tell his dad. He just leaves. He never sees his dad again.

He finds a room in a shared house in Wyken. By now, he has saved up several thousand pounds, and decides that while he needs to start applying to Barrington's and finding some other form of employment, he needs to learn how to drive. This worries him greatly, as he has avoided cars throughout his adult life as much as possible since the accident, but he knows that he has to. He's seen himself driving the pair of them on early dates (dates that were agonisingly close to their first meeting, happening only just after it, visions of them tormenting him with their near-miss nature) and begins looking into it. After six months of labouring for a local builder, he lands a job at Barrington's (to his immense relief, and wonderment; seeing the place from the inside of his head— as opposed to viewing it from without—and being able to interact with it is uncanny) and he has passed his driving test. He doesn't buy a car, though. He doesn't need one yet, and still doesn't like them.

The other staff are uncomfortable around him, but he's a hard worker, and eventually he becomes part of the furniture, if not a well-liked or popular one. They call him weird behind his back. He manages, with great effort, to curb the humming, and the occasional twitches, and he comes across as just quiet but stern. The management approves at least, and like the fact that he isn't too pally with other employees. He takes all the hours he can get, takes on shifts that the other staff want to offload, and this all helps cement his position. Working still helps him lose himself while awake, and even if he has a lot of late finishes, the lie-ins means he still gets the right amount of sleep, the right amount of time in what he sees as the real world. All that and his age mean that, after a year, he is an assistant bar manager. After another year, he is bar manager. He has to make sure he is still a Barrington's employee when he meets her; all of the other

Charlies work at Barrington's, and even if he doesn't actually meet her while on the job, he needs everything to be as similar as possible.

Now he is at Barrington's every day, he reminds himself to wash. Hygiene is big in the food and beverage industry, he knows. He is losing weight, though; he doesn't eat very much now. He forces food down, trying to keep his weight correct for meeting Minnie. He bites the bullet, and buys a car. He uses it rarely, if ever; it's an investment for the future, and nothing more.

2014 begins, and every day is a nervous nightmare.

He knows that they won't meet until the winter, or near the start of it, but just knowing that the countdown has begun—that she is likely to be in the area, in person—makes him a trembling wreck. Every day he is sick at least once.

He also has another problem, one that he anticipated all too late. He's a bar manager; how on earth can he get every Friday and Saturday night off, in order to be off work when she arrives? And he does need every Friday and Saturday; he doesn't know which one it will be, unlike the other Charlies who just happened to book off a random Saturday and bumble into the girl of their dreams. But he also needs to work there if he is to be like the others ... this is a terrible time for Chuck, during the long months across the spring and summer as he wrestles with the problem.

When autumn arrives, his mind is made up; he has to quit his job. Being there, in the bar, off work and able to talk, is more important than working in Barrington's, surely, and even then he will have at least worked there up until the winter that they meet. That might be enough? It will have to be. He wants to be as much like the other Charlies as he can be, but this is just something that has to give. It is a devastating decision. He has a lot of money spare though, having barely touched his savings—adding to them in fact—and more than enough to cover him well past the end of the year.

He goes back to factory work in the week, as he needs something to occupy his daytimes; free time is difficult for him to handle. Friday and Saturday nights from the autumn onwards are spent in Barrington's, sitting on his own and watching the door, his skin crawling while a high-pitched noise going off inside his head. He knows it said 'winter menu', but it could have been out just before winter, so he can't take any risks. As he watches the entrance, he feels like his spine could snap from the tension, and his vision often becomes blurred. The headaches are crippling.

Every one of those nights he comes away disappointed, trembling, spent, almost suicidal, but then he disappears into his night-time real world and it soothes him. Of course he can wait, next time, next time, but every next time is even worse than the last. By the time they reach October, the weekends roll around with a sense of abject dread; he is sure the tension will kill him. He has nearly fainted at least ten times, and the doctor now has him on medication for his blood pressure. He is on the cusp of it, the cusp of the greatest moment of brilliance in all of creation (the knot inside him gibbers this, for of course it is now utterly in charge and has been for years) and it is still just, just, just agonisingly out of reach. The nearness of it all is like razor wire scraping at his brain.

IN THE DARKNESS, THAT'S WHERE I'LL KNOW YOU

Until one night.

One night, when the sounds and faces and people all look familiar, and of course they do, he tells himself with his lunatic internal voice, they always do, it's the tease, but maybe yes maybe no maybe yes maybe no maybe yes maybe no (he doesn't notice how people move around him, away from him, almost smelling his barely concealed lunacy, this man with the sunken and staring eyes, this silent, twitching, rigid man who has not had a night of rest in over twenty years, no full REM sleep, no mental shut down) and then, as if it was the most effortless, easy thing in the world, Minnie is led into the bar right in front of him, right before his madman's eyes.

Dave, looking the same as before, the same clothes, the same tight-fitting low-cut metrosexual t-shirt, but Chuck doesn't even notice.

She's here. She's here. She's here.

She's here. She's here. She's here.

Ah. Ah. Ah.

Something tightens in his chest, painfully, and Chuck can't breathe. The pain doesn't stop, and it's actually getting worse. It feels like someone is sitting on his chest, an enormous weight that is squashing him, pressing him down, and he realises that it could be his heart but even then he can't register it because she's there, THERE, SHE'S THERE, and he is blinded by it, his very flesh burning because he is in the same room as her and he realises that she is freaking out from all the bustle and all the people and just like before she will leave if he doesn't stop her.

How can he stop her? How can he even speak?

He struggles to his feet, wincing, not noticing the people that move out of his way, and he tries to breathe. He just manages a gasp, then another, and totters towards her on legs that feel as if they are made of sugar glass.

It's too much. How did he ever think he could handle this, after all this time? How could he ever have prepared after twenty years of incredible, twisted build-up, and be expected to perform under the greatest pressure of expectation that any human being has ever known?

And still he stumbles, groping for the right line in his head. What was it? He can barely remember his own name. At least his breaths are coming regularly now, short, inwards jerks that sound almost like hiccups. He is five feet away.

He's memorised it all a thousand times, the opening exchange, going over his notes again and again, but now he has nothing. Before him is the prize, a thousand times more intense in the flesh than in the night, and she will soothe him and he will soothe her, relieve her as he has seen that he will, if he could only remember the words and if his chest would just stop hurting and if his body would work.

Listen, this is going to sound like the world's worst come on...

That's it, that's fucking it, but she looks like she's about to bolt, being in this room is too much for her and it's written all over her face. He can see the distress in her eyes, and it almost mirrors the pained look on his, both from the physical and mental as he thinks please wait, oh please wait, I waited twenty years so please just a few seconds more *and then he's there, he's within touching distance and even though he thinks that he may die if he actually* does *touch her, he raises one shaking hand with a superhuman effort and touches her shoulder.*

As he knew she would, she spins around on the spot to face him as if she'd been groped. Her eyes meet his, and her eyebrows raise, frightened, nervous, but he's always known that she would be, it's his job to soothe her, to bring out the sunrise. He knows this, and then when it's done she'll be his, oh God, oh bliss, but the thought doesn't make it any easier as he opens his mouth and just a shambling noise comes out.

"Aaah ..."

It's so quiet she wouldn't have even heard it, but he swallows and tries again, his eyes wide. Mannerisms? He'd been practicing the others' mannerisms? He can barely stand.

"Lerrr ... listen ... this m-might sound ..."

He doesn't get any further.

"I'm sorry, I have to go," she says, her eyes crumpling, and she brushes past his still outstretched hand and dashes towards the door, nearly falling as she does so.

He watches her go, paralysed. The door shuts behind her, and he sees her run past the window, away into the night. The crucial moment, the precise event, the correct meeting ... is ... gone?

Just like that. Over.

...

The thought is too big.

He failed?

...

Too big.

But ...

Too big.

He lets out a little pained gasp, and his left leg buckles. He drops to a knee. His chest begins to cave once more.

He stares at the door, at the path cleared by her, at the people staring at him. He is dimly aware of Dave saying something to him, saying what the fuck did you say to her, *but it might as well be another language.*

Twenty years. Twenty years.

Everything. Everything.

***

Tommy's eyes were latched onto Charlie's. "We stayed up late after the wake, obviously. Me, dad, and my Uncle Paul. Mainly positive stuff, I admit, swapping old stories and making each other laugh. It was good to see. The old boy having a laugh. Good to see." He nodded, and the film on his eyes caught the light. Despite his nerves, Charlie felt a slight jolt of sympathy for the man. He was hurting. But then Charlie remembered the message on his phone, and the moment passed quickly.

"We had a few more drinks, and the tone changed over time, to say the least," said Tommy, looking up at the lights in the ceiling. "Started talking about her later days, you know. You know, Charlie?" He turned it into a question, raising his eyebrows, and Charlie shook his head.

"I don't know, Tommy," he said quietly. "I haven't seen her for a long time. I told you." Tommy didn't say anything, and just nodded slowly instead. He scratched at the side of his face, and sniffed.

"He talked about how she was, during that last week. He beats himself up for it now, of course, convinced that she was using again and that he should have seen it. The coroner's report and the toxicology report should have fucking set him straight, of course, but he won't have it. *They've missed something*, he says. Silly old sod. This is what you fucking junkies never think about. It's not just you. It's all the people around you, the people you lot drag down with you." Charlie bristled, and shifted in his seat, but kept his cool. He didn't know why he was taking offence. He'd never been a junkie.

"I'm not a junkie, Tommy," he said, then quickly added, "I'm clean now."

"Good for you," Tommy said, "I'll be sure to pass that on to my dad."

"I didn't get her hooked, either, if that's what this is about," said Charlie, getting angrier. "She made that choice long ago, as an adult."

Tommy smiled, bitterly.

"Ohhh, no," he said, shaking his head. "Nothing to do with that, Charlie. I think you *know* what this is about." He wagged his finger at Charlie, but then took it back and held a hand up. "Actually, let me rephrase that; I *only* think you know what this is about. I'm a fair guy, Charlie. And the one thing, the *one* thing in your favour that's stopped me from having you kicked shitless and put in the hospital or worse, is the fact that neither me or my dad have ever heard your name mentioned outside of the funeral until last night, and even then I don't think he would have remembered you. He was in too much of a state to remember anyone he talked to that day. Maybe I wouldn't have either, if not for the weirdness of you claiming to be Dave's mate when he didn't even know who you were. But he's no slouch, you know, my dad. I had to be the voice of reason. I said he had to let me deal with it. He knows some very dodgy guys, and I think he'd go too far straight away. He's distraught. Even more so, after this latest ... news, and that's what's so bad. The last thing in the world he needs right now is to deal with this. But it might all be nothing. It might have just been the scribblings of a girl with a ruined brain that was winding down for good."

Minnie. Minnie said something? This world's Minnie said something?

"Tommy, I'm really sorry that your dad is having such a hard time, but you have to understand, as far as I'm concerned I'm totally innocent and have no idea what you're talking about," said Charlie, spreading his arms. "I'll be honest, under other circumstances I'd be pissed off about all this, but you've lost a family member and so emotions are going to be running high. That's why I'm taking all of this on the chin, but *I haven't done anything.* So tell me. Please. What happened?" Tommy cocked his head, looked at the table, sniffed in a business-like way again, and nodded.

"Fair enough," he said. "So Dad's talking about her last few days, you know. How we caught her rambling a lot, when she thought we weren't listening. He beats himself up for that, too, for not dragging her to a doctor, but it's a delicate subject, you know? You know, *you* certainly know. She's trying to get her self-esteem back, and maybe she's having a bit of a relapse and doesn't want people to know so she's being brave, talking to herself, maybe not even realising she's doing it ... so we pretend not to notice, and hope she comes out the other side before we have to intervene." Tommy began to rub his temples. "So Dad mentions the drawings she used to do, scribbly, messy things that she did when she was having bad days. They were these stream-of-consciousness kind of things, apparently something they'd taught her to use as part of her rehab, or maybe something one of the other addicts told her, I don't know. She hadn't done one for a while, as she'd been doing so much better, apart from the recent talking to herself thing. Anyway, Dad says he'd found one when he was going through her things before the funeral, a real messy one, and he hadn't seen it before. He said it broke his heart, because it had *I'm sorry I'm sorry I'm sorry* over and over on it, along with lots of the usual squiggles and circles. *I hope it was an old one at least,* he says, *'cos if she was going through that in her head before she died ... it'd break my heart. I can't even bear to look at it properly yet.*"

"And I just had this urge to see it, to connect with my sister—I'd had a few drinks by then—and so I asked him where it was. He said it was in the box in the living room, along with a lot of old letters and stuff. When I found it, he was right; it was just heartbreaking. It looked like it had been drawn by a five year old. The state she must have been in ... I dread to think. It was covered in nonsense phrases too, about worry and fear, and I hope to God that this really was just an unseen old note, as if she'd been like this before she died, and we had no idea ... fuck me." He took a deep breath, and shook his head. "There was hardly any white visible on the page, it was that covered. Started me crying. She was clearly terrified, or crazy, or both. And there was one note in particular that, at the time, I barely even noticed in amongst the *I just want to sleep and never wake up* and *I'm sorry for all this Dad* and *where are you Mum* and *the smack was the poison* and all these pictures of stick figures inside circles; and one with writing on it that said *Charlie's gonna kill me.*

Charlie's eyes bugged wide open and his face went pale. It was as if someone had just scooped out the inside of his stomach in one go.

What ... the ...

Tommy carried on speaking.

"I was so upset at the time that I didn't even think of the guy who'd disappeared at the funeral. I mean, *charlie,* right? Cocaine? She used to say that kind of thing all the time, back in the day. *The junk is gonna kill me, the smack is gonna kill me, the shit is gonna kill me.* I didn't even think she'd been on the charlie, but to me it was just another drug reference. But as I sat in the living room with that note, crying my eyes out, my mind kept going back to that statement, because there was something about it that I'd obviously just caught onto, you know? Something that my mind had snagged on. I couldn't forget it. And the more I thought about it, I'd never heard her mention coke as something she wanted or thought about. The way I hear it, heroin addicts see it as a very poor substitute. So it was just a weird thing to say. And then something snapped into place, and my brain suddenly decided to remember you."

Tommy paused, and laced his fingers together across his stomach, his eyes staring and wide. His lips pressed together, wrestled against each other. Charlie still said nothing, wanting to hear where this was going and still stunned by what he'd just heard, feeling light-headed.

Charlie's ... gonna kill me? I didn't even know his Minnie before she died! What the fuck is this?

"And straight away I nearly dismissed it, thought that was impossible because it was a brain haemorrhage, right?" said Tommy, his eyes wet, his voice cracking. "It happened all by itself, or at least after everything else had already done the damage. So what could you have actually done? But then ... why would she say that *you* were going to kill her?" Tommy shifted in his seat suddenly, and twisted his head as his teeth clamped down on his bottom lip, taking a deep, steadying breath. "I don't think you killed her, Charlie. Let me make that clear. There were no signs of physical assault. There was nothing to say that her brain was ruptured by external force; that sort of thing is obvious if that's the cause. But I think that maybe this *was* an old note. I think that you might have done something terrible in the past. I think you might have threatened her. Or I think you might have been forcing her to take that crap, for whatever sick reason of your own. Either way ... she *thought* you were going to kill her, at least. She wrote it down. And I hope to *God* that she wrote it a long time ago, because if you made her last days painful for her, I swear ..." Tommy was pointing his finger now, and his tears spilled over his bottom eyelid, but Charlie was barely listening.

Fuck ... that Minnie's Charlie ... the one in her head ... did she mean him? Did she just mean that Charlie was going to be angry with her for something, like Charlie's going to kill me for breaking that plate ... or did she mean ... she couldn't have meant that he ...

***

Chuck's first thought is, of course, to kill himself. He returns home, to his rented, squalid room that seems even more hopelessly empty than it did before, and wonders how he should do it. His thoughts are numb, mechanical, and that is good, as he knows that if he moves out of that mode the only feeling that he will find will be a howling, bottomless despair.

His life. His entire life. One moment. He blew it.

And her, the look on her face ... he wasn't even a consideration to her. She had spurned him utterly, when she had accepted, no, LOVED the others. How could she do that? How could she do that to him? SHE, The Woman In The Night, the woman whom he had drawn such comfort from all of these years, the woman who had soothed the loss of his mother and the abandonment by his father ... she'd turned her back on him now, and at the pivotal moment when he had sacrificed EVERYTHING FOR HER?

Had it ... had it all been a mistake? Could he have been wrong about her all this time? Was it even possible?

It doesn't matter. If true, it's just another reason to end it all, a layer of unspeakable cruelty draped over a world suddenly devoid of all hope and meaning. The bath, then, and a radio to drop into it.

But as he lies there in the water, water that has long gone cold in the three hours that he has been staring at the ceiling and crying the desperate tears of a man who's entire existence has been torn to shreds, ignoring the banging and shouting of the various housemates (strangers to him) outside who are by turns irritated, angry, and desperate to get in, he realises something even worse; he does not have the courage to go through with it. He curses himself, curses The Woman In The Night, and the world, and wonders where he will go next. All he wants is oblivion, something to make all the thoughts stop.

Alcohol, then. Drugs.

He endures the night, refusing to let himself sleep, terrified of it now, knowing that it will bring more visions of her and with them a cold blade in his chest that will never go away. He wonders how he will ever get through the nights of his future without going insane. The next day, he returns to Barrington's, though he no longer works there of course, and speaks to Jerry. Being in Barrington's again, the place where he has both seen the successful first meeting and experienced his own unbearable failure is almost too much, but he has no choice. It's for the greater good, he tells himself over and over, the only way that he will find relief. He doesn't know Jerry well, but he has overheard him talking enough to know that he is someone that can help him get what he wants. Jerry is taken aback by Chuck's maddened appearance, just wants rid of him, and asks what Chuck is after.

Chuck doesn't know; he asks for options. Jerry says he can get weed, speed, ket, and acid, that's it. Chuck knows a little about the first two (one not hard enough, the other sounds like the last thing he needs) knows nothing about ket (he doesn't even know what it is) so he opts for the acid. He just wants to get out of his head without going to sleep, without going to her. He just wants anything that will help him escape. Jerry writes his phone number down for Chuck, and says to call him that evening.

Chuck meets Jerry later, and tabs and money are exchanged, along with brief, reluctant instructions and a casual threat about Jerry's name ever being mentioned. Chuck slips off into the night, the small packet in his pocket. Once home, he immediately lies on his stinking bed and drops the acid. Almost immediately after the visions begin, he realises his mistake.

The worlds are back, floating before him in his room as if they had come to find him, to torment him. This is the worst possible outcome. This is the last thing he wanted to see. The walls of his room melt away and expose a vastness so great that it is incomprehensible and terrifying, and now the bed is gone and he is floating in an endless nothingness, and the stars are not stars but worlds, *millions, billions, countless in their number, stretching as far as the eye can see, above, below, in front and behind, and Chuck would scream but there is no air here, no, it's not a lack of air, it's a lack of* him, *like before, he is a disembodied consciousness floating in oblivion with only the myriad faces of his tormentor for company. His suspicions—that there were always more worlds just out of sight—were correct. It is far bigger than he could ever imagine. He is in hell.*

But it isn't just her. As his non-existent eyes try to take in all the worlds around him, he realises that the ones that he is closest to, the hundreds that always span around him … these are different. These are the ones he recognises, the ones he has seen, and others similar to them … but beyond those, there are others, ones without a Minnie, *he can feel it, and yes, there is his escape! These worlds in the night* were *endless after all … but not the ones in which he and she were supposed to meet, in which the potentially endless possible variables came together and ended with he and her meeting, the energy of those possible connections being so strong that they called to him from across the void and appeared to him in the night. Those were the ones that he saw, and though now he could never begin to count them all, that group is atom-sized compared to the number of other worlds all around him. He can go to them, he can flee to—*

And then he sees it, appearing before his eyes as the vision becomes deeper, solid.

The End.

It lies behind all of the worlds, vast and white, hanging in the void, the point where all the worlds diverge, the place that all the worlds lead to. It has a pull, a gentle but inexorable draw that, even though is barely noticeable, Chuck knows immediately that one day he will go to it, as unavoidable as aging and crumbling to dust. It is at the heart of all things. Though it speaks of peace, of resolution, of rest, the things that Chuck came searching for in his darkest hour, he could not face The End when presented with it in the bath with an old Bosch cassette radio perched on the porcelain, and he cannot face it now; he is terrified beyond anything he has felt in his life, horrified by the soft, gentle call of The End as it triggers an instinct as old as time itself to flee, to flee, *it is not his time yet, he shouldn't even be seeing it yet, and Chuck's essence recoils and dives head first into the nearest refuge that it can find.*

Chuck dives deeper than he ever did in the night, deeper than he ever could with the limited consciousness of a sleeping man, and plunges away from The End with the life-preserving effort and speed of a terrified, hunted gazelle. He knows that he has dived inside a world where Minnie is, can feel it all around him, but that doesn't matter in the blinding fear that comes from his seeing and feeling The End. He dives in deeper, and then somehow inside something again without even knowing what he is doing, drawn automatically to a safe haven that shines like a beacon until he comes to a stop and sits, huddled and shivering.

Eventually, he opens his eyes, and sees only a terrifying swirl of colours, lights, and movement. Panicked, he screams, tries to curl his consciousness into a ball, wishing there to be form in this place and empty shapes and chaotic imagery, and in doing so he creates an image of his body. This creates focus; automatically, his focus expands outwards and the colours and swirls settle into solidity, his mind reshaping his perception of this place, the place that his essence has found itself taking shelter in, until it becomes something he can visualise and understand. What was not physical is shown to him as being physical, his mind's need to comprehend manipulating this new, smaller void into something he can interact with. He now sees it as a room, sees himself inside it, naked, looking at the room through his own eyes.

The room is black. At one end, there is a screen.

***

"Tommy," said Charlie, dragging himself to his senses and putting this fresh news on the back burner for the moment, realising the he had a bereaved and furious man to deal with as the more immediate and pressing problem, "I have never, ever threatened Minnie. And I certainly never forced her to take anything." Thinking fast, he added: "If I was being totally honest, Tommy, back in those days, if she didn't want to touch something, the *last* thing I would do would be to try and change her mind. If she didn't want something, it only meant more for me. I never had any money in those days; leftovers were always welcome." He hoped it sounded convincing, as split as his attention was. Tommy nodded slowly, the tears rolling silently down his face at equal speed. Charlie felt a compulsion to fill the silence. "I mean ... if nothing else Tommy, I weighed about nine stone. I was skinny as a rake and as weak as a kitten. Junk tends to do that to a body. I was about as threatening as Charles Hawtrey." He saw the need to believe him in Tommy's eyes, a grieving brother wanting to know that his sister's life and last days had not been as bad as he feared.

"*Kill me quicker than greased-up lightning,*" said Tommy, quietly. Had the statement fully triggered the memory in Charlie at that particular moment, it would have shown all over his face in shock and Charlie's fate on the business end of a baseball bat in some dim future moment would have been sealed. As it was, he didn't immediately remember anything about this particular sentence in any meaningful way, and his confusion was genuine.

"What?" asked Charlie, furrowing his brow. Tommy continued to stare.

"*Kill me quicker than greased-up lightning,*" Tommy repeated, although he didn't sound *quite* as sure of it. "The last complete, legible sentence on her sheet, one of the ones that stood out at least. Seemed to me like a weird way of putting it ... not something Minnie would say, that was for certain. Sounded like someone else's words, not hers. Wondered if that meant anything to you," he said, but the fire in his weeping eyes seemed to have died that little bit; he hadn't seen what he had wanted to see in Charlie's face, even as Charlie heard the sentence a second time and a faint bell rang in his head. Now he came to think of it, he *had* heard that somewhere, hadn't he? As his mind wandered, the silence continued and Charlie became very aware of it. That brought his mind back to the present for a second time, and he again told himself that the matter could wait; the important thing was getting Tommy to believe him.

"I almost wish I could say that it did," said Charlie, looking sad and beginning to lean forward. "Tommy, I don't know what—"

Bang. He remembered. He'd heard the phrase coming from his own lips as he watched himself say it, saw himself standing behind the bar in Barrington's holding up Minnie's business card and promising to pass it on if anyone he knew wanted web design doing, promising to pass it on *quicker than greased-up lightning.* The phrase had stuck out like a sore thumb, and Charlie had written it off as his other self being nervous and trying to be funny, failing badly in the attempt. The other self that knew where Minnie lived—

Minnie. Oh, fuck me, no.

It made no sense, it was impossible, and he had no idea how it all came together, but there was no way a unique, bullshit phrase like that was used twice in coincidence. It had appeared it two places, on what was effectively a death note and on the lips of one of two men who were involved in both Minnie's worlds in one way or another. And just as only one of those Minnies was still around, only one of those two men could still actually touch her.

Minnie, Charlie thought as his nerve endings came alive as one, a unique terror crawling inside him that we only reserve for the peril of those nearest to us, *is in danger.* And with a sense of helplessness that is always that terror's worst and favourite partner—the thing that gives it power and presence and grip—he remembered that he could not be farther from her, sitting as he was on the wrong side of a divide that spanned entire worlds.

***

Chapter Eight: The Other Black Room/Chuck's Story - Part Two, Charlie Makes His Move, The Cuckoo's Horizons Broaden Even Further, and Charlie Remembers The Night Before The Night Before
***

Chuck takes only a short while to make contact with the Minnie that he finds himself inside, a shorter time than Charlie will later take when he finds himself inside his own Black Room, inside another Minnie in another world. He realises more quickly what he has done (for the incredible is a nightly occurrence to him, not to mention that he has the luxury of remembering his arrival; he therefore understands far more quickly than an ordinary man like Charlie, remembers his journey there due to a lifetime of similar travel) and identifies Minnie immediately (how could he not?) Even though he doesn't fully understand what has happened, he realises that the drug must have unlocked a part of his brain that has lain dormant; his abilities have somehow gone even further. He is no longer a ghost on the outside looking in. He is now a presence on the inside looking out.

His first action upon arrival—after hearing her voice and knowing within a moment of unfathomable wonder where he is—is to touch the walls of the

199

Black Room, almost not daring to make a sound as he does so. He is inside *her mind? Can he speak with her? He begins to do so ... but to his own surprise, he finds himself hesitating. The thoughts come again, with the logic of a man who has gone twenty years without the full benefit of REM sleep:*

She turned her back on you. She wasted your life. It's a lie. It's all a lie. She's a liar. They are all liars. *And while he doesn't believe the words, not fully at least, another knot is already growing, faster and harder this time, fuelled by a cracked psyche and the desperate need to turn hurt and pain into something that can be used as a shield against those two bedfellows; hate.*

Another thought comes:

What if ... *he's* there, in this world? If the partner is here. Can you watch that? Will you be able to watch that, knowing how it turns out for you?

The fear rushes back, and he decides right then and there that he will not let that *happen; he's on the inside, after all. He will not go through that. He will find a way.*

The view moves, to his intense distaste (the sight draws a moan from him) to a mirror, and Chuck turns his back on the screen, but not before seeing something that brings even greater anxiety; she is the right age. Soon, even very soon, she will meet her future husband. The impostor.

Can she hear you?

Not knowing if he even wants *to be heard, but helpless against his own curiosity, Chuck speaks. After everything he's been through, everything he's seen, the safety of the Black Room gives the madman the small amount of confidence he needs, the safety to think freely.*

You're inside her. You can find out the truth. You can make her tell you. You're in the driving seat.

"Hello, Minnie."

The resulting, hysterical conversation is much like the one Charlie will later have with the Minnie he knows, only a lot calmer on one side. As it continues, Chuck decides to claim ignorance of how he got there, thinking it better than admitting his nightly stalking of her for the last twenty years. He says he'd taken some drugs and somehow wound up inside her head from another world. The response is as would be expected. They go through the same rigmarole that Charlie will later with his *Minnie (specific memories to prove he isn't a figment of her imagination, followed by an online search, this time at Minnie's insistence) and, like our Charlie and Minnie, they discover that there is indeed another version of Charlie Wilkes living in that world (this Charlie has a Facebook profile, discovered online after Minnie Googles Charlie's name. Chuck has never had a Facebook profile, hates the very idea of doing so.)*

Minnie wants to go and meet this Charlie at the place where his profile says he works, to prove Chuck's existence or otherwise, and Chuck does not like this idea. Does not like this one bit. This would mean this Minnie and that Charlie meeting, would potentially mean Chuck having to watch the courtship dance that he has been teased with for his entire adult life and then denied.

She's doing it again. She's rubbing it in your face again, twisting you around, just like they all will.

"I don't want to go. We're not going," says Chuck, *and there is a determination and darkness in his voice that surprises even him.*

"Fuck you!" says a surprised and still fairly hysterical Minnie, her terror and delirium at finding a strange man inside her head only muted by the knowledge of her inability to do anything but go with it, now rising back up when this man seems to wish to take control. "As long you're in my head and not the other way around, I'll be calling the shots, I think. So get used to it. It's bad enough that you've given me this bastard of a headache since you've been here, so I don't need you actually becoming one."

Chuck doesn't like this. This is only proving his darkest suspicions, and Chuck's mind already lacks a great many of the limitations that the average person possesses. It's only natural after years of seeing the limits others take for granted swept away every night in his sleep. And isn't she directly choosing to hurt him, after all? He's made his feelings clear, and yet she still plans on going?

You were right. You were right. They were all fucking you over, Charlie. All these years. It's a big cosmic joke. *You're* a big cosmic joke. *They made you a big cosmic joke.*

"We're not going anywhere," he says, very firmly. A thin smile finds its way onto his face, stays there. "Let's stay here and talk. I want to get to know you better."

Minnie begins to get a very frightening, sinking feeling in her chest. It is immediately countered by the shield that she has thrown up these last few years to defend herself from such feelings; anger, attack, defence. Rational thought goes out the window as she begins to feel herself cornered, even though she doesn't know why. She will not have this.

"Bollocks," she says, but she doesn't sound as brave or as hard as she would like. Her voice is quiet, and trembling. Something is very worrying here, but she will not be told. She needs to either get this guy out of her head or prove that he's a figment of her damaged mind. She needs to see the real one, get some answers. She needs to leave the flat. "We're leaving."

"We're not. Going. Anywhere," says Chuck, his voice rising, and he punches the nearest wall of the Black Room with each syllable. He hears nothing in response, except the sudden intake of Minnie's breathing. It is surprised breathing. She has noticed something, and to her it is very frightening indeed.

Chuck has also noticed something; noticed the timing of each of Minnie's sharp in-breaths coinciding with each punch against the Room's wall. He looks at his fist for a second, and then punches the wall again. Harder. This time there is an actual gasp.

An idea has come to Chuck, and it is a dark one. He isn't aware of it, but the thin smile becomes a grin. Chuck now knows for a fact that which our Charlie Wilkes can only guess at, as Chuck has actually witnessed the Black Room's formation:

This place is just a physical representation of her mind.

"What ... what are you doi—" gasped Minnie, her voice barely above a whisper.

If you can damage this place, you can damage her.

"Sit down," says Chuck, his mind beginning to race with the possibilities.

Is she yours now?

"N-no," stammers Minnie, "I-I'm leaving, a-and—"

"Sit down," *says Chuck, grinning gleefully as he punctuates the second word with a kick to the wall. Minnie lets out a little cry and then drops to the floor in shock as if she had been slapped.*

Is she yours? Are you in control? What do we do with that? What do we *do* with that? Is this what control feels like, what choice feels like? After all these years?

"Please," says Minnie, "Why are you—"

"Shut up," *says Chuck, punching the wall again in the same spot, and this time there is a slight crack and Minnie cries out loudly in pain, holding her head. Chuck begins to almost hyperventilate, a mixture of crazed laughter and excitement.*

Revenge? Do we get her to tell the truth? That she was in on it from the beginning? Does she know about the others? Do they do this with lots of people? The bitch. The fucking *bitch.*

Hate stemming from betrayed love is a powerful force. In the hands of a madman it is a hurricane.

"I want you to answer ... some questions for me," says Chuck, his voice gasping like he has just completed a marathon, "because I'm beginning ... to think that for a long, long time ... you ... and a lot of ... others ... have been ... having a laugh at ...my expense. You fucking bitch. You ... you fucking bitch."

"Please, I don't—" the response is met with a swift rebuke, and so it begins.

The first thing he does is to make her tie a gag around her own mouth, and to get a piece of paper and a pen. Her responses are placed upon the paper, and disobedience is met with swift retribution. His questions are unanswerable to her, formed as they are through paranoia, madness, newfound hate and unfounded suspicion. She can't answer them, and the response from Chuck is that which you would expect. It goes on for a long, long time.

Eventually, she passes out from the pain, and to Chuck's annoyance no amount of kicking and punching of her mind can arouse her. He sits in the dark of the Black Room, and wonders, like Charlie, if he can access her mind directly, but dismisses it with a madman's logic; her nonsensical (to him) answers has proven that she, and all the rest, are liars, the best in the world; even her memories are not to be trusted, full of falsities that she will have convinced herself to be true. No, he will wait for her to awaken, and then he will bring the truth forward in his own undeniable way, in a way of pain that will eventually break down any false constructs and distorted lies that she has told herself.

He can't believe that he'd never seen it all before. How was he ever so naive.

Of course, after a while, as Minnie enters deeper unconsciousness, the walls contract and Chuck is sent home, just like Charlie, flung back across the void, The End flashing by terribly in the infinite distance. He hadn't expected to be sent home. He awakes in his bedroom to his great displeasure. He wasn't finished.

IN THE DARKNESS, THAT'S WHERE I'LL KNOW YOU

He spends the day thinking, planning, obsessing. He doesn't eat. The possibilities are so vast that he can't stop trembling.

They were all liars. They were all liars. But you can get them all. You can make them tell you why and then you can get them *all.*

But first that one. The one he started with. Can he go straight back to her? He doesn't know. He will find out. Does he need the acid again? He has some left, after all. He will see. He will sleep tonight without it, will risk seeing the worlds in his sleep because now they have been de-fanged and de-clawed. Now he can hurt them back. Now he is in control.

But what about The End? What if you see that again?

He won't stick around long enough. He will be straight inside her head, away from it. It will have to wait a long, long time to get him. Whatever comes next can wait. He will duck it for as long as he can.

That night, sleep doesn't come. He almost takes the acid again, but he resists. He needs to know. Fortunately for Chuck, his constant tension and mania throughout the day has taken its toll, and even a madman's body can only stand so much. Eventually, he succumbs.

He awakes to find himself in the void, just like before. He is elated; the acid effect is permanent then, or at least long-lasting. He then remembers the end, and the elation stops, as now he can feel The End far away. He dares not look at it. Instead, he begins what he believes to be a fruitless search for where he was before, but it turns out to be easy; the world he'd previous visited stands out like a beacon, its energy different from the others. His presence has altered it, entering not as a wraith like before but as a mind made solid, and it is clear where he has previously been. He is drawn to it quickly, the worlds flying by until it is before him then around him then swallowing him, down deep once more into the Black Room.

The world outside is dark, the curtains drawn against the daylight creating an external Black Room of Minnie's own. Her gentle sobbing is clearly audible. She has spent most of the day taking painkillers, stemming recurrent nosebleeds, and trying to convince herself that it was all just an episode, just some kind of horrific psychosomatic flashback.

"Hello, Minnie," Chuck says, the smile growing as the sense of power washes over his burning psyche like a cooling salve. She screams wildly, hysterically, and Charlie sees the blood on the handkerchief and realises that he will have to be more gentle with her. He can do this at his leisure after all, can't he? He knows he can return. He will get his answers. He will get his pound of mental flesh from her. He doesn't want to kill her, after all. Just revenge. Just a little revenge, just a little of what he's owed. And he's owed much, isn't he? They took a lifetime from him. Over the next few days, he talks with her in the down time in between interrogations, framing it as light-hearted conversation on his part, toying with her. He wants to discuss with her, to chat, finding it fascinating. The Woman In The Night? She's just human after all. The same as everyone else, with a hole in her backside for shitting out of. She's just very, very good at lying. He gets her to answer simple questions, mocking her answers gently, playing both the good cop and the bad cop.

203

On a few occasions he returns to her, he finds her in what appears to be her father's home. He considers humiliating her in front of her family, but decides that it may interfere somehow with his plans; they could be in on the whole thing after all. He talks with her there for a while, but her answers are stunted as she tries to hide her responses from her family.

After the fourth time he finds her there, he tells her that she cannot go there ever again.

He also adds that he will go to her family next—an idle threat, as he's not sure that he can—and give them the same treatment. By now, the walls of the Black Room are cracked all over, and on occasion he has broken through into the undulating layers beneath. He doesn't know what these deeper parts are— this Black Room, this visualisation of her mind, was created automatically by his own, after all—but he thinks that they must be the bedrock of her essence. He knows that he has to be careful with those. He really doesn't want to kill her, after all, but he doesn't tell her that. He tells her that he will kill her, kill her quicker than greased-up lightning. He grins as he says the phrase. That's smart. He needs to remember that one.

By the fifth day, he returns to find Minnie slowly putting on her jacket, fumbling with the buttons like she can't remember how they work, her fingers groping at them like a child. Her arms move before the downward-facing view with painful slowness, like they are full of broken glass.

"Hello, Minnie." He loves to say it. He says it every time. It makes him feel like a god. He hears her hopeless sobs begin, quiet this time. No scream. Interesting. Here is a desperate sorrow, a quiet acceptance of her doom, and Charlie realises that he's been kidding himself. He wants to kill her. The thought is almost a release.

"I need ... to eat," she says. Her words are slightly slurred. "Run ... out of food."

"No," he says. It's almost a sigh. "Back in the living room." He doesn't care about the truth for now, not from her at least. This one will never crack, not even in the face of torture and death. The next one will, though. Or the next. He has all the time in the world. And it's going to be so, so satisfying, the satisfaction that he has yearned for all these years.

There is a pause, and then very quietly, almost inaudibly over her sobs, she speaks.

"No," she whispers.

Perfect. Resistance. She's even given him a reason. All the signs are there. He gives in, knowing that he is doing the right thing.

By the time he is finished, lost in his own bloodlust and mania as he rips and tears and shatters not just her, but his own last vestiges of restraint and decency in the process, this Minnie's broken mind is drifting into unconsciousness before her ruptured brain dies. Chuck feels for it, feels again for the reverse of the process that brought him in, and heads out. He doesn't need to wait for the walls, he realised several days ago. He can come in, so he can of course go out early if he wants, and he doesn't want to stick around to find out what happens next. He leaves this world—this world where our Charlie Wilkes lives, where our Charlie Wilkes will attend that Minnie's funeral and lie to Tommy about knowing her—with a peace in his mind that he hasn't truly felt since he was ten years old.

***

"You don't know what, what?" said Tommy, repeating Charlie's words and watching him closely. It looked like the hurt man's desire to believe that Charlie was an innocent person—his need to accept that his sister had not spent her last days afraid—were all still there. Tommy would never know that the truth was far, far worse than any of his darkest fears.

"Uh, sorry, my phone is going off in my pocket, think I just got a text," Charlie lied, thinking on his feet. His pulse raced, already desperately thinking about what to do next, and he realised that he simply had to get out of there. Whatever the hell Tommy wanted to think or do, he could fucking well do it, but he had to get back to Minnie *right fucking now.*

How you gonna do that exactly, champ? Think you're gonna be sleeping comfortably after this latest little realisation? A bottle of Night Nurse isn't going to do the trick.

For a crazy moment, he briefly considered trying to goad Tommy into knocking him out, but then thought better of it almost immediately. Tommy wasn't a big guy, and the threats he'd been making weren't promises of violence from his own hands. He was going to get others to do it. Again, the bottom line: Charlie had to leave, and immediately.

"Tommy, I didn't do anything. It's not in my nature. There's nothing I can say or do to prove you wrong, because it's just not something that I *can* prove. But if you think an emaciated junkie is either A: going to force someone else to take drugs that he'd much rather have for himself and B: is any kind of physical threat, even to a girl like Minnie—who from what I remember is not the type of girl to back down easily—then you have got to realise that you were mistaken. I can't do anything other than to leave you with that." He waited for a response from Tommy, not planning to wait long, either. None came, just the staring eyes, and the tears. It wasn't an acceptance of Charlie's story by any means, but Tommy was less certain now than he was when he came in, that was for certain.

"And I guess you're going to do whatever you're going to do, based on whatever you decide. And I suppose that means that I might be getting a heavy knock on the door in the future, and I really don't look forward to that. But I don't deserve it," Charlie said as he stood, not taking his eyes off Tommy. He wondered why he was still talking, but for some reason he felt pity for the man before him. He wasn't defending himself. He was trying to reassure Tommy, the hurting bereaved brother that had made some terrible threats. "I'm going now. I *am* sorry for your loss, Tommy. I appreciate you giving me a chance to say my side of things. I suppose ... I await your response." His mind was halfway out of the door, but he didn't move, caught by a sudden image of himself and Tommy in another possible time that should have been; Charlie and Minnie's wedding day, sharing a laugh, a pint, a memory with his brother-in-law, the man who in another world could have been the brother that Charlie had never had. The moment was a body blow.

Chuck, you son of a bitch. I don't know how you've done it, but you've taken everything from me and I didn't even know it.

"Goodbye, Tommy," said Charlie, and walked away, only looking back as he exited through the pub doorway. Tommy was still watching, jaw set, unaware of the stares around him as various pairs of eyes followed the tears that rolled down his cheeks.

Once he was out of the door, Charlie reached his bike at a run while his mind was racing even faster. By the time he was pedalling out of the car park and down the street, he knew what he was going to try first, even though it meant having to deal with someone he despised. He only hoped they didn't live too far away, having no memory of ever being in their house.

As he rode, he kept one hand on the handlebars while the other found the recent calls list on his phone. He pushed the number that he knew to be Neil's.

***

His sense of excitement, no, his thrill *is only dimmed when he is back in the void the next night, within sight of The End. He fears it even more now that he is a murderer.* Murderer ... *Though he feels justified in what he has done, to take another life is no small thing. What does it mean with regard to what comes next? Everything? Nothing? Were the long-abandoned beliefs of his childhood true after all? There is a* consciousness *to The End, he's sure he can feel it. He knows on a deep, deep instinctive level that its eye has seen his actions and marked him for them. His mind-self shudders, a spasm of consciousness in the void, as he realises that either way, there is no turning back. His actions from now on, whatever he does with the time he has left, are more important than ever; he fears that no matter what, it is decided, and whatever comes after The End for him, this dark version of Charlie Wilkes, may well be endless and bleak.*

Will it?

It's done. The present is what matters. There is nothing else for it. There is only the thrill of the now; he will embrace it. He chooses a new world at random, enters it.

As he descends into a new world, drawn on autopilot to that world's Minnie, he realises with a mixture of horror and excitement that a Charlie is already there, a Charlie not much older than Chuck is now. This other Charlie is inside Minnie in a different way, and Chuck hears her gasps and moans. He hesitates in his descent, fascinated and repulsed by them both; with some effort, he manages to hang outside like their bodies in his new, controlled form. He

206

feels a growing backward pull though, and realises that, even with his post-LSD abilities, he can only do this for so long. He must get inside her head or he must ascend back to the void—

Wait, *her* head? Or just *a* head? What would happen if ... if you *dared* ... to go inside his? Could you even do it? Would you ... would you feel it ... what his body feels, if you tried? Would you finally know what it was like with her? She is a monster, but you know that you want to know.

That is something. That is really something. To feel what it was like with her—no matter how much the thought of her now boils in his head—is a thought that holds an intense fascination. His physical desire has never been truly sated by the women he has slept with.

It wouldn't even be rape if she's already consented, too. Look at her! That is not a woman saying no!

That's true. She isn't. He feels justified in his previous act of murder, but he is not a rapist. That is something else. He is not a monster, after all. He is a force for justice. But the thought of sex with her is exhilarating yet frightening, as if to touch her in that way would be to catch some of her filth, some of her poison. But he wants to know. He needs to know. Although he doesn't think this will work ...

Either way, the reverse pull is steadily growing, and he knows that he must choose a destination before it is too late to counter the force dragging him back into the void. This new form is not designed to hang between destinations, his astral evolution giving him vast new abilities but simultaneously removing old options. His mind is made up. He feels for this other Charlie's consciousness, and begins his descent.

He reaches the other Charlie's mind, and while he finds to his excitement that yes, it feels like he can *get inside the body, there is a resistance here that he didn't have with Minnie's. His first attempt fails.*

Like two matching magnetic fields. Like two magnets repelling each other.

Chuck tries again despite the pain—the effort hurts—and fails again, but he knows he can do it. He goes back for a third try, like a spoilt child who wants something only because he has been told that he can't have it. He would, he will later think, have achieved his goal purely from his own efforts eventually, but as it turns out, there is a moment of deeply unfortunate (for this other Charlie, at least) timing. This Charlie's consciousness flutters as his arousal reaches a peak and his body comes to the moment of climax; Chuck seizes his opportunity. In this brief moment of psychic weakness, Chuck is in.

There is no leisurely re-organisation of the swirling consciousness this time. All too late, this Charlie's consciousness realises that something has happened, something dangerous and deadly and usurping, and tries to fight back. Unfortunately, it is not only caught on the back foot but spent. Chuck is more prepared; while he is without form and coherence in this new destination, he has gone in as the aggressor, and understands an attempted counter-attack when he feels one. His instincts want to take over, to defend and rend and tear, and he lets them. With Chuck's advantage of momentum and surprise, this Charlie's consciousness is stamped down even as it fights for its life, caught all-too unawares and completely unprepared. As the psychic skirmish reaches its end, this Charlie just has time to dimly think Where am I going before his spirit winks out like a light. *The untamed colours of consciousness disappear, and there is only darkness left for Chuck; this is not the blackness of a Black Room though, not yet. This is merely another, smaller void, a canvas. Outside, this Charlie's body slumps on top of this other Minnie's with an outward rush of air, and is still.*

As this Minnie laughs, thinking this Charlie is playing her some sort of exaggerated, playful compliment, Chuck's gasping, exhausted consciousness takes no time to savour his victory, does not allow himself the luxury of the thrill of his new situation. The universe has opened itself up to him in new ways yet again, revealing possibilities that are so immense that they make those of the previous week seem positively mundane. He doesn't have time to acknowledge it though; if he had a body, he would be breathless, panicking in his resolve to shore up the walls of his new fortress. He does not know if this new victory is fleeting, has no idea if the former host is merely stunned and able to return, but knows that he needs to make his Black Room again to make everything safe. The cuckoo has invaded the nest, turfed out the rival, and now he must make a new nest of his own.

It doesn't take as long, whether it be from having prior experience, from instinct combined with knowing the desired end result, or from being inside a head far more ready for a connection from the energies of a Charlie Wilkes, any Charlie Wilkes. His body appears (loose consciousness becomes the illusion of flesh) and he feels the room appear and solidify around him ... but the darkness remains. There is not even a merely blackened screen; there is no screen at all. He can feel its absence as his efforts to shape one go unheeded, and he almost panics. Then it comes to him; it's because there is no input to be cancelled out by the mere closing of eyes. There is nothing coming from the outside. He feels that he walls of the Black Room are utterly still, and Chuck realises that he's inside a frozen shell. He thinks wildly, fingers and teeth full of crackling, uncatchable psychic adrenaline.

It all has to be running on autopilot, just like *your* body has to do when you leave it behind. It breathes by itself, pumps blood by itself. The body isn't dead, just the active mind, the consciousness. Don't panic. You haven't made a mistake. Don't panic.

The total silence tweaks and pinches at his already tortured and burning mind. There is absolutely nothing coming in, and he feels blindly for a wall to push against, to find his bearings.

You can always leave. Remember, you can always leave. So just take your time, nice and steady. Don't worry about the bigger picture, don't worry about what all this might mean. Step by step. Step by step. She's not going anywhere, nowhere you can't follow in a *heartbeat.*

His groping hands find a wall, and he pushes against it on instinct—

"*—arlie! Charlie, stop fucking around, this isn't funny! You're scaring m—*
"

208

IN THE DARKNESS, THAT'S WHERE I'LL KNOW YOU

The sudden sound makes Chuck jerk away from the wall in startled surprise, screaming noise piercing the darkness like a bomb going off in an empty church. As he does so, the sound cuts off just as quickly. After a few, hesitant seconds, he gingerly replaces his hands, and pushes.

"—*it! Get off ... Charlie? Oh God, Charlie, what's happened? Char—*"

The hands pull away again, and the sound cuts off like a paused recording. Chuck hyperventilates psychic air, and thinks as fast as he can.

In the last world, you never even tried to connect with her. There was no point. The lying bitch would even lie to her own mind. Fucking bitch. Fucking *cunt.* But a connection, with *yourself,* with another Charlie ... what would that do? Surely it's different in here. Inside yourself.

Ideas form.

In her, you were in the driving seat, but only because you were in the place where you could do the most damage. You could only force the monster to do your bidding through pain. But here ... *this is where Charlie Wilkes' mind is meant to be,* at the heart of *Charlie Wilkes'* body. You are also Charlie Wilkes. Are you ... are you in the driving seat here, too, but this time in a way that you never imagined?

Raising his hands again, slowly, like he is frightened of touching an unseen, electrified wire in the darkness, Chuck's hands find the wall once more. He caresses it with the fear and reverence of the desperate virgin, his breathing and nerves at an even higher peak than that. As his hands press against the wall's dead surface, Chuck ignores the continuing cries that can instantly be heard from the world outside, and he sends his mind not out but in. He gasps with an almost orgasmic cry of his own as he feels the deeper connection take hold.

Of course it does. This is no unfamiliar territory, no entirely unrelated environment like that which our Charlie Wilkes would later experience. This is the same as the body that Chuck has been in for all of his life. The grip is immediate, but still difficult and uncertain, like a toddler taking its first steps, trying to figure out how all the different aspects go together.

See.

Nothing.

See.

The screen appears and flickers in and out of existence in the dark, his consciousness reflexively taking the split-second signal from the body's fluttering eyelids and giving it a presence in the Black Room as it comes and goes in rapid succession.

See.

The screen appears once more, increases in certainty, and stays, bringing a dim light into the Black Room as it shows the half-lit bedroom in the world outside. The Black Room is already becoming lighter even without the glow from the screen though, as Chuck's own connection begins to flood The Black Room's very core. It will become lighter than our Charlie's Black Room will ever be. Chuck is dimly aware of this Minnie's voice, coming from the right this time as if she has managed to free herself from under the limp, heavy weight of this

Charlie's body. Chuck doesn't know it, but she is unsuccessfully trying to turn over the body that he inhabits, thinking in her panic that doing so will help this Charlie to breathe. She sees that his eyes are open.

"Charlie? Charlie! Can you hear me? Are you okay?"

Chuck wants her to shut up, as this is taking enough concentration as it is, but he realises that he needs to move onto the next stage anyway; speech.

Speak. Reply.

"Mourgghh."

He can't quite get it, like the control is just slightly beyond the end of his outstretched fingertips. It's maddening, exhilarating. He dare not even stop to think about what he is doing; the implications are just beyond his current state of comprehension, and to try and grasp them would mean a distraction of catastrophic proportions.

"Charlie? Oh fuck, Charlie—*"*

"Fahh. Mnnn."

Come *on.* Speak. You can fucking do it. You need to be able to do all of it.

"What's happened, Charlie? What do you need me to do?" The fear in her voice is palpable, and if Chuck had time to savour it he would have done so. How does she like her perfect Charlie now?

Concentrate. Fucking concentrate.

"I'm fine, baby. Just a funny turn. Sorry if I scared you. Come here."

Chuck freezes; a third person has come into the room. Who the fuck could that be? Was the bitch some kind of dirty three-way slut as well? But then he hears her sigh of relief, and the tears in her voice as she says—

"Oh, thank God, you scared the crap out of me, oh baby ..."

And Chuck hears the sheets rustle as she presses her body against his, then feels *her body press against his as if she was in the Black Room with him, the nerve endings of this Charlie's body now starting to connect with Chuck's mind. All of which would have been deeply thrilling both in terms of potential and physical satisfaction, if not for the fact that he has a far, far more exciting development at hand.*

Those words were not said by a third person. They had come from his host body's lips, and even more importantly, they were not words that he had chosen to say. *They had come subconsciously, brought forth by his own will for the body to speak ... but not from* his *subconscious.*

You killed the conscious mind, but the body still breathes. The heart still pumps. The subconscious takes care of all of that. The subconscious is *still there, inside this body's brain.*

He doesn't even breathe, scared to disrupt this thought process.

Think about it. What is personality? It's the subconscious mind influencing our conscious decisions, surely? Well, you've changed all that. Here, there is no conscious mind for it to act on, not built into it anymore anyway. But the memories and personality traits are all still there, stored in the brain, waiting for your conscious mind to use it like a resource. You've sent the system the *other way.* You needed words ... and they came. They were words *you'd have never thought to say.*

"Give me a hug," she is saying, *"you really frightened me. What was that? What was it all about?"*

Test the arms. See if you can hold her. Don't get carried away, do the small stuff first.

He feels for the nerve endings in the limbs, using the sensations of her skin against his as a frame of reference. He is new to all of this. Eventually, neurons and synapses work correctly and fibres twitch. It is a loose, spasming hug, but he gets the arms to draw around her and hold her tight.

"Are you crying?" she says, mistaking the vibrations in his body for shaking sobs.

What would he say if she said that? How would he lie to cover it up?

Speak.

"Just hiccups," he hears himself say. *"I think your cooking is backfiring again. I keep saying, you should let me cook—"*

Chuck feels a playful slap against his chest, and he silently whoops for delight. He can't believe that this is happening. It's like magic. And that slap felt different too, more harsh and there *than it should have been. What was that about?*

"As if you ever offer! But seriously, if you fainted just then, we need to get you to a doctor—"

Chuck has stopped listening. He's already feeling for the nerves in the other limbs, the genitals, the lips and scalp and feet, all the while reeling with this latest, most perfect revelation, and what it might mean.

He thinks that maybe he can wear his hosts' personality like a mask.

Minnie says something about getting him some water, and Chuck manages to make the body nod. He wants some time alone to get used to driving it. With shaking limbs, he gets the body to sit up and look around; he is in this Minnie's bedroom in her flat. He'd know it from several night visits of the past, but only yesterday he'd been torturing another Minnie here in another world as he carried out the interrogation. He'd felt powerful then, but this ... this ...

He brings the body's hands together, and after a few attempts, he interlaces the fingers, enjoying the delicious feel of skin on skin. Delicious? Yes ... operating a body in this manner, feeling the connection deepen as he savours the second-hand firing of nerve endings. What was it they said about it not being possible to tickle yourself? He knows that he could. Every touch is so amplified.

How would it feel to fuck her? To claim her, to finally put yourself above her and show all of those fucking *cunts* who the real fool is? To play her at her own game, to be the liar and then show her your true, all-powerful self? You can go anywhere. Be anyone. You are limitless.

Then:

How much better would it be to feel these hands come together with her neck in between them?

Thoughts of interrogation, of truth, are blotted out; desire takes over, and like an addict who has been presented with the possibility of an even greater high, he imagines taking his rightful place, slaying his tormentor.

Oh God. To show her. To show them *all ...* when everything feels this delicious ...

He feels the body's mouth begin to water. He wills the body to its feet, and it stands, swaying. Minnie returns with his water, and sees a hunger in her Charlie's eyes that makes her take a slight step backwards.

"You okay?" she says.

"Yeah," her Charlie says, lifting his left hand and turning it back and forth in front of his eyes, then looking down at his feet as he lifts first one, places it down again, then does the same with the other. He looks at the water, as if considering it, and then lifts the glass to his lips. Most of it spills down the side of his face and onto his chest as he drinks it. He looks at the empty glass, and laughs, and then drops it onto the floor.

"Baby ... are you sure you're okay? Do you need to lie down?"

She watches as he just stares at her for a long moment, that unfamiliar look in his eyes. Minnie feels uncomfortable all of a sudden but doesn't know why; this is Charlie, the man she trusts most in the entire world ... so why does she suddenly feel so weird, as if she were talking to a stranger? He is being odd though, as if he's been on the scrumpy cider again like that time in the Cotswolds, but she knows he hasn't even had a drink. Then, like a switch had been flicked, he is suddenly back to normal, smiling, the Charlie she knows seeming to appear in the room again. She relaxes, relieved; he was obviously just dazed, and she wonders why she's being so jumpy. Still, she worries that maybe Charlie's sudden collapse and brief, odd behaviour was some kind of micro-stroke. She's heard of such things.

"Sorry babe, I'm fine, just a little dazed," he says to her. "Tell you what, give me five minutes to get dressed and we'll put a late film on, how's that sound? Just need a bit of quiet time to get my bearings again. That funny turn has kind of knocked me for six. Probably need more water."

He sounds normal, and she relaxes that bit more.

"Okay. Are you hungry?"

"God, yeah," he says. "I'd love a sandwich." *She smiles, and kisses him on the cheek.*

"I'll sort it. But if you're not out in five minutes, I'm coming to get you," she says, heading for the door. "You really scared me."

"Don't worry. I think five minutes will be all I'll need," he says, grinning with that schoolboy charm that she loves so much. She smiles back, and heads out of the door ... but concern makes her look back over her shoulder, to check that he really is fine. He might be putting on a show after all, covering up any real physical trouble to spare her the worry. That'd be just like him. The door is already closing behind her, but she catches a glimpse of him, still standing upright in the dark. He looks steady on his feet, she thinks ... but it didn't look like he was smiling at all anymore. Had he been staring after her?

She dismisses the thought, remembering her previous paranoia. She had promised him some quiet minutes, and that's what he'll get. She heads to the kitchen to make his sandwich and to wait, thinking about the spectre of work in the morning and savouring the contrasting lazy evening ahead.

IN THE DARKNESS, THAT'S WHERE I'LL KNOW YOU

Chuck thinks about how he will do it. When it happens, it is even sweeter than he hoped it would be.

***

It was cold, but Charlie couldn't afford to wait. He needed somewhere that his body wouldn't be bothered, and the field he was now sitting in was the nearest place that would do. He didn't have time to mess around, and it wasn't so cold that his body was likely to be in any kind of trouble even if it ended up being left out all night. It was just past eight pm.

He threw his lightweight bike over the top of the locked gate, and clambered after it with trembling hands. The frustration was so thick that he felt as if he could almost chew it with every nervous breath that made its way from his mouth. *Minnie. Danger.* And here he was, stuck as far as he could ever possibly be from her.

How the fuck did he do it? The only Charlie in this world is me, and I didn't go anywhere near her. So how the hell is the Chuck in that world saying the same damn thing to this world's Minnie, the same—

He pushed the thought away for the umpteenth time, and pulled his coat tight around him as he made his way over to the field's corner. There he could get as near to the bottom of the hedge as possible so that he would be out of sight, and also have a windbreak. Admittedly, it wasn't an ideal place to snort ketamine, but it was the first place in the area that would suffice.

Neil had tried to play it pally when Charlie had rang, but Charlie had kept it curt and business-like. Fortunately, he had enough cash on him to meet the payment required, but Charlie had been worried that Neil might have been reluctant to hand the stuff over given Charlie's previous concerning reaction. He should have known better; Neil took his money with a smile and a handshake, on the half-jovial proviso that Charlie *didn't do it here! Ha ha!* The guy had done nothing to change Charlie's previous opinion of him being nothing but an utter fucking weasel. Once the drugs were in his pocket, and advice given on how best to take it, Charlie had left Neil's house without another word, leaving the prick standing in his hallway looking bemused.

The low temperature wasn't due to wind, at least, which was good as it meant the crystals weren't going to blow everywhere. The hedge would have helped if the wind *had* been up, but it wouldn't have blocked everything. He poured the crystals out onto a piece of paper that he had in his jean pocket (that week's shift rota, as it turned out) and used his maxed-out credit card to divvy the amount up into three even lines, as advised. He'd been very specific that he only wanted enough for one trip, and an acceptable amount for a second-timer too, as he knew he'd be squatting out in the cold somewhere without scales to weigh out amounts or even a proper flat surface. In hindsight, he wished he'd thought of getting two lots of the stuff in separate bags so that he had some for a backup trip should this somehow go wrong, but he guessed that beggars couldn't be choosers.

It worked for you the first time you took it ... but who knows what the hell is going to happen this time? You changed something for good in your brain, or reminded it how to unlock something; what if this undoes everything? What if it makes it worse *somehow, or you end up in a different Black Room than before, with a different Minnie? What if—*

He forced himself to calm down. He knew enough about ketamine to know that anxiety can produce a bad effect, even if it was a chill out drug. But how the hell was he supposed to calm down? He was desperate to get back there, desperate to let her know the danger that she was in. He wished fervently that he hadn't let her sleep, that he'd somehow stayed there—

What if he was only waiting until you were gone? What if he knew you were there?

The thought was ridiculous. How would Chuck even know that he was there in the first place?

Well, how the hell has he managed to be in two worlds, and to kill someone in another world at that?

The thought both made his previous one sound plausible, and his current worries sound ridiculous. It could all just be a coincidence, after all. People said 'greased lightning', didn't they?

Not very often. And no-one *fucking says 'faster than greased-up lightning'. They just don't.*

No. They didn't, that was true.

Charlie took a deep breath, and looked up at the night sky above him. The stars were out, and the road, even in this suburban area, was silent for a moment. Everything was very still. He felt sad then, and suddenly felt the depth of the loneliness that he'd only recently realised was there. Sometimes, it seemed, the ten percent was kept secret even from those whom it belongs to.

The moment passed. Charlie pushed fear aside and snorted the first line.

***

Once he is finished with her body, Chuck stands in the middle of this Minnie's living room. He sways back and forth, breathing through his nose and inhaling the subtle smells around him: cheap air freshener, half-drunk tea, dust, the aroma of the evening meal the couple had shared before sex, blood. It is all so intoxicating. He had no idea anything could feel like this.

The sun is coming up outside. It's been a long night. It had been so intense—far, far greater than he could have ever anticipated—that even though he had made it last as long as possible it simply had not been enough. Even with her mouth taped, she'd threatened to make too much noise, and he'd had to end it sooner than he'd liked. Not for fear of capture by the authorities—

he could just leave this Charlie's body and return to the void—but for fear of being interrupted before he could complete the deed. That had been the only down side. Still, the part immediately afterward had been intense, and deeply arousing. He remembers it again: as he'd looked at her freshly-deceased body, the frenzy still upon him (it had been a frenzy, of course, and he knows that that is something that he will have to learn to control if he is ever to extract the full amount of satisfaction possible from the deed) he hadn't been able to help himself. He'd attacked it again.

As he stands, calm and at peace, even now he knows that the need will eventually be upon him again; he is doomed forever, but that is just fine by him. He wants to keep doing it. Utter bliss. He has never known such contentment, such confidence in the future. Even his old, embarrassingly naïve self (the one that swallowed all the lies whole and put a fucking bitch in charge of everything) never relaxed about his own dreams, never trusted that everything would work out all right, because there was always the chance that something could go wrong. Of course there was; he'd let the attaining of one woman become crucial to his own happiness. How utterly blind.

He looks at the ragged mess on the floor behind him, lying there resembling so much offal.

Look at it. You let *that* be everything. You see now? You see what she is?

He does. He feels a loose droplet of blood run down his neck, and he shivers. It's like being tickled by an electric current. Everything feels so fucking good...

He wonders what to do next; he knows that he should return home at some point, or his original body, lying unconscious in bed as it is, will starve. He wonders what will happen if he lets that happen; would that set him free? Or would he die as well? Better not to risk it. After all, for now, he is sated. He can wait until the night. He had long ago mastered the art of getting his head down and getting through the days, after all. With a smile and a deeply contented sigh, he unlocks and rises from this Charlie Wilkes' body as he leaves this world behind, never to return. He heads back up into the void, where even his fear of The End can't rattle his inner peace. Not completely, anyway. Back in the world he has just vacated, Charlie Wilkes' mindless and blood-soaked body slumps to the floor.

Chuck awakes in his own body, and while the improved ease of movement is vaguely pleasant, the dull sensation of his own flesh and bones feels like he is buried. The sheer focus of will and determination it takes to manipulate a host body that he has invaded electrifies every nerve ending to the point of ecstasy (he idly wonders how pain will feel when he inevitably hurts himself, but he dismisses it; no matter how bad, it will be worth it) but the lazy, automatic motor functions of his own limbs are utterly lacking in sensation by comparison. It's like being stroked while wearing thick leather.

What to do next? He sighs, contented despite his relative physical discomfort. He rises, and moves to use the small sink in the corner of his filthy room; he wants to make some tea. He scratches at his face as the kettle boils, scratching hard enough to leave red welts, trying without realising to recreate *the heightened sensation of the skin he has recently vacated. The obvious answer is, of course, to do it again; that will be happening, without doubt. No, the harder question is how best to go about it.*

It needs to be *just* like it was before, but better. You had to kill her too quickly. You need to make sure that you have time to work, undisturbed.

This is true. He will make sure of this next time. But there was something else about the experience, something that—now he is in a calmer, more relaxed state of mind—intrigues him. The other new experience that he has just been through.

You were him. On the outside, at least; she responded to you like you were him. You used his words, his responses...

But he doesn't want to be him. Not anymore. Why would he want to be? To be with that thing, that lie in human form, that bag of flesh? No, no. But still ... there were answers to be had, weren't there? He remembers wanting them, working hard to get them. They might be less important now, but even so; surely if he's the butt of some big conspiracy, some cosmic joke, he needs to know who's responsible? So he can take care of them too? So he can get them all?

You could do both. You get her to spill her guts to you, not realising who you are ... and then you can spill *her* guts.

He laughs wildly at his own mental pun, and then giggles like a child as a shiver of anticipation runs through his skin. He wants to remember that one.

You wouldn't even have to worry about when you meet her, either. It wouldn't matter, because this time, *you can be him.* You can turn on everything that you need, just like that. It wouldn't be a case of having to make sure the situation was the same because you'd need all the help you can get ... you wouldn't *need* any help. You can wear that mask anytime you like, and you can be the Charlie the liar expects, *he thinks with a madman's logic. He is shaking now, grinning like an idiot, pacing the floor and flicking the tips of his fingers again and again. An even more exciting idea follows on the heels of the other one.*

You could do it again. You could find it, you can fly through the void and look through the worlds at will now, and find another one that has *that* meeting. This time, you follow the script, or let his body do it for you. This time, you let things go how they should go. You get close. She opens up, she lets you in the joke, she tells you who is behind it and who is pulling all their nasty little strings ... and then you punish her. And if she doesn't tell you anything, why, what do you think happens next? Either way, *you still win.*

It's perfect. It's so perfect he can barely contain himself. He hugs himself tightly, then does it even harder, wanting to feel his ribs bend and his skin push painfully onto the bone, but it's just not the same in his proper body. He needs to sit down, so he allows himself to fall backwards onto the bed, breathless and laughing. He has a brief moment, one where he wonders what he did to deserve this incredible blessing of power and endless potential physical ecstasy.

You have all the time in the world. You need to do this properly though; it could get messy. You need to eat. You need to look after your actual body.

IN THE DARKNESS, THAT'S WHERE I'LL KNOW YOU

You can only visit other worlds at night, or you will starve. If that happens, it will all be over, and she and the others will all go unpunished.

The thought is an immediately sobering one. He does need to be careful. How easily he could stay in the other worlds indefinitely, skipping from one to the other, and never coming back to his own, mundane body until it was a malnourished, dying wreck. He must be extremely strict; everything must be in moderation, especially with a high like the one he has just experienced. It would be so easy to indulge in it endlessly. No; he must return to work once more, must get a job to pay the bills and keep maintaining the food and shelter that his own body requires. He must slog through the days, and earn the nights, just like in the past.

Okay then.

He dresses, and prepares to go into town and buy some running shoes. The body must be looked after; preparations must be made.

He earns his night-time, and he once again slips into the void with his anticipation and need at a peak that even he could not have foreseen. He needs it by now, and the time before the night is almost too much to take. But back in the void, unencumbered by any kind of physical form, he literally feels a weight slip from his shoulders as he knows that the time has come again. With a thought, the worlds flip by him as he searches for the ideal starting point. He knows it will be difficult—the worlds with the timeline where he and Minnie are the right people to be together are so, so many in number—but he feels that it is worth a try. As much as he fears The End, and does not like to hang in the void for any longer than necessary, he desperately wants to find the right starting place. It's not essential (he can pick any point before if need be, as he knows now that he can be the right Charlie at any time, and could engineer a meeting; he knows where she lives and works in most of these worlds, after all) but he wants it that way so badly. He feels for it, tries to visualise it and see if that helps find the right time in the right world, and receives a dim flicker of awareness...

You felt it. You can find it if you focus. You *can* find what you're looking for. You have the power.

He strains, his ragged consciousness tearing a little in the process, and thinks he has it again. He nearly misses it as it flashes past—at any other time, perhaps he would have done—but he snags something ... wait. A Minnie walking in town ... Dave by her side, holding her hand, reassuring. Check the street; YES. She is nearly there. He has done it! He can even draw the right time and the right world to him! True, it was close and he doesn't know if he could do it again, but oh this is—

You're going to miss it. Find him. *Find him.*

Yes. He dives into the world, and wonders if, as it was when he was a child, if he cannot go too far from her, as this might stop him being able to find that world's Charlie, but in this instance it doesn't matter; he doesn't need to, because with every step she takes she draws closer to Barrington's. Inside, Chuck knows there will be a Charlie Wilkes, ripe for the picking. He travels the short distance to the bar, searches, finds him with ease.

He doesn't know how easy it will be to take this one without the same advantage that he had last time (no orgasm to take mental advantage of) but he hopes that his experience of having done it once will give him an edge. As it turns out, it's even easier than before. This world's Charlie is drunk, and his sluggish, unprepared mind is no match for Chuck's focused, experienced attack.

Oh, God yes. Perfect.

Chuck has found this Charlie inside one of the toilet cubicles. As Chuck speeds towards this Charlie's body—an invisible, swooping harbinger of death that heralds this Charlie's end—he nearly laughs as he sees what this Charlie has found on top of the cistern; a broken Samsung phone. Chuck had forgotten all about that. Just before this Charlie's hand can grasp the device, Chuck has already dropped into his mind and set about usurping the space inside.

This Charlie's body falls backwards against the cubicle door before Chuck can stop it; even though the creation of the Black Room—his workshop, his control centre—is almost instant, he is still going through the process of making the neural connections, triggering the correct nerve impulses and feeling his way like a switchboard operator figuring out what goes where. With the original host mind dead, the body collapses without control as Chuck hurries to get things moving once more. While assuming command is quicker than before—Chuck thinks that it will get easier each time—but it still takes a while, more than he had anticipated. He thought he would get in and get the body under his control straight away, but it is proving more difficult than that. He realises that if he doesn't hurry up then he's going to miss her; she will have already panicked, and fled. The body's knees buckle, despite Chuck's best efforts, and the door rattles as this human puppet slides down it onto the floor. Chuck has the eyes open at least, but that's all he's managed, and the whole thing is made even harder by the rush of deliciously distracting sensation that comes with it.

Focus. *Focus.*

It takes several minutes; the piloting of another body would be hard enough without alcohol-impaired motor functions, but eventually he does it. Once he's upright, establishing equilibrium is easier, and he opens the cubicle door before realising that he nearly forgot the most essential prop; the phone. He re-enters, grabs the black plastic object, and then exits the cubicle once more. He then moves to the sink and stares into the mirrors.

"Charrr ... " he makes the body say, looking at its reflection in the mirror. Chuck sees it on the Black Room's screen and checks the body's face for its expression as it talks. It's not a bad start, but he needs it as correct as possible, and fast. The timing here is all off. He's been overconfident. "Char. Lee. Charlie."

He tries a smile; it's passable, and it will just have to do. It's time to move.

He opens the toilet door and heads into the bar, opening and closing his left fist by his side to continue getting his physical bearings as his right hand grasps the Samsung. There is no time for nerves, and to his surprise he doesn't really feel any anyway; he wonders if that's because of his new, higher perspective on The Liar, because he knows he can wear this Charlie Wilkes' personality like a hat, or a combination of the two. Either way—

WORLD 1   OUR CHARLIE (LOVES MINNIE W?

                 MINNIE KILLED BY CHUCK

WORLD 2   CHUCK

                 MINNIE LOVED BY OUR CHARL

IN THE DARKNESS, THAT'S WHERE I'LL KNOW YOU

The door to the bar is swinging shut, and Charlie sees the shocked faces of the people near it (one woman is gesturing to her dress, and the spilled wine that now adorns the front of it) as Dave dashes towards the door now from the inside, realising too late what has happened and wanting to comfort his friend and tell her it's all okay.

He's missed her. They have been and gone. For the second time, she has left him standing alone in that bar. While he knows that it ultimately doesn't matter, he also knows that he can go to her home and wait for her (even if that wouldn't be as satisfying) but it still makes his hatred burn even brighter.

She'll get hers. She'll get it *so* bad. Oh, Minnie. The punishment I have for you...

"Charlie!"

Chuck turns instinctively at the sound of his name; someone is waving at him from the other side of the bar. It's Clint. Chuck recognises him because in his world, they used to work together, but his Clint never greeted him like this; it's so different from his own experience that Chuck actually turns around to see who Clint is waving at, expecting there to be some kind of mistake. When he turns back, Clint is rolling his eyes in a yes, hilarious *kind of way, and beckoning him over again, holding out a bottle of beer for Chuck to take.*

This was unexpected. For a second, he hesitates; he has barely shared more than a nodded 'hello' with this man before now. How could he possibly—

Don't be an idiot. You have everything you need to be Charlie right here, in the body's basement.

This is true, but even so, what would be the point? Why stay here in this heaving, suffocating bar with all the other liars when you could be killing time—waiting for her *to come out of her flat unawares, waiting with piano wire and fingernails and teeth—in a far more pleasurable way? You could eat, imagine how ice cream would taste in this body—*

But that's the whole point, isn't it? They're liars too.

The thought stops him dead in his tracks. He had already been beginning to turn to the door, to find some crappy kebab house and buy his fill of delicious, greasy, garbage food—his host body's mouth already watering at the prospect—when this new possibility springs forth. What do they know?

There's too many to do anything to them on your own. You can't *make* them talk...but they don't know who you are. They think you're him, they think you're a part of it. Why not watch, and listen? Get amongst them. Are they willing actors, or merely puppets in this grand show that's been put on for your benefit for all these years? You could walk amongst them and find out, couldn't you? Wear your mask. Punish if you can ... but otherwise, lay low. A far more useful way to spend your time, at least while you choose your moment to claim her. And you *want* to punish her correctly, don't you? She may have gone tonight, but you can easily make it so you bump into her somewhere; start the whole process, gain her trust, get inside, get the answers ... then reveal your true self and *crush her utterly.*

He shudders deliciously at the thought. Yes, that is how he wants it.

So if you want to do it that way, and you've missed the ideal opportunity tonight, you'll need to find the same moment in another world, won't you? *But,* if you really want to draw her in, you need to be *really* good at being *him,* right? You need to be able to say what he would at a split-second's notice, right? Otherwise, what kind of a spy would you be?

He nods as he sits in the Black Room, believing the lunacy as he uses it to rationalise never returning home to his numb, boring body ever again.

So why not perfect it? Why not take this time to practice, and make sure that you are the best false Charlie Wilkes that you can be? It wouldn't do to have you pausing every time someone speaks to you, freezing up while you dip down into the basement to pull out whatever garbage your host would say. Think about it; be *this* Charlie in the daytime. Live his life. Work where he works. Watch the liars. Practice the act. Enjoy the body. At night, well...you can either stay and indulge (*Oh God, oh yes*) or go home and nourish the other body (*my real body, I mustn't forget, the real, mundane body*) and you're no idiot, you know you'll be sensible and look after it.

He nods again, deadly serious. Of course he will. He can handle it. He can handle it.

And hey ... there's always that Claire at work. You remember her?

He remembers.

I bet she fucks the Charlie here. I bet they're fuck buddies, two liars together. You could do that. You could be him and do that. You always wanted to fuck her, didn't you?

He did.

Well, what better way to practice? Can you imagine *fucking* in this body?

That...oh...

If you can convince Claire, you can do it again with the *queen* of the fucking liars. You can convince her. Right?

Right.

And if you can't the first time you try, you'll be able to the next time. It's all practice.

It's all practice.

Just keep it all in perspective. Don't get carried away, and you can keep living in paradise after paradise for the rest of your life ... leaving each world after the best climax possible. You remember how that feels, don't you?

He does. Even with the firing, enthralling sensations that are all around him, now the initial hit has passed, he remembers the frenzy. Something deep inside him rumbles, and it's all he can do to stop himself from charging out of the door right there and then.

Wait. Patience. Why waste this opportunity? Prepare. And then, when you know you are ready ... strike. And then strike in the next world. And the next.

The instinctive laugh of joy that comes out of Chuck's body in the Black Room echoes outwards from his mind, and travels out of the mouth of that world's Charlie Wilkes' body. It turns, and heads towards the group of inebriated young men that Clint stands with, and takes the offered bottle from Clint's outstretched hand.

"Where were you going?" laughs Clint, a bemused look on his face. Charlie doesn't respond straight away, looking confused, but when he does Clint can see what looks like relief spread across Charlie's face as he breaks into a smile.

"Just wondering what the bloody hell we're all doing drinking where we work. Whose idea was this?"

Clint grins, and shrugs.

"Staff discount," he says, and offers his bottle in a toast. This time, there is no hesitation from Charlie; Clint smiles as Charlie accepts, even if Charlie's hand seems to falter in the toasting.

Chuck does not return to his own world that night (surely his body can last another day without getting into bother) and decides not to head to Neil's house with the others (they're going to do some 'stuff', apparently, and Chuck is terrified of even being in the same room with it, imagining that another hit while already in another world would send him spinning and tumbling straight into the heart of The End.) He takes the Samsung with him; it was a conversational opener with her once, so who knows, it might work elsewhere. A quick rummage in the body's subconscious tells him where he lives, which key he needs to get through the house's front door. He stops at a kebab house he knows (he's pleased to see that it exists in this world) and buys a large doner meat and chips with several cans of coke. He stops at an all-night garage and buys a tub of ice cream. He can't stop smiling.

He goes to his shared house and spends the night in his room (he casually notes how much nicer it is than the one he has in his world) eating, drinking, and masturbating. The first two are indescribable, and the latter is a religious experience. He doesn't sleep; he doesn't even feel tired. The body is utterly alive under his command. He wonders if it will eventually need to sleep. He will see.

The next day of practice begins with breakfast; he heads downstairs and meets his housemate, a young woman that he instantly dislikes. Work is better; he's sharing a shift with Claire of all people, and while he finds himself deeply nervous around her for some reason (she pokes and slaps at him a lot; he assumes that it's playful, but it sets him on edge) he begins to learn to lean on the system within him, feeling the responses start to come more naturally. He realises that, if he gets good enough, he can just sit back and let the whole thing run almost on autopilot, while he absorbs the physical feelings. The latter part of that is a nice idea, but the former isn't; he hates this other Charlie, loathes his easy manner and seeming need to talk to people all the fucking time.

Another one who made the lie so big that he even believes it himself.

But even so, he can't help but feel a bitter sting every time he pulls out a remark that makes someone laugh, not only because that could have been him but because doing so makes him into more of a fraud, makes him more like them.

It's a means to an end. You're serving the greater good.

He knows this is true, but Charlie keeps saying things that bring people in, that keep a conversation going. He wants to be quiet...but he knows he has to keep practicing if he is to deliver the perfect coup de grace that he wants to so very badly. He sticks with it, and later that day he even ends up flirting with Claire; his flow is, for the moment at least, absolutely perfect, as he wears this Charlie Wilkes' personality and makes it dance. Claire does not know how close she came to tragedy, however; Chuck's confusion with lust and rage is like a tripwire connected directly to his fists. He manages to contain it.

Focus. Practice.

To Chuck's complete and utter caught-flat-footed shock, Minnie walks in, and asks if he can help her.

He's already reacted the second he sees her (later, he will think about the moment and be pleased, realising that he instinctively dug deep and pulled out the correct reaction. He is internalising the motion now, go for it reflexively. This is major progress) putting on his best Charlie smile and walking over to her, standing behind the bar. The outside shows confidence and pleasure at the sight before him. The inside is freaking out; why is she here? Is this the meeting in this world after all? Was he wrong about last night? If that's the case, he hopes that the small amount of practice that he's already had will be enough, his excitement and nerves building. This could be even easier than he thought.

Okay, but keep calm. Don't blow this, now. Just let the other guy do the talking.

"Well, I'll certainly do my best to try, as long as you're not after money," he hears his voice say, feeling his eyebrows go up as he punctuates the insipid pun with his expression. *Chuck feels sick, hearing his own voice fawning already over this putrid bitch. How did he ever obsess so? She's a bag of meat and lies. She chuckles slightly, and out of sight Chuck's knuckles whiten behind the bar as he restrains the urge to slap her.*

"No ... heh, no ... I just needed to ask you—" she says, and then pauses. It's unusual, but Chuck will not allow his wildly beating heart to put him off now. He knows what to do, and can do it if he just stays focused.

"Ask me...?" Chuck hears his voice say, and as he feels his facial expression change he knows that this Charlie would be thinking that his luck was in. Chuck leans forward in the darkness of the Black Room, the ogre in his gloomy den of malevolent intent.

"Are you...is your name Charlie?" she asks, and her voice is a strange whisper. This is something unexpected. How the fuck does she know his name? We know why, of course, but then we have already seen this conversation take place, observing from another perspective.

Chuck tries to rally.

Don't panic, keep it together. Someone else on the staff might have told her, you don't know anything. Let the body respond.

"Yes, yes I am!" it says. "Sorry, have we met ... ?" Again, there is a strange pause before she responds, and then she reaches for her purse.

"Sorry, I'm vibrating," she says, pulling a phone from her purse and turning away to take a call. Chuck is surprised again, if only in a much more minor way; he didn't hear her phone vibrate, and her phone was certainly close enough for him to—

A very faint thought blips across Chuck's mind, so quick that he doesn't even really catch it; even if he had, he wouldn't have given it any full credibility. It's stupid, something he'd sometimes worried about over the years and always eventually dismissed. He waits for her to finish.

You're doing well. Stay cool. Let the body do the work.

He will. When she turns around, he's ready.

"*Sorry, you were saying?*"

An apology? Sick, false fuck.

"*Yeah," she says, smiling. Chuck bets she's happy. She thinks she's getting her liar's reward today, he knows. Well, she'll certainly get what she deserves, all right. "Apparently you're the guy to talk to about lost property stuff?*"

The idea shoots through his mind again, this time setting off a loud noise as it does so; her question lends credence to the first thought, making it bigger ... but it's still lunacy. He refocuses. Focus is infinitely important in this moment. It would be so easy to lose himself in thoughts of the taste of her flesh in his mouth, the snapping of her fingers under his own...

Stop.

"*Well, I don't know why someone suggested me specifically, but I can certainly have a look for you. Missing something, are you?" the body says.*

"*Yes, my phone, it's a Samsung, black. Has it been handed in?*"

Chuck freezes. This time, the idea flashes through and drives itself home, making a sound like a bomb going off. The body is already responding ("Hold on a sec, I haven't seen one myself, but I'll have a double check for you," and rooting around in the lost property box at the other end of the bar) but he feels like he's been hit with a psychic baseball bat. Even the body's automated movements are shaking, feeling the feedback from Chuck's remote control; Chuck hopes that Minnie can't see it.

The phone you found. The one that she can't even know about. The phone that isn't even hers. The one that was in the toilet *before she even got to the bar.* The same phone that you've seen other Charlies use as a prop to open her up for their first conversation. How the fuck would she even know? Why would she be asking for a phone *that isn't hers?*

There's only one way she could know. It's finally happened.

But that's impossible.

But it isn't, he knows ... after all, with the sheer number of worlds out there in which he and Minnie should meet and actually fall in love, it's more of a miracle that it hasn't happened already.

Chuck is scared, terrified even. What does this mean? And isn't it highly significant that, now that he has spent a significant amount of time in a host body, this finally happens? Was the other one sent by some greater force, sent to take him out?

Calm down. It could just be a coincidence. She could just be asking for a friend, a friend whom that phone belongs to. She doesn't even seem to realise that she *just answered her actual phone in front of you,* which proves that she hasn't lost anything (*and it could be a spare one, lots of people have spare phones*) and suggests that, indeed, she *is* just asking for a friend.

223

He realises that, either way, he should play along. He drops back into full control and pulls the Samsung out of his pocket, kept on him at all times like a talisman. Out of sight behind the bar, he slips it into the lost property box as his head spins.

Keep cool. Be cool.

He produces it as if he's just found it.

"Oh, no, hold on, is this it?"

She pauses briefly. To anyone else, it would just look like a moment of unexplained uncertainty; perhaps the light is bad, or they're just distracted for a second. To Chuck, however, it looks entirely different, the reason as clear as day; she'd looked as if she were waiting for confirmation from someone that it actually was the right phone. Someone that Chuck can't see, someone that only Minnie can hear.

She would know her own phone, especially one with such an immense and distinct crack on the screen. She would know it immediately, but she didn't. She had to wait to be told *it was right.*

It's finally happened.

He cannot believe it. He feels a heady, intense mix of shock, fear, and rage. He always knew it would be possible ... but ... how?

But he knows how, even though he wishes he didn't, wishes the thought wasn't undeniably true: there are many, many other worlds that share his life, and there was always the chance that someone—most likely another him, as these are the worlds where he and Minnie should meet and "fall in love", a concept almost laughable now—in another place would develop the same abilities. It's finally happened. There is another person in her head.

Another Charlie Wilkes.

Oh God. Oh God. Oh no.

He cannot believe it, and this is the most devastated he has been since he first saw The End.

You can't let it show. You can't let them know. Just ... get through these next few minutes, and then you can plan your next move. Stay calm. Stay calm. For the love of God, stay calm.

He gets to his feet in his own Black Room, his hands shaking, trying to let the autopilot continue, but it's hard. He is rattled, and it's hard to concentrate, but he just manages it as Minnie speaks again.

You should have seen it when she came in. It's written all over her face. Look at her eyes; she's listening to someone else, you can see it. Oh God, it's true. There's someone in there. Oh God.

"Oh, great!" *she says, so convincing. Of course she is. She's the Queen Of The Liars.* "Was it you that found it?"

That one nearly takes Chuck off at the knees. Is this a test? He panics; does she know? *Is that why she's here? Do* both *of them know? Oh God, what does that mean?*

Calm down, you fucking asshole! She's testing you! She's not sure!

"No, no," *he manages, the autopilot flow now totally shot. He has to consciously reach for it again.* "I don't know when this came in to be honest, I *wasn't working last night. Someone must have given it to another member of bar staff. Here you go."* He holds it out, making the body produce a smile that he takes from a memory of Charlie being given a present. He hopes that if he holds her eyes, she won't notice his hand shaking. As it happens, she's too busy looking at the phone itself.

"Ah, no," she says with a sigh, *"This isn't mine. Mine's a Galaxy II, this is the older one."* She hands it back, and Chuck, now watching every nuance in her mannerisms, wonders what the hell this means.

Maybe she really lost a phone, just another Samsung? Maybe she dropped it when she ran out?

No, the pauses, the coincidence ... but then, it could just be a coincidence ... he feels as if his head is going to explode. He desperately wants that to be true. Oh please, let that be true.

It doesn't fucking matter! Think! Either way, you need to build from this, right? She either knows, or suspects, in which case you have *got* to find out what's happening! Shitting yourself will do nothing! And if she *doesn't* know anything, and it's all just a colossal coincidence, then you've been given an inroad with which to get closer and start the process that you wanted to! You haven't had as much practice as you'd like, but you've come on so quickly, and this is too good an opportunity to waste if she *doesn't* know or suspect the truth. Do *not* let her leave without getting her number. Understand?

For a moment, the excitement of the possibility of his perfect plan being realised is so great that it blocks out even the shock of the possibility of another person being in her head, maybe even another Charlie, but then such is the attention of a madman. He remembers now, and feels sick. He's confused. He can't think straight now, needs time, wants her gone, needs her gone. This is all escalating too fast, too much pressure. On top of it all, he just wants to leap over the bar and tear her face off, and he has to keep that in check too.

"Ah, sorry to hear it," he says without thinking, and he realises that it's just his words, not the body's. He's exposed, right out in the open. Get it together! His panic peaks, and he flails around mentally, trying to re-establish the system that was so perfect only minutes ago, but he can't. His autopilot is confused, running his own thoughts out through the body's mouth.

Okay, fuck it! If you can't get it under control, just sound natural! You only need to get her number and she's gone, how hard can that be!

"Never mind," he says, and it almost sounds right. He checks her face intensely; she doesn't seem to have noticed the difference? *"Listen, do you want to leave your contact details in case it turns up?"* He hears the nerves in his own voice, hears the intent. Too much. Too keen. He's going to blow this.

"Oh, that'd be great. I'll give you a card. I knew these'd come in handy for something one day." she's saying, and dips into her purse for something. Chuck can't believe it. He did it.

Nearly there. Come on now. Don't get excited.

He takes the card, looks at it; the address is the same as he thought it would be.

"Minnie Cooper?" he says, as if he's heard the name for the first time, and it sounds so convincing that he grins at his own performance...and then catches her expression and realises that the smile has transmitted onto the body's face.

Say something! Do *not* give yourself away! You don't know what she suspects!!

"Web design, eh? Tough work to make a living from, you must be good?" The redemption is so good that he could almost weep.

"Apparently not," she chuckles, "Gave it up a while back and started working on something else. Had the cards printed and just needed an excuse to use them up. But I still do it, if you know someone who needs any." It's a bounce back, an opening for a polite response, but Chuck is spent. He has nothing, his nerves shot. What would Charlie say? He feels around, but the connection is just temporarily dead, mental impotence.

Just be breezy, get her gone. You've got what we need. Get her out of here.

Thinking of nothing else, he holds up the card and flicks it.

"Not at the moment. But if I find anyone, I'll let you know quicker than greased-up lightning," he says.

That was pretty good.

There was that line again, and it did sound good...but then he realises that he's responded incorrectly.

That's not even something that asshole would say! You're blowing it, you're leaving yourself right out in the open!

The needle of the lunatic's paranoia drops deep into the red. He knows that it's all over his face.

Fix it. Fix it.

"Uh..." he says, but she interrupts him. Normally, this would drive him to a rage, but right now it's a relief.

"That's one way of putting it," she says with a smile, the patronising fuck. "But listen, thanks anyway."

"No problem," Chuck says, waving her off, deeply relieved to be seeing her go as she turns and heads towards the door without a backwards glance. It's as if he has avoided the firing squad. Even through his relief, his broken, split mind sees that—again—she is turning her back on him. It's all he can do to stop himself coming around the bar and jamming a corkscrew into her spine.

You did it. It doesn't matter. Take a break, sit down, and plan your next move.

He watches her through the glass as she crosses the street. Checking. She just walks.

So maybe she really doesn't know—

Just before she disappears from sight, he sees her hands moving, gesticulating.

Talking to herself.

He keeps his head down throughout the rest of the day, conserving mental energy and taking pleasures where he can, soothing his stress (water from the tap running over his hands, the smell of freshly cooked bar meals) and trying not to think about it all for a while; he lost control there, and he needs to calm down and get it back. However, he can't help but think about it, of course. When his shift ends, he heads home, turning her business card over and over in his fingers all the while.

Is this one worth the risk? There's other worlds, after all. So many. You could just leave, to be on the safe side. You don't know who this other guy (*or girl*) is, what he can do, or even why he's here. He might have been *sent*, and if that's the case, it's got to be best to run.

The idea irks him greatly. Why the hell should he *run? Maybe the other guy was even here first, but who cares? If Chuck runs now, he might always be running. No ... he has to get to the bottom of it. He has to take the risk.*

If *they're* not certain about you either, what does that mean? Is that why they came to the bar? *What do they know about you??*

It continues in this manner for some time. At home, he orders pizza, pleasures himself, and in this manner he manages to get lost in sensation for a while. No, he won't be running; how could he let himself be forced to leave all this? The physical bliss relaxes him in the best way, and he begins to feel the autopilot, the connection to the subconscious, return. He feels fortified, ready to face them. He knows what he must do.

He considers returning to his own world first, to feed and water his own body, but then decides against it. His body will be okay a little while longer. This is too important. He picks up her business card and dials the number printed there.

She answers, and he speaks, wincing at the smarmy bullshit that the body brings forth ("This may be a little forward, because I know you left your card just to get your phone back, but ... well, I couldn't help wondering if you wanted to go for dinner tonight?") and struggles to quell his rage as she gives her simpering, flirtatious slut answers. It makes him sick, but he has to keep it up; he listens for hesitations, for traces of her listening to the other. She may be the Queen Of The Liars, but she slipped up earlier; he has to listen in case she does so again.

It doesn't happen (maybe he's not there now? Maybe he was never there at all?) and again there is that uncertainty ... but even if he's wrong, he's doing the right thing. He has to get close now, to get within the Queen's circle of trust and to wait for her to fuck up. He has to find out what the hell is going on with her and her internal lodger—the fraud, the potential fake *Charlie in her head— and he will do it any way that he can. It might just be that he has to simply kill them both to be on the safe side, an option that he will gladly take. He can't risk another Charlie Wilkes being in competition with him, living in between the worlds. What if the other affects his plans? What if he gets in the way? The idea enrages him, and fear runs through him as he can't help but ponder the other question:*

What if he's more powerful than you?

They continue to talk, and Chuck listens with a mixture of fascination and disgust. His desire to punish becomes a burning need once more; he even starts to wonder if he will be able to hold himself back during dinner, even though he knows that he must. He hears her laugh down the phone again, and it is like a taunt, like clawed fingernails drawn across a blackboard.

Ohhh, Minnie ... bring all the backup you like. It won't be able to help you.

But the nerves still thrum beneath the surface.

The call ends, and Chuck lies the body down on the bed, preparing to detach with great reluctance. He means to leave immediately, but then there is the feel of the bed sheets on his skin, stroking against him with every movement ... he suddenly realises that an hour has passed.

Go. You need to go.

With an effort, he detaches, travelling home through the void (don't look at it don't look at it) and opens his own, mundane eyes. The thirst hits him like an iron grip around his throat; he gets to his feet in a desperate run to the toilet, but feels faint and drops to his knees.

What the fuck? I haven't been gone that long, surely?

He sits up through the night, planning what he will do and what line of questioning he will take. Of course, he isn't tired; this body has been asleep for nearly twenty-four hours, after all. He comes up with nothing, so uncertain is he of the scenario, and instead decides to focus on staying calm and working with whatever comes up. Restless, he goes for a run. It becomes a walk; his fitness level is pitiful, but it's a start.

When morning comes, he gets into his car, which struggles to start after not being used for so long. Now the daylight has arrived, he can carry out his recon mission. He leaves the urban sprawl of Coventry behind and heads out into the Warwickshire countryside. He has a dim memory of the area he wants to reach but doesn't know its name; he can see it in the clouded-haze of his early childhood memories, from the days when his mother was still with them. They used to drive through it all the time—this place of fields and houses separated from other buildings by acres and acres—on their way to visit Auntie Sarah. She used to tell him tall tales of the countryside around them. He loved his Auntie Sarah. It takes a while, but he finds it, finds the farmhouse he's looking for; the one with the immobile windmill and white walls. It had captured his imagination so as a child, and it will be the perfect place for the evening's work. He would go and check who lived there now, check who he will have to be dealing with later, but decides that it's pointless; there's every possibility it will be somebody else in the other world instead. Either way, now that he has found it once, he can find it again in the dark, and that's the main thing.

The rest of the day drags by. Again, as it was when he was a child, only the night time matters. He just has to get there. Finally, the afternoon arrives.

He's already worked out that the times between his and her world are about the same; it's now around three o'clock. A good amount of time to get himself ready for the date, and everything else. It's far too early to sleep, however; he will need the LSD again then, the boost that will detach him and put him into the void, the body sleeping upon detachment.

Before he leaves, he takes out a certain piece of paper, memorises what's written upon it. He's not sure if it will work in the other world—the details might be different—but it's worth a try.

Nervously—it's only his second time, after all—Chuck drops the acid, and traverses the worlds. He drops back into the body, re-establishing control easily. He tries not to think about the other guy, and picks up the phone to call her.

Just check about the date. Don't do anything stupid. Leave it until tonight.

"Hi Minnie," the body says, though it takes an effort to let it do the work; he's already a nervous wreck. "Just wondered if you wanted me to swing by in a cab to get you, or if you were going to make your own way there?"

She says she has an early start, so she'll be driving. Chuck doesn't detect anything else in her voice. The conversation ends, and he idly wonders what he should wear, of course realising that he will simply let the body decide. Before he does that, however, there's something that he needs to try first. Using the information that he memorised in his own world, he tries it out in this one, hoping that his extra little plan will work; it doesn't. He tries something else; that does. He makes a short journey across town, collects the few things that he needs, and returns to his home. He now has a backup, a plan B.

By the time he is dressed, it's nearly six o'clock, so he decides to make his way to the restaurant. He wants to be there early to see if she *gets there early, to see if she and her internal fraud are maybe planning anything.*

Extra careful. Extra careful.

He spends the time focusing, sitting alone in the quiet Italian restaurant and really feeling the connections, making sure that he is at one hundred percent. When she arrives, he knows he will be rattled; he wants to at least start *with his best foot forward. He looks around for the twentieth time, again assessing the route to the exit and the fire exit and making sure he has the best seat for both. If something happens—if he gets a sense of the guy inside her pulling out any tricks of his own that might be threatening to him—he wants to make sure that he can kill her quickly and get out of there before anyone can do anything. It doesn't occur to him that to flee would be utterly unnecessary; he could just detach and leave the concerns of this particular world behind him. The lines are becoming blurred for Chuck.*

She arrives, and as he stands to greet her, forcing *himself to lean away from his own consciousness and let the body do the work—it's more important tonight than ever—his stomach turns like a Catherine wheel.*

This is going to be even harder than you thought. And you have to watch her at the same time. She's going to try and catch you. Don't give her the slightest fucking hint. Then, when she thinks it's safe, and he leaves...

The thought is supposed to comfort him, but it doesn't work. Even so, he performs admirably, bearing the toe-curling lines coming from his own mouth and the bitch's coquettish bullshit. He gets into a flow, and manages to just keep *it there. He thinks he catches her doing something at one point (perhaps her listening to an internal voice) and seizes the moment:*

"Everything okay? You seem a bit ... uncomfortable? Is this place all right for you?"

That fucking pause again ... and then she smiles, a smile so warm that he almost believes her ... then he remembers who he is dealing with.

Good work, bitch. Two can play, though. *Two can play.*

He summons up this Charlie Wilkes' response—a deeply pleased smile of his own—and listens to her reply.

"Everything's fine," she says. "I just suddenly thought that I might have left the door off the latch, but I just realised I can text my neighbour to get her to check, so no problem; and you know what, sod it, I will leave the car. Let's order some wine."

And then she's fishing out her phone, and pretending to text. But Chuck knows what she's doing.

What has he said, bitch? What did he tell you?

His anxiety nearly blows up into panic, but he keeps a lid on it. He doesn't know what to do next, how to find out what he wants to know, and that only makes things worse.

Okay. Just stick to the basic plan. Keep your head down. Convince them you're the real deal. Get him to leave. Get him to leave, or just fucking kill them both. I don't fucking know. Make your choice.

He rallies magnificently, somehow, and summons up a response, but feels a delicious sensation on his neck; sweat. Despite the body's outward appearance, his own nerves are transmitting to the sweat glands.

Lock it *down.*

He does. The evening continues, minute by tormented minute, but he walks the tightrope, keeps the connection and lets the body do the talking. He keeps it alright, just. At one point, he feels the body's instinct wanting to take her hand. He lets it, despite his own intense paranoia that the knowledge of his presence would somehow shoot down his arm and give the whole game away, causing her eyes to open wide and her mouth to say I knew it, *her finger raising and pointing in an accusatory gesture as it summons down the psychic armies from The End, The End that had spotted him and marked him straightaway, its armies coming to take him and cast him straight into the waiting entropy that lies behind all of the worlds—*

But that doesn't happen. The anxious torment simply continues without incident.

Is she buying this? Is it working?

"Someone's still being a bit cagey though," she says at one point, after sipping her wine. "I've seen your 'lack of ambition' and raised it, upping the ante with 'Minnie Cooper: My Drugs Hell.' But don't think I didn't notice how you skipped over the bit about your family, there. Come on. This has been a very on-the-couch date so far, so don't hold back on your half of it."

FuuuUUUUCK!

If she notices his free hand gripping the handle of his knife, it doesn't show on her face. He forces himself to release it.

No, don't panic. This is perfect. Tell the car story. But *change* it. Tell her that you got out. Lead them astray. Use this to your advantage. But you're going to have to do the talking.

Heart pounding, he assumes full control, feeling the expression on the body's face match his own; the smile feels stiff, forced, and his panic rises some more. He drops his head slightly to hide it, and looks up through his eyebrows as he sees a movement across the table. He nearly flinches, thinking in the fog of his anxiety that he had given the game away already, but he of course he hasn't. She is simply taking his hand.

"Hey," *she says softly, with an empathy that Chuck thinks is as see-through as rain,* "it's all right if you don't want to tell me. I'm sorry, I was only teasing. If it's hard to say, you don't have to. It's only early days anyway—"

She freezes, as if she's given away something that she shouldn't. If she thinks he's the real Charlie Wilkes, it's part of her usual suck up routine, dancing as she always does for the other *guys. If she suspects the truth, it's another masterful display.*

Fuck you. Fuck *you.* Two can play at that.

He uses the body's manner to sandwich her hand between both of his, uses its responses once more. Of course, he realises, he doesn't need to take control yet; he just needs to do it once he gets to the part where the car hits the water.

But listen to the way the body tells it. Try and match it.

"*Sorry," comes the response from the body's subconscious. "Reflex action. It's not something I talk about normally. I haven't talked about it for years. It's kind of ... well, it's hard to think about, and I don't wanna end up being weird tonight as a result. I just don't want to blow it, being perfectly frank."*

He begins the story, wearing the mask, and when it reaches the point where the car hits the water, Chuck takes a deep breath then takes over, wrapping the story up; again, if she notices the change in his voice, the new tremor to it and the fact that the rhythm of his speech is merely an imitation of the way he spoke before, her face doesn't show it. The effort it takes is immense, and when he finishes he feels like he could collapse onto his Black Room's floor. He stares at her, and to his dismay the bitch pauses once more.

Wait. She could just be deciding what to say next. It doesn't mean that she's listening to someone.

She begins to speak, sounding concerned (yeah, right*) and asks about the aftermath of the accident, what help he received as a child. He freezes, and nearly loses the connection completely.*

Calm *down!* The fact that she's asking could be a good thing. Maybe they believe your story. Maybe they just want to double check the rest of it, see how it sounds. So do a good job. You don't need *all* of the connection for this anyway, you just need enough to dress up your own bullshit as best you can. You did okay before, right? Change what you need to change, wear the mask as much as you can. You can do it.

He isn't sure that he can, not sure at all, but he hopes that any shake in his voice will sound like emotion. He fumbles his way through it, but he manages to develop a technique, a way of using his words through a filter of the body's manner; the end result sounds almost exactly like Charlie Wilkes.

The taxi journey home is like a pressure cooker. Holding her hand earlier made him paranoid, as if she would know the truth as a result, but sitting side by side, arms wrapped around each other, he feels like a man tasked with disarming a bomb. There is a moment outside her place, when she moves to kiss him and stops. His heart lurches, his mind ready to detach on the spot in a panic or instruct the body to attack. He is vaguely aware that he would have to kill the taxi driver too in the latter situation.

"I'd invite you up, but ... it's not that I don't trust you. I just want this to be ..." she says. Does she mean it? Or does she just want time alone with the guy in her head? Is he even still there, or has he left, satisfied that Chuck is the real deal after all?

"I know. It's okay," the body says, and then she is kissing him, and he forces his hands to find her back. Once, this would have been ecstasy, the culmination of a lifetime's dream. Now, he cringes away in his Black Room as much as possible, trying to be as little a presence as he can, not wanting to be sensed. The sensation on his lips is deeply pleasurable, but it's like getting a blowjob while stood in the path of an oncoming train.

Once she has left, and the door to her apartment finally, finally swings shut, he lets out a breath of relief that has the weight of all his stress inside it. A film of sweat breaks out all over his body as he slumps on the seat of the taxi, trembling and rubbing at his face. He feels like he might cry.

Thank God that's over, oh, thank God...

It was a mistake to go out with her tonight. He's learned nothing, and that was just an ordeal.

There's always plan B.

He checks his pocket with a trembling hand; it's still there.

"Where you want dropping then mate?" says the taxi driver from the front seat. Chuck had forgotten all about him. An idea forms.

He checks the brain's memories; both of his housemates in this world drive, and they both have cars. He instructs the taxi to take him home. Once there, he takes his sleeping housemate's keys from the hook in the kitchen, collects a little something else while he's at it, and then drives their Nissan Micra back to Minnie's place. He is frightened, and he knows he needs to be careful. He can't arouse their suspicions. But he has to know, and it has to end.

He clarifies his story, gets it straight in his head. Eventually, he reaches Minnie's block of flats, and parks the car a short walk away. As he approaches on foot, streetlit in the dark, his excitement rises along with his fear; the duality of a lunatic. He hopes that this will all end in a frenzy, and the thrill is tangible. It is now ten past two in the morning.

By the time he reaches her building's door, he has almost turned back twice, fear threatening to dampen the anger that fuels this entire undertaking, but the image of himself running between the worlds, harried through the void, and her being back on top is all he needs to push his shaking body forward. He pauses at the intercom for some time, rehearsing his lines, feeling for that perfect balance that he found before of half-Charlie delivery, half-Chuck lies. He pushes the button, and when she answers, he speaks the phrase perfectly; he has nailed it, sounding like a Charlie uncertain and embarrassed, with his own anxiousness making the whole thing sound even more believable.

"... fuck it, I'll just say it," he says, eventually. "Do you have ... have you been having voices in your head? Maybe even one that ... Christ ... maybe even one that sounds like me?"

The conversation ends, and the door opens.

He continues his own lies inside, waiting for a perfect opportunity to implement Plan B. Almost immediately, she confirms it; the person in her head is indeed another Charlie Wilkes. Even though he suspected it, this revelation is somehow still a shock. There is now no doubt as to what his course of action should be. He needs to find out what she knows, find out what he knows, and then they both have to die once he's sure that it is safe. There is a brief moment where she looks at him strangely, and he can't place the look, but his autopilot is running the show very nicely; too nicely, for she suddenly lunges in for a kiss and the autopilot responds. Chuck instantly panics, going to break the kiss off, but he knows that it would give the game away. He cringes like a cowering dog in the far corner of the Black Room, willing his consciousness to not be detected while simultaneously letting the body continue to kiss. The physical sensation would be highly pleasurable, he knows, but he is only keeping the thinning level of connection to the body, just enough to keep it in motion; he does not dare have any more in this close physical moment. He ends it at the earliest possible opportunity, retaking full control and praying that she doesn't notice the shake in his voice, at least until Plan B is ready.

He tells his fake story even better than the way he'd planned it, with new embellishments coming out on the fly (he is particularly pleased with saying that the Black Room is blue, with two screens...a little detail that will surely lend credence to his bullshit) as he tells a fantasy story of a Minnie arriving in his head.

It is the perfect decoy; if they sense another person in his body's head somehow—which they surely do—they will believe now that it is some other accidental, innocent traveller, and see no threat. And if by a slim chance—one that Chuck no longer fully believes—this other Charlie has been sent, he may even leave to inform his superiors to this new development. Either way, he just needs time to put Plan B into action, before either of them realise what has happened. He doesn't even know if it will work, but it has to be worth a try.

The anxiety is thrumming in his head like a thick electrical cable, but he has found his zone and he is performing admirably. He is back on the tightrope once more, enduring an ordeal like he did at dinner, but he has set himself on his course and will not be intimidated. Even so, he can only take so much, and becomes desperate for a natural-sounding break in things to put his plan into action. When she appears to be waiting for another kiss, he takes his chance. Another kiss would just be too much. Something would tear again in his mind.

"Wait ... wait. There's other stuff to talk about. Coffee. We need coffee, we need clear heads. Right?" He follows this statement with a face that Charlie

would pull, knowing from the information in the basement that he would say this if he was trying to be 'noble,' but know that this Charlie would also let his face show what he really wanted.

Idiot. What a pair of fucking lying idiots.

She agrees, and Chuck heads for the kitchen, trying not to slip over in his current state.

Here we go. All or nothing, but this *has* to give you an advantage.

He'd told Jerry that he needed something to act as a tranquiliser, and that he wanted to be able to drink it. After memorising Jerry's phone number in his own world, he'd tried it out in this one. It hadn't worked, but then it occurred to him to check this *Charlie's phone for Jerry's number. They worked together, after all; they didn't need to be friends to have each other's numbers. The number was there, in the phone, and Chuck had made the call. Jerry had seemed surprised that Charlie was asking for such a thing, but hadn't asked questions in reply; Chuck thought that Jerry probably didn't get the business he did because he enquired a lot about where the drugs were going. When Charlie had crossed town that morning to collect it—along with a side trip to pick up the plastic ties that he will later use to secure Minnie, and an uncomfortable visit to a sex shop to pick up a ball gag—Jerry had kept conversation to a minimum, answering his door in vest and boxer shorts. That was fine by Chuck. He had just wanted to pay the man and get out of there; the house had somehow radiated the nature of the person living there, and Chuck had been certain that Jerry does not really give a fuck about anyone. Chuck doesn't know much about drugs, but he knows what people use drugs like this for, what other people do after slipping the powder into ladies' drinks. Jerry gives those people these drugs, and asks no questions. That says it all. Chuck knows that he himself is terrible, but he is not like those people, he thinks. They are the monsters.*

Chuck isn't sure about what the heat of the coffee might do to the effect of the powder, but he's at least sure that it should dissolve fairly quickly. Even if it doesn't and a lot of it ends up sitting at the bottom of the mug, enough of it should get into her system before she realises.

See how you like that, you little prick. See what this does to *your* Black Room.

If nothing else, it surely has *to effect the connection between them, to slow her thoughts and close her eyes, cutting off the False Charlie in her head and plunging him into darkness. If he needs to do so, it will give Chuck enough time to kill her—and the False Charlie with her, he hopes—before either of them can do anything. But more importantly, it will let him get close to her without either of them being aware so that he can test the waters ... to* feel *the outskirts of her mind, to check what's going on. To get some fucking* answers. *It's far from a perfect plan, but he has to do* something. *He has to take a first step.*

He is staggeringly anxious as he hands it to her, continuing to do a marvellous job of walking the tightrope and keeping it all looking natural. She takes it, and he sits, dying a thousand nervous deaths inside his head as she sips from it. Her expression does not change; she has noticed nothing. Yet.

"Well. Well, well, well. This is a fine old load of bullshit, eh?" the body says, and to his absolute disbelief she asks for some quiet time to take it all in. It couldn't be more perfect. He offers for her to lean on him, wanting her to believe that she is safe, and the second that she does he once more retreats as far as he can from the connection to the body. He lurks in the shadows of the Black Room, his web spun, almost drooling in anticipation as he waits for a lunatic's resolution, wanting failure or success as long as there is a result.

Time passes. Only when she lets out a slurred murmur—one that is clearly not the utterance of someone half-asleep, but the stoned drawl of the deeply drugged—does he decide that it's time.

She's gone. You've got away with it. Take a look at her.

He moves her torso, propping her up against the sofa's opposite arm. It is clear from one glance that she is under, or at least well on her way; her efforts to move end up as mere sluggish twitches. But while the connection should be ruined, he hopes (and maybe you've even sent him away, maybe the tranquiliser has moved out of her him the way the LSD moved you out of your own head) *and the first part is achieved, he wants her fully out. This, at least, is easily resolved. He will enjoy this part.*

"Yeah ... I think you're about ready," he says, his own true voice clear and open and delicious in his throat. As a gleeful little Fuck You *occurs to him, he lets her know the undeniable truth, lets her know what he knows she fucking suspected all along, the Bitch: "So tell me; how long has that cunt really been squatting in your head?"*

He thinks he sees a little flicker of realisation flash across her slack-jawed, lolling face, and almost laughs as he punches her in the face as hard as he can. He feels a tooth break beneath his hand, and the pain of his knuckles against her bone is excruciating, amplified like every other sensation from the body. He tries to completely disconnect from it, to let it shut down until the pain has passed, but to his surprise he finds that he can't do it. Now that he tries complete disconnection, tries to cut off as far as he can without leaving the body altogether ... he finds that he can't. Even when he disconnects from controlling the motor functions, when he pulls away from the subconscious too, when he pulls away from the nerve endings, he still feels pain. It is far less no—a normal level of pain in his hand that he would feel if he had punched someone in the face using his own body's knuckles, and a far cry from the amplified sensory experience that he has had since piloting someone else's frame—but it is still there just the same.

Has the bond to the body grown now that he has spent a long amount of time in it? Does he now experience any intense sensations that affect his outer shell? Would that happen to the guy in her head too?

Enough. Get on with it.

Yes. He waits until the blistering pain has subsided in his aching hand, and then fully reconnects, taking control once more. The first thing he needs to do is secure her, and he does so using the plastic ties that he picked up earlier that day. Once she is bound to the seat, he kneels in front of her, resisting the urge to take her ears with both hands and slowly pull, pull until they tear off the side of her head like gristle from a carcass.

He looks into her eyes, rests his elbows on her thighs and leans the body's weight onto his forearms. This should support the body when it has no controller. He is so focused he is barely even aware of his own trembling, of the outer body doing the same in growing symbiosis. Cautiously, very cautiously, he sends his consciousness out.

Just a little, at first, darting out of the body and back in like a rabbit poking it's head from its burrow. Then a little more, growing in confidence slightly, reaching almost to the edge of her head and feeling, probing, checking. Still nothing. Over a long time, he keeps going slightly further, sniffing at the air, scanning the meadow. Eventually, after a deep breath and a few half-started attempts that ended when his nerve was lost, he dives through her mind and out again, checking as he does so like a child daring to open their eyes underwater for a moment.

There is no-one else there, only her own consciousness. Either her inhabitant believed that Chuck was the real deal and left, or the tranquiliser sent him away. Chuck returns to his Black Room, the rabbit darting back to his bolthole, and squats inside as he tries to regain his composure.

You can't assume that it's the latter, and even if you did, you don't know how long he's gone away for. And you can't assume it's the former, because you don't know for certain and if they *don't* believe you they might still turn up elsewhere.

She will be under for some time, he knows, the combination of the drugs and the knockout punch working together most effectively. Time to get the car.

He departs, fetches the car from around the corner, returns. While this Charlie's body feels stronger, healthier than his own, he thinks that even in his normal body he would have just as little trouble carrying Minnie's unconscious body down the stairs. She's too damn thin. At this hour, they see no-one in the stairwell of her building. If they had, Chuck would have killed them and carried on. He has to get where they are going, has to make sure that he has all the time he needs to interrogate, work, and ultimately enjoy the process. If the other Charlie comes back in the meantime, he will just have to deal with that as it comes. He's too nervous and excited to care now, almost on the verge of frenzy.

With Minnie in the boot of the car, the drive to the farmhouse seems to take an eternity. He can't fucking wait; he's terrified, he's aroused. The swirl in his head makes it hard to concentrate on the road, the central white line speeding past the Micra as it travels through the night carrying two bodies but taking three passengers. Twenty-five minutes later, they get to the farmhouse.

Chuck kills the headlights and parks the car at the top of the drive, then disembarks and walks quietly up to the building. It's very dark, and silent; out here, at this time, passing cars will be extremely rare. The night sky above is surprisingly clear, with light pollution only coming from the motorway some distance away. He lies the body down outside the house—he thinks that, even if he is tethered to Minnie in this world to an extent, she is close enough for him to do this—and detaches himself from the physical, floating up and through the walls of the building and going through the rooms until he finds the current inhabitants. They are old, asleep. This will not be difficult.

He returns to his body, and withdraws the paring knife that he had collected on his trip home. Small, easy to hide and transport. Quick. Nasty. His hands shake as he rings the doorbell, not through fear but through a nervous excitement as his skin squeezes against the knife's metal handle.

The door opens on the chain; a face peers through the gap. A man, elderly but broad. He is considerably shorter than Chuck, however, and Chuck already knows that this Charlie's body is strong. He doesn't realise that he is giggling frantically as he shoulders the door fully open, snapping the ancient chain out of the even older doorframe. The man jumps back in surprise, and it's all the opening Chuck needs to jam the paring knife into his throat and pull sideways. He doesn't enjoy this, not like he does when he hurts Minnie; he is dimly aware that this is probably wrong and he shouldn't take pleasure in it anyway, but the frenzy is on him and he doesn't care. He will later convince himself that it all serves a higher purpose, serves his important work.

The old man's hot blood spurts out wildly, spraying Chuck's clothes as he leaves the man gasping and clawing at the air in the hallway. He finds the old woman still sitting in the bed, clutching at her sheets in terror and confusion. She's too frightened to scream; instead, she just repeatedly whoops the inward breath required *to scream, but never manages to make the outward sound. She pulls her bed linen up to her chin as he approaches, looking almost comical as Chuck lunges onto the bed and pulls the sheets away. The knife finds her throat, leaving a wound that matches that dead husband's.*

Only once he is done, he fetches Minnie's unconscious body from the car and secures her to a chair once more, this time in the farmhouse's living room. He removes the makeshift tea towel gag and replaces it with the ball gag, fastening it nice and tight. Only when the car is stashed behind the building does he allow himself to pause for a moment to take stock. He shuts the farmhouse door, and breathes quietly in the now pitch-black hallway. The darkness and silence of his outer surroundings mirror the inner chamber in which he stands, and creates a double-womb effect. He feels supreme.

They are secure. He has all the time in the world.

He undresses, wanting some air on the body's skin. After washing the knife clean, he allows himself some time to gently draw the edge of the blade across the body's skin, not cutting but merely tickling. The action sends little electric trickles of pleasure coursing through the body's nervous system. Time slips away for a while. When Chuck comes back to his senses, he thinks about molesting her unconscious body, but manages to resist. He does what he does out of justice, he thinks, out of a desire to righteously punish the wicked (and if he enjoys it immensely, that's his right) but he will not be a rapist. That is something else, a step too far. Having sex with a willing Minnie as Charlie Wilkes is one thing, and that will indeed happen with the next one (oh God, oh yes) but he will not commit rape. He is not a monster. Not like Jerry's other clients. His mind calm, he finally decides upon his course of action. It is not perfect, but then, he is figuring all of this out as he goes along.

The other Minnies, the other liars, they might not have broken when questioned about their role in all of this ... but if they had been questioned about the Charlie in their heads, would they have been more forthcoming? She might be the Queen Of The Liars, but that doesn't mean that she wouldn't confess all she knew about someone else to save her own skin.

He will wait for the tranquiliser to wear off, and then he will pump her for information. If she reveals that the other Charlie is too much of a threat to risk confronting, then he will kill her and leave, and plan his next move from there. He will have no other option. If there is no threat, then he will wait until the fake Charlie returns and kill them both; her by the knife, and him by his connection to Minnie as she dies. He just hopes that he can do it before the fake Charlie realises what is happening and detaches himself off into the void ...

Satisfied, he begins to make his way back to the living room, when he hears her stirring. She is awake. He waits in the hallway, to see if he hears her talking to the other, to see if the fake has returned.

***

Charlie floated in the void, and wondered, amongst other things, how he'd ever forgotten *this*. It was beyond description, beyond hyperbole. Before him hung all of creation, all the worlds, and if he'd had a body in that moment, the shock and awe of it all would have killed him instantly. As he was, a suspended consciousness presented with the true universe, all he could actually process was a supercharged sense of déjà vu.

It fucking worked. The second dose of ketamine worked, just like before ... and this *is where you came the first time. This is where it took you before you woke up in the Black Room.*

Being back there, as a mind and nothing else, brought it all back. This is where he ended up after he took the ketamine at Neil's, and it was no wonder that he forgot it. It was too crazy for his mind to fully comprehend now, even after all the madness of the last few days. Compare that to when he'd gone there the first time, unprepared, just a guy on a night out, it would have been an immense psychic trauma. His mind must have blanked it out to protect itself; either that, or his consciousness reforming itself as a body had somehow reset his brain.

It doesn't matter; bottom line, are you really surprised that this was too much of a shock for your brain to remember? And my God, no wonder you started screaming about The Woman In The Night; she's almost everywhere.

And she was, presented before him in hundreds, no, *thousands* of worlds, at different times and ages, filling his vision. He was aware of other worlds beyond those as well, behind and in front and on all sides, but he could feel that they were different; they did not call to him the way that these did, did not have a connection to her that called across time and space. In those worlds, he would be another few seconds in the toilet at Barrington's, someone else would find the phone, he would trip, he'd never even be out, he'd have moved cities, he'd have contracted cancer, he'd have never made it out of the car, he could be so much more than the nothing he had allowed himself to become.

But in these *worlds ... you always find her.*

Not you. You should have found her in your world, but she was taken.

The anger began to build, his hurt and rage and disappointment and sense of profound injustice beginning to deafen even the incredulous voice in his mind that kept saying *it's all ... it's all ... it's all ...* but he got himself under control. Minnie was in danger, and even if she wasn't his, he loved her and had to save her.

But ... how the fuck do I know which world is hers?

And that was when he saw the other thing; saw it beyond everything else, waiting patiently and calling to him in its soft, reassuring voice, singing to him of peace and rest. It told him that everything might not have a reason, but that when his trials were over, everything would be all right. It would wait until his time came, and then it would draw him to itself and bring him home. *For you,* it called to him without words, *in The End, everything will be all right.*

Charlie felt that he should be frightened, that some primal survival instinct was telling him to rebel at all costs, to flee to the furthest place he could ever find and hide ... yet he knew that this would be wrong. No matter what instinct said, on a purely conscious level he knew that there was nothing to fear here. But there was also no time to waste, and The End was not something that could be investigated; he knew this in his very essence. It was something you went to only once, and that was it.

This ... more than any of the other madness ... is just too big. You ... you can't deal with that. That's too much. Too much.

Indeed it was, and he simply could not waste time contemplating it. Any attempt would be fruitless. As insane as it was to simply ignore something as revelatory as that, he just had to. Minnie was in trouble. But how the hell did he pick the right world?

What did you see the first time? What made you pick that world out of all the others? Can you remember now you're here? Hadn't there been ... there was a reason, wasn't there? You saw something ... something had left a mark...

As if the act of remembering it transported him there—and maybe it did, as here he was just a mind controlled by conscious thought after all—the worlds flicked by at a blur, and Charlie gasped as he realised that he was travelling to where he had already been once before. As he approached his destination and the worlds slowed, Charlie instantly noticed what he had seen the first time. He remembered his original curiosity. Seeing it again, it confirmed his worst fears; Minnie was definitely in trouble.

He looked from the first one, then to the next nearby, then the next, then the last; a closely grouped quartet. These were indeed different to the others, distorted in such a slight way that it was *almost* unnoticeable. It was as if there were a slightly more filmy quality to each one, as if something had changed about them. More than that, each one looked progressively less so, as if the first's change was the oldest and the fourth the youngest, suggesting that—

Maybe it's not even a sign of change. Maybe it just shows where something came out of one and where something went into another. Either way, it looks like whatever happened, happened in the one on the left first and then and moved along to the others.

His thoughts echoed those of his first time in the void, reminding him of them as they returned.

It only moved into other worlds where she is, Charlie now remembered thinking the first time, remembered interpreting the same sight before him. *Whatever happened in that first world, it's done something else in the next one, then the next, and it's still there doing it in the fourth. And if it's only going where she is, it might be doing it to* Minnie ...

He remembered his response now, the memories unlocked like boxes containing grenades. The first time here, he'd followed, wanting to be sure and wanting to explore. Except when he'd entered the fourth world, he'd followed instinct, allowing it to draw him where it wanted to go; of course, that turned out to be straight to her, wanting to be close to her ... and then, removed from the effortless energy existence of the void, he'd gone too far. In the confusion, he'd ended up right inside her head, crashing into it.

Oh my God ...

His consciousness had gone into autopilot, created a visualisation for him that would allow him to understand at least *some* of where he had ended up, and then, perhaps overloaded, had shut down to prevent him from going crazy. And like every victim of an accident involving unconsciousness, like everyone who had over-indulged on their intoxicant of choice, he'd forgotten the whole thing. Or maybe it was just from the mind's effort of creating the Black Room, or maybe just because he wasn't used to jumping between whole fucking worlds, he didn't know.

But one thing he did know now, one thing that the four tainted portals before him proved; he knew what had left its mark on the worlds, knew who had been travelling from one to the next, and who was still in his Minnie's world right now. With a slight tremor of fear, he also knew that—due to them having a physical presence, as opposed to just a psychic one like Charlie— they were perhaps in possession of abilities of which Charlie did not know the limits.

Chuck.

***

240

Chapter Nine: Minnie Runs Her Mouth, Wilkes Meets Wilkes, King Arthur Had It Easy, and The End Of The Black Room

***

"And that's about where this conversation started," said Chuck breezily, staring into Minnie's eyes and grinning with a manic smile that contained no trace of humanity. "I think that gets you pretty much up to speed ... and from the little I was told, your head should be clear by now as well. I guess we'll see if he turns up, then."

Minnie, who had been sitting in weeping, bug-eyed silence throughout Chuck's unbelievable tale, tried to find her voice. His account had made things infinitely worse in one way, and only slightly better in another; it meant that this man was definitely not *her* Charlie, and that her Charlie was not a lunatic pretending to be a sane man. This was *another* Charlie, one who had developed the ability to take over and control the body that his mind had projected itself into, able to access a brain that was of the same physical structure as his and to use the subconscious memories and mannerisms that it stored. It also meant that everything she had seen at dinner, every nuance and response that she fell even more in love with, was from the true Charlie

241

Wilkes, and the lunatic before her had robbed that Charlie Wilkes in the worst possible way. These were the good aspects, and they still didn't really come close to balancing out the very, very bad aspects of it all.

The idea of the whole thing was insane; a man who can possess a body and wear its personality like a suit? But after the past two days, it was no more crazy than anything else. And *crazy* was the problem here, the main, bad aspect of Chuck's story that didn't just make things worse, but spelt her doom. He hadn't said so yet, hadn't explained what his 'two options' were, but she knew that both of them would involve her slow, drawn out and agonising murder. The fact that his story was now complete also meant that she was now closer to that end, perhaps about to start down the dark road of pain that would culminate in her death. As her terrified mind ran through all the ways that he might start, it threatened to become utterly unhinged at the prospect.

Minnie knew that if she allowed that to happen, it would mean her definite slaughter. As soon as she let her mind collapse, she would begin to scream and not stop until she was dead at Chuck's hands.

At least that way it would be quick. Your mind will go and it will be over soon. That could be best.

Shut the fuck up. Don't lose it. You can stall him. Get time to think. Please.

"No-one can hear us out here," Chuck was saying, matter-of-factly. "I just don't want you making noise, I want quiet for the sake of my own sanity. I like it quiet. That's why I picked this place. Nice and out-of-the-way." He pointed out of the window. "You can see the nearest cottage over there, a good few fields away. They'd never hear us. Aunt Sarah told me about that place once, said that some crazy old guy with one arm had lived there for decades and never left his house in all that time. Old people, eh? That's our nearest neighbour, and I don't think he'll be bothering us."

Minnie tried to speak again, but as she looked into his utterly insane eyes and saw no hope of mercy or restraint there, seeing only the barely hidden yearning, the *need* to tear and wound and hurt, it was all too much. She felt a warm wetness spread across the back of her thighs and buttocks as her bladder let go. She thought the tears would intensify again as a result, but strangely they did not. Instead, the shock of realising that she had wet herself clarified her feeling of rapidly approaching complete capitulation, and this knowledge brought her back to herself slightly. She did not want to die, and knew that after bodily malfunctions, complete gibbering surrender would be next. An extremely painful death would be the end result, and the piss dripping off her chair made her realise that her fear of that painful death was stronger than her need to retreat into the comforting mental shutdown of panic, to indulge in the luxury of the loss of control.

She now knew she'd made a mistake listening to his tale when she should have been trying to think of ways to escape—not that there appeared to be any—but not only had she been hoping to hear some information that she could use, this madman had been explaining the secrets of the universe. What was it they said about the hypnotic, charismatic power of a psychopath?

The fact that he'd been doing it at knifepoint had also greatly affected her concentration.

It doesn't matter now. Stall him. You have to stall him. Try to think when you can, but please girl, stall him or he's going to hurt you so badly and you're going to die.

"You've ... you've got everything so wrong," she said. "I'm not any of those things you said. I don't know anything, I'm not ... I'm not part of some conspiracy, *I don't know who you are!* You're making a terrible mistake, I'm just ... I'm innocent." She hated using the word, hated justifying herself before such madness, but it was the only thing that she could think of. Chuck nodded and smiled that lizard smile again.

"So, the way I see it," he said, talking as if Minnie hadn't even said a word, "is, as I say, that I have two options. The first is that I ask you some questions, you tell me what I need to know, and then I decide what to do from there." Minnie thought she knew exactly what he would do from there, but said nothing. "The second is that I wait for the *faker* to come back, and just kill the pair of you together. That's how it works, isn't it? Now he's been there a while? I hurt you, it hurts him ... that's true, isn't it? I hurt this hand earlier, which made my hand hurt inside ... it's the same for him I bet, isn't it? You know. Tell me."

"I ... I don't ..."

"This is only going to take longer if you fuck around, Minnie. Shall I motivate you?"

"No! No, please ... I think ... I think that's ... true?" She had no reason to think so—Charlie had never said anything to her about pain—but she had to give Chuck something. She'd seen the way his hand had tightened upon the knife's handle, the complete readiness to do unspeakable things with zero hesitation. Chuck smiled again, but his breath quickened. Minnie saw this, and her heart seemed to pinch in her chest, to physically bite at her in its anxiety.

"So you *do* know things," he said, not with surprise but with the sound of a man finally getting the confirmation that he knew was long overdue. He almost sounded relieved. "Good. Let's continue with this, let's continue along these lines, this is good."

"Yes, yes, I know some things, but only the things that have happened to me," Minnie babbled, feeling her brain creak and lurch. "That's all I know, that's all I can tell you." Again, it was like she hadn't spoken; Chuck seemed lost in thought for a moment.

"Should have worn off by now ... " he said, as if to himself. He suddenly looked at her, examined her face. "Still alone there, cheeky?" he said, face now utterly blank, his voice flat and at odds with the words he was saying.

"What ... what did you give me?" said Minnie, hearing the fear in her voice, reminding herself again to lock it all down, to keep control ... but he'd drugged her, forced chemicals into her blood stream, and after what she'd been through at the rehab centre, the hell she'd gone through to leave all that behind—

Please, you may be scared, but please, *keep it together.* Stall him.

"Answer me," he said, ignoring her, and advanced. Minnie let out a gasp that would have become a scream had she not bitten it back, but then Chuck suddenly stopped just short of the chair. He bent quickly, and his hand shot out and grabbed her right ankle, but even as one half of her mind cowered in terror at this action ... the other half had noticed the uncertainty in his movement, the last-minute halt of his approach.

He just stopped himself getting any closer. Just like when he undid your gag ... it was all done at arm's length, like someone dealing with a dog that might be dangerous. He really doesn't know what he's dealing with, does he? Is he ... is he scared of Charlie? Is that something you can use? Do you dare use it?

Immediately, the thought was followed by another one, reining in the glimmer of hope that had shone out for a second:

He can still kill you at arm's length. He can still torture you at arm's length. You don't have to be within kissing distance of someone to stab out one of their eyes. If you're going to try something, be very fucking careful.

All of these thoughts flashed through her head in milliseconds, her consciousness already returning to the terrifying present as Chuck's grip on her ankle tightened. He knelt in front of her, resting one knee on top of her bound foot and putting his weight onto it. She gritted her teeth against the pain as she felt the bones in her foot bend, and this time a scream did pass her lips as she felt the cold tip of the knife rest just between the flesh of her big toe and the protruding edge of her toenail.

"This will just be the start," he said, staring at her with eyes that were now totally dead. He looked like a man-fish in that moment, a glassy-eyed bottom dweller that only saw her as something completely alien. "This will be the very least of what I will do. Do you understand? This is pain that you will remember with great fondness when I am doing the worst that I can to you. I will hurt you on your very inside. I will poison your dreams. I will turn your mind inside out and make every thought into a shard of barbed glass. Do you understand me?"

But can he though? Oh God, can he? Do you dare? Do you dare call his bluff and threaten him with Charlie?

She didn't know if she could, as helpless and petrified as she was. The world around her turned grey and small lights danced before her eyes as she thought she was about to pass out. She *had* to call his bluff, for it was clear that he wouldn't listen to any protestation of ignorance. She was the Queen Of The Liars to him, after all. She opened her mouth as hot tears ran down her cheeks like a betrayal, not knowing what she was going to say but knowing she had to try something, and that was when Charlie arrived in her head like the cavalry cresting the brow of a hill.

"Minnie? Minnie!" He sounded out of breath.

***

IN THE DARKNESS, THAT'S WHERE I'LL KNOW YOU

She is in the void. The worlds rush past her, but they are of no consequence; she already knows of these, knows of their existence, told of them by the dark man, but travelling to them are not an option to her. There is only one destination that she can have, only one that she is inexorably drawn towards, and this has always been the case. It calls to her now, speaking of comfort and warmth and light, of a welcome at a journey's end; she sees it filling the endless horizon before her, and to her surprise she is not afraid. This has all happened so fast, so unexpectedly, that she hasn't had time *to fear, but even if it had been available she thinks that she would have known that all is well ... for people like her, at least, and this thought makes her think of those for whom it would be different. Those like* him. It was him, *she remembers for the hundredth time, the dark man, the one who took it all away ... but it is too late now to think of such things, things that cannot be undone, and soon she will be at peace. The End is waiting, and she goes to it like an old friend.*

***

Minnie was so relieved to hear Charlie's voice that she would have wet herself all over again, were it not for the fact that her bladder was now empty. She let out another cry, one of surprise this time, and this too was bitten back; not for fear of retribution from Chuck, but to conceal Charlie's presence. She wanted to call his name, to cement the fact that he was there once more, there with her. She knew that, together, they might have a chance; above all else, she ached to tell him that she loved him before her ability to do so was torn from her, but of course she could not. His arrival had to be kept secret.

As for Charlie, within the few seconds that he allowed himself to take in Minnie's surroundings, he already had enough of a grasp of the situation to understand that his suspicions were correct. This was not the building that he had left Minnie in, and the mad-eyed dark mirror of himself that crouched before her clearly meant Minnie nothing but harm. Chuck was clearly far from being just another version of Charlie Wilkes.

But how the fuck did you share responses like that? Talk exactly the same, react exactly the same—

These wild questions could wait, he told himself, as his eyes already whipped around the room and checked for any possible accomplices that Chuck might have. He scanned for unnoticed weapons or escape points. Around him, the walls of the Black Room churned at an unbelievable pace that he had never seen before; Minnie was clearly almost mad with fear.

"Minnie! Minnie, can you hear me?" he said, desperate at the thought of her in distress and still trying to get a handle on the full situation as he called her name.

Why isn't she doing anything? The guy is clearly fucking nuts—

The view panned downwards without a word, and that was when Charlie simultaneously saw the plastic ties cutting tightly into Minnie's legs

245

just above the ankle, Chuck's hand gripping her right ankle, and the knife about to thrust in under her toenail.

"*Fuck!*" Charlie screamed, helpless. "*Get off, you fucking cocksucker!! Minnie! Minnie!!*"

He felt utterly impotent, full of useless rage and possessing only of limbs that could do nothing but flail wildly and pointlessly in the Black Room when they wanted to be caving in Chuck's skull.

Why the fuck isn't she responding to you? She can't be worried about sounding crazy in front of this lunatic, so—

The thought was immediate and forceful, and stopped him dead in his tracks.

She doesn't want him to know that you're here. He knows that you've been here before ... or suspects it ... and she doesn't want to let on yet. She's showing you the knife to let you know how dangerous this is. Clever girl ...

"Fuck, oh, oh fuck ... okay, okay, I got it, he knows, right?" he said, his hands on his head and tightening in his hair. "Okay, don't say anything, don't panic, uh, let me think ... just ... just keep him talking a second, okay?"

SHIT, this is bad, this is really bad, if only you knew what was going on—
You can know what's going on. You know how.

He did. She hadn't liked it one bit before, but this was an utter emergency, so bollocks, he was doing it.

"Minnie? If you can hear me, blink three times."

The screen flashed three times in rapid succession; it would look like the fluttering eyes of panic to Chuck, but nothing more.

"Okay, just ... just tell him about when I first arrived. Fill for time. Tell him the truth. Drag it out as long as you can, okay? Act like you don't *want* to tell him, but you are doing, right? I'm going to try something here." There was silence from Minnie, and Charlie stared desperately at the screen as he waited for her to start speaking, checking she got it. As he did so, he looked straight into the wide, unblinking eyes of Chuck as they stared back into Minnie's face. Charlie wanted to kill him, to commit full-blooded murder on the spot. He knew utterly and without question that he could go through with it, too. This fact did not concern him.

"He's not here now! You know he's not!" shrieked Minnie breathlessly, her fear genuine, the words coming out so fast that they almost slurred together. "Why are you pretending that you don't already know? Why are you tormenting me?" She didn't know if Chuck knew or not, but she thought that it might be what he wanted to hear, a confirmation for him of her fear and compliance. "I don't even know when he's going to turn up! The first time he did, it was completely out of the blue, I knew nothing about it! I was just at home, getting ready for work, and then he just pops up, asking if I can hear him!" She paused, and Charlie froze; would Chuck buy this, or would he just get to work with the knife? Charlie didn't even know what they'd been talking about before he'd arrived, so this was a big gamble; in his head, he'd assumed Chuck would hear it as the verbal explosion of a terrified woman, but would still take interest. Now, it seemed far riskier than when he'd suggested it just a few moments ago. Everything was happening so fucking fast, and there was so much he didn't know. He intended to take care of that immediately, however, as soon as he thought that Chuck was paying attention, but there was a very big chance that Chuck was about to carve up the woman Charlie loved before his very eyes.

And you, as well. Don't forget that.

His body in the Black Room was so tense that it hurt. Chuck's face didn't move, but the knife didn't either.

"Really," said Chuck, and his voice was unreadable. "Let's hear the whole story, then." It was neither sarcastic, or curious. When he didn't say anything else, it became clear that he was waiting for her to continue.

"Y-yes," said Minnie, hesitantly. "I thought I was going crazy, at first ... I freaked out completely, and thought I was having a, a kind of flashback or something ... " As she continued, Charlie turned away from the screen, almost tripping over his own feet in his haste to reach the nearest wall. He had every faith that he could at least begin to do this, knowing full well that he could read her memories if he needed to, but before he'd only got as far as grabbing at whichever emotion had come through the strongest, and seeing the associated memory. If he was going to be successful, he had to *search* her memories.

He quickly placed his hands on the wall, focused, pressed. Immediately, it was in him, even stronger than before. A hurricane of thought—a tsunami of awareness—smashed onto him, and if he could have found his voice he would have screamed. This was too intense now, the connection too strong.

Suck it up, you fucking asshole. What's going on? What does she know?

Even hearing himself, however, was next to impossible against the roar of Minnie's mind. Her life both lay before him and ran through him ... but differently, this time. It wasn't her *whole* life, it was just the last few days that he was seeing. They were flowing by at breakneck, mind-bending speed however, catching up to *now* at an incredible pace. He realised it, then; yes, the connection was stronger than ever, but it was more than that. Before, he'd gone in uninvited and tried to look. This time, Minnie *wanted* him to know all that had happened, and not only that, it was fresh in her mind as well. He was already caught up to their date together, and how *she'd* felt, seeing Chuck wearing his smile and his laugh but feeling the intensely warm glow in both Minnie's heart and her loins, and he just had time to realise that he was inside the last ten percent when he reached Chuck's story, hearing it as it was told to Minnie. His eyes widened in horror as he heard a tale of his own life but twisted into a dark, mangled, murderous mess. It hit home with added force, coming as it did at a speed of knowledge that the human brain cannot normally process.

Suddenly, it was past, and the horror was briefly replaced by an intense flash of relief and love as he caught up to the immediate present, to the moment just now when he arrived in Minnie's head, seen from her point of view. The following shock to Charlie of seeing both a dark version of himself and a memory of his true self at the same time brought him back to his senses.

He was done. He broke the connection, and fell to the floor gasping for non-existent air.

Chuck ... oh, Chuck ...

Now, as well as rage and fear, there was disgust, and pity; too small an amount of pity to concern him, however, and there was no time to waste. In knowing Chuck's story, he now had an idea of what he was going to try, as risky as it might be. He didn't even know if it had a chance in hell of working, but couldn't see any other way out of this. The only problem was that it required Minnie to show a hell of a lot of courage, and show it in amounts that he wasn't sure he'd be able to pluck up himself if he were in her shoes.

"And then I went to sleep, as my head was hurting so much, and when I woke up he'd gone," Charlie heard Minnie saying.

"Gone?" said Chuck, speaking for the first time since Minnie's account had started, and sounding genuinely intrigued. "You mean he'd left? When did he come back?"

Minnie hesitated. She hadn't heard anything from Charlie since she'd started her story, and was already terrified that she'd given away her only ace upon Charlie's advice; Chuck now knew, or at least had heard her saying (whether he believed it or not was another matter) that Charlie didn't know why he was there, that he wasn't an agent of some other, higher power. Did she go further with the truth then? She'd already thought about bluffing, guessing that Chuck was wary, but what if he called her out on it, and she was revealed to be lying? She shuddered at the thought of what would happen next.

"Minnie," she then heard Charlie say, sounding shaken and drained. "I know what he is. I read your memory."

Minnie didn't reply to either Chuck or Charlie, waiting in silence and thinking that she was about to pass out. The walls of the Black Room spasmed and shook around Charlie's head.

"Whennnn ... did heeee ... come baaaack?" said Chuck, speaking deliberately, slowly, dangerously. He leaned forward and set his jaw.

"Tell him I'm back," said Charlie quietly, trying to control his breathing. "You have to."

"No," whispered Minnie reflexively, responding in immediate fear at such a wild suggestion, but her eyes widened in panic when she realised what she'd done. Chuck's brow furrowed for a moment, and then he leapt to his feet like a gun had gone off in the room. He'd seen it on her face, heard the word and seen her own dismay at her slip, and had known that she wasn't responding to him.

"He's fucking there now, isn't he?" hissed Chuck, but there was something else in his eyes as well as madness and fury: fear. "You fucking lied again!"

"You don't have a choice Minnie, you can't move and it's the only thing you can do!" shouted Charlie, speaking quickly and trying to make clear what he wanted before Chuck could react any more. "You have to get him in here! You have to get him to come in here with me!"

"He's only just got here!" shouted Minnie at Chuck, straining at her bonds, "he's just got here and he wants me to let you know!" She spoke without thinking, both answering Chuck and giving Charlie what he wanted.

Charlie, what the hell are you doing? You're going to get us both killed.

Chuck's eyes widened even more, looking now as if they were about to fall out of his head, and he took a step backwards. He pointed the paring knife at her, holding it at arm's length and gripping it with a shaking hand.

"You tell him ... " he began, but then stopped himself. "Impostor," he said, speaking more loudly as he narrowed his eyes. There was a tremor in his voice, "I know you can hear me ... so listen up." The words were meant to sound tough and in control, but all they seemed to do was channel the scared ten-year old from the two Charlies' shared past. "If I think for one second that you're trying anything, I'll stick this into her eyes. You understand me?" He turned the blade back and forth in the air, catching the light. "I'll blind her. I'll fucking blind her." For the first time since she'd come to, Chuck seemed really uncertain. His eyes were shifty now, darting here and there as he thought on his rattled feet.

"Minnie," said Charlie, as calmly as he could, walking slowly towards the screen, eyeing his enemy and trying to get himself psyched up at the same time. He didn't know what he intended to do next, but at least if he got Chuck on the inside he might have a chance of hurting him. Left out there, Chuck could definitely kill both he and Minnie with ease. In the Black Room, there might be something Charlie could do; there was just the slight issue of Chuck clearly having a greater mastery and knowledge of his out-of-body form. Charlie didn't know what that might mean if it came to a straight-up fight, or if they could even hurt each other in there. It wouldn't be their actual bodies, after all ... but then again, an injury to Charlie's Black Room form did mean an injury to his own body ... would it be the same for Chuck? Plus the small fact that he'd never been in a fight in his entire life. "Listen to me, baby." The word came unbidden, surprising him and making his heart ache. "This is gonna be really scary for you, but you have *got* to do as I say here, or you're going to die, okay? We have to be a team on this. We need to save you, both of us, together. You want to live, don't you?"

Minnie did. She tried to calm down as best she could, but her chest was so tight that it hurt. She knew what Charlie would be thinking—he wanted to get Chuck where he had a chance of hurting him—but she was frightened for Charlie, and also for herself if Chuck went inside her head too; what would having two of them in there do to her? She nodded, knowing that Charlie would see the motion and hoping that Chuck would take it as acknowledgement of what he'd just said. He didn't.

"*Don't fucking try that!*" Chuck screamed, backhanding her across the face with his free hand and reigniting the pain in her injured jaw. It was intense enough for Charlie to feel it too, just like the cut from the broken cup in Minnie's kitchen. Had he time to consider that memory, it would have felt like it was a lifetime ago. He let out a cry in the Black Room at the same time that Minnie did, and staggered backwards. "Do you think I'm a fucking idiot?"

Chuck was saying. "What is he telling you? What the fuck is that little cunt *saying?*"

Charlie opened his mouth to prompt her, dizzy as he was from the sudden and stabbing agony in his mouth, but he heard Minnie already doing it for herself.

"Yes," she gasped, spitting blood from her lips as she did so and ignoring his second question. Her voice was hoarse, and the view, for Charlie, was partially obscured by her hair hanging in front of her eyes as she looked up at Chuck furiously through her eyebrows. "We *do* think you're fucking stupid."

Chuck looked startled again, but suddenly the knife jumped over to his left hand as he slammed his right fist into her stomach. The air whooshed out of her with a groan, and Charlie slumped to the Black Room's floor, clutching at his own guts. It felt like he'd been kicked by a mule. He heard Minnie coughing, and Chuck screaming in a high pitched screech of a voice.

"*How's that? How's that then, you fucking bitch? You pair of fucking bitches? Who's stupid now? Who's stupid now? You think you can make me look stupid again? Never again! Nevaaaaaaaahhh!! You're nothing now! Nothing! You think? You think? Fuck you! Fuck you! Fuck yooooouuuuuuuuu!!*"

"He's ... he's ... laughing at you," gasped Minnie, her vision swimming as the view pointed at the floor.

Charlie couldn't believe her sudden display of balls; Minnie's back was totally against the wall, and it was almost as if every blow was heightening her survival instinct, bringing out her animalistic will to live. "You can ... hurt me ... all you want, but you can't hurt him. You're nothing to him. You *have* nothing on him." She looked up, and the view showed Chuck's beet red, boiling face. He held up the knife, his whole body trembling, and then suddenly stopped. His finger came up, pointed in the air.

"Do I?" he said, his eyes goggling in his head, his voice now low and cracked. He had gone even further over the edge, the change from calm lunacy to all-out mania coming as fast as the punch he had put in her belly. "Do I have nothing on him? I have you. I have *you.*" He pointed a wagging finger at Minnie, but the uncertainty in his voice was clearer than ever.

"I'm no one to him," she replied, her voice too rough to betray any fear. "I'm just a vessel. He came here for you, Chuck. He came here to find you *out.*" Minnie heard her own words, and even she couldn't believe what she was saying. She'd always been able to bullshit when the chips were down, but this was life and death. When staring oblivion in the face, she'd found herself trying to blag it. "You're such a big man? Come on in and face him. If he's nothing, come on in. Come on, if you've got the *balls.*"

Oh God, let this work. Let Charlie be right, let him be alright.

Charlie had his wind back (*how can I be winded in here, I'm not even breathing air*) and got shakily to his feet. She was doing it. Would it work? He had to be ready himself, if it did. He felt his own fear grow, felt his stomach turn liquid, and he began to hop lightly, nervously, on his toes as his legs felt like they wouldn't support him.

Okay. Be ready. Be fucking ready. Get ready to go. Oh, shit. Oh, God.

Something occurred to him.

"Minnie, if he's coming in here, you're gonna need to know which one is me, all right?" Charlie said, his voice shaking with adrenaline. His thoughts were verbalised as they came, turning into a babble. "We'll use a keyword, and it's ... it's ... wait, he could read your memories and find it out ... but he'd have to know what he was looking for, and he wouldn't know that I'd even mentioned a keyword ... uh, the keyword is ... " It needed to be something obscure, something unusual, and the only one that came to mind was the title of an old ELO song. "Xanadu, right? Minnie? Xanadu. Did you get that?"

"I got that, Charlie," said Minnie, being deliberately loud so that Chuck could hear, and it worked; Chuck jerked like he'd just been goosed.

"If I have the balls?" whispered Chuck. "The balls? The balls? The *balls?*"" He narrowed his eyes and leaned forward to intimidate her, to intimidate them both, but Minnie could see the action for the empty display that it was. Chuck was downright scared, the bonds on her wrists and ankles forgotten, thinking only of the thought of facing Charlie. His bravado was utterly shot, and his breathing was now rapid and shaky. "Oh, I've got the balls. I've got the fucking balls, little girl," he said, breathlessly, eyes widening again. Minnie looked back at him fiercely, trying to give away none of her own uncertainty. She really, really hoped that Charlie was ready.

Please, Charlie. Don't get hurt. Don't let him hurt either of us. I love you.

Chuck started to mimic Charlie's own action without realising it, bobbing on his own toes and nodding repeatedly, holding Minnie's gaze and breathing heavily through his nose.

"I've got the balls," he said again, nodding faster and faster, convincing himself as best he could. "I'll show you both. Watch this. You won't make me run. The only one. I'm the only one. The only one." He cocked his head for a moment, then stopped dead. He dropped to one knee without a word, raising the knife at the same time and then driving it downwards to bury it in the meat of Minnie's right leg, embedding it up to the hilt.

Minnie screamed like a banshee, the white-hot pain of tearing flesh and sinew boring deep in her right leg, and Charlie bellowed in agony himself as a hole an inch wide and nearly three inches deep tore open in his thigh. The pain was blinding, the waif-like thighs of Minnie carrying so little muscle and fat that the blade scraped against the bone on the way in. He rolled around on the floor of the Black Room as Minnie yelled and bucked in her seat.

Chuck stood up, breathless and grinning, covered in sweat, and grabbed a fistful of Minnie's hair as he did so, pulling her head back. He pushed his face right up against hers, breathing into her face; his breath was putrid, his body dehydrated and riddled with adrenaline.

"*You feel that? Does he feel that?*" he gasped, his lips brushing against her face. "Maybe he does, maybe he doesn't, eh?! But you do, and if this all works like I think it does, I think he *has* to feel that, right? Maybe more than feel it; there's a hole there now, isn't there?" He wiggled the knife's handle, and Minnie's and Charlie's combined screams rose up to an even higher pitch. "I think maybe he has a hole too. The connection between the host and the *intruder!"* Minnie didn't answer, instead simply screwing up her eyes and bellowing like an animal at the solid object lodged in her thigh. The pain was indescribable. Chuck straightened, shoulders moving up and down with each heavy, rapid breath, and began nodding and bobbing once more. His smile was gone. He was preparing.

Charlie saw none of this in the Black Room, the screen blank due to Minnie's closed eyes. He clutched at his leg and gritted his teeth, trying to keep his cries to a minimum, knowing that Minnie would be deafened by them and making her even more terrified. It was just so fucking *painful.*

He's coming. He knows you're hurt. He's coming. You have to get up. You have to be ready. You have to save her, you have to save the both of you.

He tried to sit up, fell back down again, every movement sending a bolt of pain through his leg.

Where will he come in from? Where will he appear? You have to get up!

He sat up again, and this time he stayed up, getting a hand down behind him to prop himself upright. As he pitched forward and got his good leg behind him, letting out a cry as he moved his torn thigh in the process, he tried to lurch to one foot via the strength of one leg. The pain made everything so incredibly difficult. The screen blinked into life, lightening the room and revealing Chuck looming over Minnie, Charlie's angled point of view making Chuck look like a giant.

"Here I come, you pissant," said Chuck, then his eyes glazed over, his body went limp, and fell out of sight.

"Charlie!" screamed Minnie, her voice shredded with pain and adrenaline of her own, *"he's coming!"*

And indeed he was; there was a change in the pressure of the Black Room. The skin of Charlie's body began to tingle, sending fresh pain through the wound in his leg. Charlie nearly fell down again, but remained upright as Chuck's head began to appear through the floor of the Black Room, just a few feet away from where Charlie was balancing on one leg. Charlie had time to crazily think, *so that's why the floor's different, it's the exit and entry point* before Chuck's entire, naked body had risen into sight. The image of Chuck's true form made Charlie's mind go blank. He hadn't really expected there to be any differences between their Black Room forms. There was.

Chuck's eyes were set in almost hollowed-out sockets, far more than would be humanly possible in an actual body. His cheeks were gaunt to the point of being stretched paper-thin over protruding cheekbones, and his body as a whole looked emaciated. His shoulders were hunched, his skin was milky-white, and the overall impression his appearance gave was that of a lurking, brooding troll. He didn't look weak; he looked dangerous, coiled and sinewy, like Gollum at the height of a grown man.

This is what his mind looks like. This is what happens to you when you don't sleep properly for twenty years, when you chase something beyond the point of obsession. Oh, Chuck.

Chuck laid eyes on Charlie, standing as he was on one leg, holding his wound with one hand and wincing as he did so. At first, Chuck's eyes widened again, enhancing the gruesome effect of his sunken eye sockets, but then he saw the fear in his enemy's eyes, saw Charlie's inability to defend himself, and his lips parted in a grin that made his face look like a death mask.

But only for a moment.

"You're in biiiig trouble, Charlie boy—" Chuck began, but his expression suddenly changed to one of confusion, then surprise as his body buckled at the waist and fell over.

What—

Immediately, Chuck tried to get back up, pushing his torso clumsily off the ground. One arm gave way, and his shoulder dropped back to the floor with a smack, taking the rest of his body with it. His eyes glared up at Charlie from the floor, full of impotent fury, and he tried to speak, but whatever he meant to say came out in a useless, drunk-sounding slur. One hand rose, swiped uselessly at the air in Charlie's direction, and Chuck then began to roll back and forth on the floor, making frustrated, enraged-sounding noises. Charlie balanced on his good leg and watched, amazed and stunned into inaction.

What the fuck is this?

Chuck had clearly lost all control of his form in the Black Room, as if he had somehow been struck down with some kind of psychic cerebral palsy. But it didn't make any sense; Chuck could do things that Charlie could not—he could float his consciousness out of his host's head at will and back in again, for starters—and his experience and control of all of the different aspects of an out-of-body existence were clearly far greater than Charlie's. So why the hell was this happening? Chuck had even evolved to the point where he was controlling the host body, having wired himself into the connection and nervous system in a way that Charlie never had—

That's right. He has. He's fully calibrated himself to his own Black Room, his own host, in a way that you never have. He's gone even further in, and now come out of there and into a Black Room that doesn't belong to a Charlie Wilkes but a Minnie Cooper ... he's fucked. He's had to reset, to adapt to a Black Room that already exists rather than make his own. You knew this wouldn't be a fair fight, but not this way round; you can win, you can—

Charlie was already hobbling over to Chuck's inert form as fast as he could, knowing that the advantage could be lost if Chuck managed to get his shit together. As he reached Chuck's squirming body, the fear inside him gave way to rage at a level that he had never experienced before. Not only had this man, no, this *creature* abused, terrified, hurt and *stabbed* the woman he loved, but he'd also destroyed his only chance at getting to have the version of her that should have been his. Chuck had destroyed *this* world's Minnie's only chance of getting to have a Charlie of her own too, by killing that Charlie's mind and turning his body into a puppet. He was a monster, taking and tearing any chance at happiness, and worst of all, Charlie thought of the countless others across the worlds who would feel the effects of his poison if he were allowed to continue. The bitterness and fury and injustice of it all found its way into Charlie's fists, and fuelled their onslaught into Chuck's face as Charlie fell upon him, screaming and punching as hard as he could. He didn't even notice the stabbing pain in his thigh as his bodyweight landed on top of Chuck's helpless body.

Please don't let him get up. Let me get as much in as I can. Please let me win.

"*You—*" was the only word Chuck managed to form, but even that was lost as Charlie's knuckles mushed Chuck's lips against his teeth with all the force he could muster. Chuck squawked in unintelligible, garbled utterances of pain as Charlie rained blows down onto his head, wanting to cave it in if he could. A distant part of his mind wondered what he was actually punching; what was he damaging, if this was only a representation of Chuck's body? His mind? His very self? He didn't know, and didn't care, as the conscious part of Charlie's mind was only interested in doing as much damage as it could. He needed to satisfy the raw need for vengeance that flowed down his arms and through his knuckles. And he *was* doing damage, Chuck's face beginning to swell slightly and change colour as Charlie pummelled it like a heavy bag, and Chuck's limbs feebly flopped in a fruitless effort to protect himself. All Charlie knew was that he had to kill Chuck, there and then, while he still could. Chuck had to be stopped, and this was not only the only way that Charlie knew how, but the only chance that he would get. Chuck would not make this mistake again, would not give Charlie this opportunity.

Eat this, you fucking cocksucker. Die. Die.

"You fucking bastard! You killed them! You killed her! You killed my Minnie! I won't let you kill any more! You're not! Killing! Any! More!" His blows crashed home as Chuck's head rocked back and forth, now making no sound at all and ceasing his attempts to fight back. Charlie knew that he was about to commit murder, and while this registered as a big deal in his mind, it came with no need for consideration, no need to double-check his intention. He knew, without doubt, that it had to be done, and that was apparently enough to quell any remorse over taking a life. Even in his rage, Charlie noted this, and was a little surprised that he felt so effortlessly prepared to do it; he wondered just how thin the divide between himself and Chuck really was. If he could do what Chuck could do ... if he could learn it, and know as Chuck did that she was out there, another Minnie that he could have ...

Maybe you don't even know your own ten percent, Charlie.

Over the sound of his own screams and Chuck's battered moans, he could hear Minnie screaming his name.

"*Charlie! Charlie! What's happening?!*"

"*I've got him!*" Charlie screamed, jerked from his rage-fuelled thoughts and realising that he was, undoubtedly, winning. He was almost laughing with manic delight now, as he continued to smash Chuck as hard as he could in the face, his knuckles singing with the pain of smacking bone onto bone. "*I've fucking got him, he's completely shafted himself by coming in here, and he's—*"

Charlie didn't have him. When Chuck had stopped flopping uselessly on the spot, Charlie had taken it as a sign of impending victory. He had been wrong. Chuck, it appeared, had been playing possum while he got enough focus together to escape; his body was beginning to sink back through the floor, the failed attack abandoned. Chuck was retreating, and if he got back into his body—

He's just going to kill her, and you as well. He's not going to take any more risks.

"*Oh ... oh fuck!*" yelled Charlie. "*Minnie, he's leaving! He's getting out of here!*"

"*Stop him! Stop him Charlie!*" screamed Minnie, knowing just as Charlie did what would come next.

Charlie grabbed onto one of Chuck's arms and pulled, but it was like trying to dislodge a streetlight. The floor of the Black Room was halfway up the sides of Chuck's head now, and whatever force Chuck was using to depart was far stronger than Charlie's ability to pull against it.

"*I can't! The transfer is too strong!*" he yelled, still pulling uselessly at Chuck's arm as he watched the face begin to disappear from view. He just had time to catch Chuck's swollen eye and see the monster's ruined lips part in a broken, lopsided grin of triumph. Then the head was gone, and the body and legs, and only the arm remained sticking up from the floor like that of a corpse badly hidden in tar. Charlie still held it, and still it descended. "*Minnie, I don't know what to do! I can't stop him!*" The arm was almost gone too now, sunken up to the forearm where Charlie's knuckles desperately grasped it with all of his might. Then the forearm was in the floor too, along with Charlie's hand.

Charlie screamed, expecting pain, but there was no sensation at all, save for the continuing irresistible downward pull. It was the strangest feeling, but Charlie also realised that he felt something else. The flesh of Chuck's arm under his hand.

"*Minnie!*" he yelled, as his upper torso began to dip towards the floor as well, following Chuck's arm. His knees remained on solid floor, his body bending further and further at the waist, leaning after Chuck's point of exit. Charlie knew he only had a few seconds. "*I'm going with him! I've still got him, but ... I'm going with him!*"

"*What?!*" yelled Minnie, her voice bellowing into the Black Room. "*But ... how? How will you get back?*"

"*I don't know!*" Charlie yelled, fear welling inside him like ice cold water as his head drew closer and closer to the jet black floor before his eyes. "*I just ... Minnie, remember the word, the keyword—*" and then Charlie's world went black as his head was pulled through the floor too, then his upper torso, then his legs and feet. He felt nothing around his head and body, as if the solidity of the floor had turned into mere air the second they had passed through it, and then suddenly he was out, a mind without form as he was already floating across the room towards Chuck's unconscious body. Even though he had no shape, somehow he could still feel Chuck's arm, gripped tightly in his fist. He wondered what would happen if he let go, but already they were nearly at Chuck's head, looming huge before them like something on Mount Rushmore. The next moment, Charlie was in the blackness once more.

It passed just as quickly as it had when he had exited Minnie's head, and then there was the same pulling sensation as before but in reverse. He felt Chuck weakly trying to shake him off—he was clearly already through, and trying to make sure Charlie couldn't follow—but Charlie held on for dear life. He had no idea what would happen if he let go while he was in the blackness *outside* the Black Room, and he wasn't going to find out. Then his head was through, his reformed body rising after it, but he had no time to take in his surroundings as he felt a sharp pain in his fingers. Chuck was biting Charlie's hand, lying on the floor next to Charlie's rapidly rising body.

Aaaaaaaagh, son of a bitch! Has he got it back together already?!

Charlie yelled in pain, and began to strike at Chuck's head again, hoping that Chuck would still be weakened from the previous assault that he had endured. Charlie's legs popped free of the floor—the stabbed one yelling a fresh agony at him as it emerged—and then the biting pain in his fingers gave Charlie a desperate surge of strength as he drove his knuckle deep into Chuck's left eye. Now he was clear of the floor, Charlie let go of Chuck's arm as the lunatic yelped and pulled away, clutching at his sunken eye socket. Charlie, clutching his wounded hand, skittered away on his backside and tried to get his good leg under himself to get up. As he did so, he looked at Chuck's Black Room properly for the first time, expecting the worst. Had he more time, he would have appreciated how wrong he was; he'd thought it would look like something out of Dante's inferno, full of hellfire and brimstone and wailing bodies hanging from the walls. It didn't. It looked almost exactly the same as Charlie's, if considerably brighter, the walls looking more grey than black. Formed automatically by the subconscious, each of them obviously visualised being inside another person's mind roughly the same way as the other.

Charlie realised that he couldn't hear Minnie, or anything else outside for that matter. Even with the screen off and the body unconscious, Chuck now had enough of a connection to make this Black Room have just enough light of its own. The shapes and ripples in the walls were clearer as a result, but there was far less movement to them.

Of course the room's lighter. He's running *the whole body from here. His connection goes way beyond yours, that's why he got so screwed up when he came to visit just now. And it looks like he was bullshitting about the blue walls and double screens as well,* thought Charlie crazily, recalling Minnie's memory of Chuck's tale as he painfully struggled to get to his feet and resume the assault. His pulse was racing now, thinking that he only might have seconds to get on top of Chuck before he could—

"That's ... that's a new trick, even on me," gasped Chuck, getting to his feet more easily and chuckling gently. Whatever effect coming to Charlie's Black Room had on Chuck, it had clearly vanished now that he had returned home. Charlie watched his adversary move, and tried to prepare himself once more. He knew that he was now deep in the lion's den.

IN THE DARKNESS, THAT'S WHERE I'LL KNOW YOU

Oh shit ... he's got himself steady again. You just have to hope that you did enough damage already, that you already messed him up enough to keep him from being fully in command of his abilities.

Chuck was breathing steadily now, standing a good ten feet away. He was holding his pummelled head and having to squint through one swollen eye, but despite the shake in his voice he sounded more confident now that he had himself back under control.

"So how the hell does that work, then?" he said, a crazy guffaw coming from his throat. "We're obviously different in some ways, you and me, aren't we? I mean ... she was telling the truth, wasn't she? It was written all over your face when I showed up over there." He pointed a weary-looking arm at Charlie, let it drop loosely back to his side. "You were shitting it. You had no idea what was going to happen. You're just some guy who woke up inside her head. You aren't like me *at all*." He stretched slightly, wincing, and arched his neck around, testing his mobility. He rolled both his shoulders gingerly, and felt his jaw. Charlie watched, trying to mask his own pain.

Good God, it hurts so much to stand ... how the hell are you going to get out of this?

"I was actually scared of you," Chuck continued, the grin coming back to his now even more distorted face. "*Me.* How did you get there then? Drugs? That's how I went the extra step. The first time, at least. I had full control after that. But I don't think *you* do ... you don't, do you?" That weaselly, lizard-like look crept into Chuck's eyes as he searched Charlie's face, who was still yet to say anything in reply. Chuck's tone sounded confident, but it was also theatrical in its manner.

Like a TV villain, or rather what he thinks a villain should sound like. Is he trying to shit you up?

Charlie was now steady on his feet, but only just. He didn't want to look as vulnerable as he actually was in front of Chuck, but hoped that the damage he'd done to Chuck's face already might make the man think twice about attacking just yet. His left leg felt like a dead weight though, and he wondered if he could even lift it. His blood pounded like a bass drum in his ears, and his heart hammered in his chest, but he just about managed to keep his poker face. He worried that if he spoke, his knowledge of his own desperate situation would be clearly heard in his voice.

You missed your window. He's back on his feet, and however badly banged up his face is, he has four working limbs. You don't. What the fuck are you going to do?

"So what was that, then?" asked Chuck, shaking his head and looking annoyed. The question sounded genuinely curious, not asked in the smug arch-villain tone that he'd been previously trying to put on moments ago.

And what's that all about, anyway? Is he also trying to cover up worse pain? Is he also putting on a show of bravado so that you won't know how hurt he really is? He still hasn't moved, after all.

It was true; Chuck had made no attempt to close the distance between the pair of them.

"Just a desperate grab that paid off?" said Chuck, going back into serial-villain mode ... but this time, it sounded like less of a put-on and more like Chuck was starting to enjoy himself, enjoying his own swagger. Charlie's stare intensified, as did his thoughts.

He's working it out. He thinks he can take you. Can he? He must know that you at least can't move as fast as he can with a bum leg. Even if you've beaten him enough to put you both on a level playing field in terms of Black Room stuff, you're up shit creek physically.

"Maybe you *can* travel then...maybe you have the same abilities in the void that I do?" said Chuck, shrugging. The growing confidence was unmistakable. Charlie shifted his shoulders, made sure he was facing Chuck more directly. "Maybe yours are just ... less?" He raised his eyebrows and grinned, his ragged breath making his head shake slightly, and Charlie registered that continued rough breathing as it gave him a flicker of hope. Chuck may or may not have been in more pain than he was showing, but the encounter in Minnie's head had certainly taken something out of him, and he wasn't healing up over here either.

"Locked away? You can do it with me as your training wheels, but not on your own?" said Chuck, his grin widening as he spread his arms. He was enjoying the sound of his own voice, of his own show. "Hell, maybe that's the same for everyone, right? They just don't know how to do it, unless somebody takes them by the hand. Or lets them take *their* hand, in this case." An idea seemed to occur to him, and he pointed a hand out to the left. "So, really ... there's nothing to stop me jumping out of here, going into the bitch's head, and having a good stomp around? Sure, it might take me a while to get control of myself back over there, but it'd come eventually. Meanwhile, you'd be stuck in here!" He gestured to the walls, the floor, but through the theatrics Charlie saw another wince.

Maybe. Maybe.

"Hey, you might even learn to control this body, too," said Chuck, "it's the same as yours, after all. But you couldn't get into where it counted, could you? You couldn't get out of *here* and into *there*. You couldn't stop me stomping her brain to bits from the inside." The grin had turned into a grimace by now, and this last sentence had been spat through gritted teeth. Charlie heard the desire in it, the sheer hatred. Chuck closed his eyes briefly and rocked gently on his feet. Clenching his jaw like that clearly hurt him. Charlie had definitely done some damage that was more than cosmetic, then.

"You don't know that I can't," said Charlie, breaking his silence. His voice was shaky, but not *too* shaky.

Don't let him know how badly you're hurt. Don't let him see.

Chuck nodded, a smirk replacing the scowl.

"I don't, that's true," he said. He threw his hands up into the air, let them flop back down to his sides. "Have a go. Pop over there. Hell, just leave this room and come straight back in again. I don't mind. Show me. Show me what you've got."

... shit.

258

Charlie stared back at Chuck, desperately trying to think of a covering reason, a cocky counter that might distract Chuck's crazy mind enough to forget about his little test for a moment. He needed anything, anything to buy him some fucking *time*, but nothing came. Chuck slowly raised a finger, and wagged it at Charlie.

"I. Don't. Fucking. Believe it," he said, shaking his head and beginning to snort out a series of little gasping giggles. The serial-villain swagger was gone, replaced by the glee of an unpleasant child. "I was worried about *you.* You don't know anything! *She's* the brains of this outfit, and I'm wasting my time talking to you! Why the fuck did I let you alter the plan of action in the first place? She's the one that knows! *She's the Queen Of The Liars!*" The last part came out as a screeching cackle of laughter, Chuck's hands flung wildly over his head as tears streamed down his face. Chuck took several steps in Charlie's direction, making Charlie want to back up, but he didn't dare move. He wasn't sure that his leg would support him, and the worst thing he could do would be to fall over.

Keep it together. Watch him. KEEP IT TOGETHER. YOU ARE NOT GOING TO DIE IN HERE—

"The fucking bitch!" laughed Chuck, a nasally cackle that made Charlie want to smash his skull in. He hated Chuck, hated him more than he would have thought himself capable. "You stay here, Charlie boy, while I go take care of business. I'll even put the screen on for you so you can watch! Oh! Oh! How does that sound?"

"*She doesn't know anything you fucking twat!*" screamed Charlie, his rage surging through him as he forced a shuffling step forward of his own. His bad leg screamed, but he wouldn't let Chuck see that. Even though Chuck seemed to have the upper hand physically with Charlie immobilised as he was, Charlie wanted to be within grabbing distance. If Chuck was talking about going back, Charlie was damn well going to be latching onto him. "*She's just a normal, scared girl, who has two fucking arseholes showing up in her head! She doesn't know anything! She doesn't know* anything, *you fucking paranoid loony nutcase pathetic loser dick!*"

Chuck let out a hysterical, braying cry in response to all this, sounding like an excited hyena.

"*I'm* the loser? Me?" he said, his eyes wide and triumphant and utterly, completely insane. "I can go anywhere. *I can be fucking anyone I choose.* I can wear a person like a, like a fancy dress costume or something. What can *you* do? How can you be me? How were you and I *ever* the same? You're *nothing!*" he cried. "You're an imitation, an embarrassment, a fucking, a fucking ... stain, a fucking stain on my name, that's you! *You have to be rubbed out! First I rub you out, then I rub her out, both of you rubbed out!*" He cackled, wildly, and took another two steps forward, clawing at his own cheeks with his fingernails. One more step, and he would be within striking distance.

His eyes. You have to go for his eyes. That's your only chance. His eyes or his kneecaps, oh man, oh here we go, oh shit.

"Tell me, Charlie boy," hissed Chuck, his voice low now, his breathing fast again and oh-so eager, "how's that bum leg of yours?" Chuck darted around to Charlie's right with snake-like speed, and struck.

***

As Minnie felt Charlie leave her head, she let out a scream of desperate fear and frustration. She knew that it was just Chuck and Charlie now, together on Chuck's home turf ... and that Charlie was hurt. But hadn't he said that he had hurt Chuck as well? It was hard to think with the horrible torn sensation in her right leg screaming at her, combined with her terror for Charlie; it left her thoughts whirling in a chaotic maelstrom. She wanted to start crying again, and the appeal of that action was great in her mind. Her previous determination had floated away with Charlie's departure, her impotent fear on his behalf drawing her bravado from her like a syringe. She needed to release. Oh God, her leg hurt so much, she'd been stabbed, she'd been *stabbed—*

You haven't got time for that shit. You need to help Charlie. What can you do? Think. Just take emotion out of the equation and break it down. Fix it piece by piece. You can do it.

Now she did start crying. She couldn't do it.

Yes you fucking can, and you don't have the luxury of feeling sorry for yourself, even though you have every right. Charlie's in trouble because he came to save you. Help him.

But what could she do? They were inside Chuck's head, so anything *she* did on the outside could affect them both! And even if she wanted to get over there, she was stuck in the goddamn chair!

Okay, that's problem number one. Is there any way you can get out of the chair? Now Chuck isn't standing over you waving a knife in your face, you have a moment alone to think. Is there anything you didn't notice? How tight are your bonds?

Very. There was no give there.

Can you tip the chair over?

Probably, but with her hands lashed behind her, the only thing that could break her fall would be her head, which was a good way to get a broken neck. She could fall sideways, meaning her shoulder would take the blow instead, but even then she'd still be pretty much as immobile as she currently was sitting upright.

You need to get your hands free then.

Minnie instinctively began to try and blot it out as it arrived, self-preservation automatically kicking in. Then she remembered the reasons *why* she wanted to get free, who she was doing it for, and the thought arrived as clear as a jagged bell:

You have a knife.

IN THE DARKNESS, THAT'S WHERE I'LL KNOW YOU

A shudder that was almost a whole-body spasm rippled through her as she forced herself to look down at the metal handle sticking out of her leg. The knife. The kind that chefs use, shaped from a single piece of steel or aluminium. There was a small amount of blood pooling around the point where metal met flesh, but she knew that there would be a lot more blood if she managed to pull out the knife. She knew the worst thing a person could do with a stabbing was to pull out a still-embedded knife. It would most likely cut again on the way out, the veins would be left wide open, and anything that it might have missed on the way in would most probably be snagged as it came free. Plus, it would really, *really* fucking hurt.

You can reach that with your mouth, can't you? You can bend down and pull it out.

She could, but she desperately didn't want to. It already hurt such an unbelievable amount, the worst pain she'd ever felt. She realised that she'd actually even stopped noticing the pain in her face as a result, the ultimate spot-specific painkiller.

Want a way to lose that stubborn toothache? Stab yourself in the leg.

She realised that she was already bending down towards the knife's handle. It jutted out stubbornly from her thigh like an ugly and perverse Sword in The Stone. She'd listened to herself, and listened well; there was no other choice, so why waste time dithering about it? Even so, her lips pursed together tightly as her jaw trembled, as if her body was rebelling against the will of the mind. Gingerly, she forced her mouth open, and wrapped her jaw around the stubby handle of the knife like the world's most reluctant blowjob. Hot tears coursed down her cheeks again, but she was silent. She gripped it with her teeth, feeling a faint crunch as enamel dug into metal. She winced, both at the sensation in her injured jaw and the jolt of pain that shot through her leg as the action of gripping the knife moved it slightly, a teaser of the far greater pain that was about to commence.

Don't think about it. It's pointless. Just don't drop it. Count to three. One ... two ...

She tried to surprise herself and went on two, gripping harder and suddenly yanking upwards as fast as she could, getting it over with quickly as if she were tearing off a Band-Aid. She screamed hoarsely around the handle as the blade came free, letting out a deafening guttural bellow as the knife sliced a few extra millimetres out of her thigh on its way out. The blade was very sharp, and Minnie's action was desperate and clumsy. Blood spurted slightly from the now fully open wound and began to trickle down the sides of her thigh in fresh, warm rivulets. Minnie sobbed as she threw her head back, trying to ride out the first wave of sharp, sharp pain and holding the knife aloft. The knife pointed towards the ceiling, held high as if in triumph, but Arthur was not revelling in his new-found regal status; Minnie wept and moaned in pain and relief that it was over, even as the wound in her leg sung anew.

You did it. You did it. You did it. Well done, oh, well done. I know it hurts, but you have to keep going. Just a little more.

Minnie moaned once more, and bent again at the waist, turning round to her right hand side. The blood from her thigh was now soaking the edges of her pyjama shorts. She was trying to reach behind her, and even though her right side was the one where the pain was, she thought that maybe her right hand was bound slightly higher than her left. That was therefore her best chance of transferring the knife to her fingers.

Come on, stretch. You can do it.

Her leg burned incredibly badly as she reached, but almost immediately, she realised that she couldn't do it. Bending forwards was one thing, but getting round to the rear side of her to pass the knife to her hand was another entirely; she couldn't get anywhere near it. The knife was too short, and her hand was too far away. She was screwed, and so was Charlie.

You'll have to drop it. You'll have to drop it straight down to your hand, and that means sitting upright and dropping it behind you from shoulder height to get the angle right.

But what if she missed?

You mustn't miss, or you're both dead.

Sweating heavily now, she slowly straightened up and tried to calm her breathing. This was going to be hard enough without her shoulders pitching and lurching with each breath. She turned her head gingerly back over her shoulder, lifting the knife up and over in the process. Looking down along her triceps, she saw her backward-turned fingers as if they were looking up at her, waiting. They seemed a million miles away, as if they belonged to someone else. She flexed them slightly, testing them; they moved, but felt numb and senseless.

This is impossible. I can't do it.

Shut up. You've got to try.

She waited there a few more seconds, her shoulder becoming wet with her tears. She wasn't hesitating or procrastinating, she was trying to focus, continuing to get her breathing steady.

Don't blow it. In fact, wait, don't think about not blowing it, think about getting it right. Visualise it dropping perfectly into your hands. Visualise your fingers snapping shut around it like Mr. Miyagi snapping a fly in his chopsticks.

She tried to see it working in her mind. She couldn't, instead only seeing the knife slipping straight past her clumsily grasping fingers and tumbling utterly out of reach onto the floor below.

That won't happen. Come on.

She leaned her head out over her hand as far as she could, trying to ignore the dizzying pain in her thigh, and saw her fingers a good two feet below the knife. She opened her mouth.

The knife dropped like the blade of a guillotine, and as she turned her hand to catch it without the blade stabbing into her palm, the first inch of the knife fell almost perfectly into the space between her thumb and forefinger. She snapped them closed and caught the tip of the blade, but it was too early; had she waited a split second longer, she could have gotten three fingers onto it. As it was, the heavy metal handle of the knife overbalanced it, momentum lending it extra weight, and that combined with sweat that covered her fingertips like an oil slick led to the knife pitching over itself and tumbling free of Minnie's grasp. It fell the remaining two feet to the floor, and landed on the carpet with a damning and very final thud.

Minnie stared at it dumbly for a moment, her breath caught in her throat. The knife stared back up at her like a condemnation.

You had it. You fucking had it.

Minnie threw her head back once more and let out a scream of rage, her hands forming into fists behind her back.

"*FUUUUUUUUUUUCCKKKK!!*" she screeched, and then it hit her.

Topple the chair over sideways after all. The knife is on the floor; topple the chair over and get yourself on the floor too. Then you can wiggle the chair so you're close enough to it to grab it behind you, and then turn it against the tie on your wrist. You don't have a choice now. You have to rock the chair over.

It was the only option. Not giving herself time to think about it, Minnie began to rock the chair. She knew this was going to hurt a lot too; she would have to fall onto her stabbed-open right hand side to get the knife into her more capable right hand, as well as have the combination of her weight and the solidity of the chair falling against her right arm, bound as it was around the outside of the seat's back support. There was no time to waste thinking about that, and besides, she was already hurting a hell of a lot.

Just a bit more. You can take it, Minnie-moo. You can do it. You can take it.

She wasn't sure she could, but regardless, Minnie pitched first left, then back towards the right, creating enough return momentum to get the two left legs of the chair into the air. She hung there for a moment, suspended in the calm before the pain, and dizzily and sleepily wished that she could just stay there forever with everything turning out all right. Then gravity won the battle, and then Minnie and the chair fell towards the floor. She had just enough time to think:

Shit, what if the chair breaks my arm?

***

Chuck's foot smashed directly into Charlie's wound before he could react, and even though he swung a fist wildly at Chuck as he fell, Charlie's leg betrayed him and buckled under the pain.

Oh, shit. Oh, get up fast or you're fucked. Minnie—

Making strange whooping sounds as he gasped in non-existent air, Chuck was immediately upon him, stamping on Charlie's head with his entire body weight. Charlie immediately felt as if he'd just been run over by a pickup truck, the weight of a full-grown man battering into him with devastating effect. He couldn't cry out; each blow was simply too jarring. The strange nature of the floor of the Black Room meant that the stomps to his skull weren't as lethal as they might have otherwise been, Charlie's head jarring

263

against it with each kick, but the sheer force behind them dwarfed that of any of Charlie's previous blows to Chuck's head. Each time the foot went down, it was as if a bomb had gone off inside Charlie's skull, stunning thought from his mind and sending a white flash across his vision. He felt as if his head were about to crack open. A distant, detached part of his mind wondered:

What would happen if he split my skull in here? There's no actual brain in there, but does it surely represent the core of whatever I am in here; would I just die? Would my consciousness be destroyed? Would my brain be damaged back in my actual body? Would I just cease to be?

Charlie rolled on the spot, unable to move away as stomp after stomp pistoned onto his head, each attempt to get out of range cut short by a blow that reset his bearings and made him wonder for a second where he was. As soon as he realised, he would start to move, but then the next blow would come and the process would begin again.

"*Fake! Fake! Fake! Fake!*" screeched Chuck, using the word to punctuate each stomp. In his excitement and mania, he jumped into two-footed stomp onto Charlie's body, one onto his stomach and one onto the stab wound in his leg. This time, Charlie did make a sound, somehow able to scream from the pain in his leg and stomach even though he normally would have been winded by such an attack; again, there was no air in the Black Room. Thanks to this brief reprieve from attacks to his head, Charlie had a moment without being stunned again, and managed to quickly roll away,

Can he kill me? Can he actually kill me in here?

Charlie felt like something had given slightly in his skull, and there had been a definite and unmistakable crunching sound as he rolled. He dimly realised that *kill* was perhaps the wrong word in the Black Room. *Destroy* would be more appropriate. Charlie was nothing but his own consciousness in here, and if Chuck could tear him to bits, so he would cease to exist.

Get up man ... you can do it ... shit, this was a bad idea ... get up ...

His thoughts felt broken, but the instinct came through clearly enough. Chuck followed Charlie as he crawled across the floor, and jabbed his heel agonisingly into Charlie's kidneys, knocking him back down every time he tried to get up. Charlie focused on the wall as he drew close to it, hoping to be able to use it to help him stand, but then felt another, different attack to his leg. There was a horrible, tearing sensation in the wound as he looked round to see Chuck on top of his thigh, his fingers dug deep into Charlie's leg wound and pulling at it. Charlie screamed, and loudly.

JESUS! Get him OFF YOU!

Despite the pain, Charlie wildly swung his good leg around and smashed it into the side of Chuck's bruised head. Chuck screamed and let go, but the scream was not as loud as Charlie would have liked. Clearly, Chuck had already done far more damage to Charlie in here than he had received in Minnie's head.

Chuck sat back up, and his hands came away from his face, wincing as he did so. The grin came back as he stood and advanced once more. Charlie

264

frantically tried to rise on shaking limbs, but they felt weak and unreliable now, as if they weren't responding properly.

Oh God, what has he done to me? What damage has he done? You have to get hold of him, you have to stop him stamping on your head—

"That ... that was a mistake," breathed Chuck, gasping in air as he wagged his finger at Charlie again. "I admit it. Let's be honest, neither of us are fighters, so *mistakes—*" he leapt across the few feet of space that was now between them, landing one foot back on Charlie's injured leg and then dropping another awful, crunching blow onto Charlie's skull. Something else gave in Charlie's head, but he still flailed to try and catch one of Chuck's legs in an attempt to topple him over. It didn't work; Chuck skipped out of Charlie's reach.

Think   dying   get up

"—are going to happen. One opponent immobile, the other not ... the guy on his feet doesn't then get down to the other guy's level and give him a chance to get his hands on him. *Right?*" Chuck darted in again, stomped, jumped back. Charlie's vision flashed over to whiteness, and took several seconds to become clear. During that time, he felt another blow against what he thought was his head. There was a bigger, worse sounding crunch, and something felt like it had fallen out inside his head. He tried to move his arms, his legs. There was barely a response.

minnie

"*Yes!*" screeched Chuck, "You fuck with me? *You fuck with me? You can't even get up! The pair of you! The pair of* wait—I want you to *see* her, you failed, you *failed—*" Chuck went quiet for a second, and then the room was suddenly a lot lighter; Chuck had turned on the screen, opened the body's eyes. Charlie looked towards the light, his thoughts dim, his vision hazy, but even before he looked, he knew that Minnie was no longer in the chair.

Once Chuck had re-ignited the connection, the ears had activated as well, and the volume of her voice was so deafening that she could only be close by. A glance at the now-appeared screen confirmed it, Minnie kneeling so close that she almost filled the image entirely. She was calling Charlie's name.

"*Charlie! Charlie! What can I do? Tell me? Can you hear me? How can I help you?!*" The desperation in her voice was at a manic, fever pitch. Chuck turned fully to the screen now, his brow furrowed but amused at the same time.

"You think this makes a *difference?*" he yelled, and Charlie couldn't tell if the question was aimed at himself or Minnie. "She got out of the fucking chair, so what? Don't you twats *get it?* She can't go *anywhere! There's nowhere she can go that I can't follow! There's no-one she can talk to that can do anything to stop me!* I can go right into her head! The only person I was worried about was *you,* Charlie, and I've already beaten you 'cos you're *nothing.* I *will* have my answers from the Queen though Charlie boy, and if not her, then the next one, or the next one, or the next one, or the next one, or the next one, or the next one, *or the next one, or the next one,* and I win either way because it *feels*

... so ... good. Even if I let you go, you can't always be in her head. You have to go home eventually. You think it would take me a long time to recalibrate over there? No sir. I could wait until you're not there, and then take my time tearing her apart. She's already dead, Charlie. Already as good as dead, already dead, already dead, already dead." He scuttled back towards Charlie and kicked him in the face with the instep of his foot this time, yelling a little in pain as the bone of his unpadded instep cracked into Charlie's face. Charlie felt his nose break, and despite his fear and injuries, he suddenly felt very, very tired. He had done his best, hadn't he? Did he deserve all this? Hadn't he earned a rest, after this whole, tiring, confusing, frightening experience?

minnie

Yes. He couldn't just let her...

what   can   do   think

He tried moving his limbs again, and there was only that slight flicker of motion. Hardly anything. He tried again, and his arms flopped up off the floor and onto his chest. It took a herculean effort.

Arms   legs   mouth   body

Charlie's eyes caught sight of something on screen, something on the floor to Minnie's right. He'd only glimpsed it for a split-second as her head moved slightly out of the way, and then he had it. He didn't know if he had anything left to do it with, though. If he did, it would take everything. All that he had left.

"*Look at her face!*" screamed Chuck, his head seeming to swell with his own mania. "*Look at her face, look at her frightened fucking face! Are you looking! Are you fucking looking—*" He stepped in for another stomp, and Charlie rose to meet it with a final, concentrated push, taking the blow as it glanced with a vision-blinding scrape off his broken head. Charlie's attack caught Chuck's body off-balance. There wasn't much strength in the move, but Chuck hadn't anticipated it; he stumbled and fell, and Charlie crawled immediately up Chuck's fallen body as fast as he could, clambering up his torso like an eager zombie upon fallen prey. Every movement was agony for Charlie, his head screaming and grinding with each inch that he gained, but he didn't stop. He knew that as soon as he did, he would be finished, and there was too much to do. He focused his thoughts, rage and desperation lending him temporary clarity:

Here   comes   motherfucker   no idea   if this   work   going to make   hurt you either way

Chuck's own head had banged off the Black Room floor as he fell, unprepared, but already he was sitting up and screeching as Charlie advanced. Charlie flopped up a hand and drove his thumb into Chuck's eye socket, the injured one this time, and Chuck twisted and bucked as Charlie ground the digit home. His thoughts spun like a drunk's:

Thumb   to eye   classic   Ric Flair   woo

Charlie knew that he had to press his temporary advantage, for as banged up as he was, he couldn't keep this up very much longer.

Just   little   further   nearly there

Charlie pulled himself up agonisingly over the rolling sea of Chuck's body, using his other hand on the top of Chuck's head to gain the last few inches. Chuck's fists beat at Charlie's shoulders and head, causing further white flashes and horrible grinding sensations in his brain.

This   it

Charlie's mouth reached his target, and he clamped his teeth over Chuck's throat and bit as hard as he could, pinning the monster to the floor. Chuck squealed like a stabbed pig, and stopped beating with his fists. His hands flew to Charlie's jaws on his throat, trying desperately to prise them apart, and Charlie knew that the countdown had begun. He could only bite with this force for so long, could only keep Chuck occupied for a short space of time before his strength ran out. Sticking his good leg feebly out behind him, he fumbled around with it, an action made harder by Chuck's own bucking and thrashing limbs. Charlie found what he wanted, knowing that this was the easy part; he already knew he was close enough to the wall to touch it. What he *didn't* know was whether Chuck's deeper connection ran both ways; did the body and brain store Chuck's memories too? It was time to find out. He pressed against the Black Room's wall with his foot, and searched, as Minnie's yells from outside rang in his ears.

He found it. Memory slammed into him again, but deeper, further, a connection so deep that, for a moment, it was like the memories were his own, coming to him like something that he should never have forgotten. Now he had it, he used it, stealing experience, stealing memories of technique that made the whole thing effortless. Nerve endings fired into life but in a distant, alien way that was just ... *electric.* Despite his body's weakness, the vitality of the connection fired his mind into life as if he had just had a good night's sleep.

***

"Charlie! What do I do? Can you get back? How can I help?" repeated Minnie, feeling useless, desperate, and frustrated in a way that she had never known before in her entire life. She wanted to grab the unconscious head of the body before her and shake it, but that brought a wild image to her mind of Charlie rattling around in there like a porcelain figure in a glass jar, shattering and breaking.

Then Chuck's body opened its eyes, and Minnie shrieked and drew away. It opened and closed its mouth a few times, soundlessly, and then it found its voice.

"Xanadu," Charlie said. "Xanadu." He blinked his eyes a few times, the mouth flapping uselessly again, and then he spoke. "This ... this is harder than I thought it would be." He rolled his eyes around, looking, then they fell upon his left arm. The hand twitched, and then the fingers opened and closed, opened and closed.

"Ch ... Charlie?" gasped Minnie, still drawn up into a ball on the carpet a few feet away and goggling her eyes at the sight before her. She was now even more pale than she normally was, making her look corpse-like. Charlie's eyes went back to her.

"Yeah," he said, blinking. "I don't have much time. This ... this is so hard, doing two things at once. I'm talking to you here, but I've also got ... Chuck pinned down by the throat ... with my teeth. I can already feel ... my body tiring again in here." His hand flapped around on the carpet, fumbling. Even as he concentrated intensely, the sight of her took his breath away. He saw a future as he looked at her, a life lived together; a first home, a first child, growing old. He wanted it so badly that he nearly wept.

Come on, old son. Time to man up, now. Time to man up like you never have before. For her sake. It's okay. You know it's okay.

"Charlie, oh my God, *Charlie*," scrambling forward on her hands and feet, taking the hand that was flopping around on the carpet and grasping it tightly. "This is ... this is ... how did you ... what can I do? How can I help, *what can I do*—*" Charlie limply held up the other hand, cutting her off, his eyes still blinking in that strange manner.

"Chuck's memories. Deeper connection, works both ways. Learned what he knows. Might not ... .be able to leap around from body to body, but ... I can connect with ... own body. Have to be quick. "

Don't let her realise. Please. Don't let her know.

"Okay, okay," gasped Minnie, leaning forward, intense and wide-eyed, nodding frantically and rubbing his hand. "Tell me quickly, what are we—"

"Just listen," said Charlie, gripping her hand back. "At the back of all ... the worlds. There's something else. Chuck ... was afraid of it, but ... he's different to me. Different to you. I'm not afraid of it. You shouldn't ... be either."

"I don't understand—"

In the Black Room, Charlie felt Chuck's body come off the floor slightly, pushing Charlie's back, but Charlie managed to get him back down again. He knew he wouldn't get a second chance. There was no time to explain, and other things to do and say first.

"It's alright. But please ... hold me. I want to know ... what it's like. Quickly."

At the absolute fucking least, we're owed that. We're having that.

Minnie stared at him, terrified of what he was saying, but there was such urgency in his voice that she didn't hesitate. She released his hand, and held him viciously tight, as Charlie's arms found her with a strength that surprised even him. The embrace was perfect, like coming home, just as he knew it would be, but there was no time to savour it. After a moment, he kept one arm where it was and released her with the other, extending it out behind her. He felt for what his hand had been previously fumbling for, and found it. When he released her with his other arm, she sat back quickly, looking into his tear-filled eyes.

IN THE DARKNESS, THAT'S WHERE I'LL KNOW YOU

Will she figure it out? Will she understand that to use the connection means to be bound by the effects of the connection? Will she know that there was no choice, that she had to be protected? That Chuck would never stop?

There was no time to ask, no time to clarify. There was only time for one thing.

"I love you ... Minnie. And I think that means ... I don't even need to know ... your ten percent. I think people need ... just that little bit left ... for themselves. That little bit ... of darkness. And that's okay. We all have it. That's what makes ... accepting it so important ... and giving everything else up ... easy. I love you."

"Charlie, I love you too, but—"

His free hand came up and interrupted her, limply caressing her face as he stared into her eyes. He smiled gently, a mix of tenderness and sadness. It just wasn't fair.

Ah ... ah, bloody hell. It's not ... if only ...

"I have to save you, Minnie. And the rest ... come to think of it."

Now. Now or never. You can do it, man. Oh God, you can do it.

He could. Charlie's smile threatened to collapse into tears. He closed his eyes, and gritted his teeth as he lifted the knife from where he had been holding it behind Minnie, out of her line of sight. As the other half of his mind heard Chuck screaming in the Black Room, felt him squirming frantically as the monster began to push Charlie back for the final time, Charlie made the body grip the handle even tighter. Using all of the force that he could muster, he pulled the knife up and stabbed its blade deep into the body's heart.

Minnie screamed like her life was ending, and inside the Black Room Chuck and Charlie's forms simultaneously arched and locked up as if they'd been electrocuted. Charlie's connection was direct; Chuck's, just like Charlie's had become to Minnie, was ingrained. The effect was the same. A thin hole appeared in each of their chests.

The body before Minnie's eyes juddered for a second, its eyes rolling backwards in their sockets, and went limp. She grabbed its shoulders in clawed fingers, screaming Charlie's name over and over in a voice that had descended into torn, hysterical and all-consuming sorrow. In the Black Room, Charlie just had enough time to look down into Chuck's stunned, terrified eyes for a moment, and gave him a shaking, pained, but wide grin of triumph. He nodded gently, confirming what Chuck knew was happening. The horror and fear in Chuck's eyes said it all.

That's right, motherfucker. I got you. You don't get her, or any more of them, and I really wouldn't like to see where you're *going now. Suck my bal—*

And with that last thought, Charlie Wilkes—and his dark reflection—died.

Chapter Ten: Epilogues
***

Coventry Evening Telegraph

STABBED TO DEATH

The body of a Coventry man in his thirties was found in a field on the outskirts of Coventry in the early hours of Tuesday morning. Charlie Wilkes, 33, of Radford, was found with a lethal stab wound directly to his heart. His death is being treated as suspicious, as no weapon or suicide note was found in the vicinity. A bicycle, believed to belong to Wilkes, was found nearby. Friends and colleagues describe him as being 'very outgoing, friendly and happy' and said that there had been 'no sign' of him being involved in anything illegal or unsavoury. "We're all devastated," said Clint Rushton, a friend and co-worker at Barrington's Bar and Restaurant in Coventry city centre. "Nobody can understand why this would happen to somebody like Charlie." The investigation ...

Elsewhere

Coventry Evening Telegraph

271

STABBED TO DEATH IN HIS OWN HOME

The body of a Coventry man was found in a Coundon house on Tuesday afternoon. Charlie Wilkes, 33, was found in his bedroom with a lethal stab wound directly to his heart. His death is being treated as suspicious, but highly unusual, as although there was no weapon in the vicinity and no suicide note, no signs of a struggle or a break-in were found. His housemates have been taken in by police for questioning. A friend of one of his housemates said: "They didn't really even know the guy. He kept to himself, never came out of his room. They wouldn't do anything like this to someone, they didn't even know him." Wilkes, a former employee at Barrington's Bar and Restaurant ...

Elsewhere again:

The Guardian

INNOCENT: Cooper Cleared Of All Charges, Civil Rights Groups Celebrate

In the dramatic conclusion to a trial that has gripped the nation, Minnie Cooper left court today a free woman, cleared of all charges, including manslaughter. "It's a triumphant day for the rights of British women everywhere, and a landmark day in the history of the British court system," said Marie Corn, spokesperson for women's rights organisation WAVA. "This is someone who has been through an experience that we wouldn't wish onto our worst enemy, and who has been hounded afterwards as a result by a biased and prejudiced judicial system. Ms. Cooper has always been the victim here, and her treatment by the courts and the press has been nothing short of horrific." The prosecution had portrayed Cooper as a willing participant in a 'night of criminal misadventure that had gotten wildly out of hand,' claiming that she had not been kidnapped but was in fact a willing accomplice of Charlie Wilkes, whose naked body was found stabbed to death along with that of Michael and Edith Adams, the elderly owners of the Stratford home in which Miss Cooper's ordeal had taken place. Her defence had regularly pointed to a lack of evidence to justify the prosecution's claims of collusion throughout the trial, as well as the deep wrist and ankle restraint marks found on her body after she called police to the house. The jury took almost no time in reaching a unanimous, not guilty verdict, accepting that Miss Cooper had acted in self-defence and that she had no choice but to kill Wilkes in order to escape being murdered herself. In passing sentence, Justice Stephen Calloway, said that Miss Cooper "had acted in the only way that she could," and that she could leave court with "her reputation beyond reproach." Upon hearing the verdict, the public gallery burst into cheers and applause, as well as her father and brother who hugged each other and wept. Miss Cooper showed little outward emotion, instead simply closing her eyes and putting her head in her hands. Miss Cooper declined to talk to the press as she left court, but her lawyer read a prepared statement saying that she "thanked the people of the UK for their unending and full-hearted support." It asked that she be allowed privacy, however, as she and her family wished for "time to reflect on the ordeal" that Miss Cooper had suffered, and to "decide how best to begin to put it behind them."

Even further elsewhere:

It has been a good, long life. She has never been married, never felt the compulsion to do so; she'd even considered it once or twice with good men, willing and eager suitors who made the usual courtship movements in such kind, expressive patterns, but all were eventually—and politely—declined. She had experienced something far beyond such trivial, tawdry gestures. Hers had been an all-too brief, but deeply intense and world-altering love that had crossed universes. How could they, for all their fine and worthy and admirable traits, ever compete with that?

She had travelled, she had lived. It had been many, many years until she even brought herself to leave the house once again, living during that time under a black cloud of seemingly endless and unfathomable loss. She doesn't know what ended it; perhaps it was the result of all those dreams of him, the culmination of all the painfully bittersweet nights that she remembered all too well. He came to her in those dreams, and they would sit and talk, sharing a Black Room in the night that vanished in the morning like mist against the dawn. She would wake, weeping and full of a dull, terrible ache that never fully went away.

Whatever the cause, something changed. His sacrifice would be made into a sick mockery if she wasted that which he had died to give her. She would live. And so she did, even if that last ten percent of her would always be filled with the heavy, heavy weight of his absence. It had been a good life, as long and as happy as she could possibly make it, but the knowledge of his departure always made her feel as she was being held a long way from home, all of the time.

The nightmares about the dark man eventually passed. Discovering that the previously solid reality that she had always relied upon—with no reason to think otherwise—was actually as thin and as permeable as a nylon sheet had at first had threatened to turn her back to where she once was, back into being the trembling, wretched thing that thought only of its next fix. But with each day, the knowledge lost its edge, like a memory once vivid that slowly dulled. Eventually, it became merely another huge but accepted cosmic fact, like the sun being impossibly big or the universe being impossibly vast. In the long run, it didn't matter; her world was solid enough for her to live in.

She sometimes wondered if another dark man would come. She consoled herself on those few, dark nights with the thought that if he did, surely the other one would come as well.

She often thought about what he was trying to tell her, just before he died. She felt that, on some level, part of her knew exactly what he meant, that everyone would, even if they didn't know that they knew.

She had lived, and lived well. No children, no partner, but a lifetime of friends and partnership and laughter and tears. She never saw the truck skid as she crossed the street. She was sixty-two years old.

She opens her eyes to find herself streaking past a blur of visions, images of things moving too fast to mention. She doesn't know it, but this is the place that has touched her life in such beautiful and terrible ways. Others that she has met have been here, but they didn't travel through it like this, not at this speed, not passing through on their way to the place behind it all like she is; again, this is knowledge that she doesn't have. What she does know is where she is. She was told about it by the dark man, but even if he hadn't, she would know. Everyone does, the instant that they arrive here, but only when their time has truly come. She realises what the blurs are; they are the other places, speeding by. Of course.

She is in the void. The worlds rush past her, but they are of no consequence; she already knows of these, knows of their existence, but travelling to them is not an option to her. There is only one destination that she can have, only one that she is inexorably drawn towards, and this has always been the case. It calls to her now, speaking of comfort and warmth and light, of a welcome at a journey's end; she sees it filling the endless horizon before her, and to her surprise she is not afraid. This has all happened so fast, so unexpectedly, that she hasn't had time to fear, but even if she had she thinks that she would have known that all is well ... for people like her, at least, and this thought makes her think of those for whom it would be different. Those like him. It was him, she remembers for the hundredth time, the dark man, the one who took it all away ... but it is too late now to think of such things, things that cannot be undone, and soon she will be at peace. The End is waiting, and she goes to it like an old friend.

It swallows her, and everything is white.

There is silence. There is a brief moment of confusion, and then she finds to her surprise that she is standing upright, and naked. She looks at her hands, her breasts; her wrinkles and stretch marks and lines that she has always despised so are gone. She stands, nude in an endless horizon of white, and she is not afraid. She is uncertain. Is this The End? Is this the place that sang to her so across the void?

No ... she can still hear that call, coming from somewhere in the distance away. A little further, it says. Almost there. You've come so far, but just a little further now. To reach it might take some time, she thinks, but that might not be so bad? Perhaps a long way to travel alone. In any case, she begins to walk—

There is a figure approaching. Too far away to make out the shape properly, but from the height and gait of its walk, she thinks that it is a man.

She breaks into a stumbling run, comfort replaced by a fear that this is all another cruel dream, another repeat from a childhood sequence of nightmares where her mother was calling from a horizon that she could never reach. But

274

this figure grows larger in her sight; he is approaching. No; he is running too, running towards her.

Tears are streaming from her eyes, tears of a mixture of terrified anticipation and barely restrained joy. The shape is right, the walk is right, but oh God, oh maybe it's the wrong one, the one who hurt her so and tore a hole in her life that was never ... no. He can't be here. She knows that he can't be here. This place isn't for him, she can feel it all around her so this must be the right man, it looks like him it looks like him it looks like him—

He'd tried to tell her, after all. Theirs was a connection that had already drawn them together across the void, had already led them to one another across the endless abyss; why would this be any different?

Her hand extends in front of her as she runs, seeing him mirror the movement as she draws close enough to see the tears running from his own eyes, to see the desperate grin on his face. She reaches him, sobbing wild cries of self-pity and loss and boundless relief as he takes her in his arms, the man laughing as he does so and sobbing and holding her so tightly, so tightly, and he will never let go again. When they have embraced for what seems like an eternity—and perhaps it is—they stand locked together in a weeping, bawling, joyful mess of humanity. He looks up into her eyes where he holds her aloft, the man that will travel with her to the distant call, hand in hand.

"Xanadu, gorgeous," Charlie says, grinning and laughing and looking impossibly youthful, *"You got here in the end then. What took you so bloody long?"*

If you enjoyed this book, *please* leave a star rating on Amazon; the feedback that I've had is not only the thing that keeps me writing, but also means more people are likely to buy my books and that *also* keeps me writing. You can also find out about my other available books while you're there. Follow Luke Smitherd on Twitter (@travellingluke or @lukesmitherd) or go to Facebook under 'Luke Smitherd Book Stuff'. Most importantly visit lukesmitherd.com to sign up for the Spam-Free Book Release Newsletter, which not only informs you when new books are out (and *only* does that) but also means that you get new short stories for *free!*

Hi there. I really hope that you enjoyed reading this book, whether you first read it in the original, four-part individual versions and are re-reading it now (thank you) or whether this complete volume is your first time round with Charlie and Minnie. I've been meaning to compile them together for a LONG time, but 2014 was such a rollercoaster year for me that I never got round to it until now.

By the way, hello! My name is Luke Smitherd, and I wrote this story. This afterword is my little segment (as always) to sincerely thank you, the reader, for your interest, to let you in a little on some of the ways this story came about, and to claw and weep at your feet for an Amazon review (as ever, more on that later.) Some people, for some reason, really find these an offensive concept, going so far as to downgrade the book as a result. I don't really get that at all, but in case you think that might be you, probably best to sign off here but, sincerely, thanks for your time.

... right. Are they gone? Fuck me, *geez*, those guys ...

Now only the really cool, awesome, well-read, well-dressed, gropeable and caressable (and gullible?) people are left, hi guys. Long time readers (or Smithereens, as they call themselves, some actually without rolling their eyes and sighing at the same time) and Facebook followers know a bit about me by now, but for the uninitiated, I am now a full time writer for a living (*just*) and those who have been there ever since The Stone Man or even The Physics Of The Dead will know that's it's all been about getting to this point. It's only happened thanks to the support (and reviews) of people like yourself. 2014 had some of the biggest lows of my life so far, but also some very exciting times, the biggest of which being that I have reached a point in my "career" (cue my own eye-rolling and sighing) that I am able to now dedicate pretty much all of my work-time solely to writing. In fact, as I write this part, I'm sitting outside Stacks' in the Hayes Valley area of San Francisco, on Day Two of a very, very long-awaited trip around the U.S. (yeah, the writing didn't pay for *that,* but it'll keep me in cheap rooms in crack-den hotels and overpriced cider. The Pontiac Hotel; it's cheap and clean, but man, you have to run a gauntlet outside to get there ...) The fact that I even came to this part of town today because of a recommendation by the second-ever Smithereen that I've met in person, and by complete chance at that, says a lot about how much of a difference both the writing and the support I've received from complete strangers has made to my life (thanks Patty!) Writing and travelling is basically a bit of a dream come true, and I still can't really believe that it's happening. By the way, if this is your first book of mine, then I would probably go for The Stone Man next.

Some notes on this story then, the majority here lifted straight from the original part four afterword:

—You may also be curious, after all the drug references in this story, if I take them myself. As any experienced drug takers who have already spotted the no-doubt numerous errors in my depictions of the logistics of drug use will know, I don't, and I'll be sticking to that story in court, thank you. No, but seriously, I don't, and I find weed to be quite a boring experience if I'm honest. I'd rather be drunk than stoned. There's lots of drugs that I'd like to try, but I know that I have an addictive personality and that if they turned out to be amazing, I'd keep taking them. I'm sure that a night on relatively uncut charlie is incredible, but I just can't afford the habit, and I genuinely worry enough about my own detachment from the actual experience of life as it is.

—There is no Barrington's in Coventry, as Coventrians will know. I made it up. Cov people, if you want to know what I had in mind for that, I'd probably say the Weatherspoons opposite the council house in town, or the old Yates's (remember that?) that used to be just down the road from there, if both of them weren't a national chain pub. And Yates's would be on the other side of the street.

— The line about Minnie feeling that Charlie's absence (after his death) made her feel like being far away from home all the time was lifted from a documentary about the comedian Dave Allen. It was something that his widow said about being without him, in a gentle and throwaway moment of such sincere longing that it broke my heart to watch. What made it far worse was the easy way that she said it, like she'd been living with that feeling for so long that she was just used to it now. I really wanted to put that in the book.

—At the end of Part One, I said that I knew some of you would be wondering why this book is nothing to do with any of the other books that I said I'd be working on after TSM, and said that I'd say why at the end of the complete series. Well, the reason is simply because, as I say, the idea was just so appealing, and I thought it would take so little time to write, that I got into it and never came out until it was done. In the meantime, I've also had so many other little ideas for short stories and novellas (who knows, maybe they're also whole books after all) that I've kept a little list. 90% of them are probably fucking useless, but we'll see. No, I've no idea why I didn't just give that answer in Part One either.

—WAVA, as mentioned in the news article about Minnie at the end, is a fictional organisation. It stands for Women Against Violent Assholes.

—The part four in this version has been edited down a little from the original version (it was, even by my allegedly overly-verbose standards, a little wordy) and some of the more brutal elements of Chuck's back story have been toned down just a fraction; on a re-read while editing, even I was surprised by some of those and felt that they were a bit too much. Also, as I said before, I like my work to be as watertight as possible, and that's why Chuck's back story was quite long. I've trimmed as much as I felt comfortable with. There are a lot of elements of this story that, unlike a lot of the mystery elements of The Stone Man, *have* to be explained for me to be happy with the logic. I didn't want people to finish this book and think 'Hang on a second ... why did Chuck bother to go to work behind the bar?' If a story doesn't make sense—at least from my point of view, and I'm the one writing the damn thing—then all emotion and immerison is killed in the reader.

—I've never liked The Black Room as a title. Not least because there are other books with the same title, but it doesn't say anything about the story itself. In The Darkness, That's Where I'll Know You (or, of course, to use a now-traditional Smithereen acronym, ITDTWIKY, which is easily the worst one so far as I have to check it's right every time I type it) conveys the themes of the book—loneliness, intimacy, how much of ourselves do we really give to those close to us—and also can be taken as romantic, sexy, or straight out creepy. I like it.

—Some people said that releasing them in four parts, the first being free, is a money grab. Due to Amazon's royalty and pricing structure, I made *less* by selling them as four smaller parts than I would as a whole novel. It was purely done to see if a free part one would entice new readers to my work, and to experiment with a serialised release. *This* collected edition is the money grab. :-D

What's next, you may ask? Again, long time readers will know just how accurate my predictions of when new material will be out are. Extremely fucking inaccurate. Hell, I was supposed to be writing a book of short stories by now ... well, that's *kind* of still true.

Basically, from day one, I've told readers to sign up to the Spam-Free Book Release Newsletter in order to A: get emailed when, and only when, I release new stories, and B: to get FREE short stories. They will also know that in three years there has not been one single short story sent out ... (sorry.) It's high time that is addressed, and heavily, and so here is the plan for the rest of this year. I'm going to focus on short-form novellas for now (if you've read The Man On Table Ten, then they'll be about that length) that will be released on Amazon. This will repay the long-overdue short story debt to the Newsletter subscribers. These releases will *not* be initially announced on the Facebook page (Luke Smitherd Book Stuff) or Twitter (@travellingluke or @lukesmitherd.) The day after release, they will be free for one day, and only Newsletter subscribers will know when they are coming out. The day after *that,* it will be announced on Facebook etc. The deal therefore is that subscribers get a free book, then leave me a review. Based on the number of people on the Newsletter list, there should be quite a few reviews going up quickly. If they don't, the free novellas end. Fair?

Speaking of reviews, let me give you an example of their importance. TSM has the highest number of reviews, and therefore is by *far* my biggest source of writing income, probably accounting for 70 percent of it. Last year, I didn't make anywhere near as much money from UK sales as I did from US sales. Now ... once The Stone Man passed the 700 review mark, a funny thing happened. The numbers of reviews coming in dropped massively. Worse, people that liked it stopped reviewing it, presumably thinking that there was no need because it was already doing well. That meant the only people reviewing it were people that *hated* it. It's entirely possible that that analysis is wrong and that by some amazing coincidence everyone that bought the book from a certain point were people that hated it, but that seems a very strange and sudden turnaround to me. Whatever the reason, the book dropped from four and a half stars to four.

US sales plummeted by two thirds.

I would have been screwed, if not for the fact that UK review numbers had slowly passed the 400 review mark, while remaining at an overall score of 4 and a half stars.

UK sales shot *up* by two thirds.

However ... if the same thing that happened in America happens in Britain, then I have to go back to singing songs and prancing like a tit for a living. So A: if you've read TSM and liked it, *please leave a star rating saying so,* and B: see how star ratings are really, really important? :-D

I see every review you guys leave, and starting today, now I have the time, I will finally be going through the backlog of reviews that I need to reply to. Sorry if you thought I hadn't seen yours, I promise you that I did, and will be replying shortly (if it was nice, or at least constructive in its criticism.). Some of you have even started leaving personal messages in your reviews, which is great, and yes, I DO see them, and they were very much appreciated! Make sure that you hit the 'Track replies' box under your review though so that you get alerted when I reply! Melissa Quimby, you who are one of the few who have reviewed every single book that I have written and even wrote in one that you were delighted to see your name in the review acknowledgements at the start and very end of the book (if you left a review for AHFOK at the time of me writing this btw, your name is in this book right here) STILL haven't seen any of my replies, so I am now at the point of putting your name in this afterword! TICK THE FREAKIN' BOX! And thank you :-)

2014 saw the first meeting of Smitherd and Smithereen (I think I managed to be not *entirely* disappointing) and Neil Novita is now Chief Smithereen of Brooklyn. I also had a nice message come to me from Macedonia, and so Emil is now King of the Macedonian Smithereens. These got me thinking; seeing as the Smithereen army (well, more of an angry mob) is growing, I need to probably start assigning more ranks. You can be Chief Smithereen of whatever you want, providing it isn't already taken; fancy being Lord Smithereen of the work water cooler? Perhaps General Smithereens of the number 83 bus? How about being Lord Smithereen of Snodgrass, Bumgrape and Fuckface Solicitors? (Providing of course that you actually work for SBGFF PLC.) Put your title in your review or email me at lukesmitherd@hotmail.com, and I'll rubber stamp it. Let's get organised!

2014 also saw the highs of me cracking the top 100 books on Amazon UK (briefly) for the first time, the prep for the audiobook version of TSM, and the low of—and I mention this because her stories involving her (and her words!) have come up in these afterwords—the end of my years-long relationship with Angela. It wasn't something either of us wanted but what we both needed from life would take us in two separate directions, and we both had to acknowledge it, as horrendous as it was to do so. We remain on pretty much the best terms that it's possible for ex-partners to be, and will always be extremely close. Some people wouldn't agree with that, but to me it seems fucking stupid to just throw a bond like that away only because you have to adjust the parameters of your relationship and get through some tough stumbling blocks. It's perhaps strange to share something so personal here, but you guys are always so personally supportive I feel like I want you to know what's going on with me.

As ever guys, as long as you keep reading and reviewing, I'll keep writing. I can't thank you all enough. Watch this space; 2015 is going to be busy.

Stay Hungry,
Luke Smitherd,
San Francisco,
March 25th 2015

Luke Smitherd Book Stuff on Facebook
@travellingluke
@lukesmitherd
lukesmitherd@hotmail.co.uk

Also By Luke Smitherd:
The Physics of the Dead

What do the dead do when they can't leave ... and don't know why?

The afterlife doesn't come with a manual. In fact, Hart and Bowler (two ordinary, but dead men) have had to work out the rules of their new existence for themselves. It's that fact—along with being unable to leave the boundaries of their city centre, unable to communicate with the other lost souls, unable to rest in case The Beast should catch up to them, unable to even sleep—that makes getting out of their situation a priority.

But Hart and Bowler don't know why they're there in the first place, and if they ever want to leave, they will have to find all the answers in order to understand the physics of the dead: What are the strange, glowing objects that pass across the sky? Who are the living people surrounded by a blue glow? What are their physical limitations in that place, and have they fully explored the possibilities of what they can do?

Time is running out; their afterlife was never supposed to be this way, and if they don't make it out soon, they're destined to end up like the others. Insane, and alone forever ...

Available now on the Amazon Kindle Store, and in traditional book format

novel. A HEAD FULL OF KNIVES is a supernatural mystery that will not only change the way you look at your pets forever, but will force you to decide the fate of the world when it lies in your hands.

Available now in both paperback and Kindle formats on Amazon

24167642R00176

Printed in Poland
by Amazon Fulfillment
Poland Sp. z o.o., Wrocław